BISON
BOOKS

QUIET STREET

A NOVEL

By Zelda Popkin

INTRODUCTION TO THE BISON BOOKS EDITION BY

Jeremy D. Popkin

UNIVERSITY OF NEBRASKA PRESS
LINCOLN AND LONDON

First Bison Books printing: 2002

The introduction is revised from the article "A Forgotten Forerunner: Zelda
Popkin's Novels of the Holocaust and the 1948 War" in *Shofar: An Interdisciplinary
Journal of Jewish Studies* 20:1 (fall 2001), 36–60, and is used with the permission of
the University of Nebraska Press.

The Bison Books edition follows the original in beginning chapter 1 on arabic
page 9; no material has been omitted.

Library of Congress Cataloging-in-Publication Data
Popkin, Zelda, 1898–
Quiet street: a novel / by Zelda Popkin; introduction to the Bison books ed. by
Jeremy D. Popkin.
p. cm.
Includes bibliographical references.
ISBN 0-8032-8770-4 (pbk.: alk. paper)
1. Jerusalem—History—Siege, 1948—Fiction.   2. Jewish families—Fiction.
3. Kibbutzim—Fiction.   4. Sieges—Fiction.   I. Title.
PS3531.P634 Q54   2002
813'.52—dc21
2001057392

For
Helen, Sascha and Dan

AUTHOR'S NOTE

Although this book derives from certain historic events which took place between the first of February and the end of July, 1948, in the country now known as Israel, its characters are all fictitious. Actual happenings and personalities offer a novelist only cues and any resemblance herein to people, living or dead, stems from the fact that persons as disciplined, as brave and as bewildered as those in this book were among the human components which made Israel.

Introduction

JEREMY D. POPKIN

More than a half century has passed since Zelda Popkin wrote *Quiet Street*, the first American novel about life in the independent state of Israel. Much has changed since then, both in Israel and in American Jewish literature. Although it tallies up the high human cost of the war in which the new country defended its independence, *Quiet Street*'s account of the siege of Jerusalem in 1948 reflects the high hopes that surrounded the Jewish state at its birth. Popkin was aware of the Palestinian issue, but she optimistically believed that it would not have a lasting impact on Israeli life. If she failed to foresee how heavily the conflict with the Arabs would weigh on Israel for decades after its founding, however, Popkin did understand that the creation of a Jewish state would bring with it new problems. Even as she celebrated the courage of those who fought for the country's survival, Popkin strove to create Israeli characters who were mixtures of good and bad, determination and doubt. Subsequent American Jewish writers have delved more deeply into the Israeli psyche, but *Quiet Street* already strove to avoid casting all Israelis as simple heroes. And although she was no feminist in the present-day sense of the term, Popkin's decision to tell her story primarily through female characters gives *Quiet Street* a surprisingly contemporary flavor and offers us some genuine insight into how women experienced the drama of Israel's birth.

Zelda Popkin was born in Brooklyn in 1898, the daughter of Jewish immigrants from eastern Europe; she grew up in several small towns in New Jersey and eastern Pennsylvania where her father ran a series of unsuccessful businesses. Her parents named her Jenny; her decision to rename herself Zelda was one of the many ways in which she expressed her determination to break with her background and fit herself into American society. Her writing career began with a job at the local paper in Wilkes-Barre, Pennsylvania, when she was just sixteen. Soon afterward, she moved to

New York, where she met and married Louis Popkin. Together, they founded one of the city's first public-relations firms. The business prospered, leaving little time for writing, but Popkin never abandoned her literary ambitions. In the late 1930s, she published the first of what became a series of mystery novels featuring an independent-minded woman detective, Mary Carner, who solved her cases while her obliging husband looked after the couple's child. When her own husband died in 1943, Popkin closed their public relations firm and set out to become a professional author. A dramatic personal experience—she had been riding on the Pennsylvania Railroad's *Congressional Limited* when it crashed in 1943—provided the framework for her first "straight" novel, *The Journey Home*, which appeared in 1945. This story of a soldier just returned from World War II and an attractive young career woman who were brought together by a crisis on the home front struck a chord with the reading public and sold close to a million copies.

The Journey Home appeared just as Americans were grappling with the most shocking catastrophe in Jewish history. In the winter of 1945–46, the American Red Cross dispatched Popkin to visit the "displaced persons" camps in which Holocaust survivors were being housed. What she saw "shocked her into Zionism," as she later told an interviewer, and drove her for the first time to put a Jewish theme and Jewish characters in a central place in her writing. Her novel about the unfavorable American treatment of camp survivors, *Small Victory*, appeared in 1947 and was one of the first fictional works by an American author to deal with the Holocaust, although she used Gentile characters to convey her message. Like Laura Z. Hobson, whose *Gentleman's Agreement* had been published a year earlier, Popkin understood that anti-semitic attitudes were still widespread in the United States, and she hesitated to write a book that would seem like special pleading for her co-religionists.

No such evasion was possible when Popkin turned to the theme of Israel. Popkin had long had a direct personal tie to the fortunes of the Jewish population in Palestine: her younger sister Helen had made *aliyah* in the 1930s. Throughout the war years, Popkin and her elderly parents had exchanged worried letters about the dangers facing her sister and her family. As the conflict in the Middle East moved toward a climax, Helen lobbied her novel-writing sister to take up the subject. "The story needs to be put down and you're one of the persons who could do it," she wrote in June 1947. Popkin, who was at work on another novel, delayed until after the declaration of Israel's independence in May 1948; she did not personally witness the dramatic events that would make up the plot of *Quiet Street*. But those stories were still fresh when she arrived in Jerusalem in October of that year to begin the research that gives her book its documentary value.

Popkin was impressed by the courage of the outnumbered Jews, who had fought off the invading armies of five Arab countries, but she wanted to tell a story that would be more complicated than just a recital of heroic deeds. Memories of the Second World War were still fresh in her mind, and she knew there was no victory that did not bring personal losses with it; her original title for her book was *The Silver Salver*, a phrase from a poem in which the young soldiers who died in the fighting were memorialized as "the silver salver on which the Jewish State is handed you." Finally, she wanted to dramatize the way in which the achievement of statehood forced Jews to confront the moral dilemmas of power. Her book would ask, "When one gains a miraculous victory, does one become arrogant, hard, proud? Here, too, will idealism go by the board before the practical realities?" she told her editors.

A half century after the publication of *Quiet Street*, such questions inevitably make one think of Israel's treatment of the Palestinians. Popkin was aware of "the problem of Israel's relation with 300,000 dispossessed Arabs," as her correspondence shows, but, like Leon Uris in *Exodus*, her sympathies were unmistakably with the Jews, and the Palestinian question plays little part in her story. Instead, she focused on a controversy that divided the Jews themselves. To show how "a new nation grows into responsibility," Popkin built her plot around an actual event: the Tubiansky affair, the story of the one Israeli soldier executed for treason in 1948. When she started her writing in early 1949, Popkin thought that putting this story in the center of her novel would give her a way to show that the Israelis had achieved the right to be like other people, to have both their heroes and their "sons of bitches," as her Israeli brother-in-law phrased it. Tubiansky's punishment, she thought, proved the new country's willingness to deal firmly with its own problems. As Popkin was working on the novel, however, the Tubiansky story took a turn that she had not anticipated: Prime Minister David Ben-Gurion announced that the Haganah officer had been unjustly executed on trumped-up charges. Popkin changed her plot accordingly, and in the final version of *Quiet Street*, the haste with which most of the novel's characters turn against the supposed traitor and harass his family demonstrates that the Israelis are no more immune to unreason than any other people.

Popkin's emphasis on the Tubiansky affair made *Quiet Street* something other than a simple celebration of Israel's military success, and the mixed message conveyed in her book may have been one reason for its failure to find a wide audience. Popkin's way of portraying the dramatic events of the 1948 war may also have disappointed readers. Unlike the heroes of Leon Uris's *Exodus*, her characters were not shown carrying out daring guerrilla raids or defeating heavily armed Arabs. Instead, she emphasized the heroism of ordinary civilians who endured the siege of Jewish Jerusalem and of the isolated kibbutzim in the Negev. In our post-Vietnam age, Popkin's unheroic depiction of war and its toll rings truer than Uris's epic treatment, but her approach drained the story of Israel's independence of much of its excitement.

Popkin's novel was characteristic of its day also in downplaying the Jewishness and the foreignness of her Israelis. She had been determined from the outset to create characters who would be "believable and identifiable in American terms," as she told her editor. She set her story in her sister Helen's middle-class Jerusalem neighborhood of Rehavia, whose Bauhaus-inspired architecture was similar to that in many American cities, and the people in the book are mostly middle-class professionals and housewives who were shown doing activities familiar to middle-class American readers: going to work, shopping, caring for their families. Her approach underlines the dilemma that faced Jewish novelists trying to reach the general American public in the middle of the century. Popkin's whole life had been an effort at assimilation; her strategy for presenting the Israeli case to American readers was to argue that statehood was a way of assimilating Jews to other nations. "They're people like us," she told Eleanor Roosevelt in a radio interview. In making her fictional Israelis so familiar, however, Popkin probably reduced the appeal of her book: it lacked the exotic element that would be one of the major selling points of *Exodus*.

Ironically, the aspect of *Quiet Street* that seems most relevant today was not something Popkin had consciously planned. Although she had written detective novels with a female protagonist, she had originally conceived of the male characters in her Israeli story as the dominant figures. As the manuscript evolved, however, its women took over. Edith Hirsch, the sensitive Jerusalem housewife, Dinah Hirsch, Edith's kibbutznik daughter, and Carmela Levine, the wife of the wrongfully executed Haganah officer, became the moral centers of the book. In Dinah Hirsch, she created a stereotypical representation of the Israeli woman soldier, and she wrote one of the first versions of that clichéd moment in which an American Jewish male finds himself unnerved by the country's "bosomy babes with the sparkling eyes ... with their Stens." Dinah Hirsch is the Jew without complexes, the one who has dedicated herself to "the straight line. . . . Build the Land. Defend the Land," and her heroic, if senseless, death—an incident based on the actual death of the daughter of one of Popkin's friends—emphasizes her dedication to the cause. Carmela Levine, widow of the unjustly executed Haganah officer, forces the other characters in the book to confront the possibility that their new country was less than perfect. As she says to a judge who is debating whether to respond to her demand for justice, "Our State is young, like a small child. It, too, must be punished when it does wrong. Otherwise how will it learn what is right?"

Finally, it is Edith Hirsch who experiences most fully and painfully the dilemma that struck Popkin most in her encounter with Israel: the fact that the country's independence had to be purchased at the cost of so many lives. Unlike her daughter Dinah, Edith is a divided soul. She joins her neighbors in shunning a Rehavia couple who have encouraged their son to stay safely overseas rather than returning to fight, but she understands their feelings. She admires her daughter's courage but is in agony every minute that Dinah is out of sight. Her sensitivity to others' pain makes her the one person in the neighborhood who refuses to boycott the family of the supposed 'traitor,' even when there seems no doubt about the justice of his execution. Although the book stresses the depth of Edith Hirsch's Zionist convictions—we are told that she is the granddaughter of one of Theodore Herzl's earliest associates—she never forgets that states are made up of individual people, who may suffer painful losses even as they share in collective triumphs.

Quiet Street won the Jewish Book Council's fiction award in 1952, and it had received a burst of nationwide publicity earlier when Frank Frisch, manager of the Chicago Cubs, expressed his opinion of an umpire's call by tossing his copy at the offender's head. Despite generally favorable newspaper reviews, however, the book was not a commercial success. Like many unhappy authors, Popkin blamed her readers. "American Jews, like American Gentiles, limit their reading to the sex and sensationalism which tops the best-seller list," she complained to one journalist. It was left to Leon Uris to give readers a story, similar in many ways to that of *Quiet Street*, that did a better job of satisfying those appetites. *Exodus*, published in 1958 on the tenth anniversary of Israel's declaration of independence, also provided a more convincing context for the events it described, linking the creation of Israel both to the Biblical drama that provided its title and to the Holocaust. After Uris had shown that American audiences would respond to stories about Israel, younger American Jewish novelists, less constrained by the shibboleths of assimilation that had inhibited Popkin's generation, created images of Israel and of Israelis that had greater psychological complexity and depth than hers.

Now that the body of American fiction dealing with Israel has become so large and so varied, *Quiet Street* can be read with new interest. The book's value as a record of the experience of the 1948 war was acknowledged even by Israeli reviewers; it recreates the mood of a time increasingly obscured by the many traumas the country has experienced since. In her own way, Popkin grappled with many of the big problems that have continued to preoccupy both Israelis and Americans who care about the fate of the Jewish state. Finally, realizing that the first major American novel about the making of Israel was written by a woman author and that its central character was not a gallant freedom fighter but a middle-class housewife requires us to revise our notions of how the image of Israel developed in American Jewish literature.

FOR FURTHER READING

For a more detailed analysis of *Quiet Street*, see Jeremy D. Popkin, "A Forgotten Forerunner: Zelda Popkin's Novels of the Holocaust and the 1948 War," in *Shofar* 20:1 (fall 2001), 36–60. In her autobiography, *Open Every Door* (New York: E. P. Dutton, 1956), Popkin provides details about her background and career; one of her later novels, *Herman Had Two Daughters* (Philadelphia: J. P. Lippincott, 1968) covers much of the same ground in fictionalized form. Andrew Furman, *Israel through the American Jewish Imagination: A Survey of Jewish-American Literature on Israel, 1928–1995* (Albany: State University of New York Press, 1997) is a useful account of the development of American fiction about Israel, although it makes no mention of *Quiet Street*. The Tubiansky affair, which looms so large in the plot of the novel, is explained in Israeli historian Shabtai Teveth's *Ben-Gurion's Spy: The Story of the Political Scandal That Shaped Modern Israel* (New York City: Columbia University Press, 1996), 3–58. I am grateful to the Mugar Library of Boston University for permission to cite from Zelda Popkin's literary papers, part of their Contemporary American Authors research collection.

Quiet Street

Part One: February

I

WHEN YOU MET Edith Hirsch for the first time, you were apt to observe that she had once been very pretty, that she had elegance and that she was tall. The last was not so. She was small boned, thin, and no more than five foot three. It was the proud lift of her head which gave her both height and elegance.

However, her daughter, Dinah, had another explanation. "When you speak, *Imma,*" Dinah had said, "I think you are tall because you talk the way a tall woman talks."

"And how does a tall woman talk?" her mother inquired.

"As if she means what she says."

That was true. Edith meant all she said, though she spoke sparingly. Talk is too often sheer nervousness, an aspect of need for approval or reassurance, and what Edith Hirsch thought and observed she habitually kept to herself, even within her own family. And so, before they were well acquainted, people would say she was snobbish, cold, colorless, although it was merely that she had elected reserve. Discrimination, a Wellesley professor had taught her, is a *for* word, not an *against* one. It means choosing what happens to be best for you.

Her voice was low pitched and agreeable, and the very care of her phrasing, in Hebrew or English, was part of her elegance. You could not know, since Edith herself would never have mentioned such intimate facts, that hers was blue blood, a lineage of culture, rabbis and scholars on the maternal side, and on the father's, professional men, doctors, lawyers and journalists. Her own grandfather had been Theodor Herzl's good friend, had worked with him on *Die Welt,* that historic journal which sounded the clarion call to build a Homeland. That was where Teddy, her son, got his name, and it was one of

9

two reasons why she had lived in Jerusalem for the last twenty years.

The other reason was Jacob, her husband. From the twilight when he had stumbled down the streets of a village in Russia, a terrified child, hearing the howls of a mob, Jacob Hirsch had known he had to live in a land of his own. The terror of pogrom was in him and not Harvard's prizes and honors nor New England's free atmosphere could exorcise it. He took a Boston schoolteacher rowing on the Charles River one night. "Naturally, Edith," he told her, "if you decide to marry me, we shall live in Palestine." "Naturally." Could the granddaughter of Herzl's colleague and friend have replied otherwise?

Edith's delicate features were like fine porcelain and her rare smile was sweet. Her eyes were slate blue, clear seeing, intelligent, her forehead high, appearing higher in the way she brushed back her hair, center-parted, drawn to a bun at the nape, once the burnished brown of horse chestnuts but now sun-faded and with a patina of gray.

Time had not dealt with her kindly and the fault was her own because she refused to appease it. The Middle East's climate with its strong sunlight and parching *khamseen* is cruel to fair skins and the veil of the Arab woman is as much precaution as modesty. Yet Edith went hatless, except to the more formal teas, and since she used neither make-up nor creams, as lacking in feminine vanity as any woman in a farm settlement, the sun had dried and wrinkled her skin and made her look older than her calendar years. A poor complexion and graying hair are self-evident. A passer-by seldom can glimpse a soul's radiance.

Certainly, had you seen her that Sunday morning, clutching the arm of the barrel-shaped man with the button nose and thick lips, tar-black hair, eyes and shaggy eyebrows, who was Jacob, her husband, racing down Keren Kayemeth Street to King George Avenue, down King George to Ben Yehuda Street, down Ben Yehuda to Zion Square, weaving between pedestrians, bumping a few, neither her charm nor her elegance would have been visible. Her nose was beet red from February's cold; the loose ends of her hair blew every way. Her attire was dowdy, the venerable tweeds in which she went marketing. And she was in an undignified hurry, since Jacob's bus was to leave from the Egged depot on Jaffa Road, off the Square, at eleven, and there was not one second to waste.

Ida Goldstein, the druggist's widow, almost crashed into them. She was pushing Tamar, her youngest grandchild, up Ben Yehuda Street's hill in the chipped white pram which she used to deliver the cookies and strudels she baked to earn bread. When she saw them running, she thought of trouble, of an emergency, something happened to Dinah, perhaps. But Jacob waved to her gaily and she went on, relieved that whatever it was, it was nothing sad. Gordon Leake, meandering, for want of better to do on a Sunday, around Zion Square, saw them dash into the depot and realized his neighbor was taking his life in his hands. "I wish he were not going on the bus," Gordon said to himself. "That man is too good to lose."

Edith had thought the same thing. She, too, had kept the thought to herself.

Jacob had said, "Yes, I will deliver the speech. Depend upon me." A promise made is a promise kept. Men might be coming from Haifa, from as far as Afula or Safed, to hear what Dr. Hirsch had to say. No obstetrician in all Palestine had had such success in preserving the lives of both mothers and babes in the ordeal of birth. From Beersheba to Dan and in even Beirut and Damascus, people spoke highly of Jerusalem Hadassah's Dr. Hirsch.

However, in December, 1947, when his Tel Aviv colleagues had asked him to address their meeting on February the second, 1948, Dr. Hirsch had planned a quite different trip. "I shall leave around four," he had told Edith then. "I shall warn all my women not to dare to go into labor that day. I shall take my car. . . . Please do not start nagging about slippery roads. . . . One hour on a hard surface highway . . . *Nachon,* agreed, I'll drive slowly. An hour and a half. Satisfied? . . . A leisurely supper. Where do you think the best food will be? At Kaete Dan? Or Gat Rimmon? . . . Tell me, how is it possible all the world's worst cooks managed to move into Tel Aviv? . . . You are right, little one, supper at Armon, on their terrace, facing the sea. Beautiful! . . . It will probably be raining that day. . . . Well, then, make my speech. Browbeat the few imbeciles who always disagree. . . . Argument is our national sport. . . . Afterwards coffee. At Cassit? . . . Yes, Cassit. Cassit is amusing. . . . Then slowly drive home by starlight. . . . What more can I ask? Little one, you come too. Let's make it a holiday."

Edith said yes, she would like to go, too. Carmela Levine would surely give Teddy supper (he half-lived in her house anyway), let him sleep the night with Asi, his friend. All arranged, even a letter sent off to Dinah who lived in Gan Darom, a communal farm settlement, a *kibbutz,* in the Negev, reporting on plans for the trip, and Dinah's reply, *"Good! You will enjoy it. Too bad we do not have a big hospital at our small kibbutz. We, too, would like to invite Doctor Hirsch."*.

By February, however, the Doctor's petrol ration was barely enough for the trip every day from the Rehavia quarter where he had his office and home, up to Mount Scopus where the hospital stood, and he was traveling on foot or by bus to visit his patients in town. Moreover and more pertinent, the Jerusalem–Tel Aviv road had become a deathtrap. Since the end of November, 1947, when the United Nations had voted to partition Palestine into Arab and Jewish states, Arab gangs, from Latrun and the Castel and the Bab-El-Wad gorge, had filled the highway with the wreckage of blasted and burned vehicles. When one had to travel, one traveled in convoy, behind armor plate.

The Doctor used pull. Through Yora Levine, his neighbor across the street, and Benjamin, a driver for the Egged bus lines, who lived in the house on the corner, a chit was obtained, authorizing him to occupy one place in an armored bus, departing Sunday morning, February first, to join a convoy to the coast. With good luck, he might find passage back on the third or the fourth.

The first was Teddy's birthday. It was a pity, Jacob agreed, the boy's own father couldn't be home on that day. But what is one birthday in a long life? The boy will have many, we hope. Yet in a small family, when one member leaves, there is a great void. They were just four, counting Teddy who was going to be ten and Udi, their brindle boxer, who at three was already much larger than Teddy and better behaved. They had been five until last October when Dinah became eighteen and went off to live in the Negev. Dinah was missed very much.

On his departure morning, Jacob rose earlier than usual to the pleasant ding-dong of Sunday bells from Terra Sancta and Ratisbon, a few blocks away. Udi heard him, got up from his mat beside Teddy's bed and padded down to the garden to take care of affairs of his own. Jacob washed quickly, shaved, dressed, ran out to call on a patient who was in her sixth month and had started to stain, commanded her not to stir out of bed, stay flat on her back, a week, two, as long as required. "You want a living child?" he thundered. "Then do as I say." He dashed home to rouse Teddy, with ten whacks and one for good luck, give him a bear hug, a loud kiss and a Scout pocketknife, ordered the boy to get up, hurry, dress, off to school, and wash well. "The neck, the elbows. It's a shame I must tell a ten-year-old boy to be clean." He sat down to breakfast in a dining room stately with polished mahogany and Sheffield plate and looked out with pleasure on the green lawn and the wall of blue morning-glories in his back yard. Because he was going on a trip, Edith had made a large meal—an orange, oatmeal, a scrambled egg, coffee and toast.

Teddy stomped down the staircase. Except for his meager girth and cup-handle ears, he was Jacob in fair duplicate, the black hair and eyes, the stubbed nose, the bubbling excitement over all that went on in the world. In honor of the day, he wore a white blouse and the pocketknife swung from a chain at his belt. His hair was slick and damp from the brush; his eyes were sparkling and his cheeks glowed. "*Abba,*" he announced. "I could kill a man with this knife."

"Don't try," his father said laconically. "Leave that to our cousins at Jaffa Gate." He popped an orange slice into his mouth.

Teddy swung the knife vigorously, made it clank on the table-top edge before he sat down. Edith carried the cereal in. "No *kvacker.*" Teddy fenced the porridge bowl off with his palms. "Why can't I have egg for my birthday breakfast?"

"For a very good reason, my son. *Tnuva's* been short of fresh eggs. If you have your egg now, what will your supper be?"

"Humor the beast," Jacob said. "If he eats his kvacker, let him have egg."

The boy dipped his spoon disdainfully into the porridge. "Abba," he began again, "be sure to remember it all. You will tell me and I will tell Asi. *His* father has never been in an armored convoy." He swallowed a spoonful, purposely gagged to prove his contempt for oatmeal. "Abba, what do you think Asi is bringing me?"

"Eat," his father said sternly. "I am a busy man. I have no time to listen to, 'Asi, Asi' today."

"Eat quickly," his mother warned him. "You'll be late again," and squeezed his shoulder before she returned to the stove. Asi, Asi, she thought as she beat up an egg for Teddy and poured it into the pan, all we hear in this house is Asi. Such an attachment, such love! They squabble, Asi calls Teddy a donkey, Teddy says Asi's too fresh. That's merely boy jealousy. Asi has the advantage. So our Teddy thinks. Asi's father has twice been a soldier in two different armies—German in the first World War, British in the next, not by choice, by the turn of events. But poor Teddy, his father has never worn a uniform, nor fired a shot. And now, Yora playing two parts, cool, capable— Yes, it's amazing that Asaph Levine even notices Theodor Hirsch. We Hirsches are so unexciting. . . . Leaving out Dinah, of course. But Dinah's a farmer, not a soldier. . . . Very well, I choose to think farmer. Let me think farmer, please. . . . Teddy has Dinah to brag about. . . . Even now, she seemed to hear Teddy yammering at Asi as he did time after time, "My sister is *Palmach* and your father is just *Haganah.*" Is it not distinction enough to serve in Haganah, our secret defense? Only the bravest young are the *Plugot Mahatz,* the striking arm, the Palmach.

She shivered. She knew why she shivered, yet she told herself, our winter mornings are brutal. What good is an oil burner down in the basement, just gathering the dust?

"Abba." Teddy laid down his cereal spoon. "Are you taking your pistol along?"

Jacob looked up. "What pistol?" he asked warily.

The boy's sleek head ducked to conceal a blush. "I just happened to see it one day in your room. . . . You will take it, of course?"

"Of course not . . . And in the future don't you go prowling in your parents' bedroom."

"I never do, Abba. . . . But if you need the pistol?"

"See that you don't. . . . I will not need it."

Edith carried in eggs and Teddy's *leben,* the fermented milk on which the children were raised.

"Abba, how soon can I start learning to shoot?" the boy asked while he forked up his egg.

"Finish, get done," his father replied.

"I am ten years today. Dinah was twelve when she—"

"Teddy, please!"

The boy glanced at his mother curiously.

"Edith, sit down." Jacob pushed back a chair for his wife. "Where's your own food?"

"I'll have coffee and toast." An ache had begun in her back and was circling around. She smiled resolutely to belie the pain. Her husband looked at her sharply.

"None of this I-am-not-hungry, madame, if you please."

He could not say more, because a boy's voice, from the living room, shouted, "Hey, Teddy! *Shalom!* . . . Happy birthday to you!"

"Asi!" Teddy started up from his chair.

Jacob pushed him back down. "Sit, finish, get done."

A plump boy in khaki shorts and sleeveless sweater, golden-haired, with a cherub's round rosy face and lively blue eyes, leaped up the two steps to the dining room. His mother was with him. "Good morning," she sang out. "And good appetite."

"Asi, see the knife my father gave me." Teddy gulped the last of his food.

Asi came around the table. "How many blades?"

"Six," Teddy said.

Asi examined the knife. "Only four. Learn to count. Good but not as good as the Scoutmaster has." He rolled his eyes. "Wait till you see the birthday present I have for you."

His mother gave him a shove. "Run. Talk on the way to school. The girls are already there."

"Those *fistukes!*" Teddy said, with hearty contempt.

"Those peanuts are very nice girls," Edith retorted, and what an outrage it is, she thought, that Asi's sisters, Aviva and Shoshanna, chubby small girls with shining black plaits, existed for both of the boys merely as objects of torment and scorn. "Run, both of you, you are late." She gave her son a quick kiss and hug and Asi a squeeze.

"Teddy!"

The boy wheeled at the peremptory sound. He ran back, flung himself into his father's arms. "Come home soon, Abba." His voice was thick. "Come back to us."

Carmela Levine took Teddy's chair. As soon as the boys were out of the house, she smiled at Jacob. *"Habub,"* she began. (His heavy brows rose at the cajoling, affectionate greeting.) "Habub, do a favor for me." She said it charmingly, in the precise, school-taught local English, whose accent is half Oxford and half guttural. Carmela Levine was a *sabra,* which is native-born Palestinian, bearing the name of the fruit of the cactus. Moreover, she was fourth generation sabra, in effect Mayflower stock, and a descendant of Spaniards. Persians and Roumanians had married into her family, mixed with the Spanish strain. As a result, in a country of striking women, she was one of the handsomest. Painters and photographers had made her perfect features, her cream and black coloring, famous throughout Palestine, the oval face, the deep-set expressive eyes, the passionate mouth, black lacquer hair, drawn away from the wide, lovely brow, curved around tiny ears to drop in a heavy knot on a long, slender neck. She walked with a dancer's litheness—and dancer she once had been—but she kept her hands at her sides, ashamed because she bit her nails. When she said, "Do a favor for me," it was hard to resist Carmela Levine.

Nevertheless, Jacob had to save face. "You see, Edith," he grumbled. "A man goes to Tel Aviv on his business and the whole world wants favors from him."

Carmela put her hand on his arm. "Only I, Jacob. Just me."

"Edith, bring coffee," he shouted, as though his wife were not here in the room. "A cup for Carmela . . . Well, woman, speak."

"Please, Jacob, call up my brother. His office has a telephone. Call him up, make an appointment, see him, please. That is essential. See him personally. Tell him—" she bent forward—"the children and I are very well, but Yora's ulcer—" her small bosom rose—"is more troublesome."

"Let him stop drinking," Jacob growled. "Must he be like the English and the foreign press, always at the King David bar?"

Her brow creased. She looked away toward the wall of morning-glories. "You know better, Jacob," she said. She made herself smile. "Tell my brother to be a brother, once in a while write to me."

"Be a sister," he muttered. "Write to your brother occasionally."

"Bring him my message, please."

"Since when am I the postman?"

"Who trusts His Majesty's Government to carry the mails?"

Edith brought in the coffee. "He will do it," she said. "Jacob will see your brother."

His heavy eyebrows wagged at her eloquently.

Carmela tilted her chin. "Who knows that better than I? When has Jacob Hirsch refused a favor? But why does he scream as if it is a mortal insult?"

"Have I not the right to protect myself?" He sipped his coffee, remembering to keep muttering into his cup but aware, as all of them were, what Carmela desired her brother to learn behind a closed door, from a trusted friend. One could not send through His Majesty's mails information that Yora Levine who holds a post in the Mandatory Government, does a quite different job when his day at the office is done, that his burdens are heavy, his strains severe and, therefore, he spends the start of each day, doubled with pain, retching into his W.C., and that Carmela, fearful for him, has chewed her nails to the flesh. He drained his cup, set it down. "One minute, Edith, no more, I'll be back. I must see Doctor Kaufman. He is a *Yecke* and young, but I think he will do my patients no harm in the few hours I'm away."

Carmela rose with him, "Edith, you will wring my neck, I have done you a terrible harm." She laughed. "I have bought a flute for Asi to give Teddy for his birthday." She kissed Edith's cheek before she followed Jacob out of the house.

Rifle fire crackled as they came to the street. In the bowl of hills in which Jerusalem lay, single shots echoed, sounding like more. Jacob cocked his head to guess the direction from which the noise came. "Ours?"

"Theirs." Carmela shrugged. "Jacob, if you know how little we have."

"I know." He raised her chin with his thumb. "Go home. Feed your husband. That's all a woman needs do."

There is a woman who loves her man very much, he said to himself as he watched her crossing the road. It is a pity this terrible country will not permit her to relax in her love.

The "one minute, no more" stretched to an hour before he was back. Edith had time to bake Teddy's cake and fix sandwiches, olives and white cheese, and sausage, *nacnic,* for Jacob's lunch on his trip. Shifra, the buxom Kurdish girl who did the housework, arrived, helped herself to coffee, olives and bread, before she took her place at the sink. Margalit, the Yemenite laundress, who at thirty had an old woman's body and face (bearing ten children, watching five die, working too much, never eating enough) came, took the primus stove out of the cupboard, and carried it into the yard to boil the week's wash.

Edith glanced at the clock. Jacob was taking too long. She looked out the door. An American Cadillac car, light green, brand-new, stood in front of the office entrance. Good Lord! she thought, the Nassairs. Now Jacob surely will be late for the bus.

He tore at his hair when he saw the green car. *Katzenkopf!* You forgot they were coming. They will take half a day.

Madame Nassair was pregnant with her fifth child. When a pregnant woman makes her visit, one examines blood pressure and specimen, asks "How do you feel?" hears two or three trifling complaints, five minutes, finished, "Shalom." But six Nassairs, Mama, Papa, three sons, a daughter, came to consult Dr. Hirsch for one office fee.

Nassair was an importer of various things, all American-made, nylon hose, fountain pens, electric refrigerators, motor cars, which entered the country informally over the unguarded Trans-Jordan frontier. The man had a mansion in Katamon, an exclusive quarter, beyond Rehavia. Ten years ago, while he was still poor, he had brought his wife into the Hadassah wards and Jacob had delivered Madame's first child. Thereafter no other obstetrician would do.

Madame was violet eyed, statuesque. She wore Western clothes, out of Paris, and wobbled on tight, imported, spike-heeled shoes. When Dr. Hirsch tried to tell her that if one is carrying an unborn child, one should walk on low heels, her husband shrugged airily. "My wife does not walk. We have always the automobile." Though she wore no veil, Madame was closely guarded, and whatever required discussion, regarding her health or her children's welfare, was handled by Papa Nassair. Hassan, the eldest boy, for instance, still wet his bed. Suggestions for limiting fluid intake at night and exploring the roots of anxieties had to be made tactfully and over again, on every visit. Fatima, the daughter, skinny and brown as a monkey, had a capricious appetite; left alone, not beaten or bribed, she'd have tried to live on cookies and grapes. Her small size and listlessness were ominous. Papa Nassair heard the Doctor's warnings about rickets and tuberculosis, received his instructions to feed Fatima milk, fresh eggs, buttered bread, paid for the advice and fed his child as he did usually. All three of the boys had BB guns, gifts of a kinsman abroad. They thought it advisable to carry weapons when they came to visit doctors.

A spray of lead from the waiting room casements greeted Dr. Hirsch when he ran up his path. Nassair shook hands with him warmly. "Well, Doctor, we are here at the time." He tried to bluster. "We are surbrise"—like many Arabs, he had difficulty pronouncing the letter "p"—"you make us wait for you."

The family paraded, Papa first, Mama next, gripping Fatima's hand, then Hassan, Yussef and Aram, into the consulting room.

While the Doctor wound the sphygmomanometer bandage around Madame's plump arm, Nassair hovered over the chair. "Doctor," he commenced, "I am most sorry to tell you—" something in his tone made the Doctor look up—"you will not have the honor to welcome a new little baby for me."

"Madame is changing her mind or her doctor?"

"No, Doctor, no." Nassair clapped Jacob's shoulder blade and joggled his arm. "It is only we go away. Now, this week, we go."

The Doctor managed to keep his voice casual. "Where do you go?"

"To Jericho, first. Then, berhab, Cairo. My wife have cousin in Cairo. Berhab, we go to him, *Inshallah,* we come back before new baby is born. I do not know."

"Seventh month is no time for Madame to travel." Dr. Hirsch squeezed the rubber bulb, watched the quicksilver shoot up the tube and recede. "Why do you go?"

Nassair hunched his shoulders. "I have wife, many children. If shooting come bad, big trouble."

The Doctor glanced up again. "Are you afraid?"

"Afraid!" The man's sputter revealed his squirrel-pointed teeth. "Me, I am never afraid." He brushed Fatima's hand from his arm. "Wait, we take you bibi one minute. When Mama is finished, she take you. . . . No, Doctor Hirsch, we go because we mus'. We get the instruction to go. *Bas,* Yussef, *bas* . . . Stop or I kill you! Not in the face of the Doctor. He is a good man. You hear me, but down the gun. One minute, one secon', I ask you, no noise. We go, Doctor, and we come back. . . . I will be bleased to remember when it is finish', you have always been good friend to us."

"And suppose—" Dr. Hirsch smiled gingerly—"it does not go that way?"

Nassair shrugged again. "How else can go? You are a clever man, Doctor. Why you do not understan', the Arab, he will not sit quiet and let United Nations take his country from him?"

Jacob unwound the bandage, rolled it up carefully. "Madame is in perfect health," he said. "She must remember to keep down her weight, not eat too much."

Nassair indulged him with a smile. "That she know better than you, how much she and the not-born mus' eat." He took out his wallet. "Doctor, blease—" his grin had faded—"blease, you do me big favor. Blease tell to your friends, Nassair, he is not a bad man. He only do what he mus'. He has spend all his money on his beauti-ful house. Blease to take care of my house. My wife—" Madame, escorting the little girl toward the W.C. in the corridor, stopped to add a beseeching glance—"she is more afraid to go as to stay. Blease, you know, bossibly, some good doctor in Jericho or Cairo?"

"Your cousins will find one, I'm sure. Your cousins will take care of everything."

Nassair sighed. "Doctor, how you think the children look now?"

"Like always." The patients are leaving town; the doctor can afford to sound bored. "You always know what is best for your family." Yet he had to wait patiently until Hassan and Yussef and Aram trailed out to the W.C., straggled back. He shook hands with Nassair and Madame, wished them good luck, gave the boys each a shove, in affection, as much as relief, patted the girl on the head and glanced at his watch. Now there was one more errand, another few minutes to lose. Yet he waited until the limousine could no longer be heard, before he went, swinging his black leather bag, down the street to the corner, where there was a three story house of small flats.

A Tommy, lounging against a light tank at the street intersection not ten yards beyond the building entrance, watched him go into the house and assumed the Doctor was paying a professional call. This house had visitors at all hours of the evening and day, but no one could guess, from their casual coming or going that they came with news and left with directions for things to do.

On the middle floor of the house Dr. Hirsch knocked on a certain door in a certain way. A man with a tired, pleasant face and pinned-together left sleeve, opened the door. "Shalom, Nathan," Jacob Hirsch said.

"Shalom," Nathan answered him. He locked his door carefully before he went ahead of his visitor into his living room. It was the room of a family of modest means, two couches draped with coarse woven spreads, a modern easy chair, a low table for coffee, breakfast cup on it still, a narrow bookcase, a small radio, nothing to stir suspicion if any stranger chanced to drop in. Here lived a one-armed ex-soldier, veteran of North Africa, whose identity card stated he worked at a night watchman's job at a bank down in town and whose income was augmented by his wife's work as a public health nurse.

He waited for Jacob to begin to speak. Jacob began. "An Arab patient was just in to see me. His family is going away. He says they all have orders to leave Katamon." He watched Nathan's face. There was no change of expression, no flicker of surprise or even of especial interest and he had no way of discerning whether he had brought significant news.

"*Toda*," Nathan answered. "Thank you." He nodded curtly. "That is all?"

"That is all." He was disappointed. There had been no speculation, no invitation to weigh or discuss or surmise whether this order for Arabs to leave was actual fear or a new craftiness.

Nathan unlocked his door. "You are going on a journey. Shalom," was all he said. But before his door shut, he added one other word, more meaningful than the simple "shalom" for "hello" and "goodbye." He said, *"L'hitra'ot*—hope to see you again."

Edith had everything ready, a briefcase packed with the notes for Jacob's lecture, this morning's *Palestine Post*, at which she had been too busy to glance, a clean shirt, a toothbrush and comb and the lunch. She announced she was walking Jacob to the bus.

He scowled. "I go to Tel Aviv only, not to the moon."

"I want to be with you," she said. "As long as I can."

His gaze sharpened. Does she seem frightened? No, merely peaked and drawn. That was not new. So she had been since the day Dinah left. He tscked to belittle her anxiety. "An important man! Hirsch needs an official escort."

Udi whined, nuzzled the briefcase which reeked of nacnic. Jacob cupped the dog's flat, ugly snout. "Udi," he ordered, "take care of this house. That's what Dinah said you should do."

At the mention of Dinah's name, the animal's ears stood up, for he had been her dog. She had personally chosen that puppy out of a litter at the breeding kennels, had carried him home, wrapped in her sweater, held to her breast. Her smell had meant protection and love. She had fed and housebroken him and he had slept at the foot of her bed. There had been mention of taking him with her when she left with her comrades October last to start Gan Darom, but it was discussed, and it was not practical. A new settlement's budget cannot provide for feeding an enormous, non-productive beast. If he'd been a donkey or camel, for instance, from whom one could get a day's work—"Take care of the house, Udi," Dinah had said. "Take care of my family."

The day Dinah left, the dog had loped up and down the staircase, whimpering whenever he met anyone on his rounds, but that night without urging, he crossed the upstairs hall, stretched beside Teddy's bed and became Teddy's dog. Much better than human, this animal was, Jacob frequently said, because he listened and never talked back, and an amiable dog, barking only with joy, and a wise one, who had learned the day Dinah left that people you love go away and sometimes they do not return and each departure possesses that threat. No one except Udi knew that when he strained after Jacob, he was trying to say, "Please don't you go, too."

Shifra, the maid, seized his collar. "I will tie the dog up."

Jacob frowned. "Not necessary. Udi has discipline."

"Margalit is washing. She is afraid of Udi. He will knock over the primus. He will step on the wash." Shifra's voice held the broad hint of a sneer, the contempt of one who has learned Western ways of housekeeping toward a primitive creature who still washes clothes as her grandmother did, squatting on earth and pounding wet cloth.

Dr. Hirsch shook his head. "Do what you must. Only never be cruel to our dog." Then he scowled at himself. Why am I leaving last messages? I am merely going to Tel Aviv to make a dull speech. "Shalom, Shifra," he cried. "Shalom, Udi. . . . Edith, come if you must. Run, woman, run, we are very late."

As it turned out they need not have hurried. The bus did not leave until one o'clock.

It stood, a cumbrous gray van cased in thin metal sheets, in an alley behind the Egged depot. Its driver was not yet aboard and the passengers were still getting on, showing their chits to a harried young man in a tight battlejacket of old olive drab, delaying each other to turn back for final shaloms. For each person going, at least a half dozen were seeing off.

Jacob kissed his wife's lips. "Shalom, little one." He pressed her hand. "I shall send you a cable, 'Safely arrived.' Go home now. Don't stand here. It's cold." He kissed her again, "Shalom, *haviva* —good-bye, darling" (endearment even in sound!), waited for her smile and her "l'hitra'ot" before he muttered, *"Slichah,* excuse me," to the crowd, and used his elbows to plow a path to the bus.

The young man in the battlejacket was being harassed by a stout old woman in a young woman's wig. "But I wish to know," the old woman insisted, "if there will be shooting today."

"I wish to know, too," the man answered her.

"Give me an advice, should I go?"

"Grandma, I give no advice." The young man, Jacob was pleased to observe, was handling himself with fine self-control. "Go or not go, be good enough to step back. Let the others get on."

"My daughter, my oldest daughter—" the woman kept talking while the young man reached past her to take Jacob's chit—"she is married three years. God has blessed her at last with a son."

"Mazel tov," Jacob murmured. "Congratulations!" He beamed at the woman.

Unreasonably encouraged, she plucked at his sleeve. "You see, *Adoni,* if I am not there for the *Bris,* her husband's family may say—"

"Come, *Sabta.* Grandmother, come. Do not worry. We will bring you to the Circumcision." He hoisted himself up the steps.

The thick aroma of people and food welcomed him into the dark vault of the bus. Slits in the sides admitted mere fragments of light. As far as he could see, while he stumbled on valises and shoes, all the places were filled. Between a *Hassid,* with corkscrew earlocks and broad black pancake hat, and a neat, elderly man in a gray business suit, there was a small space, but neither man moved to make room for him. The Hassid was busy, holding a book toward the light, mumbling the prayers for God's protection on a dangerous trip.

"Slichah," Jacob said courteously. He raised his voice. "One seat per passenger. Move over, please." The gray man squeezed against his far neighbor to make a few inches of space and Jacob edged back on the bench. The crown of his head reached the light slit. Target for today, he thought wryly but he put his briefcase on his knees and looked round to see whom he recognized in the bus.

Across the aisle were two Jewish Agency officials whom he knew well. He nodded at them, called a cheerful "Shalom." The young woman with the child at the rear of the bus lived in Rehavia, near him, come during the war, lucky ones, out of Europe's charnel house, bringing cash, diamonds, fine furniture and high self-esteem. Mother and daughter were dressed for a journey, in new traveling coats. Luggage was heaped at their feet. The young woman held a handkerchief to her eyes.

Why do you cry, *G'veret?* he wondered. Because our world is disturbed and you and your diamonds must find a new hiding place? Because you are leaving your husband? Because you are leaving this land? Or because you feel sorry for your own self that you lack the courage to stay here with us? He frowned at himself. Hirsch, this is not your affair. You are not a judge. Everyone does what he must.

Herr Doktor Prinz who lived in the corner house, was up front, haunches spread, taking more than his share of the bench. *He* can't run away, Jacob thought sourly, no place to go, nobody wants him but us. And we could spare him very well. He despised Doktor Prinz and knew why he did. The man mourned for München. He blamed Palestine and not Adolf Hitler that he earned his livelihood here at a bookkeeper's job. A Herr Doktor of Economics! Aah, Yecke! His mind spat the derisive epithet and was immediately ashamed of itself. The man was born German, raised German, acts German. He knows no better. Must you therefore sneer "Yecke" at him?

Something scratched the back of his head. He wriggled to see what it was. An envelope came through the slot. "Mail this for me, please." He stood up, accepted the letter, and then peered through the opening to see whether his wife was still there.

Yes, there was Edith, on the edge of the crowd.

Patient, composed but aloof. That's Edith. This pushing, this semi-hysteria of saying good-bye is distasteful to her. Then why does she stay? . . . Poor Edith, one by one we leave her. First, Dinah. Then I. We will be back, both Dinah and I. . . . She is a pretty woman, my wife. She *was* a pretty woman. She looks old, sad, too thin. Is she sick? . . . Edith is never sick. She does not need to be sick. She is a complete and happy woman. . . . I do not like the way Edith looks.

He ducked down to the gray man. "Keep my place, please. I have to go out."

When Edith saw him, she cried, "Have you changed your mind?" and he caught the lift of relief in her voice.

"I came out to tell you, go home. It's foolish to stand to watch a bus leave."

"Is it? Then half of Jerusalem is as foolish as I. Get back on, you'll lose your place."

"Promise me you'll go home."

"I promise nothing."

He scowled, squeezed her arm, scooted away to ask the young man in olive drab, "How soon do we leave?"

"When we are ready. Maybe five minutes, maybe two hours."

"What's the delay?"

"We are waiting for people."

He returned to his wife. A dirty and ragged man with a face like a walnut pushed toward them, thrusting forward a tray of small bottles and bleating, *"Mitz nylon. Mitz!"*

"Mitz nylon!" He mocked the vendor. "What are they doing to our language, to *Ivrith?* Nylon is stockings. How can it also be orange juice?"

The hawker made an "O" of his dirty mid-finger and thumb. "Nylon. The best!"

"Madame—" Jacob grinned at his wife—"may I buy you a drink of nylon fruit juice?"

"Get on," she answered. "The driver is here. Our neighbor Benjamin is driving this one himself."

"You see." He stroked her cheek. "The best driver. What's to worry about? Well, shalom, l'hitra'ot!" He kissed her again, started off, and came back. "Little one, a bit of advice. If I do not return, take a lover, a young, handsome man, and live happily."

A boy had Jacob's seat and made believe he was deaf. "It was not for me to say no," the gray man ventured. "Each one has the same rights as everyone else." Jacob had to roam the length of the bus, both sides, and finally beg the Herr Doktor to push his thighs together, so there might be enough room for him. The old woman with the wig who was going to the Bris, was on his other side. *"Oi,"* she moaned as Jacob wedged himself in. "Oi, it should be already the end of this trip."

He sighed heavily. Fine companions I have, he said to himself, for this pilgrimage.

"Why do they not close the door?" Doktor Prinz muttered into his ear.

He half-turned. "Cold or afraid?" he inquired.

"I am afraid, certainly. If I did not have an important appointment—"

"If the driver is not afraid to drive the bus—"

"It is his business to drive the bus."

He wanted to say something caustic. Men like our Benjamin risk their lives to transport Yeckes like you. Stay home. How important can your business be? But for once he held his tongue. "Have you read the newspapers?" Prinz was asking him.

"Have I had the time?"

"Then you do not know the news?"

The superior tone nettled him. The Herr Doktor's life is arranged efficiently. He can read the papers before he leaves on a trip. "Well, then, speak up," Jacob said. "What is so terrific today?"

Prinz settled back on the bench and cleared his throat as though he were about to deliver a speech. "Cadogan of Britain in an interview at Lake Success—" he gave each syllable emphasis—"has announced that the Mandatory power will not give protection to the Partition Commission of the United Nations when it arrives in Palestine."

Jacob lifted one shoulder. "Are you surprised? I am not."

"*Natürlich,* they are right. They are in authority. Cadogan says they will maintain civil administration and public order until May fifteenth, when the Mandate is done."

"Very good." Jacob lunged for his briefcase as it started to skid off his knees. "Let them keep their word. But suppose our cousins attack?"

"Our cousins? The *Araber?*" The man seemed to shudder. "The British will defend the country. Cadogan assures us of that."

Jacob made a rude noise. "Good. Let them do that."

A youth and two girls, all in olive drab, climbed into the bus. The girls were hippy and with full breasts. Jacob nudged Doktor Prinz. "See! Our daughters do not trust Cadogan. Their bosoms are pomegranates, their hips are steel." It struck him that Prinz had turned pale. "Go on with your news," he said quickly. "What else was there?"

"What else?" Prinz squirmed to reach his handkerchief and mopped his face. "*Ach, yah,* I forget. Gandhi was shot yesterday. Gandhi is dead!"

"No!" He was stunned, then sad, then confused. Why is it, he asked himself bitterly, that men who truly want peace inspire so much violence?

The motor whirred harshly. The van started to roll. The hiss of indrawing breath ran along both sides of the bus. "Shalom," Jacob found himself calling out to whom it concerned. "Shalom. L'hitra'ot."

Rifle fire chattered in several parts of the city as the bus pulled away.

The crowd broke slowly, scattering to go home for dinner, queuing up for the local buses to distant quarters.

Edith stood until the tail of the bus, rattling up Jaffa Road toward the hills, could no longer be seen. Then she turned and went the opposite way, toward Zion Square.

II

Zion Square, a small irregular oval, bulging in the New City's main artery, Jaffa Road, was drowsy with noon and Sunday. Jerusalem belongs to the semi-tropics where men take siesta plus lunch. It is also a city of three official Sabbaths, the Moslem Friday, the Jewish Saturday, the Christian Sunday.

On this Sunday, the Jewish-owned shops around the Square were all open but because it was midday, pedestrians were scarce. A quartet of laborers, Arab and Jew, all of a similar bronze, crouched on the curb, eating lunch. The bootblack warmed himself against the sunniest wall. The doors of the Café Vienna stood open and an occasional business man strode in, to lunch and to kibitz the chess games which have been going on there for the length of the memory of man. The thud of small explosions and the clatter of guns, near the foot of Jaffa Road where there was a gate to the Old City, echoed sporadically but the few passers-by in the Square scarcely noticed the noise.

No place in all the world is more used to the sounds of combat than Jerusalem. Its wars have been everlasting, like the city itself: King David's war, one thousand years before Christ was born, Nebuchadnezzar's sack of the town, Antiochus' slaughter, Titus' siege which destroyed the Temple, Godfrey de Bouillon's conquest, Tamerlane's raids; Hebrew, Babylonian, Greek, Roman, Crusader, Egyptian and Turk, for three thousand years shedding blood for this place.

In 1917, Allenby came up Jaffa Road, dismounted, strolled, with a scholar and gentleman's reverence for history, through Jaffa Gate and ordered the Union Jack raised above the gray walls built by Suleiman, the Turk. Then Jerusalem entered an era of uneasy peace under a League of Nations mandate to England which promised too many too much.

Outside the walls where ancient history languished in foul, crooked alleys and lanes, a New City grew, sturdily built of Jerusalem stone, broad thoroughfares—Jaffa Road, Ben Yehuda Street, King George Avenue—fine quarters for residence of prosperous Arab, Briton and Jew, and slums where ten persons lived in one room. But the ambiguous Mandate, enforced by fumbling colonial administrators and indifferent troops and police, satisfied no one, brought further bloodshed.

Yet the peace for which every man longed might have eventually come had not circumstance struck a crushing blow. An Austrian madman, in Berlin, announced that he would massacre Europe's seven million Jews and Whitehall replied, in 1939, to urgent pleas for a place of refuge, with a White Paper, proclaiming that, in security's interest, it was closing Palestine's doors.

Two tramp steamers, with eighteen hundred men, women and children aboard, steamed into Haifa in November, 1940. His Majesty's Government transferred the passengers forcibly to another ship, the *Patria,* and ordered them taken to Mauritius, in the Indian Ocean. The *Patria*'s passengers preferred to die. They blew up their ship in Haifa bay. The following year, an old cattle boat, the *Struma,* crept into Istanbul with 769 persons crowded into cages on a sixty-foot deck. The ship lay in Istanbul harbor while the Jewish Agency pleaded for Palestine visas. At the end of two futile months, the Turkish authorities ordered the *Struma* to sea. It sank with all aboard, a mile off the coast.

Yet until the second World War's end—out of need to close ranks to destroy the common foe, the Nazi—Palestine's Jews (and the world's) fought the White Paper only with words and with tears. In 1945, a young man who had seen the *Patria* sink, murdered Britain's Lord Moyne. After that the sound of the bomb and the Sten began to be heard continuously in Jerusalem's streets. There were those who felt that the Haganah—the name meant simply defense and the purpose, at first, was no more than that—was far too mild. A policy taken by those groomed in patience, bred on the Commandment, "Thou Shalt Not Kill," could gain nothing, these others maintained, but more degradation and violence. The time was here to demand eye for eye. *Irgun Z'vai Leumi* (the *Etzel*) and *Lohmey Heruth Israel* (the *Lechi*) moved to change Whitehall's mind by bombings and floggings, kidnapings and planned individual homicide. The Mandatory struck back and the Holy Land became a police state. Habeas corpus was ended; men were held without trial; settlements, houses were raided and searched; youths swung from gallows for membership in the Etzel or the Lechi. All of Jerusalem, the capital, became an armed camp.

In July of 1946, the Etzel dynamited the King David Hotel where the Mandatory had its Secretariat. Ninety-one—Britons, Arabs and Jews—died by that blast. Then a shocked world demanded that justice and peace be restored in the Holy Land. His Majesty's Government, exchequer depleted, nerves frayed and dignity lost, asked for release from the Mandate and proposed that the United Nations decide Palestine's fate. Commissions came, surveyed, reported. In November, 1947, the General Assembly of the United Nations gave a Solomon's answer. Divide the land between Arab and Jew. Britain had declined to vote on partition. The Arabs opposed and rejected the vote. Out of Jaffa Gate Arab hooligans streamed with knife, gun and torch, to nullify the General Assembly's solemn and earnest decree. And here, in the tranquility of February's first Sunday, the tired Mandatory was ticking off its last days, harassed by the noises of undeclared war.

Being inured to gunfire, Edith Hirsch heard, without hearing, the sounds of that war as she crossed the Square and began to climb Ben Yehuda Street.

A block up the hill there was pain in her back and she reduced her pace. Was it foolish not to wait in the queue for Rehavia's Number Five bus? It was not. More important to get home to Teddy, on his birthday.

The pain circled her middle and nagged at her abdomen. This had begun after Dinah left, this backache which dragged through her entrails and left her tired and cross. But it came and it passed, and therefore it wasn't worth mentioning. I should have told Jacob about it, she said to herself; I think of it now, when he's gone, it's too late. . . . Stop, she told herself sharply. Don't make something of nothing at all.

"G'veret Hirsch!" She paused at the sound of her name and saw a woman half-dragging a cross-eyed small boy into an apartment house. "Schmulke will not come in to eat. Play, play, all he knows is play." She couldn't at first recall who the woman might be—a patient of Jacob's, no doubt,—but she nodded and stroked the child's head. "G'veret Hirsch, you look tired. Come in my house. Have a coffee and rest."

She said she was in a hurry, no thanks, and tried to move on, but the woman stood in her path. "G'veret, you will be so good as to tell the Doctor, we will take his advice. The operation on Schmulke's eyes. After *Pesach,* if God wills—"

"When he returns, I'll tell him."

"He has gone away?"

"To Tel Aviv. Just a few minutes ago."

"How did you let him, G'veret? It is so dangerous."

"Shalom," she answered and began to walk fast.

The upper half of Ben Yehuda Street was concerned not at all with either Sunday or noon. The pavements were crowded, in the hustle and bustle, shoving and crowding of Jerusalem's own rich design, a mosaic made out of pieces and bits of each century, every land. Against the Atlantic Hotel's front wall, a Yemenite squatted, brown-skinned and scrawny, whose white beard and cameo profile might have come straight from a Bible portrait, wearing a turban, a skirted robe, selling nothing more exotic than American, English and local cigarettes. A German, in plus fours and homburg, carrying a leather briefcase, strutted into a block of flats. A black-eyed Susie, olive-skinned with jet curls, barefoot, in red pantaloons, white *keffiah,* silver chains on her wrists and throat, was plodding uphill on a donkey. Was she Persian? Bokharian? Easterner, certainly. Here the twain meet, Edith thought, and we have proved that Kipling merely made a rhythmic phrase. East and West meet in New Jerusalem's streets. And one people they are. There go Hassidim, swishing along in kaftans, earlocks flapping beneath pancake hats, out of the ghettos of Poland, Galicia, costume unchanged for hundreds of years. Why should it change? Have they not the same right, precisely, as nuns or priests have to habits of gray, brown or black? Or I to the taste I acquired in Boston? Or Madame Malkoff to her beaded long gowns, left over from Czarist Moscow and let out in the seams? Or Ida Goldstein to the prim black hat, the black cotton gloves like those she wore when she shopped on Budapest's streets?

Our pasts are the baggage we've brought to this place, for amalgam, never for loss.

Out of the mixture, our sabras have come, our children, sturdy, straight-standing, with skin like ripe peaches warmed by the sun. Out of one cloth . . . Olive drab.

The street was full of their color, odds and ends of old uniforms, leftovers from everyone's wars. The boys were wearing knitted peaked caps made for Italian prisoners of war, a bit pixyish but rather nice. . . . Our defenders! Our brave! Nothing but courage in their bare hands.

The pain was full in her middle, almost tearing her body in half, and she halted again, before she wheeled to go up King George Avenue.

On the arc of a high ridge the avenue swung, from Mamillah Road to the Street of the Prophets, a broad, dignified thoroughfare, lined with tall apartment buildings and young carob trees. Across the way from Yeshurun synagogue, the green lawns and the gravel paths of the Municipal Gardens sloped steeply down toward Mamillah graveyard where living Arabs crouched with their dead, waiting, guns at the ready; and not far away—what is five hundred yards to a powerful rifle?—was the Generali Building's towering flatiron, within a British Security Zone. Walk fast here, she admonished herself. Run, crouch.

Yet she stopped, as she always did, at the crest of the Gardens and looked toward the hills, ancient beyond man-clocked time and, in this midday, as sere and brown as barren old women. Once those hills were terraced and green with vineyards. There holy men walked in the freshness of dawn and cool of twilight. They cradle our city, she said to herself, the honey-hued walls of our dwellings, our roof tops of rose.

Her glance slanted down, toward the Old City walls, surrounding King David's Tower, the Dome of the Rock, the Church of the Holy Sepulchre, the Wailing Wall. Her throat swelled. This vista, she thought, is my well, is my spring. It makes a poet of me. This is why I am here. My hand, my heart, to Jerusalem. There lies *its* heart, inside those gray walls. Ironic and strange, the heart of the Holy City is a mighty stone fortress built by a Turk! From King George, you can't see the mortars and shining new guns. You can't see Glubb's

Arab Legion. You can't see the reeking filth, the crowded misery and hate. From this distance, it's easy to think holiness.

She lifted her head and looked at the sky. Always, no matter how often Edith Hirsch walked King George Avenue, she was awed by the sweep of the sky, a great azure arch, not just overhead, but on every side. Winter had streaked it today with feathery white clouds. Here we are closest to heaven, she thought. God's own ineffable grace is in our sky.

Somewhere in the Old City church bells were tolling. Their faint and sweet sound reached the ridge.

She moved on.

Ahead, just beyond the stone quadrangle of the Jewish Agency buildings, were the looped coils of wire, the high steel fence of a British Security Zone, and high above the wire, Terra Sancta's Madonna raising her head toward the firmament. Terra Sancta is inside the Zone, she realized. Our synagogue is outside. It is their fence which keeps us separate.

As she crossed the road, two British policemen, with their caps of silver on blue, left the wire fence of the Zone and asked her to stop.

"Your identity card?"

She bit her lip, angered, impatient, while she fumbled inside her handbag. They must have seen me go by this corner dozens of times, she thought. This harassment is petty, a pin-prick of spite. Yet she waited, head up, not saying a word, while each in turn read her name and address, occupation, housewife, place of birth, U.S.A., on the card, and stared with cold insolence at her features, before they gave the card back and let her go on.

She hurried up Keren Kayemeth Street and entered Rehavia.

The greengrocer, the drygrocer, sweetshop, florist and tailor, as well as the branch post office, the school and café, were on Keren Kayemeth, and there she shopped quickly: at the sweetshop, a kilo of boiled sweets, a half kilo of freshly roasted, salt almonds, a box of Elite's best chocolates, festive in wrappings of red, blue, green and gold; at the greengrocer's, the small, sweet tangerines called *clementinas,* and bananas no larger than a man's thumb. Arms loaded, she went past the café and the school, around the tennis courts, inhaling the resinous pungence of Rehavia's pines, and turned into the street where she lived.

It was a quiet, green street, inconspicuous and unimportant, a single long block between two thoroughfares. It had been named for a poet who became immortal in Spain, five centuries before its Inquisition.

All the streets of Rehavia bore the names of poets, philosophers or wise men of one kind or other—Don Abarbanel, Alharizi, Ibn Ezra, Sadya Gaon, Ibn Gabirol, Rambam, even Ushisskin, whose wisdom belonged to more modern times—all the streets except Keren Kayemeth, whose title meant simply Jewish National Fund, the organization devoted to purchase of land.

The street was unpaved and without sidewalks. Its pines were tall, its lawns wide, well tended; its gardens bloomed the year round, boldly, as though this mountain city could not possibly know a sudden freeze. It was fragrant most of the year with roses and jasmine, the biblical flower.

On the corner, where a British light tank or a Bren carrier was usually parked, was the big house of small flats, in one of which Nathan lived with Rachel, his wife, a high-bosomed maternal woman, who ran out at sunup each day in her green uniform to care for the babies in the slum quarters of Mea Shearim or Beit Yisrael. A variety of other people also lived in that house; the Atanis, Tamar and her husband, Elia, Yemenites who ran a gift shop in town where they sold the exquisite pins, bracelets, necklaces, rings made by their brothers and sisters, cousins and uncles and aunts; Benjamin, the Egged bus driver; Herr Doktor Prinz, his wife and his mother-in-law; Rosensweig, a nervous, twitchy man who taught school and had the blue-green concentration camp brand on his arm, and new plastic teeth, replacing those knocked from his jaws by a guard at Dachau, and a treasured concertina which he played badly at night; two Viennese blondes, dressmakers' apprentices, who were reported to have Arab boy friends, and their timorous mother who invariably kept her window blinds down.

Past the apartment house, the block had five dwellings in which seven families lived. Henry Winkleman, a district judge, his spinster sisters, Maida and Janet, and Isaac, his aged father, whom everyone called "The Afrikaaner," had the mansion cater-corner opposite the flats. Ida Goldstein, widow of Moshe, the Jaffa Road druggist, whose son Arieh was a university student and a member of the Palmach, owned the two-family dwelling between Judge Winkleman and Dr. Hirsch, a house subdued and lonesome after Moshe and his daughter,

Deborah, both died and Ida and Arieh lived there alone, but now bursting its seams because Ida's oldest son, Max, and his family— wife and three little children—had moved into the place. In its second story flat, Gordon Leake, who held an administrative post with the Mandatory, had lived with his daughter and wife for several years and Gordon still stayed there, alone, since last year, when his women-folk had gone home to England.

Opposite, another two-family dwelling belonged to Madame Malkoff (she had a first name, Leah, but was referred to, invariably, as "Madame") and there Madame dwelt in perpetual rancor with Ephraim, her son, who wrote poetry and spent his days sitting with Isaac Winkleman before the Keren Kayemeth Street café. Ezra Gross who taught philosophy at the Hebrew University on Mount Scopus and Lillie, his wife, lived on the second floor of the house and they were sedate and reserved. Their son, an only child, was away, in Canada, studying medicine at McGill, where the Professor himself had taken a Bachelor's degree, and Mrs. Gross at this moment was an invalid.

The last house on the street was Yora Levine's, window to window facing Jacob Hirsch's.

At night, when everyone slept, the street was silent, but all day its children laughed, shouted and wailed. Old Isaac Winkleman, an endearing white-bearded wisp, was rather deaf, so that his daughters had learned to shout. Madame Malkoff quarreled with her succession of maids and her son. Jacob Hirsch liked to sing, basso, off-key. Every dwelling and flat had at least one radio. Arieh Goldstein had a violin, Rosensweig a concertina, the Hirsches a piano, the Levines a piano and Asi's flute. Moreover, numerous birds had pre-empted the trees and were talkative. Yet, because the sounds of living can't be considered rude noise, everyone called this a quiet street.

All of the dwellings had been built at one time, designed by the same architect. He had been German. His blueprints stemmed from Bauhaus, square graceless boxes, with balconies and flat roofs, and an ugly iron water tank on each roof, but because of the warm honey stone, quarried out of the very same hills from which Solomon dug for his palace and Temple, and the foliage and sky, the result was not European at all, but had the sensuous flavor of the Middle East.

Henry Winkleman's house was the most ornate, a red tile roof, and large gates and hand-rails of ornamental wrought iron which gave it a Moorish effect, but Hirsch's place, at the end of the block was largest, since it was his office as well as his home. There, a rise of ground had been the architect's problem and so he built on two levels, with a dropped living room, a narrow outside entrance staircase of stone, leading up to the dining room level, and a cellar below the dining room wing. A separate path led to the office and waiting room wing. From the roof, on the water-tank side, it was possible to see the Old City walls.

Jacob had planted cypress trees at both ends of his lawn, to insure a privacy he neither needed nor wished and since everything rooted in Jerusalem's earth feels an urge toward magnificence, the trees had to be thinned each two years. A fig tree which had established itself long before the first modern settlers had climbed up this ridge was allowed to remain in the yard and bear its sweet fruit and an almond tree bloomed in the spring. There was a pepper tree on the front lawn, a graceful fan of branches whose thin leaves and red berries looked as if they had been sprayed around the slim trunk. Purple bougainvillea had climbed over most of the wall on the dwelling side of the house, reaching the second floor balcony. On the other side, hibiscus grew tall, with flame-colored blossoms dotting the green. There was an excellent flower garden at one side and in back, and a hedge of red geraniums from the gateposts all the way to the house.

Tacked to those gateposts which had no gate was a blue-on-white ceramic sign, "Dr. Jacob Hirsch, Surgeon and Specialist in Obstetrics and Diseases of Women," in Arabic, English and Ivrith. Being Boston-born, and reared by parents who could recall when Victoria sat on a throne, Edith had, in the earlier days, blushed at that sign, finding it blatant and indelicate. The metal plaques beside apartment doorways in the States, the discreet "John Jones, M.D.," left the nature of whatever illness a doctor treated, anonymous, as it should be. Yet, suppose, she had occasionally thought, the sign had read "Specialist in Nervous and Mental Disorders," then everyone would have known the sad truth about each poor wretch who came up the path to the door at the left. Well, suppose. Would that have mattered? For all the headlines it made throughout the world, Jerusalem was a small town. Here there were no minor secrets, only the very big one which was shared by each man, woman, child, who lived outside the iron spiked fences of His Britannic Majesty's Security Zones.

III

TEDDY RAN TO meet his mother as she came up the path. He called out Dinah's name and her hand flew to her heart. "Dinah is home!"

He stared. "Of course not. A man came."

She dropped her bundles on the hall table. "Where? Who?"

"He came when I was in school." The boy sounded impatient. "See what he brought for me." He wagged a book under her nose. *"Doctor Dolittle!"* he cried.

She snatched it from him, flipped to the title page. Yes, there was *her* writing, *her* words. *"To a son of Eretz Israel. May he help to build a great nation. With love from his sister Dinah."* Her fingers were trembling when she gave it back.

"It's *yoffee,* Imma," he said. "All about a man who talked with animals. The way I talk to Udi and Udi talks to me." She was not listening to him. "Shifra saw the man," he hurried to add. "Maybe he told her something."

Shifra was in the yard, helping Margalit bring in dry clothes. *"Ken,* G'veret," Shifra said. "I saw the man. He was from Gan Darom. In on business, he said." She smirked over that. "Dinah asked him to bring things for her family. Such things! Wait, you will see! Carrots. Tomatoes. Yoffee! He said tell you she is well. They are all well. His name was Reuven, he said. He was very handsome. And intelligent." She paused to sigh reminiscently. "I asked him if he was married. He said yes, he was. Then he laughed. You should have seen how his eyes glistened when he laughed at me. They are so good-looking, these *kibbutznicks.* 'You are a strong, pretty girl,' he said to me. 'Come join us in Gan Darom. We will find a husband for you.'" She beamed at Margalit, seeking confirmation, and finding none, she went on, "Was it not nice Dinah remembered her brother's day? Such an expensive book! They have not much money, these kibbutznicks. Was it not good of her?"

Yes, it was good of her, fine, wonderful, Edith agreed, but how much better if Dinah had come herself. It's more than four months since our daughter was home. She went back to the house, into the living room, to comfort herself with the photograph.

Framed in silver, it stood on the old Kashmir shawl which covered the Steinway grand, in a rank of its own, ahead of the family pictures —parents, grandparents, brothers and sisters, of both sides of the family. She had been sixteen when that picture was taken by Orushkes, of Zion Square, and she had chosen to pose in her Scout uniform, the *Ata* blue scarf loosely twisted around the sturdy throat, the khaki blouse taut on the tumescent breasts; an earnest, round face, on which time had had little to write, unsmiling, untasted lips, eyes serene, a girl child waiting in beauty, as in the old fairy tale.

Her nose was small and well shaped. She wore her hair long, sabra's hair, thick, vital, lustrous. Her large, dark, almond-shaped eyes were arresting. "Some female in my family misbehaved with a Tartar," Jacob always explained. "It couldn't have been Edith's side. They were the *pure* idealists."

How has she changed? Does one grow much taller in only four months? She was taller than Jacob and I when she went away, five foot six without shoes. And well-filled-out, bone and muscle, not fat. Her breasts were a woman's. A woman! Think of Dinah as woman! Ridiculous. She's a child. *My* child. My unique and brave, lovely girl. Who that has not a daughter can understand the dearness of another woman of your own blood?

Teddy came up behind her. "Imma, why are you wasting more time?"

She set the photograph upright on the old tapestry.

"I looked in the packages," Teddy said. "I think there will be enough. When will you make my party?"

"When my work's done."

He followed her upstairs while she hung up her coat. "How was the bus, Imma?"

"You know how the buses are."

"Was it covered? You know what I mean."

"It was covered," she said over her shoulder. "Don't worry, Abba is safe. Benjamin's driving. He's the best driver we have."

"How brave can a driver be, if there is a mine?"

She whirled. "Don't talk so much," she cried.

The sound of her dread frightened him. "I will not speak about it," he said. "I will not even think." Nevertheless, when he tagged after her, down the steps, he said softly, "Just the same, I wish Abba had taken his gun."

There was only the dusting to do. The stone floors had been *spongehed*—the time-honored flooding with water, wading in ankle-deep, swishing a *smartout,* a thick, grayed old rag, around with a circular motion, which kept Shifra's waistline so supple and slim. The rugs had been beaten; the woodwork gleamed. But because Shifra's hands were heavy, there were things Edith chose to do for herself.

She was proud of her house. In its living room, she had mingled the East and the West. The sofas and chairs, the grand piano which she played well, were from the apartment she and Jacob had furnished in Cambridge when they were married. The rugs were Persians, rich blues and deep reds; the window hangings had been woven on Palestine looms; the small tables on which coffee was served, hand-carved by gifted craftsmen of the East. Jacob sometimes painted in oils, for relaxation, and one of his works, lowering gray-purple storm clouds at sunset over the crenelated Old City walls, hung over the powerful radio which occasionally picked up New York.

On the window ledges were foot-high glass jars, blue, pale green, opalescent white, blown wafer-thin and preserved for two thousand years beneath desert sands. The Roman glass picked up each morning's sun and worked alchemy, so that the long living room was a web of rainbows. On the tables, the bookshelves, the radio cabinet, stood ewers, bowls, plates of lustrous old copper on tin. The shades of the lamps through which electric light streamed were of venerable parchment, the clay Menorah on the bookshelf of the Maccabaean period.

Living thus, with the old and the new, Jerusalem's thousands of years in one room, Edith derived her own comfort, the assurance of life's continuity, that man lives forever through what he creates, the work of his hands as well as his loins. I, Edith Hirsch, in Rehavia, am dusting a pitcher from which some woman who lived in a goat-skin tent may have poured wine for a shepherd or warrior or even high priest. And it stands on a radio cabinet out of Boston's Filene's. I, Edith Hirsch, have given a daughter and son to this Land. Here their seed will flourish, bringing forth children and children's children, a stream widening to feed the parched wilderness, so that new life may spring. We are immortal, Jacob and I, because Dinah and Teddy were born in this Land.

When Edith wrote to her sister Belle in Brookline, Massachusetts— which was not often, since when you are far away in miles, you grow distant in other ways, too—she wrote principally of this house and the garden, such agreeable details as, *"You will not believe it, but my garden paths are lined with hedges of red geraniums as high as my waist. My pansies and nasturtiums are as big as saucers and I have more kinds of roses than we used to see in the North Shore gardens in June. They bloom practically all year round. And the morning-glories at the back of the yard, a wall of extraordinary blue, must be seen to be believed. Jacob doesn't like our jasmine. Too sweet, he insists. A flaw, the bride is too beautiful, our mother used to say.*

". . . I have been combing the town for fabric for my living room chairs. Two active children and a growing dog wear out whatever isn't cast iron. One of the decorators turned up a beautiful piece of old tapestry from Kashmir that I couldn't resist but when I brought it home, I realized it was too delicate for chair cushion. It will go on the piano."

"Edith dear," Belle had answered. *"What else do you do in Jerusalem except tend your garden and re-upholster your chairs? Why don't you write us about your life, yours and Jacob's and the children's? Why don't you write us the interesting things?"*

Belle had not been using her head. Surely, in the States, they must surmise that outgoing letters often were opened and could you venture to write that Dinah, at fifteen, was already an excellent shot with a Sten? Moreover, what are the *interesting* things? Every detail of life is absorbing, important. Yet while Edith told herself that, making excuses, she knew well enough what Belle was eager to read, but she phrased her reply with evasions which seemed to tell all and told nothing whatever.

"Life in Jerusalem is much like life in Cambridge or Brookline. Jacob spends his days at the Hospital and seeing private patients and since he still does obstetrics, he's often out the whole night. When we have a free evening we go to the cinema or to visit our friends. Or they come to us and we play bridge and have coffee and cake. The Levines

*who live across the street come in at least once a week for contract.
The town is not lively, you know. No night clubs. Occasionally
theatre, Habima, on tour. We have a little car, British make, and
when Jacob's not busy, we sometimes drive in the hills, up to Mt.
Scopus, for instance, on the Sheikh Jarrah Road, past the Grand
Mufti's house, to stand on the portico of the University and admire
our entrancing town. A busman's holiday, Jacob grumbles. He goes
up that hill, to the Hospital, every day. A staid, peaceful city and our
Rehavia most refined of all. A Middle East Cambridge. Can you picture that?*

*"The children are superbly healthy and we think, beautiful. If all
goes well we may send them to you for a holiday and you'll see for
yourself what odd chicks we've hatched. Typical sabras. Fruit of the
cactus. The prickly pear. Rough on the outside and sweet within. A
vigorous, forthright, original breed. There has been some talk around
the house of sending the children to college back in the States. I've
talked Wellesley to Dinah but she hasn't exactly been joyful about it.
She seems to have other ideas at this moment. However, if things go
well and these quiet times last, we shall see."*

That was three years ago, just after the big war had come to its end,
when peace seemed all at once, natural and permanent, when one
regarded the occasional bombings as nothing more than the dangerous sport of out-of-hand boys. A lulling dream, for an hour. And
now our girl is a soldier, in a garrison outpost in the desert. No, a
farmer, tilling the barren soil, hoe in one hand; in the other, a gun.
Can I write my sister that?

Teddy was at her elbow. "You don't need to clean up so much. We
won't play in the house. We'll be out in the yard."

"I'll dress now," she said. "And make your party."

Upstairs, in her many-windowed front bedroom, with its Boston-
bought mahogany dresser and chest and four-poster bed and its ruffles
of English chintz, she changed swiftly to a print frock, brushed out
and pinned up her hair, before she stepped into the bathroom and
Teddy's bedroom to make sure they were tidy for guests. Both the
children's rooms (is not Dinah still child of ours?) were austere in
the way of the country, with hard-as-rock studio couches, graceless,
huge wardrobes and plain Gaza rugs, stripings of crimson or forest

green on oyster white. Everything here was neat and spotless, a blessing to have a reliable maid.

"Only twelve places." Teddy hovered around while she set the the dining room table. "Not the Scoutmaster. We didn't want him. He thinks he's too much. . . . I'm glad we're not having girls. I hate all girls. Except Dinah. Dinah was never like those fistukes. She was always Palmach."

Asi came first, bringing the flute. When the rest straggled in, scrubbed and hair-slicked, fair and dark, gangling and chunky small boys, the wailing of Teddy's new flute greeted them.

After they had had their cake, lemon squash, candy and fruit, the boys got up abruptly and ran from the house, down the street. Edith fretted about them while she cleared the table, because there was gunfire and it seemed near.

Teddy came back alone, in an hour, out of breath, somewhat pale. He found Udi, lay down on the living room floor, and snuggled against the dog's chest.

"Where are the boys?" his mother inquired.

"They went home."

"So early? Did you have a fight?"

He rose and went for his book. "Not exactly. I wanted to read my new book."

She kept after him. "What happened?"

He looked at her coolly, taking her measure. "The soldiers chased us," he said.

"Teddy!" She seized his hands. "Tell me what happened."

He avoided her eyes. "Nothing happened. Nobody was shot."

"Tell me. I need to know everything."

"Nothing, I tell you. Asi said, 'Let's go out and sing the anemone song.' That's all, Imma; I tell you the truth."

She let out her breath. The song was a charming, inoffensive tune about the flowers that bloomed in the hills in the spring. When the children had first seen the Sixth Airborne Division, it had struck them the soldiers' red tams looked like those flowers and sometimes they trailed the soldiers around, singing the anemone song.

"So we went down to the Zone," Teddy said. "And we sang the

anemone song." He gestured expansively. "They didn't like it." His eyes lighted up. "They hollered at us, 'Go away.' Then Asi said, 'They think we make fun of them. Let's not go away. Let's sing it again.' So we didn't go away." He giggled. "We sang it again. They were mean. They started to shoot."

She gasped. Strength oozed from her legs.

"Don't be afraid." Teddy grinned. "We could run faster than they."

She sat down beside him. "Son, don't do that ever again. Don't provoke the soldiers in any way."

His nose wrinkled up. "Why not? Etzel and Lechi do it."

"You're not Etzel or Lechi." She heard her voice rising in a half-shout. "You are not a terrorist. You are a Boy Scout. And you are a child. I don't want you hurt."

He listened, nodded, though his very agreement seemed to make fun of her. "Did we eat all the cake, Imma?" he asked when she stopped. "Or is there still some for me?"

"There is. But it's going to Lillie Gross; she's been sick."

He made a face. "Good, so then bring it to her. And ask her when David comes back for Haganah."

On her second floor balcony, swaddled in blankets and a heavy tweed coat, Lillie Gross was receiving the last of the afternoon sun. Rest, nourishment, the Doctor had ordered, a modest prescription. Yet, Edith realized as she crossed the road, the ordinary things have become hardest to get. Lillie's own illness proves that. Our stone floors are always cold in the winter but usually we do have some heat to take the chill off. There's not been a drop of fuel oil this winter and Lillie Gross got frostbite. Chilblains in Jerusalem! Imagine that! And turned into gangrene! That's because she's so heavy, circulation is poor. How lucky the hospital had penicillin! It saved her life. But with David away, poor Ezra has had all the work and the worry alone. Madame, downstairs, isn't the best of good neighbors and I haven't helped all I should.

"Birthday cake!" Lillie's pain-bleached eyes lighted up before they started to drip. "All these years it was I who baked for the birthdays. And now—" She gestured toward her legs.

"You will again, very soon." Edith drew a chair up for herself.

"Tomorrow," she promised," I'll come and fix you a good lunch."

Lillie was pleased, but being an invalid, had to indulge herself with a bit of a fuss. "You have no time. No one has time for a useless old woman like me."

"We take care of each other. Remember when Teddy was born? You traipsed to Mahne Yehuda Market to buy the freshest, best chickens for me. You made me good soups. . . . We've been such close friends." She paused because it hurt to remember how close, not merely come at the same time, from the same hemisphere, but raising the children in a joint dream. That's over, that's past, she told herself. David's at McGill, away more than a year, a brilliant boy, handsome. They're so proud of him. We're all proud of him. Yet last fall, before Dinah left . . . I had no right to hope, no right to pray, David, come back, come home, save Dinah for us. . . . Come back for Dinah's sake and for mine.

"Here! My invalid's tea!" Professor Gross, a spare, fussy man with salt and pepper goatee and steel-rimmed spectacles, brought in a tray, which he carried clumsily because a fresh bandage was on his right hand.

"Ezra, you've burned yourself!"

"It is nothing. As many years as I have lived here, the primus is still a lethal weapon to me. . . . Lillie, you were fretting that Edith left you alone. Here she is." He beamed fondly while he handed his wife her teacup. He looked tired and worried. These were difficult days for him, too, hurrying to Keren Kayemeth early each morning to shop, running to the windmill on Rambam Road for the kerosene ration for the primus, traveling up to Mount Scopus to the university, and after his classes, nursing his wife.

Lillie Gross tasted the cake.

"Edith! You used powdered egg!" She made it sound like a crime. "For the children, I suppose, good enough. But in my condition, for me!"

There was an awkward silence, before the Professor asked gently, "Did the boy have a good day?"

"Dinah sent him a present, a book."

Tears marbled Lillie's eyes. "How lucky you are to have Dinah so near."

"Near? We have not seen her since October."

"We have not seen David since long before that." Lillie dabbed at her puffy face with a moist handkerchief. "When the weather improves, you can drive to her, or she come to you. But we—" She set her cup down, blew her nose. "Last month when I thought I was dying, I asked Ezra to cable David. True, we had not the money for his passage, but we would have managed somehow. . . . When I came to my senses, when the fever was down, I knew it was impossible. We have made a decision. We must bear with our loneliness until he has finished what he needs to do."

Teddy wasn't hungry, didn't want supper, said he was tired, but because his conscience was bothersome, asked, "Imma, do you have to water the garden tonight? Can't it wait till Abba is home?"

"You're excused," she said. "You don't need to help. I can do it myself."

He went upstairs with Udi, took a chair out to the balcony and sat there tootling his flute.

There was still ruddy glow in the sky, gilding the clouds, and garrulous birds were having their evening *cumsitz* in the trees.

Edith carried her watering can out to the rose beds. Usually Jacob insisted on bringing the watering cans out, maintaining that women's insides weren't built for hauling such loads and please remember we can't spare a hospital bed. He was right. The water was painfully heavy. Only the roses tonight, she decided, wait for rain for the rest. The rose bushes looked sturdy, stems thick and green and innumerable buds. If there is no killing frost, there should be flowers before the end of this month.

"Ephraim!" Madame Malkoff's voice crossed the road, hoarse from a lifetime's strong cigarettes. "Bring me my shawl. . . . Not that one, idiot!"

Ephraim fetches and carries, Edith said to herself, yet his mother is never pleased. Such a difficult woman. A prima donna, because in her father's house in Moscow she once had a salon—or imagined she did.

She set the watering can down, pulled a few weeds and strolled over to inspect her pansy borders. They were at their best, lush purples and yellows and coppery browns. She picked a handful of pansies, brought them in for the dining room bowl. When she emerged, Yora

Levine was just leaving his house. She called out, "Shalom," to summon him. He waved, stiff arm, like a salute, seeming vaguely annoyed to be hailed, yet he started across. It was singular, she thought, while she waited for him at the hedge, when people talked about Yora, they invariably said, "There's a clever one." Why clever? Because he had come home from the North African war with officer's pips, to a big desk, a good job with Government? . . . Because he serves two masters so skillfully? "Clever" suggests quick and deft, and this man is heavy, he's florid and bald as an egg, with a clipped Prussian mustache. He walks like the soldier he was, shoulders back, abdomen in. Self-important, stuffy, a bit ponderous.

"Have you heard—" with Yora one didn't waste time on amenities— "whether the Tel Aviv convoy arrived?"

Yora's long forehead creased. "I have not heard it did not."

"But there was difficulty?"

"That, I cannot say." His gray eyes met hers. "That is all you wish to know?"

"That is all."

"Shalom," he said and started on up the street toward the apartment house.

Max Goldstein, Ida's elder son, red-haired, like all her children and she herself, came out of his mother's flat. His own children— Tamar, Naomi and Shlomo—piled out after him, competing to see who could yell loudest, most shrilly. "Shalom, Abba. Shalom, shalom."

"Get in the house." He shooed them back. "Go to sleep. *Lila tov*. Good night."

He fell into step beside Yora, straightening his spine to match the ex-soldier's bearing, and Edith watched them marching together toward the end of the street

Max was a printer at the *Post* and he worked nights, a strapping fellow, taller than Yora—you don't realize that till he straightens up. He's gotten the stoop from hunching over linotype keys. Is it good or is it bad he's now living in Ida's house? Ida's husband had bought the place in the years when his drugstore was prosperous. When he died, Max was already married, with a wife, a family and flat of his own, Arieh had started his studies up on the Hill, and Deborah was seventeen, completing high school.

Graceful Deborah, with shimmering auburn hair, she wanted so badly to help her mother support all of them. Gordon Leake had found her that job, clerk at the Secretariat, in the King David Hotel. She'd been one of six typists and clerks who had begged their department head to let them go out (into the courtyard, at least) after the Etzel had telephoned to warn that in half an hour the place would be blasted to bits. They had begged, had implored (one had been flung free to tell what occurred), but the official refused and so they had linked their young hands and stood in a circle, waiting for death. Even now, after nearly two years, remembering that day brought a chill. Of all the young blood spilled in this Land, none had been more wanton than this.

Gordon himself had come down to urge Ida to file a negligence claim against His Majesty's Government but she had replied, "Will money bring my Deborah back? Can you change the ways of an empire by making them pay a few hundred pounds for the bull-headedness of one official?" Then His Majesty's Government had commandeered blocks of dwellings for troop quarters within their new Security Zones and had put Max and his family out of their flat. They had moved in with Ida. Miriam, Max's wife, was slovenly and not *kasher*, besides, and Ida had always been meticulously neat and rigidly Orthodox. It took all her patience and back-breaking work to manage the flat and the hard work helped her to forget.

Forget? Edith thought. Does one ever forget a lost child?

She stooped to pluck a few yellowed leaves from the geranium hedge.

Little Shlomo was wailing, objecting to going to bed. Miriam was spanking the child and screaming at him. Gunfire, spattering from Katamon's direction, beyond Rehavia, made a strange accompaniment to Shlomo's wails.

Teddy called down from the balcony. "I can play '*Hatikvah*.' Listen to me." He piped a few notes.

"Yoffee!" she called up to him.

From the balcony across the road, Asi answered him on *his* flute, playing the song perfectly. Teddy blew harder and worse. "*Sheket.* Be quiet," Asi shouted at him. "Practice before you play in public."

She laughed to herself. With two flutes there will be no peace at all in this street.

The lights went on in Carmela's kitchen. Supper dishes were about to be washed.

Judge Winkleman came up the street slowly, on his habitual evening stroll. A slight man, on the sallow side, a narrow, sharp nose and thin lips, in his robe and curled judicial wig, Henry Winkleman might have stepped from a Daumier print, but in old Harris tweeds, he merely seemed shabby, undistinguished and tired. He walked on the opposite side of the street, halted and seemed to be interested in the silvery leaves of an old olive tree in the Levine back yard. His glance shifted, inch after inch, to the kitchen window. He walked on, paused again. The oleander on Yora's front lawn was worth studying. Then, for several seconds, he stood on the pavement considering the outside of the house.

Some dreams never die, Edith said to herself. When he first came, Henry Winkleman was fresh out of Oxford and South Africa, and Carmela Benatar the most courted girl in this town. Those two went strolling by moonlight on the Old City walls, danced outdoors on spring nights, took long walks in the scented evenings. But the flame never lit. "He wants me and is afraid to want me," Carmela had said. "He is frightened even to give me a kiss."

She had married Yora and Henry had buried himself in his work, had done well as a barrister, become District Judge, yet there had been no wife, no whisper of other romance. It was taken for granted he would not marry until his sisters did, but the girls were as hard to please as they were unpleasing and they held their heads high. Jacob had had his own theory on Henry's bachelorhood and it came to her now as she watched the slight, wistful man. "The bell doesn't ring because the clapper is missing," Jacob had said. My husband's so vulgar sometimes, she thought. Why do I put up with it? You take a husband as is, you'll never change him. Then why do I keep thinking the right wife would have made a great difference in Judge Winkleman?

Carmela might have done worse than to marry him, Edith thought. The man she had chosen was by no means an amiable husband and there had been that gossip during the war. The military censor had tattled, had told a few trusted friends, that a fading but distinguished lady was writing amorous letters to Captain Yora Levine in North Africa, and word got around. Naturally, Carmela had heard the gossip—how else does our city amuse itself?—but she'd shrugged it away.

"Who does not flirt in this country?" Who? For one, Carmela Levine. Even when Yora was off at war, many men tried but not one could boast he had so much as bought the lady a drink.

Henry Winkleman crossed the road and paused at the geranium hedge. "Shalom," he said to Edith. "A mild evening for this time of year. Your flowers are doing well."

She thanked him. She said, "I'm terrified of a frost."

He smiled faintly. "Would our God be so cruel as to send us a freeze in a winter when we have no fuel?" Then he pursed his thin lips. "Has your husband phoned he has arrived in Tel Aviv?" he asked.

"Why should he phone?"

He had alarmed her, he saw, and he tried to retreat. "No reason whatever—I merely assumed that he might. You will hear from him, I am sure."

"I am sure. . . . Would you care to step in for coffee?"

"Thank you." He bowed. "I should like it very much. But tonight I cannot. My sisters are off to the cinema. We prefer not to leave Father alone. There is, have you noticed?, a bit of disturbance around Katamon." He shook his head. "We shall have to do something about that. Cadogan's promise is not good enough." Then he smiled again, said, "Shalom," folded his hands behind his back, and walked slowly toward his gaudy house.

Why Henry Winkleman had built himself the most ornate house on the block was anyone's guess. Maida and Janet had probably insisted on that. I try to be generous but social climbers are hard to admire. The girls are so pleased with themselves because some of the ladies of the Mandatory have condescended to sip their tea. Poor dears, she decided, now they'll have to content themselves with *our* society.

The old man who goes shuffling to the café each morning with his gold-headed cane and sweet smile is the best of that family. The Afrikaaner! He likes to be called "The Afrikaaner" and he tells Ephraim Malkoff fascinating tales about South Africa and teaches him Zulu songs. It took courage to come out from Poland to that primitive continent, start out with a peddler's pack, build up a big dry goods store, and again tear up roots to come here. If he could give some of that courage to Ephraim Malkoff, she thought, and rebuked herself. Courage cannot be given. It is or is not. And for every man whatever he has is as much as he will ever have.

"Imma," Teddy called down from the balcony. "I'm going inside to read my book." Light streamed from the second floor of the house and flung glittering arrows into the darkening trees. Across the road, light flared in Madame's living room.

"Idiot!" Edith heard Madame Malkoff again. "Why do you turn on the lights? Come out here and sit." Madame was smoking, her cigarette a crimson pinpoint on her balcony. The light within the house was extinguished. The rumble of quarreling voices came from Madame's balcony.

Ephraim is almost forty and still a poor thing. Has she broken his spirit entirely? Yes, probably. It's a misfortune to be that woman's son. Sweetheart of the regiment, Jacob calls her. She hints that whoever you mention or she herself does was once her lover or panted to be. It's vulgar, ugly. That's the Boston in me. Her sort of bragging might be indecent in a young woman but let's be indulgent when the female is beyond seventy.

Yet, really, now, she considered, why shouldn't a grown man put on lights if he wishes to? Everywhere else there was light beyond the drawn window blinds. Except in Gordon's flat, over the Goldsteins'. Those rooms were shuttered and black. The man slept there nights, but without wife and child it wasn't a home. How stupid the Mandatory had been to send the English women away! To shame us before world opinion. See, Jewish terrorists have made the country unsafe for our tender British females. Malice and stupidity. (Where is it written that all statesmen must be endowed with flawless judgment?) Five years ago, gladly, we might have been a faithful Dominion or a Crown Colony. Bright star in the Empire, bringing it riches and loyalty. That's over now. . . . She brushed her hands. . . . They're leaving, in shame and in pique.

Gordon will go. And he will be missed. He's lived in Rehavia almost as long as anyone else. He's one of us. Strange thing to say of an Englishman, but he isn't quite like the rest. He hasn't the fabulous British charm. He's gauche, but sensitive and considerate. Veronica his wife, was plain, unexciting, yet we liked her, too. And Betty—why, Jacob had delivered that baby—that imp with buttercup curls.

Gordon must be fearfully lonely without his family.

Let it never be said we hate Englishmen. That is the truth. Why, see here, it was the Englishman, Balfour, who promised a Homeland to us. And there was Orde Wingate, Bible-loving soldier and mystic and seer. I can remember him in this town, walking about in his sandals and robe. Yora knew him well, talked with him often, learned much from him. Orde Wingate. Captain Wingate. General Wingate. How tragic that he died on the Burma Road. But he left us a great heritage. He left us Palmach. An Englishman, godfather to our Palmach! And he left us faith in our destiny. . . . He was one of us.

So is Gordon Leake in his way. . . . Oh, he's no Wingate, good heavens, no. He's ordinary. Just a Civil Servant, modest and shy, who says "Shalom," not "Cheerio." He's accepted us and we've accepted him. Why, he lives under one roof with Arieh Goldstein who is Palmach, and nobody gives that one anxious thought.

What a curious mixture we are on this block! Out of so many lands, such different backgrounds, here for only one reason, that here we wish to be. Not necessarily friends, merely living close.

She rested her back against a gate post. In the gray dusk, she could barely make out the gleam of the ceramic sign and she let herself wonder an instant whether her husband would telephone.

The cypress rows at the end of the lawn were sharp silhouettes against a dark curtain studded with stars. The night was soft and still, the birds and the Goldstein babies hushed finally. Leaves rustled in a light breeze. Down in the corner house, the concertina wailed.

There was a whistling noise. In a tree high over the hedge, a twig snapped. It fell near her feet. She stepped back. Even here, in this quiet street. How fortunate that Teddy is in the house!

She turned and went quickly up her path into her house. The long day's weariness gripped her there and she sat a while, numb with fatigue and a sudden loneliness, before she switched on a lamp, drew the casements shut, the blinds tightly down. She turned the radio dial carefully, until she heard the musical signature. The first bars of "Hatikvah," clear, sharp, with a saucy lilt, like a gamin whistling in a sunny street; then the voice. "This is *Kol Hamegen Ha Ivri,* the broadcasting service of Haganah, calling on a wave length of—" She kept it turned low and crouched close. "*Yesterday at Lake Success,*

Cadogan speaking for Britain announced that until the end of the Mandate on May 15, His Majesty's Government would be responsible for the defense of all Palestine territory. May we therefore call to the delegate's attention that on the day following his statement of policy, there was persistent firing from Mamillah Cemetery, and from other Arab-held sectors of Jerusalem. When we attempted by our fire to disperse the cemetery snipers, British police and soldiers, on guard on top the Generali Building in Security Zone B, began to shoot indiscriminately. . . . May we also call to his attention that traffic on the roads between—"

She tensed so that she could barely hear the place names. She sat abruptly down on the floor. "Not mine," she breathed. "Thank God, this time, not mine."

"Every hour," the voice went on, *"it becomes incontestably clear that if the country is to be defended we must not rely upon promises and we do not intend to rely any longer upon promises. Let this serve notice upon His Majesty's spokesmen that we shall defend this country and defend ourselves. . . ."*

The small boy goes down the street, bravely whistling "Hatikvah's" first bars.

She clicked the radio off, put out the lights, went upstairs. Teddy was in bed, reading and chortling, "Imma," he barely glanced up, "it's nylon!"

She reached for his light. "Save the rest for tomorrow."

"One page more, only one."

When she passed his door again, coming back from the bathroom, his light was out. He was crooning softly to Udi, the *"Udi Chamoodi"* song. "Sweet little Udi," indeed, to a boxer as big as a donkey with an appetite like a horse!

"Imma!" She came back to his doorway. "You heard our broadcast. Did they mention Abba's bus?"

"No, darling. Lila tov."

"Lila tov." He yawned. "I would like to have a birthday every day," he said. "Imma, how many birthdays do you think I will have before I have to die?"

IV

EDITH HAD NO more than dozed off when a violent blast shook the house. She sat up. She snapped at the switch. The lamp did not light. She groped for a torch, heard Teddy's sleep-drugged voice. "Imma, what was that boomp?" Udi was alongside them when they ran to the balcony.

The night blew cold, the stars were icicle tips; but to the left, down below, where Zion Square was, the yellow of fire warmed the sky. The blast had aroused the whole block. Down the road, she could see figures in night clothes, leaning over the balcony walls. The boy and the dog pressed her side, shivering.

"What is it, Imma?" Teddy's teeth rattled. "That was a big one. What have they done to us?"

Candlelight flickered across the road. A telephone rang. A torch's straight beam cut the night. Yora ran down his front steps. "Yora, what was it?" Edith cried out to him from her balcony.

"The *Palestine Post* has been bombed." His voice was like a trumpet in that hushed street.

A woman screamed. A door banged. Miriam Goldstein, in her nightgown, ran out to the road. "Max!" she cried hysterically. "The *Post!* Max! Max!" She began to run up the street.

A man and a woman were strolling, arms linked, down the street. The man saw Miriam, moved to her side, stretched his hand out to make her halt.

"Don't touch me!" She clawed at his face.

"What's the matter with that crazy one, Gordon?" everyone on the balconies heard the other woman ask and Gordon Leake snap at her, "Millie, shut up."

Just after dawn, Yora brought the facts to Miriam and Ida Gold stein. A truck had driven up Hasollel Street, off Zion Square, where

53

the *Post* building was, had parked beneath the newspaper's windows. Faceless men lighted a fuse, leaped, ran away. The *Post* building stood gutted, blasted apart, and the near-by buildings were wrecked. Three people were already dead, and scores in the hospitals.

Max was not dead, Yora told his mother and wife. He was in the hospital on Mount Scopus, and the doctors were doing their best. His face and body had been terribly burned by splashing hot lead. His ribs were smashed, how many they would not know until X-ray pictures were made. One eye was gouged out by a metal slug; the other eye seared. Yora suggested that, since the sniping was bad, his family should wait a few days before they tried to see Max.

Miriam, his wife, sat at the dining room table, her head on her arms. "My children!" she wailed. "My poor little ones. Who will take care of them?"

"Be quiet." Her mother-in-law put a comforting hand on her head. "Arieh and I will take care of you." She bit her lip before she added, "Max is also my son."

A lanky, spectacled, red-haired young man came out of the kitchen. "Imma, I have given the children their breakfast," he said. "What else do you wish me to do before I leave?"

Ida clutched at his hands. "Arieh, darling, son! Be well, be strong. Now you are father in this house. You are my only one."

The newsboy delivered the *Palestine Post* at his usual time Monday morning. When she took it from him, Edith said, "But I don't understand. The *Post* was destroyed last night."

"I know only, G'veret, they gave me the papers today."

"What wonderful people they are!" she said.

On Tuesday, the procession of the *Post*-bombing dead, crawling up toward the venerable graveyard on the Mount of Olives, was attacked at the corner of St. George's and Nablus Road. A mine exploded under its convoy. The police failed to arrive in time to catch those who detonated the charge.

On Wednesday evening, Gordon Leake met Judge Winkleman on the street while the Judge was taking his stroll. Gordon said, "Shalom."

The Judge halted. "Yes, Mr. Leake?"

"Judge, I find my position difficult," Gordon began.

Judge Winkleman's eyebrows arched, though he said mildly, "I am not surprised."

"I mean living here. After what happened to Max—"

"Why do you stay? Rehavia can spare you. Why not move into one of your zones?"

"This is my home." The man's face, usually bland as a custard, wrinkled up with acute distress. "These are my friends."

"Were those also your friends who set fire to the *Post?*"

"Bloody bastards! They shame all decent men."

The Judge clapped his hands delicately. "Bravely spoken." He bowed. "Forgive me," he murmured, "if I do not exactly feel sorry for you."

"And wh-why-why n-n-not?" Whenever he was greatly disturbed, Gordon stuttered. "Wh-wh-when F-F-Fascist b-b-bastards p-p-pull off a s-s-stunt, y-y-you people b-b-blame all of us."

Judge Winkleman's attention sharpened; his head came up. "You know then who set the *Post* bomb?"

"D-d-don't you?"

The Judge shook his head. "I can only surmise. 'Bloody bastards,' as you so well said. And doubtless Britons."

"Th-there y-you g-go." Gordon swallowed hard, struggling to control his stammer. "As I said, blaming all of us. When slimy Fascist bastards crawl into our ranks—"

"They are accepted with open arms, are they not?"

Gordon flushed. He could, at the moment, think of no retort.

"Do you know," Judge Winkleman asked quietly, "that what you have just implied is a fact?"

What is a fact? And what is loose talk? It was Millie, the girl he'd been with the night the newspaper was bombed, who had mentioned the matter and with positiveness. "Gordon, I tell you a secret, because I love you. I know who did the *Post* job. You can guess, can you not? The gang that hangs out at the Ritz Hotel. Who else? Wait, you see, there will be more. I know." Yet can you pass on as evidence, to a dignified judge, the boastful chatter of a strumpet? He looked Judge Winkleman full in the face. "It's generally spoken," he said.

"In our circles or yours?"

"In both, I believe," Gordon said.

The Judge smiled meagerly. "In any case, it will be denied, and with vehemence, all the way from the Jerusalem P.I.O. to the House of Commons. However black and heinous their crimes may be in this land, the sons of Empire will depart, sinned against, lily-white. Gallant England, point of honor, you know." He bowed again and began to move on, paused, turned his head. "Shalom," he remembered to say.

V

It was past midnight on Thursday when Jacob unlocked his front door. Edith woke when she heard him on the stairs and she clicked on the torch. The white circle of light framed his unshaven cheeks and bloodshot eyes. She fell into his arms and kissed his gray face. When she drew off, she noticed brown smears of dried blood on his shirt.

"I am not hurt, haviva." He was so exhausted he could barely get his words out. "It was a young man. A student. Haifa Technion." He sucked his breath in. "An expensive business, this keeping open the road," he said painfully.

Teddy heard them talking. From his bed, he called out, "Abba, did they shoot at you?"

"Certainly."

"Was anyone hurt?"

"Certainly."

"How long were you on the road?"

"Ten hours."

"I'm getting up, Abba. I need to hear everything."

"Don't you dare. Go to sleep. Tomorrow is time. . . . Edith, would you make coffee? I am too tired now to sleep."

Downstairs in the kitchen, she remembered to ask, "How did the speech go?"

"There was no speech."

She gaped at him.

"There was no meeting. They called it off. The way it is on the roads, they did not expect anyone. Not even me."

Her anger flared. "Why didn't they notify you?"

He shrugged. "Why bother to tell a man you do not expect him? My fault, thinking sensible men would risk their necks to hear the great Doctor Hirsch." He stroked her cheek. "Calm down, little one.

57

They too have much on their minds. Tel Aviv is also at war."

That didn't appease her. "You risked *your* life," she stormed. "You wasted your time."

"Wasted my time? I had two hot baths. I dined on the Armon terrace. I talked with many people." He clasped his hands, bowed his head over them. "Edith," he said urgently. "There is still time. Take the boy, go to your family in the States."

She raised his head between both her hands and looked hard and levelly into his eyes. "You're so tired you talk nonsense," she said. "Finish your coffee and come upstairs."

When he had stretched between the sheets, he said, "Carmela's brother. That Benatar. They are such snobs, these old-time sabras. 'My sister chose to marry that Koenigsberger,' that Benatar said to me. 'What is he, German or Polish, from Koenigsberg?' Imagine, holds it against the man, too, that he came from the Corridor! 'I never liked him,' he said to me. 'Arrogant like a German, unreliable like a Pole.' (Can you understand it, Edith, such chauvinism?) 'She chose him. Let her not complain. She had many chances,' he said. 'One is now District Judge. A fine, sober man.' He believes his sister's husband is a woman-chaser, a sot, a God-only-knows. The proof, he says, is the man still remains in his post with Government. 'If he had character,' he had the gall to tell me, 'he would never have taken their job. If he had character, he would not have stayed.' Such a brother! Why did Carmela make me see him?"

She did not answer his question. "Will you tell Carmela?" she asked instead.

"Am I a fool?" He yawned, turned on his side, rolled back. "Haviva, you have told me nothing. The *Post*, Hasollel Street, I know, but the wireless did not report how you and my son behaved yourselves."

"Tomorrow, tomorrow we'll talk."

"How was his party?"

"Dinah sent him a present, a book."

He sighed as he stretched down the bed. "I want a present. *Herself*. My beloved wife, I would feel that much more safe, if I had all my loved ones under my roof."

When she served his morning coffee, he gave her a long, searching look. "Edith, sit down," he ordered.

Surprised at his tone, she sat down.

"Are you sick?" he demanded.

"Certainly not." She tried to rise but he held her wrists. "I do not like how you look. You have lost weight. You had none to spare. Sometimes you grimace as if you were in pain."

"Have I not the right to have a pain?"

"Not permitted. My wife does not need to be sick."

"I am not sick. I have no time to be sick."

"True enough," he replied. "But we will find out. Get in my car."

"Doctor Kaufman," Jacob said to his young colleague. "My wife is jealous of my patients. She wants a doctor, too."

"She has a doctor. May I say, a most capable man."

"Correct." He wagged his eyebrows. "Will you kindly do that most capable man the great favor of making a thorough check-up? He does not trust his own judgment in the matter of his wife's abdomen."

While Edith was dressing, Dr. Kaufman angled his finger tips and announced, "There is nothing. No mass. No tenderness." He looked up. "It is my impression the Frau Doktor is unhappy," he said.

"Mrs. Hirsch is never unhappy. She has the good fortune to be married to me."

Dr. Kaufman ventured a smile. "That is not enough, obviously. She appears to be laboring under severe strain."

"Another thing altogether. There I am inclined to agree with you."

"How would you like to go to Brookline, to your sister Belle?" Jacob asked in bed, before sleep, that night. This time the suggestion shocked her so that she answered him sharply. "Do you want to get rid of me?"

"Sheket." Then he altered his manner and tone. "Certainly, Mrs. Hirsch. I'll send you and Teddy away and settle down in this house with a young concubine." He propped himself on an elbow. "Seriously, little one, you have not been in the States for a good many years. If you were to go till this disturbance is over, peace and quiet, good food, no bombs, no tension . . ."

Out of that very tension, she cried, "Don't talk to me. Let me be."

He pressed a kiss on each of her eyelids, but said nothing more and the rest of the night they lay side by side, awake yet pretending to sleep, neither daring to move for fear of revealing he was not asleep. In the morning, when they were dressing, he said, with planned casualness, "This began after Dinah left, didn't it? The womb aches for the child who is gone."

Her eyes misted. He put his hands on her shoulders. "Now it is spoken, it will be cured," he said.

VI

THE PATIENT WAS ready for sun. Dr. Hirsch himself wheeled her chair to the solarium and settled her where she might have a good view. Only a handful of convalescents were up on the roof, enjoying the ultra-violet, the soft, easy chairs and green plants, hardly aware of the shadow which moved across the glass, vanished, returned, a guard slowly pacing the broad stone ledge, his binoculars trained across Wadi Joz toward Sheikh Jarrah.

It was so pleasant up on the roof that Dr. Hirsch lingered to tell his patient a joke, about the prize bull of a kibbutz whose prowess was so spectacular, that the Mandatory commandeered him for a stock-breeding farm. "The most beautiful cows were brought in to him," Jacob wriggled coquettishly, hands on his hips. "He scorned them. He turned up his nose." Jacob turned up his own nose. "The officials were puzzled, outraged. They sent for the herdsman of the kibbutz. 'Talk to your bull,' they said. 'Find out why he will not perform.' 'What's the matter with you?' the herdsman asked the bull. 'Why don't you do what you're supposed to do?' 'When I was a member of a kibbutz,' the bull replied, 'I worked hard, just as you do. I did my job. I am a Civil Servant now. Why should I work?' "

The patient was laughing so heartily that Jacob started to warn her her stitches might rip when he was silenced by gunshot and crash of glass. "Sit still! Whatever happens, don't move!" he ordered before he ran to the broken window. The guard lay, face down, half on the ledge, half in the room, staining the stones with crimson.

I must not tell Edith that a guard was killed on our hospital roof, he decided as he drove home. She must not worry for me more than she does.

There was intermittent gunfire not more than ten yards from the Russian Compound where the courts sat and with all that noise Judge

Winkleman found it hard to follow the case.

One Avrum Kopelowitz, an importer of English woolens, had sold to one Abdul Mussa Daoud, a tailor, bolts of cloth priced at one hundred pounds, in the month of March, 1947. Kopelowitz declared he and Daoud had done business together satisfactorily through many years. Consequently, knowing the man, he neglected to press for payment. In September, the tailor died. That demise was the single fact upon which plaintiff and defense both agreed. But is not the wool merchant nevertheless entitled either to return of his goods or to payment and interest, courts' and advocates' fees, from the tailor's estate?

Amin eff Khoury, Daoud's widow's attorney, denied the debt. The man is dead, his widow and children know nothing about his affairs. Counsel said that loudly, with waving of arms and face mahogany-red. Amin eff Khoury's degree of passion in a civil suit troubled Judge Winkleman. He knew counsel well. The man had appeared in this court many times, a good lawyer who took a good fee. This is a small case for him, the Judge realized. Why then is he spending so much energy? One hundred pounds. It is not a little and it is not a lot. And why has he filled all the benches with the family's kinsmen and friends?

Swarthy men, some in Western clothes, some in *keffiahs* and robes, crowded the benches and kept their eyes on the plaintiff and the Judge.

Avrum Kopelowitz was clearly distressed. A hunchback, with a large bulbous nose and thick-lensed spectacles, he sat far down in his chair and he also kept his eyes on the Judge. Judge Winkleman felt himself growing warm. He fussed with his robe, as though the weight of its pleats were what bothered him.

"Who knows if the goods was actually sold?" Khoury yelled. "The one man who can tell us the truth is forever silenced. And now to take the morsel of bread from his widow and orphans comes one of a race, long known for its—"

The Judge struck the desk sharply.

Khoury bowed low, before he swept the bench with an insolent stare.

The Judge felt himself reddening. "We will have no such remarks in this court," he said acidly.

"If the Honorable Judge seals my lips—" Khoury spread his arms wide. "When we entered this case, it was a matter of serious concern to us whether justice might be found in this court."

A low rumble rose from the crowded benches. Avrum Kopelowitz looked at his counsel anxiously. His counsel looked at the Judge. The Judge permitted himself a side-glance toward the door. Two policemen stood there. Only two. They looked rather bored.

"Continue," Judge Winkleman said wearily. "A bill of sale has been offered in evidence. It is contended the merchandise was not paid for. Proceed. Confine yourself to the facts." He rested his chin on his hand. Facts, he thought, do we still deal with facts?

Rifle fire crackled so close to the courtroom windows that the lawyer's voice was drowned out and the Judge asked Khoury to repeat. "We ask you to consider—" the man flailed the fusty courtroom air—"that just as there is no evidence the debt has been paid, there is also no evidence it has not been paid. I shall offer witnesses, trustworthy men of Jerusalem, who will give evidence that the deceased Abdul Mussa Daoud was honorable in all his dealings. Are we to permit his memory to be defamed by such a one as that—"

The heads on the benches swerved, following Khoury's accusing forefinger. The warning rumble swelled. Kopelowitz slid down in his seat.

Judge Winkleman brought his gavel down again and once more glanced toward the doorway. One of the policemen was smiling. The sight unnerved him and he tried to brace himself against the back of his chair, hoping that from the room below, it would merely appear the Judge wished to look as rigid as justice itself. In the courts on Queen Melisande's Way, he had learned, they were putting up grilles to separate Moslem and Jew, justice in cages, behind iron bars. Avrum Kopelowitz, he thought, is one hundred pounds so important that you place all our lives in jeopardy? Believe me, a few weeks from now you will wonder why one hundred pounds mattered to you. Why should we not adjourn the case, wait until passions cool? . . . No. He set his jaw. This is still government. There is law. There will be justice as long as I sit in this court. He drew his robe about him, and stared, unblinking, into Khoury's flushed face. "Proceed," he said crisply. "Get along with your evidence."

Jacob came home early. His face was blanched. "Where is Teddy?" he demanded at once.

"He's out. The Scouts are collecting binoculars and cóts."

"Make him stay home. Let him not run about. I am away the whole day, I depend upon you to protect our child." He paced up and down the long living room. "Edith." He came to a sudden halt. "Two days ago a sniper killed a guard on our hospital roof." He saw her hands clench, the knuckles grow white. "I did not want to tell you, believe me," he groaned. "But just now, I learned Nehemiah Mizrachi, the greengrocer's son, was killed not three blocks from here. At Ibn Gabirol and Rambam Road. I only tell you, so you will take extra care." He began his nervous pacing again. "Why does not Dinah write to us?" he cried. "Why don't we hear from the girl? It is too dreadful to be always worried about everyone."

Mail was in. Professor and Mrs. Gross had a letter from Montreal.

"Dear Mother and Father," David had written, *"At last mid-terms are over and the marks are posted. You will be pleased to learn that your son is in the first tenth of his class. Your air-mail letter reached me, after three weeks. Mail service, I realize, is getting bad. I was distressed to learn of Mother's illness, but relieved that the Hospital did such a fine job. (Our Hadassah is excellent, is it not?) It is too bad that this winter when you have no fuel has been so rigorous. We have had a severe winter in Canada, too, but the central heating is efficient and there is no lack of coal. If it were only possible to send Mother here, for rest and recuperation—I know it is useless to bring that up. It would take more pounds than our family could possibly muster. Do not think I do not appreciate the financial sacrifice you are making for my career.*

"Dear parents, now I come to the gist of what I have to write. I am greatly disturbed by what is happening at home. I am torn. It is unbearable to be so far away. I think of my friends, Arieh Goldstein and Dinah Hirsch, with whom I went to school. I think of what they are going through and what they are preparing to do. And I wonder, have I the right to sit peacefully in my classrooms? Dear parents, help me make up my mind. Shall I come back? Please cable me as soon as you get this letter. It is, I hear, hard to get passage. If I am to go home, I do not wish to delay."

Lillie Gross sat with the letter in her hands, in a freezing house, until her husband came home. He read it. He looked at her. He asked, "What shall we tell him to do?"

"We cannot advise him," she said.

"No." His teeth chattered. "We cannot tell him what he must do."

"We will send him a cable, the choice must be his. Just a few words. 'Make whatever decision is best for you.'" She laid her head on her arms. "How I should like to see David again!" she moaned.

Professor Gross touched her shoulder. "Lillie, I'll make your tea. Then I shall go down and send the wireless. I think, I am certain, he wants to come back."

By the time tea was out of the way, gale winds had risen and sleet dashed against the casements. The Professor tied his hat on with a scarf and raised the collar of his old overcoat. When he came back there was ice on his beard. He hung up his things and put the kettle on the primus to make another hot drink. "I could not send the wireless," he said. "The storm. The cable mast was blown down."

"That may be an omen," Lillie said softly. "We cannot answer. We cannot tell him. Let him assume that his letter was never received. Then he will do what he needs to do."

"Have you heard from David?" Edith Hirsch asked when she ran in to fix Lillie's lunch.

Lillie averted her eyes. "Not a word."

"Nor we from Dinah," Edith said. "But it is not the same thing."

A patrol of His Majesty's forces found four Haganah men in a secret defense post near the Grand Mufti's house at Sheikh Jarrah and took them into custody. Their bodies were later found riddled with bullets on the Jericho Road, near St. Stephen's Gate.

"Henderson," Gordon Leake said to his superior the day after the bodies were found, "we are bastards."

Henderson who had grown paunchy and gray in His Majesty's service, replied carefully. "Speak for yourself, and take my advice, hold your tongue."

"We t-t-took those p-p-poor d-d-devils out," Gordon's voice rose, stuttering, "t-t-turned them over, n-n-never gave them a chance."

Henderson glanced toward his clerk, bent over a desk in the corner. It seemed to him the clerk's ears were twice their normal size. "Pipe down," he said uneasily.

Gordon drew a chair to the desk. "The man who lives under me was b-b-blinded in the *Post* b-b-bombing," he said.

Henderson lifted his shoulders. "Am I to blame?"

"No," Gordon hurried to say. "Of course not. The Ritz boys. I'm sure of that."

"Are you?" The man scowled. "Who is sure of what in this bloody place?" He inhaled and exhaled noisily. "The begetting of this nightmare is already lost in the fogs. Who did what first? We came here in good faith, the Administration and you and I. We worked hard. We did not write the bloody White Paper. We did not set Hitler's fires. And we sit in a Government office on Mamillah Road, not in Whitehall. When a sniper lets go, his bullet is by no means instructed, 'Avoid Englishmen.' Suppose the bastards decided, this afternoon, to give us the treatment they gave the King David crowd." He glanced over his shoulder and shuddered. "It will please me very much," he said after a moment, "to be out of this place."

"But, sir," Gordon rubbed his chin uncertainly. "If you were in their spot—"

"I am not in their spot," he answered sharply. "And I thank God for that. I did not applaud when two of our sergeants were hanged and their bodies were booby trapped. Therefore you will kindly excuse me from weeping over St. Stephen's Gate. Gordon—" He rose, put his hand paternally on his subordinate's shoulder. "Keep your nose clean," he said. "You are a Civil Servant, not a statesman."

Yora Levine spent an hour with his children after supper each night. Carmela insisted on it. "Otherwise they forget they have a father," she said.

He tried to protest. "In how many ways can I divide myself?"

She stroked his forehead. "I had them alone all through the big war. Now, day and night, they see only me. Two parents every child needs." And so, each evening the Levines hurried through supper and Yora sat in the living room, hearing what the teacher had said in three separate classrooms that day, how many cots Teddy and Asi had dragged to headquarters, how Asi had pulled his sisters' pigtails and Teddy had shoved the girls into the dirt on the way home from school. He approved when approval was called for, and when censure was needed, he took care of that. He admired his children's intelligence and good looks. In a less busy month, he might have enjoyed thoroughly being drillmaster at home.

He was pained as well as surprised when Gordon Leake came up the front path one evening during the family hour. The man said, "Shalom," and, "I'd like to talk to you privately, sir."

Yora found himself tensing, for reasons he did not understand. "Girls, help your mother in the kitchen," he said quickly. "Asi, up to your room. I will come later and see the arithmetic."

The children went, muttering, disgruntled and glancing back.

"Well?" That sounded rude. "Well, come in, sit down," Yora hurried to add.

Gordon sat, on the edge of a chair. "Levine, I do not know how to start." He opened and closed his hands nervously.

"I cannot assist you." Yora towered over the chair, staring down at the Englishman's thinning fair hair.

"It is d-d-difficult to b-b-begin." Gordon's stutter was troublesome. He gulped before he glanced up. "Please, sir, it's hard to be stared at, you know."

"I memorize details. In a short while, with God's help, a British Civil Servant will be a curiosity to us." He saw Gordon flush and was somewhat ashamed of himself and therefore he opened a cigarette box on the coffee table. "Will you smoke?" he asked.

"Thank you." Gordon waited for the flick of the other man's lighter. He drew in once, laid the cigarette down. "All that has been going on these last days—" he began again.

Yora finished the sentence for him, "—is far from new." He sat down, opposite, facing the man across the low table and leaned back in his chair.

"Believe me, sir—"

Yora smiled. "Shall I tell you what you are about to say? You will say what the Germans said when they lost a war. 'We are small people. We had no choice.'"

Gordon reddened. "You're not fair," he stammered. "Some of us honestly feel—"

"Be careful." Yora wagged a forefinger. "You and I both work for Government."

The man ignored the warning. "The *Post* bombing, the murders at St. Stephen's Gate," he went on.

"Shadings. Degrees." Yora shrugged. "Are these worse than what happens on the Haifa docks, in the Cyprus camps every day?"

The man studied his shoetips. "That's policy. Whatever you and I may think of that policy—" His eyes rose again. "Don't ask me," he begged. "I don't really know black from white any more." He braided his fingers. "I only know that this savagery—"

"Nice people don't do such things." Yora was mimicking Gordon's accent. "Where is it written that all virtue or vice are the property of any one race?"

Gordon tamped his cigarette out. For a moment or so, he sat quietly staring at the opposite wall. "And now the currency matter," he started again. "Dropping Palestine out of the Sterling bloc, without the slightest warning . . ."

"Somehow we will manage." Yora's grimace was faintly supercilious. "The distress may turn out to be on the other foot." He got up. "Have you come here to talk about current events? I am busy. Some other time, possibly."

Gordon shifted as if he too meant to get up but he did not. "Levine, you and I have been neighbors. I think you know what I am." His stutter was really bad now, the words emerging tattered and chewed. "I've liked it here very much. I have been contented in Jerusalem."

"The Yanks would say, 'You never had it so good.' "

Gordon chose to ignore the nastiness of Yora's tone. "When I think of the little island, with the fogs and the cold and the austerity," he went on. "Or starting again in Kenya, Tanganyika, without any heart in my work—"

"What is it you want?" Yora broke in.

Gordon looked at the wall for a long moment before he shifted his gaze to Yora's steel eyes. "Levine, I've been turning a matter over and over in my mind. Not all of us are unfriendly, callous, indifferent. There was, you may remember, one great British soldier—"

"Be careful," Yora said sharply, "how you use a sacred name."

The man turned scarlet again. "No," he conceded. "I am no Wingate. You don't have to rub that in. . . . But, I, too, would like to build up this country. I am an experienced administrator, and whenever you people set a government up—"

For half a minnte, Yora Levine could not speak and when he did, it was with cold rudeness. "Why don't you go to Amman? Abdullah should have room for more Englishmen. You pay him enough."

"I don't wish to go to Amman," Gordon stammered. "I like it here. I feel at home."

"A fine thing, if we are to suffer to create a Homeland for Englishmen. No, you will leave and you will forget us, just once in a while remember over your tea, how fair Jerusalem was. . . . You will forget us and we will forget you, I hope."

While he was walking the man to the door, he added in a gentler tone, "You placed your life in my hands, coming here, speaking up. You know that, do you not?"

Gordon half-turned. "Oh, I trust you," he said wearily. "We've been neighbors, you know. And I understand how you feel." He stopped and smiled faintly. "Your bark's much worse than your bite, you know."

"Go home, back to England," Yora Levine answered him.

Arieh Goldstein rose quickly when his name was called. He strode forward to face the military court, gave his address, stated that he was a University student, and then surveyed the room. It was crowded, with soldiers and uniformed police. This student is a desperate character, he told himself. He listened with mild unconcern while the military prosecutor stated the charge, possession of a pistol and two rounds, discovered on this defendant in the search of a convoy on its way to a settlement in the Hebron Hills. Arieh's impatience grew. Nachon, he thought, I had a pistol. Impose the fine, be done, let me go. Max is coming out of the hospital. I should be home to give Imma help.

His counsel was making a speech. That was sheer waste of time. They fine an Arab five hundred mils, half a pound. They fine us thirty pounds. We have had many pleaders. Have words ever helped?

The counsel was motioning to him, indicating he was to speak. "Well, then." He hitched his shorts up. "What have I to say in my defense? Only this. Like every Jew in Palestine, I want peace with our Arab neighbors, but we must defend ourselves and the country and establish the safety of all peace-loving persons." He heard the sound of his voice. It was calm, dignified. He was pleased with himself. "Like every Jew in this city, I am subject to Haganah orders. I tell you no news. It is a source of regret to each of us that His Majesty's forces are not fulfilling their obligation to safeguard a peace-loving population. It is therefore our right and our privilege to defend ourselves."

He glanced at his lawyer. The man was scowling. Have I talked myself into prison? he wondered.

"We fine the defendant, Arieh Goldstein, twenty-five pounds."

He let his breath out. He smiled. Good. Finished. No more time is lost.

"I am disgraced," he said to his counsel as they walked out. "No *Palmachnick* should lose his weapon. It is the worst thing."

Dr. Hirsch drove Max Goldstein home when he came down from the Hill. Dr. Ginsberg had done his best. Part of the sight of one eye might be saved. Meanwhile, rest in bed, at home, with loving good care.

Ida had fixed Max's bed in the living room on the couch where Arieh usually slept. My son is so seldom home, she decided; when he is home, I will give him my bed. She was horrified when she saw Max. His face was bandaged, just slits in the cloth for his nostrils and mouth. There was so much to do for him quickly; she had no time to weep.

"Ida needs help," Jacob told his wife. "Go to her, when you can spare time from Lillie Gross."

"I don't go to Lillie. I've asked her is David returning. She does not reply. She cannot face me. Nor I her," Edith said.

The following morning two men rang Edith's bell. "G'veret Hirsch," one of them said, "we need to go up to your roof."

They went up, stayed fifteen minutes, came down. "Toda, G'veret. We may be back."

She went in to Shifra. "Remember," she said. "No one has been here today."

"*Bachayeye,* G'veret, you insult me. Did you think *I* would tell anyone? Look somewhere else for enemy spies."

There was a small meeting in a house in Rehavia, a handful of sober-faced men, no more than might ordinarily call at a dwelling on a winter night.

A new Commander was present, sent up from the coast to take

charge of the city's defense.

"I asked them, 'With what shall I defend?'" the new Commander declared. "'Have we soldiers?' No, we have old men and Yeshiva students. 'Have we weapons?' No. We have empty hands. 'Can Jerusalem be defended?' With difficulty. Our roads are funnels through Arab territory. And so—" he shrugged, smiling the defiant, set grin of those who have nothing to smile about—"we use the poor man's choice, courage and intelligence."

A Jerusalem man answered him. "Much can be done. Nothing will be left to chance. Nothing will be overlooked. Every man, every woman, will be mobilized. There will be planning. And discipline . . . So, let us begin. Water is a weapon of war. Our pipe line runs through Arab areas. Every well and cistern in Jerusalem is to be cleaned, filled and sealed in case they cut our pipe line. . . . Next, electricity. The fuel is so dangerously short, the power will surely be cut. Arrangements must be made that whatever power is available will serve our most urgent needs. . . . Above all, discipline. Each man will proceed with his assigned duties. But will not speak." He laid his finger across his own closed lips. "What each one does, he does. But tell no one, not even your wives, your nearest friend. Understood?"

To Yora Levine fell the matter of the electricity, since he had a long-time acquaintance with those who controlled light and power. He was not too pleased. This will take great cleverness, he realized. This will mean further close contact with them. Whom among *them* can I trust?

He walked home from the meeting, tied in a knot of anxiety, and in his mind ran over names, appraising, discarding, until he hit upon one. Duncan could manage the matter. Duncan was elderly, amiable, and dull. Not a conspicuous enemy nor a blatant friend. A business man, merely. Conscientious and unimaginative.

Unimaginative. That was the essential thing.

Old Isaac Winkleman stood on his balcony and looked into the road. It was Shabbat. Synagogue services were done long ago, the siesta time past, and the café was closed. There was nowhere to go. He watched two couples, a man with a white beard and a gold-headed cane, and a big-bosomed woman in a dress which swept up the dust, march up the road, and a man in a morning coat, with a gray beard, and a stately female on his arm, parade after them. Madame's friends, he thought enviously. Statesmen. Idealists. They were attending Basle congresses while I was running a Capetown dry goods store. He was shaken a little by the profundity of his awe. How dignified they look! How they walk! They will sit around her samovar, drink Wissotsky's Tea and eat cake. They will discuss politics and world affairs. They will remember how this great man looked, how that great man talked. When we have our State, they will be honored statesmen. And I shall be merely the old Afrikaaner who sits before the café in the sun.

"Ephraim," Madame shouted. "The guests are here. I am not dressed. Go open the door."

Ephraim laid down his pen. He shuffled in carpet slippers down the hall. His mother's bedroom door was open. He caught a glimpse of her white pompadour, her yellowed flesh rolling obscenely over her bulging brassière, and he gritted his teeth against rising nausea. He opened the front door. "Shalom," he mumbled. He held the door ajar. "Imma is not dressed," he said.

He saw one of the women look at him and wink. "The son, the poet!" he heard her whisper. He shrank against the wall, into the corridor's shadows. "How goes the poetry?" The gray-bearded man tried to clap him sociably on his back. Ephraim edged away. "Come in, sit," he mumbled at them.

"Sit with us," one of the women said coyly. She tapped his wrist. "Read your poems to us."

"I am too busy." He let them go ahead of him, into the dining room, and ducked sidewise, toward his own room. "Where has he hidden himself? Where is Leah's idiot?" he heard a woman asking, before he slammed his door.

He stalked to the old kitchen table on which he wrote and picked up his pen. The white sheet, with paper's infinite patience, lay waiting, two sentences, scribbled, crossed out. He could not write. He could not think. He crumpled the paper in his fist. "Leah's idiot!" How would they like it, if I told them what they are! Museum pieces, dialecticians, chewing over the fat of the past. Has-beens. Hangers-on. Nobodies. My mother's friends. Old Russian *demi-mondaines*.

And what is my mother, herself? A lump of flesh, a white pompadour, a big bust, a big mouth. A cultured woman! What good is it to have read all of Shakespeare if one cannot control a foul tongue?

Who is my father? She smirks and she leers.

What is my life in this house? Old furniture. *Her* furniture. Russian brass. Her samovar. Her candlesticks. Her red satin bows on lace curtains and spreads. The stink of her sachet and her greasy cooking. I have no home. This is a hovel, of gross memories. Why do I stay? Where shall I go? I am in Jerusalem. I am already here. A world prays, next year in Jerusalem. So I am here. What do I have? I eat. I sit with an old man at the café. And I write poetry. Who reads what I write? Is it my fault the world is illiterate?

There is one who would read what I write. She has blond hair. She is soft spoken and kind. She has the green-blue letters on her white arm.

He came back to his table, dipped the pen into ink, and wrote rapidly,

"Fortunate woman, chosen by fate to remind,
You lived when six million died.
Each time you bring my glass of tea,
I think of them."

He crossed out "think of," scribbled "remember," inked it out, changed to "think of" again, wrote at the top, "To a Waitress" waved the page to dry it, and folded it up.

So! I have written a poem for her, and she will be pleased. So— He folded his hands behind his back and began to pace in his room. So I think of them. They were tortured and murdered and burned. While they died, I wrote poetry and now I write poetry still. Do I save one single life when I write poetry?

A child on this street does more than I. He runs; he fills sandbags; he brings messages. I sit and I write and cross out. So— What else can I do? Am I strong? I have weak eyes, a weak chest? Am I brave? I am a coward. I sit outside the café only because the old man sits there. But he is deaf and he cannot hear when they shoot. I can hear. But I stay. Then, I am not a coward. There must be something a poet can do.

VII

CARMELA SAID, "Edith, come with me to the concert tonight. I have two tickets. I am tired of sitting alone and wondering when Yora will come. You and I both need to hear something besides the Katamon guns."

She came by after supper, dressed in her long fuchsia dress with dangling silver earrings and she was as she had been in youth, beautiful. "Take off your old suit," she commanded Edith. "Put on a nice frock. We have been drab long enough." She was right. The crowd which streamed into the hall was dressed in its best.

The concert began with César Franck. I know that Prelude, Edith thought, I've played it often. The girl does it well. But she's young. Too much loud pedal, not enough intelligence.

She shifted restlessly. Carmela glanced at her and put a hand on her arm.

The Brahms was relaxing, the violins sweet. A violin is plucked heart-strings, she told herself. She closed her eyes. The melody seeped into her.

Another night, a spring night, we were sitting near the radio and listening to Brahms. It was a warm night of curfew, with windows wide open, letting in a fragrance of jasmine and roses and the noise of small arms.

Dinah had clicked the radio off. "Imma and Abba, I have something to tell you." Jacob laid down the paper and I put my sewing away. "This summer, I shall be away, and in October we go to the Negev. We shall be ready to start Gan Darom." The girl's eyes were shining, her lips parted as she waited to hear what her parents would say.

What could we say? You told us. You stated a fact. Dinah, darling, we weren't surprised. We expected that. Yet we dreaded it, in a way. One hopes one's child will be brave, you understand that, conse-

74

crated, self-sacrificing. But always one hopes she will not need to be.

That's why we sat frozen, like statues. It was here. What could we say? Only Teddy. He is a child. He feels things differently. His eyes were like bugs. He kicked over his chair. *"Eisen beton!* Iron concrete!" He pounded your back and you gave him a shove. Like children. Still children. Our boy and our girl.

There was only one word in my mind. "Grandfather." The old man who had been Herzl's friend had brought this about. Let him be happy, let him be proud.

Jacob got up first, always first. I think, I wonder, debate with myself; he acts. He hugged you so tightly, I thought, he won't let her go. "Abba! Abba!" you cried when he kissed your face. Dear, do you really love him so much? Why not? I love our Jacob, too.

"Imma, why don't you say something to me?"

"Haviva, what is there to say but to kiss you and give you our love."

There was much to say, very much. I think of it every day. When I'm cooking our meals, or dusting the glass, I ask my questions, I hear your replies.

"Haviva, we never objected but your parents have the right to know why you are doing this."

"The Land needs me, Imma."

"But you are in the Land. There's much you can do, here from this house. You're giving up all you're used to, comfort, security. What you're doing is like taking the veil (such an odd simile but in its way true), renouncing all worldly pleasures."

"It is not so. We'll have a hard life for a while. And a good life afterwards."

"Haviva, you must not be angry because I want the best for my child."

"This is the best. . . . Imma, do you wish I would not go?"

"Of course not, haviva. It is merely that I need to know why. Have we failed that you want to leave us?"

"No, Imma, believe me. You and Abba are the best parents in the whole world. I love you both very much. But I am grown. I have decided what is best for me."

"No, haviva, no. Your grandfather decided. Long before you were born."

Yes, those very questions and answers should have been spoken. But they were not. Our girl went away, a person, unknown, with her private dreams and her hopes and our fears.

It all happened so naturally. Out of the Land. My sister Belle never understood how that was. She thought I was mad, and that's very strange. We came from one household, a common background. Papa's faith and our grandfather's creed. The Land. This Land.

Belle, do you understand that our Dinah belongs to Palmach? She's in the Negev, the most dangerous place, building, defending the Land. Our papa died too soon. He would have understood and been proud. In that old brownstone on Beacon Hill—have they turned it into flats?—that rich house with the old brass Menorah on the fireplace mantel and the morocco-bound prayer books on the shelves, Papa said it over and over in his own way. Remember the night we had company for dinner and someone banged on the table and shouted, "You substitute Zion for God! You abandon the faith that has kept us a people for five thousand years. You would sell all our souls for a strip of sand!"

Papa's eyes twinkled. "The trouble is the heirs of the Turks refuse to take souls. They demand hard cash for each miserable *dunam*. Buy land. Yes, buy, buy land. Buy it with dollars and pounds and francs, or else you will buy it with blood."

How right you were, Father. But we haven't abandoned the other faith. Our children are raised on the Bible, you know. It's their reader, geography, history book. It's our poetry and our ethical code. That puzzles Belle, too. *"Do you mean,"* she once wrote, *"you're raising your kids on an eye for an eye and a tooth for a tooth?"*

Not intentionally. But, if it happens to work out that way. I suppose you would call the matter of speaking English, a case in point. Dinah reads it and knows it so well, but she won't speak a word. I tell her it's nonsense to carry an anger against politicians all the way to their language. But there she's a mule. "I can't help it. That's how I feel." When you hate and have reason to hate, even the hated one's speech is loathsome.

Belle, don't think my daughter's unusual. That's how all our sabras behave. Really, Dinah's just a nice girl. If you had seen her growing up, struggling with homework, fussing about it, not a brilliant student, merely as conscientious as most growing girls are.

She learned to dance. She went on *tremps* in the hills with her boy and girl friends. Sometimes Arieh was along. Sometimes David Gross. No special boy friend, just boys and girls having wholesome fun. She rode a bicycle, an English one. Inconsistent? That's how children are. She nagged Jacob to teach her to drive his car. There was even the dreamy phase when she tried to write poetry, about the hills and the sky and the stars. Always busy, yet a quiet child, with a self-assurance that didn't require affirmation in words. I am what I am. I think what I think. Everyone knows what I am. We're all alike, in this country. We know why we're here and what is expected of us. And so what's to talk about?

She had something to tell us, but she did not tell and that is the hurt. When she said so casually, "We're off to Galilee next week. We are taking a course," we might guess if we wished she was studying nature or historic ruins, not target practice and how to lay mines. When she went on a tremp wearing sneakers and not walking shoes, I preferred not to think she was being taught to walk quietly, and against the wind, so that the sleeping dogs of an Arab village would never wake up and howl. . . .

She did not tell us. We had to find out. By accident, when I went to her room while she was taking her bath, to see what was lying about that had to go into Sunday's wash. . . . Beneath yesterday's khaki blouse and skirt, there were the two parts of a Sten.

Dinah darling, I'll never forget how cool your father was, when I told him, and he asked you at breakfast, "How well do you shoot?" and you answered, matter-of-factly, "Arieh says I do well." Nothing else matters, Arieh approves. Must I be angry with him, that he brought you into Palmach? A child has no right to go into Palmach at fifteen without her parents' consent. Without talking it over at least. It was almost a rudeness, my dear, snubbing us as though you considered us not worth your trust. Jacob thinks I am silly. He says, "Dinah's a sabra. What do you expect?" True. You're a child of this Land. But I wish he had said, "She is our daughter. What do you expect?"

Expect nothing. We had you three years after that, still a child in the house, squabbling with Teddy, saying, "Beat me with a stick, break my bones, I will not eat squash pooding, it makes me vomit." Three years in which to know you were ready . . . and hope you would not need to be.

What was this sound like crashing waves of the sea? It's applause, clapping hands. We're a staid town, we restrain ourselves. Carmela's applauding like mad. That boy and girl on the stage must have been excellent. What was it they played?

When they came from the building, Carmela said critically, "For my part they could have omitted the Scriabine. What did you think of it?"

Edith made an evasive, non-committal sound.

Carmela linked her arm through. "Well, they played Gershwin especially for you. Did you like?"

"Which Gershwin?"

"Edith, where were you tonight? At the Beit Hechalutzot Hall or in the Negev?"

Jacob was waiting at the gate posts. "A fine thing! A man comes home from work and no wife." His arm circled Edith's waist as she started to go up the path. "Stay, love, pretend we are young. Enjoy the beautiful night."

A full moon rode high, over a bank of thick cloud and the gardens were drenched with silver light. There was no rifle fire, no sound at all, except the breeze whispering in the bushes and trees. "It's so light, I should take out my brushes and paint," he said. "It's not the same Jerusalem. I can't recognize it without the gunfire."

As the day broke, an explosion flung them out of their beds.

Rachel, Nathan's wife, had all but seen it occur. She was hurrying down Ben Yehuda Street's hill in Sunday's cold drizzling dawn when she saw a police armored car draw up before the Atlantic Hotel. Two canvas-hooded lorries halted just back of it. She had time, as she passed, to notice the men in the car and the trucks. They wore uniforms of the British Army. She caught a glimpse of a beret with the insignia of a flaming grenade. The man in the armored car's turret was young, blond and with a fair mustache. She heard the first lorry's driver ask, in English, "Is this it?" 'and her nerves flashed signals to her brain. What are Englishmen doing with lorries here on this street at this hour? They're with police escort, she tried to reason, it must be all right.

When she had gone several feet she heard shots and stopped and looked back. She was certain she saw a body sprawled on the pavement. She began to sweat. Find a telephone. Report this to Nathan at once. She glanced back again. Men were jumping out of the lorries, climbing into the armored car. A spiral of smoke rose from one of the trucks. She ran toward the Square. A crash split her eardrums. She fell flat, on a heaving pavement.

Nathan sped through the street, banged on every door. "They have bombed Ben Yehuda Street. Come, come at once."

"Me?" Ephraim Malkoff quavered. "What can I do?"

"You!" Nathan glowered at him. "You have two arms. You can carry the dead."

"Not you, Teddy," Jacob said firmly. "You will stay home. This is no sight for a child."

Nor was it for anyone. Flame and smoke soared to the leaden sky. Hotels, apartment buildings and shops lay in jagged heaps of rubble and stone. The roadway was a lane of splintered glass, between hedges of roaring fire.

On the fringe of the fire, spectators massed. They saw men and women, in nightclothes, crawling, hand over hand down ropes of knotted bed sheets, shaking ladders and drains, from buildings broken in half. They saw frantic mothers and fathers raking the rubble, calling out children's names, a couple in nightdress, strolling like lovers, embraced, on the carpet of glass, unaware they were leaving bloody footprints, and a gaunt man, tears streaming, holding a limp child, blue-faced, with sightless, open eyes, sobbing to her, *"Sha, sha,* Yehudit, Abba has found you. Don't be afraid."

And they saw above the half-wrecked Atara Café, the blue and white flag with the six-pointed star, still dangling from its flagstaff, a fragile, tenuous thing, but there, defying the fury which had reduced stone.

Within the monstrous disorder, there was discipline. A cordon linked hands at the head and foot of the street to keep the crowd back. Loud speakers rasped orders: *"Let the water carts through. . . . Stay away. . . . Stay away. Please do not come into this street unless you have urgent business. . . . Clear the way for the ambulance. . . . Stay away. Stay away. . . . Please do not come into this street."*

Human chains passed broken stone, hand to hand, to waiting lorries. Nurses and doctors moved swiftly, bringing stretchers empty, carrying them out, weighted, full. Down a side alley, British policemen marched toward the wrecked street. The watching crowd turned into mob, flung itself at the police, pummeling, tearing ferociously. "Out murderers! Englishmen, stay away!"

Gunshot and bomb tore at the city from every quarter all through the day. Jew attacked Arab and Briton; Briton and Arab fired upon Jew. It was as though all of Jerusalem had gone off its head, with the sorrow and shame and the stench of blood.

"Don't leave the house," Jacob phoned to his son from the hospital.

"But, Abba," Teddy protested, "I cannot sit like a dummy next to the wireless. I could be of some help."

"No. There are enough wounded and dead without adding my son."

This is how many: forty-four Jewish men, women, children found dead, one hundred and fifty gravely injured in Ben Yehuda's ruins. Twelve—Moslem, Christian and Jew—killed and thirty-three wounded that day in other parts of the town.

By night, when the cold moon was full, the passion was spent. Under hugh searchlights, men crawled like ants on the rubble heaps. Acetylene torches sputtered, cutting twisted metal away. Drills ripped through slabs of concrete, fallen ceilings which mashed down debris.

"Sh . . . Sheket. Is that a whimper, a moan?" The doctors and nurses waited all night. Only occasionally, now, was there a silent form to carry toward an ambulance. In one of the smashed restaurants, women had set up a canteen, to serve coffee and soup to the workers and the searching families.

In the canteen, Jacob met his neighbor, Yora. The men stared at each other, each shocked at how haggard the other one looked. Then, they clasped hands. "We must close ranks," Yora said. "The worst is ahead."

The Arabs at Sheikh Jarrah barred the road to the Mount of Olives where the graveyard was. The dead lay unburied for days, until a new resting place might be prepared, on a slope beyond an open plain near Rehavia.

On a bone-chilling, sunless day, the red earth was broken to receive Ben Yehuda Street's dead. Gray lorries, stacked high with boxes of pine, white shrouds belling out in the wind, rolled through Rehavia's streets. One thousand mourners marched back of them.

They stood massed on the slope, in a bowl of the ancient brown hills, averting their eyes from the massive stone pile of the Greek Monastery of the Cross, staring across a wadi toward the New City's honey-hued homes. They stood in absolute silence, hands pressed on mouths to stifle anger or grief, listening, as a rabbi cried out, with the words with which dying Moses had quoted God,

"*Warn all the nations. Beware of the justice of heaven. I kill and I make alive. I wound and I heal. . . . I will render vengeance to mine enemies and will reward them that hate me. I will make mine arrows drunk with blood and my sword shall devour flesh. . . . Rejoice, O ye nations, with His people. For He will avenge the blood of the slain and of the captives. . . .*"

While the clods of earth were falling on the pine coffins, a disheveled woman plucked Jacob's sleeve. "Look!" She held up a framed photograph. "Is this not the most beautiful child in the world?"

"Sheket," he hissed at her. "Have respect for the dead."

The woman slid over to Edith's side. "G'veret, my child. You saw the beautiful boy."

Edith gave the photograph a quick glance. She whispered the woman's name to Jacob. "Yes, yes," he replied irritably. "After Pesach. Ginsberg has said he will operate. I told her. Why does she bother me now?"

"The boy is dead. Don't you understand?"

He stretched out his arm and swept the woman into its circle. She rested her head on his shoulder. "Rejoice," he whispered to her. "You have known the joy of a child." His throat filled and he choked.

"My beautiful child," the woman sobbed brokenly.

"Mine too." He caught himself. "Every child is the child of all of us." He pressed his wife's arm against his side. "You must be strong and I must be strong," he said, as much to himself as to anyone.

Part Two: March

I

JANET WINKLEMAN BEGAN to suspect that her venerable father was a bit of a fraud. Whenever she wished he'd finish his porridge, go upstairs for a nap, or put on a clean shirt, she had to scream herself hoarse, but when the Haganah broadcast was on at nine-fifteen every night, there he sat, in the living room, glued to the wireless, apparently not missing one word.

It was he who said, "Jenneh, don't make me afternoon tea. No kerosene for the primus is on sale today. We must hoard what we have." How, she wondered, did Father know that? He did not read the paper; cataracts on both eyes made reading too hard. He conversed with few people, no more than exchange of shaloms and l'hitra'ots, except, of course, the long talks with Ephraim Malkoff, the poet, and these, everyone knew, were just monologues on Papa's part. And at the synagogue, if God spoke to Isaac Winkleman, it is hard to conceive that he discussed modern Jerusalem's shortages.

Obviously, what he had was the convenient deafness of self-protecting old age which, out of ennui, eight decades of hearing complaints and nonsense, now listened only to what it preferred to hear. Whenever Janet bellowed, "Please, Father, stay home. The sniping from Katamon quarter is bad," his face wore a placid vagueness. "What shooting, Jenneh? I find it quiet, like in the tomb." Yet it was *he* who told *her* at the beginning of March, "Jenneh, you remember the Lucullus Café on Ben Yehuda? They had a big ice box there. That was the storage place for the hospital blood. It was blown up and now there is no blood to help people live. Jenneh." The look on his face told her what her plain duty was. "They are asking people to go give their blood."

"Yes, Papa," she faltered. "Maida and I have thought about it. If we weren't so badly run down nowadays—"

"Why don't you speak up? You mumble. I can't make out a word."

He was crabby, too, these first days of March, and restless, and that, Janet had to conclude, was both hunger and lonesomeness. The poet, like everyone else, had defense obligations and little time to enjoy the café. Father missed the companionship, such as it was. His appetite, too, had grown poor. In one way, that was good, because there was so little to put on the table each meal. But was he getting sick, the decline, the final illness? When you're very old, a breeze can blow you away. "Papa, don't you feel well?" she asked.

"Feel well? I feel fine."

"You're tired. You should rest. Lie down more."

"I can't hear you. What did you say?"

Yet he did hear, and for once, he seemed to obey and began to spend time in his room, more than he had formerly. But when she peeped in, one afternoon, she found him, not napping but bustling about. He had cleared out his wardrobe, opened the musty valises and baskets brought years ago from Capetown. His room reeked of camphor, was littered with junk. "Jenneh," he said. "I am glad you came in." He held up an ivory-tinted, soft woolen square. "Try it on, Jennele. Mama looked like a picture in this white shawl. It's the finest kashmir. . . . If you will take this, then Maida can have the sealskin sacque I bought for Mama when we were fifteen years married. . . . Mama's gold ring. The first one of you who is married, I would like she should use Mama's ring. . . . Mama had also a diamond ring and a pin. The one who uses the gold ring, will take also the pin. To the other one, I give the diamond ring. . . . Henry will have my gold watch and chain and my cane. It is fourteen carat, the top. I have also cuff buttons with small diamond chips. They are not now in style here, but maybe some day. . . ."

She was alarmed and she spoke to Maida and Henry about it. "Papa is preparing to die. He's dividing his things."

"How old is he, Henry?" Maida asked. "Does anyone know?"

"He won't admit, but he's past eighty, I'm sure." Henry sighed. "This is what is known as the fullness of years. We should resign ourselves. We can't keep him forever, you know. Any strain, any shock . . ."

"Any bullet," Maida said crisply. "I'm getting bored with being shot at."

On Shabbat, when Isaac Winkleman came from the synagogue, Maida and Janet, looking for him from the windows, were surprised to see him walk past the house. He went spryly, beard up, catching the breeze like a miniature sail, and not resting his weight on his cane, all the length of the street to the house of Dr. Hirsch.

The Doctor was in his back yard, smearing a canvas with cobalt paint. He had an audience. The three Levine children and his own son were watching him. "Come in, come," he shouted. "Join my art class.

"*Shabbat shalom!*" The old man stroked Aviva Levine's patent-leather pigtails before he examined the canvas. The Doctor seemed to be painting flowers; it could be the morning-glories in his back yard. "Very good for handwork," he announced courteously.

Jacob held the canvas up and squinted at it.

"Abba, you put too much red in the blue," Teddy said. "Let me show you."

"My art connoisseur!" He gave his son an affectionate push. "Go bring out a chair for the Afrikaaner to sit."

"No." The old man caught Teddy's arm. "I don't wish to sit. I have something to speak to the Doctor about."

Jacob glanced at him quizzically as he laid the canvas down. "No one is to touch it." He glowered at the children and they blushed, as if he'd been reading their thoughts. "Come into my office," he said. "Away from those hooligans."

"Well, what is it?" he yelled, when the door was closed. "Your daughters are pregnant, I hope?"

"God should only will it." The old man's blue eyes twinkled. "You do not need to shout," he said mildly. "You can speak normal. You have a voice I can hear. . . . Jacob, I come on a matter. About me."

A facetious remark was on the tip of his tongue but something in the blue eyes facing him made Dr. Hirsch choke it back. He smiled and waited for Isaac Winkleman to speak first.

"Doctor, a man like you, you know the human being." The old

man was talking distinctly, with care, as though he had practiced this speech. "You know every person is happy only so long as he is sure he is worth something in the world." He bobbed his head vigorously, agreeing with his own self, and then hitched forward. "I am a miserable person," he admitted. "The most unhappy man in Rehavia. Here, we are making a Nation, and all I can do is sit in the sun."

"Who do you hear complaining because you sit in the sun?"

"I." He tapped his chest. "I complain to myself." He shook his head. "That is not enough." He paused to prop his cane against a chair. "Doctor," he began again, earnestly, "they are asking all people to give a little blood."

Dr. Hirsch sat up straight. "Yes," he agreed. "Our blood stocks were destroyed. We must quickly get a new supply."

"I know. And therefore, Doctor, here, I have come." Isaac Winkleman stretched out his hands.

Dr. Hirsch stared at them, at the thickened purple veins beneath wafer-thin flesh, and he smiled. "Not you, Isaac," he said gently. "From men of your age, we would hardly expect this sacrifice."

"Jacob." The old man wasn't listening. His speech meshed with the Doctor's an instant, before it moved on, alone. "From everyone they are asking a little. I wish to give all I have, whatever still runs in my veins. My blood is old but it is clean. All my life, I am never sick. I am strong as an ox. Why should only the young be asked to sacrifice for this Nation of ours?" His faded blue eyes were intent. "I have been in the synagogue, Jacob. I have told my God what I wish to do. I have arranged my affairs. Tomorrow morning is the right time. Jacob . . ." He halted because his voice had begun to tremble and when he had steadied it, he went on. "No man is altogether a hero. I should like to have an old friend at my side." He laid his hands over Jacob's. "You are a doctor and friend. Come with me, if you can spare me the time. Manage this business for me."

For a moment, Jacob Hirsch could not speak and his own eyes fogged over so that he could no longer see the venerable face, merely the other man's eyes, like sapphires now, brilliant and clear. "No, Abba, no," he cried out, before he rose and kissed the wrinkled forehead. "Abba." He embraced the old man. "How can I talk to you? What can I say?" He gripped the man's shoulders. "No, Abba," he said emphatically. "We need you more than we need your clean, healthy blood. As long as you can, keep doing what you always do. Sit in the sun before the café. . . . Yes, Abba." He gripped the man's hands. "Sit. Sit every day. That is all Jerusalem demands from you. And that will mean more to us than you can ever know."

II

"G'VERET," NATHAN TOLD Edith Hirsch on Monday morning. "To-day you will shop on Princess Mary Avenue." Since he had spent the night in the hills and had a bad cold, Nathan was still in bed. He reached down to a box beside his cot. "Will you take a pome-granate?" he asked.

"No, thank you," she said. "I am more uneasy with a grenade than without."

"I was not thinking of you, G'veret." He glanced down at his own empty sleeve. "Which is better to lose," he asked drily, "an arm or a dozen lives?"

She was embarrassed. "I'm so flat," she tried to explain. "People would notice if my figure changed."

"As you choose." He put the grenade back in the box. "G'veret, I wish you good luck."

What was going on on Princess Mary Avenue was by most defi-nitions war, yet a queer kind of war, against haberdashers, milliners, sweetshop proprietors, hairdressers and interior decorators, a war to make shopkeepers cowards and force them to abandon their street, leave plate glass to be smashed, merchandise to be looted, as the Commercial Center, a few blocks away, had been ravaged in the week after the Partition vote, a war to establish a new Arab front, well up in the New City's business district. It was *little* war, un-declared, unofficial, going on directly across the street from a British Security Zone.

The Arabs in Mamillah Cemetery at the base of the Avenue fired up the road. Whenever they fired, His Majesty's soldiers atop the Generali Building, on the triangle across the way, opened up. Their bullets were neutral, impartially aimed toward the graveyard and toward the shops on the street. Anyone going in or out of a store or just passing along might be caught in cross fire or nipped by a bullet, ricocheting off a wall. Yet, every day, men and women who had nothing to buy and lives to lose strolled up and down Princess Mary, hour after hour, and inside the shops, middle-aged ladies, much better at fitting a hat, a girdle, or hem of a skirt, than at armed defense, fingered grenades beneath their counters and trembled, expecting a crash of plate glass or a bullet's whine, not reassured in the least by the knowledge that behind the walls of their shops was a warren, cut building to building, where young men in the nondescript khaki and peaked knitted caps waited and watched.

When Edith Hirsch reached the street, it was quiet and listless, all but deserted. The morning sun glinted on dusty plate glass. At the head of the slope a stout man in tweeds was studying a haberdasher's display, as though all he had on his mind was selecting a new cravat. Further down, Maida Winkleman was looking at hats.

Maida had not bought a new hat since year before last, which was tragic for her, since she and her sister tried to look smart, no less than the duty his womenfolk owed to the office of a District Judge. Moreover, a spinster's hope never fades in a country where men outnumber females, and it is well known that good tailors can mitigate nature's cruel facts—a big-boned frame, sagging breasts; and a down-sweeping hat can take off the curse of a horsey jaw. Maida was fifty, though she pretended to forty or less. In profile, as she stood at the window, her figure was odd. Her bosom bulged in the center. She has more nerve than I, Edith thought. She wears the pomegranate.

Maida wheeled. "In desperation," she said, "I'll one day buy that blue hat. I've been looking at it for three months. Well, shalom." She shook hands. "It's a beautiful morning. Perfect weather for shooting." She laughed nervously. "Janet's little joke. Sister was feeling chipper today. All she had on was to stand in the kerosene queue. . . . Shall we walk?"

They walked, down the slope, half-glancing now and again at the building on the opposite side. Each time she looked, Maida, without knowing she did, touched her gloved hand to the bulge on her breast.

Edith paused at the upholsterer's, said, "Let's go in."

The shopkeeper came out of his curtained workroom cubbyhole, pleased to have visitors. Edith said the frame of a living room chair had worked loose and if he had time—

"I have time. More time than I have customers. But I cannot leave here, you understand." He glanced back at his workroom curtains. "Perhaps one day when I go home for lunch—"

"If you'll be so kind."

He bowed. "Thank you for coming, ladies," he said. "It is boring with no customers. Stay, look around. You will find it more safe inside than out."

They lingered, thumbing the squares of brocade and chintz they had seen many times and finally emerged to the sunswept pavement. They noticed two pretty young women, prancing down from the crest of the street, dressed in suits with skirts long and full and tight little jackets, thick-soled, high-heeled shoes and perky small hats, set high on hair rolled up in a style which was new.

"Shirley and Joan!" Maida laughed sourly. "The new striped-pants set!"

"I haven't seen them a long while," Edith said.

"They've been in the States, don't you know? on holiday."

The girls were cousins, Americans, young, one once a secretary out of Brooklyn, the other a social worker, reared in the Bronx. They had come on a visit to an aunt in Jerusalem before the big war, had remained as brides, married to bright young men who held responsible posts with the Jewish Agency. Since the Agency was a government, too, a government within The Government, the girls moved in the world of political affairs. They had foreign correspondents and visiting commissions to dinner and lunch, to tea at the Eden and brandy and soda at the King David bar and enjoyed the illusion that history hung on whatever impressions they made. Possibly so. What else is public relations except the art of courtesy? It's time, Edith often had thought, the world learned to think of us without horns—and without their pity or guilt or fear. It's time, overdue, for them to take us as people, asking no more and no less than all other men. And so if the girls by their charm, by their wit, by their dinner tables—

Maida was jealous of them. It was in her eyes as she watched them, stepping like ponies, down Princess Mary. She envied their youth and good looks and the fact that they'd gotten their men, but the jealousy, Edith was certain, ran deeper than that. Their husbands were bright young men with futures, if future there was in this Land. When the State happened, if it could happen, there would be Cabinet posts and embassies to be filled and who better equipped than those bright young men? The old-timers? They were old, rooted in Eastern Europe and in the last century. Certain old-timers like Henry Winkleman might well remain in their posts. They had vested interests, experience and moral right. But would they rise, rise and shine? She laughed to herself. . . . Here I am parceling out jobs in our State. Cart in front of the horse. Let's first have the State.

The girls halted together. They chirped, "Shalom, shalom," and shook hands.

"Well!" Maida Winkleman looked them up and down. "Is that the newest style in New York?"

Joan swung on her heels and let her skirt flare. "New Look!" She made a snoot toward the Generali Building. "Have a look, soldiers. New Look from New York."

"It'll be old as Methuselah before it gets here," Shirley said. "Jerusalem's like an old dowager." Miss Winkleman reddened, cleared her throat, making room for a catty remark, but Shirley swept her aside. "What fun to walk Fifth Avenue, see all the marvelous clothes! Those beautiful, beautiful shops. And sleek, stunning women! More chic than Paris, I swear. Joan, don't you think they're more chic than Paris?"

"Of course, dear." Joan preened herself and adjusted her hat. "My family begged and begged me to stay. They kept saying, 'How can you bear to leave this?'"

"Indeed, dear, how could you?" Miss Winkleman asked through pinched lips.

Joan raised her plucked brows. "Why, this is *home*. I couldn't wait to get back. You can't imagine how hard it was to make them understand."

Shirley nodded. "They have such funny ideas. They can't believe we really live here. We belong. Here to stay. They thought I was crazy, utterly mad, 'At least wait till it quiets down,' they said."

"They thought I was criminal," Joan said, her face suddenly grave, "to bring Dovidl back. 'Leave him, at least,' they said. Dovidl would have been willing, I'm sure. He fell in love with New York.

The subways, the buses, the buildings. Why, he even talked English. It was American and that made it all right." She laughed. "Dovidl's having a terrible time, now, in school. The kids won't believe one word he says. All right, Empire State was something they'd swallow, they'd seen pictures of that, but when he talks about the tunnels—the Holland, the Lincoln, roadways under the river where motor cars ride—" She rocked her head in her hands. (Her nails were nicely done, Maida noticed, with a new eggplant-red.) "Dovidl begs me to come to school and tell the children he isn't making it up."

Shirley hunched her slim shoulders. "He should have no worse troubles than that. Nommie won't eat, can't get used to our food. Over there she had fresh bottled milk. I can't get her to touch our powdered stuff." Maida humphed again, but Shirley headed her off. "Of course, she's still upset from the trip," Shirley said.

"The convoy was awful," Joan said. "Twelve hours from Tel Aviv here."

"We were attacked, you know," Shirley said. "Luckily, no one was hurt."

"Dovidl wasn't afraid. These boys, these tough little sabras of ours."

Shirley lowered her head. "Nommie was. She cried all the way and hung on to my skirts. There were times I wondered had I the right. And Moshe says we may have to go back, the same way, to Tel Aviv, if the Agency decides to move there." She gulped, then brought her head smartly up. "We went out to Flushing and Lake Success, Joan and I, several times. You should have heard the U.N. A dream world. Gabbing and gabbing as though they meant to talk us to death."

"They'd counted on the Arabs being good boys, all big talk but no guns," Joan put in. "Now no one knows just what to do."

"They know perfectly well what *they* want to do." Shirley's pretty face had grown stern. "Embargoing arms to the Middle East! That means only us and they know it does. Great Britain's giving the Arabs whatever they need."

A sharpshooter down in the graveyard decided these women had talked long enough. His bullet whooshed over their heads. As one, they scudded back to the wall of the shops and crouched to their knees. "The bullet you hear never gets you," Shirley said through chattering teeth. "Aren't we funny?" She giggled. "Four Jerusalem ladies backed to the wall."

Joan stood up. "Let's go into the sweetshop. Dovidl's nagging for some boiled sweets."

"Shalom, shalom," Shirley said, swishing off. "Let's meet for coffee some afternoon and gossip a bit."

Maida pulled herself straight. "Well," she said, puffing a little. "Didn't the girls put on a show!" She adjusted the grenade in her blouse.

"They did, indeed. They are brave. Very brave to come back." Edith saw Maida flush.

"I'll step into the hairdresser's and make an appointment to have my hair done," Miss Winkleman said to get out of that.

Edith walked on, for the moment, alone in the street, stopped at the dress shop window and stared at the frocks. Those girls brought their children back here, she thought, exposed them to fire on the road. *"We belong."* You can move mountains when you know you belong. If we must die, if death is our portion, let us die together where we belong. . . . No . . . The children deserve something else. It's life they deserve.

She abandoned the window. God in heaven, protect our children, she prayed as she moved up the slope. Help us, please. . . . Are we desperate enough to pray to God? I haven't prayed in so many years. How cheeky of me! If He's clever, He'll think, Oh, ho, Edith Hirsch is in trouble. When she wasn't in trouble, she didn't need Me. He'll be perfectly right to shrug off my prayers. Yet is it asking too much, if there is a God, He find it in His best interest to keep our children safe. Surely that isn't too much to ask. Teddy and Dinah. Dinah is a wonderful girl, my dear God. She'll do great things for mankind if You give her a chance.

As she went daydreaming along, rifle fire started again from the graveyard and the guns on the Generali Building promptly replied. A bullet whined over her head. In a reflex of panic, she flung herself on the pavement. She heard the tinkle of glass, the spatter of lead. She lay flat, her hands clawing the pavement and she heard her own voice. "God damn them! God damn them to hell! God damn the bloody foul sons of bitches!" She was shocked by the voice, for she abhorred profanity and had never known she could swear. She lay prone, until out of a sudden quiet there was a titter. "You'll have to learn to do that more gracefully," she heard Joan say. "Your pink bloomers show." Joan picked her up. Shirley dusted her off. "Are you hurt?" Shirley asked.

She tried to smile. "Just my dignity." She wondered if they had heard her swear and hoped they had not.

"Might have been." Joan pointed. At the height of her head, in the glass over pink lingerie, were two round holes, spiderwebbed with cracked glass. She put her hand over her heart.

"A miss is as good as a mile," Shirley said. "Joan, dear, how brave are you? Would you duck over to Spinney's with me and see what they have?"

The girls said, "Shalom" and she answered, "Shalom," and started again, down to the foot of the street, and up one more time. At the crown of the street, she ran into Ephraim Malkoff, the poet, starting down. He goggled at her, his myopic stare taking in her soiled dress. She smiled at him. "Princess Mary's pavements are dirty," she said. "I must learn to take this standing up." Then she asked, "How are you?"

"How should I be?" he replied.

"How is your mother?"

"How should she be?"

"She is old. This is hard on the old."

He seemed to be struggling out of a trance. "She makes it hard," he blurted. "She runs, runs, runs, from one store to another, buying more tins. Like a crazy woman, she runs. She must fill up the closets, like for a siege."

For a siege! Change the subject. "You're shopping today on Princess Mary?"

"What else should I be doing here? Is this a way to create a State, walking up and down on a street?"

When she turned into Jaffa Road, going home, a woman jostled her purposefully. The woman was decorously dressed, except that candy-box pale green ribbon bound up her gray hair and her suit coat lapels were adorned with small flags. In the crook of her arm, she carried leaflets. She thrust a paper beneath Edith's nose. "Peace! Give me a shilling for peace."

Edith tried to edge past but the woman clutched at her sleeve. "Don't you want peace?"

"Of course I want peace." She pried the hand loose.

"Then give me a shilling. Is a shilling to much for peace?"

She brushed by, moved on quickly, thinking, she's crazy, poor thing. That's one of the evils of cities like ours. Its madmen run in the streets. Mad? She's the sane one, not we. A shilling for peace? A fortune for peace. Our lives, our treasures, for peace. The longing for peace we can't get drives us mad.

She heard noon-day bells and walked faster, for Teddy would be on his way home from school. The bells were ringing in an Old City steeple, sweet and unhurried, as if they were totally indifferent to the changing tune of the times.

III

On their way home from school, Teddy and Asi found a bully beef tin in the road. They spied it simultaneously—it would have taken a Solomon to say who had first—but it was Asi who cried, "There's a good tin!" They lunged together. Teddy touched metal and yelled, "I got it. It's mine." He held it high, over his head. Asi jumped up to get the arm down, and they stumbled, rolling over and over in the dust, pounding and pummeling each other. Asi had the best of the fight because his two hands were free and Teddy was about to give in when Asi ripped his thumb on the jagged edge of the can. The sight of the blood sobered them. "Here, take it," Teddy said nobly. "You don't have to bleed for any old bully beef tin. You saw it first anyway."

Asi sucked his hurt finger and gave the trophy a skeptical eye. "It's not very good. It's not much." He was still unappeased. "Tell you what. Let's make a hand grenade and blow up their tank."

They scooped up dirt, packed the tin full and Asi, because it was technically his, got the first throw. Dust flew back in their nostrils and mouths. "It's no good." Asi gave it a contemptuous kick. Teddy picked the tin up. Their shoulders slumped, disappointed. They scuffed up dirt clouds as they shuffled along. "Let's play soccer with it," Teddy proposed. "Then we can both have the fun."

That was good. They promptly cheered up and came to the corner, butting each other, kicking the tin, banging it wildly from curb to curb. They made so much noise people looked out to see what was happening. The teacher with the concentration camp brand on his arm screamed at the boys to cut the racket.

Teddy stuck out his tongue. "Stop your own noise," he yelled.

The man shouted he'd come down and beat them if they didn't quit.

"Come, catch us," Asi jigged teasingly. "Yah, yah," he squawked.

The man's wife appeared at the window with a bucket of water. "Get away or I'll scald you," she screamed.

"You don't dare," Teddy shouted. "His father is—"

"Come on," Asi said. "Leave the old fools alone."

The man and his wife stood unsurely a moment, before they banged the window shut.

"I don't like him," Teddy announced.

"I hate him," Asi replied.

"I bet he's a spy," Teddy said.

"Donkey!" Asi shouted at Teddy. "We don't have spies."

"Why not?" Teddy bellowed. "It's a war, isn't it? You always have spies in a war."

"I bet that Yecke, Prinz, is a spy," Asi said.

"I bet he is too," Teddy said.

"Let's watch him," Asi said.

Teddy stuck his thumb in his cheek. "How can we? We don't know which office he's in."

"We can watch him when he comes home from work. We'll watch him at night. I'll sneak out one night and you'll sneak out next night."

Asi's brow knotted. "That's no good. Imma won't let me go out after dark. She's afraid."

"Me, I can go out whenever I want," Teddy boasted. "My parents let me. They don't care where I go."

Asi nudged him. "Don't you wish it," he said. Then his face brightened. "Let's play spies," he said. "You be the spy." He nudged Teddy again. "I'll be Haganah and I'll catch you."

"You be the spy," Teddy answered unreasonably.

"I will not," Asi said. "My father is a commander. How can I be a spy?"

Teddy cocked his head, sidewise. "Look at him. He will not be a spy but he wants me to be. My friend, my good pal, he makes a spy out of me." He nudged Asi back. The matter was settled, for ten seconds at least, until he had a new inspiration. "There are good spies and bad spies. Good spies are for *us.*" His eyes started to shine. "Let's both be spies." He came to a halt. "We are both spies," he announced. "We will inspect their tank and go up and tell Nathan how their tank works."

Asi took a step forward, toward the British tank near the apartment house. Teddy took a step back, unobtrusively, picked up the bully beef tin and caught up with Asi.

Because the noon sun was full, the Tommies had emerged from their tank and were leaning against it, trying to look watchful and not sloppily hot. They eyed the dusty small boys at the curb. The small boys eyed them. Nobody spoke. The Tommies turned around, made believe something needed inspection on the outside of their tank.

The boys shuffled forward and stood silently, not friendly, nor unfriendly, aloof, yet not uninterested. Teddy started to giggle. Asi silenced him with a glare. After a moment or so, the Tommies felt eyes on their backs. "Well, nippers," one of them growled. "What is it you want?"

The boys slid another inch forward but said not a word.

The Tommy rested the heel of his hand on his hip. "What're you lookin' at, the both of you?"

"What's so interestin'?" the other one asked.

Teddy's cheeks ballooned, got pink, as though he were about to burst. Asi looked at him, rolled his eyes, struggled to keep a titter down in his throat.

"What's so funny?" the Tommy demanded of both of them.

"Don't waste your breath," the other man said. "They don't unnerstan' wot you say."

"The 'ell they do not. Watcha bet?" He crooked his finger. "Come 'ere, nippers. Wanna see wot the inside looks like?"

The two on the curb still didn't speak, but a look of triumph traveled between two pairs of eyes. Yet they drew the purse strings of their lips, stiffened their arms at their sides, stuck out chests and bellies, and stared at the Tommies and tank.

"Come 'ere." A Tommy strode forward, tweaked Teddy's ear.

Teddy looked injured but he did not object.

"Whyncha answer a man when he speaks?"

Not a syllable, nor a change of expression to answer him.

The Tommy sighed. "Aw right, aw right, you bloody kids win. Come 'ere. Now, 'ere, put your foot up on 'ere." He gave Teddy his hand. "Up you go."

"Me, too," Asi cried.

The other man clapped him on a shoulder blade. "Heh! So you blighters speak English, do you?"

Asi looked guilty but he shook his head.

The Tommy grinned broadly. "'Ave it yer way. Come on, then, climb up. 'Ere you." He seized Teddy's arm. "Chuck away that old tin. I don't want yer dirt in my tank."

"I will not," Teddy said, distinctly, in English. "I found it. It's mine."

Edith was home before Teddy arrived. She found that the postman had been, had left mail from the States, two airmails from her sister, Belle, both with Miami post marks, an airmail from a cousin of Jacob's in Los Angeles, a surface mail letter from *Life* magazine, asking renewal of subscription expired months ago, and two American Medical *Journals* to which Jacob subscribed. She carried Belle's letters back to the kitchen, told Shifra, please be so kind as to heat up what remained of yesterday's bean soup, and take out some leben, for Teddy's lunch, agreed wryly that she had mussed her dress but she could bear even that, better a dirty dress than a bullet hole in the back of one's head, and sat down at the dining table to open the mail. One of Belle's letters had been written three weeks ago, the other a week after that. That was not bad. Air mail, air travel, the radio, the telegraph, phone, kept families joined. We're not yet cut off, we can still write, send a cable, make a phone call, get on a plane, reach New York in two days.

Belle's first letter was chit-chat, about Miami, the high prices at the hotel where she stayed, and her arthritis, which she used as a pretext for a holiday every year, when the New England winter became difficult. Her second letter had been penned the day after Ben Yehuda Street had been ripped apart. Its tone was quite different.

Teddy came in just as his mother had finished the letters. He dashed upstairs, dumped the bully beef tin into a chest with his treasures, gave his hands and face a lick at the basin and dashed down again.

"Imma," he panted. "I was in a tank."

"That's fine," she replied absently.

He yanked at her sleeve. "I know how it works. I can tell Nath—"

He bit his tongue. "I can tell anyone how their tank works."

"Good, good." She laid down Belle's letter. "You've ripped your shorts."

He scowled. "Asi did it. We had a fight." Shorts aren't important, his tone of voice said and mothers are a pain in the neck. "You're not listening to me. I am telling you I am a spy. I was in their tank."

"Sit down," she said. "I want to talk to you."

He saw the letters under her hands and snatched them up. "From America!" His nose wrinkled. "The same old air mails. Write her, Imma, I need other ones. Everybody has these. I can't trade a one."

"Teddy," she said. "Aunt Belle has written to beg me to send you to her."

His big eyes grew bigger. "When?" he breathed.

"Now. Right away."

"Now? When I am being a spy?"

She laughed and patted his shoulder.

"What for?" he persisted. "Why does she want me to come? Does she need me?"

"She read in the newspapers, heard on the radio about Ben Yehuda Street. She's afraid we're going to have more of that."

"We are." Teddy nodded. "That's why Asi and me, we're being spies. We're going to follow Herr Prinz. Tonight and tomorrow. We're going to . . ."

"Aunt Belle thinks you'd be safer in Brookline, in Boston, with her," she interrupted. What Belle had written was undeniably so. *"It isn't just physical safety—but believe me, if I could bundle all of you up, bring you here, keep you here, I would do exactly that. The first instinct—the truest instinct of each human being is to protect those he loves. Whenever I read of a bomb going off in Jerusalem— you're front page over here all the time—I go out of my mind. If you only would learn, as soon as anything happens, to send a cable at once, saying you're safe. I worry, especially, about your children. We elders haven't the right, I'm convinced, to ask them to take risks for what we believe. You decided to have children and raise them in Palestine, because you believed in the country, the Zionist ideal, but you did not foresee the grave physical risk. Or maybe you did and refused to believe, until the facts banged down on your head. Now that the tempo of danger is rising (Yes, the United Nations did vote for partition, but did they provide for enforcement? Another cruel hoax, like the Balfour declaration, which promised so much and gave nothing whatever—'Great Britain looks with favor'—My eye!) Will the United Nations lift one little finger to defend you against the armies of six Arab States? You're too close to the thing, the old business of not being able to see the forest for the trees, and so I must write you that everyone here is certain May 15 will bring a catastrophe, massacre, the destruction of the Temple, the Diaspora, all over again.—I hate to write thus to you but perhaps by not mincing words, by giving you some of the feeling so strongly held here, by our leaders, our thinkers, even our military strategists, I can shock you into a sense of reality. The feeling here is that you'll all be slaughtered or driven into the sea. What can your brave little hand- ful do against six Arab nations? Against Brigadier Glubb and the British-trained Arab Legion? Edith, you must think of your chil- dren. Dinah is probably old enough to make her own decisions, and she may not be easy to handle, but Teddy's a child and you can decide what is best for him. Send him to me ,at once, while there still is a chance. , , , "*

"Why, Imma, why does she want me?" Teddy was demanding of her.

"Why? Because it is safe. No bombs go off there. No shooting."

Teddy looked bored but he gave it reflection. "How would I go?" he asked.

"On the plane, probably."

"By myself?"

"By yourself."

"Without you? Don't you want to go?"

"I do want to go. But I can't leave Abba, you see."

He glanced at her curiously with the strange old-man look he occasionally had. "But I can leave Abba? Is it all right for a son to desert his own father?" He sounded injured, a bit too much so.

She smiled. "If his parents decide it is best. Under some circum- stances—" she winced at what she was about to say—"it might even be better for Abba and me if you were away, if we knew you were safe." She averted her gaze from his accusing eyes. "We'd manage somehow to get you on a plane at Lydda."

He sighed, a much deeper gust than one might have expected

from his narrow chest. "How would I get to Lydda?" he asked. "In the convoy?"

She nodded. He stood still, before her, knuckles doubled beneath his chin, Rodin's "Thinker." "Yoffee!" he burst out. "Wait till I tell Asi! *He* and his *father!* Wait till he hears I'm going in a convoy. Yoffee!"

"And a plane, transatlantic, remember." His excitement was infectious, but she was disappointed in him, just a child, all he lives for is excitement, a thrill. "You'll go on a boat or a plane. That's how you get to Boston."

He kicked the side of a shoe with the side of a shoe. "Where is Boston?"

"Get the map and find out."

While he scampered to the living room bookshelves, she brought in his leben, bean soup and bread. He snatched up a slice of bread, bit it, savagely hungry, but he let his soup cool while he flipped the atlas.

"Where do I find Boston?"

"Look for the United States first."

He turned the large sheets. "It's big." He sounded dismayed. "Much bigger than Palestine."

"Much." She smiled. "Now find the Atlantic coast."

He chewed and swallowed while he located the coast.

"Good. Now find Massachusetts."

He pushed the book toward her. "You find it while I eat my soup. I'm too hungry to look. . . . What do they have in Boston?" he asked while he ate.

"Why, houses, stores, schools and trains, and boats and docks. It's a big city, you know."

He glanced up. "As big as New York?"

"Big. But not as big as New York."

"Does it have an Empire State?"

"No. It has big buildings but no Empire State."

"Bigger than those on King George?"

She smiled, stroked his hair. "Of course. Much bigger. With lifts."

He raised his dirt-ringed chin. "I know lifts," he said condescendingly. "I've been in a lift on King George. Does Aunt Belle live in one of the very big buildings?"

"She lives in a small house like this. In a suburb—a quarter—of Boston called Brookline."

He shrugged. "No Empire State. I'd rather go to New York." He scraped the bottom of his soup bowl, drew the leben cup toward him. "Does it have a road under the water? Dovidl told all the boys in school New York has a hole under the water with roads where big lorries can go. Nobody believes—"

"It's true. Even Boston has a tunnel like that."

"Nylon!" He laid his spoon down. "I could ride through a tunnel like that. Wait till I tell Asi I'm going to ride on a road that goes under the water."

"They have a subway, too, trains that run under the ground."

He shook his head, awed and wondering. "Miracles! What a country America is!" He licked a drop of leben from the tip of his spoon. "I should like very much to see these American miracles." He put down his spoon. His eyes grew remote.

Of course he wants to go, she said to herself. What child would not? He's already there. This will be a house without children. But he'll be safe, and having a wonderful time. Belle will make him fat, with meat, fresh milk, spinach, eggs and ice cream.

"What else do they have in Boston?" Teddy suddenly asked.

She drew up to the table. "History," she said.

"What kind of history?"

She propped her chin with her hand. "Something like ours. The people of America were ruled by the British, you see, long ago, nearly two hundred years before this. They thought the British were tyrants and so there in Boston, right there, they started a war to make America free. The British made them pay taxes on tea and some of the people said it wasn't fair to pay all those taxes when you had no part in governing yourself—"

"Like us," Teddy breathed.

"And so," she went on. "Some of them got together in secret—"

"Like Haganah," Teddy said.

The Adamses, the Hancocks and Lowells, she thought, might object but this is almost true. "They dressed up like Indians one night and when a British tea ship was in the harbor, they went out and dumped all the tea in the water."

"To show the British!" Teddy crowed. "I told you, like Haganah."

He finished his leben, looking pleased and thoughtful. "I think Boston is a good place to be," he said finally.

"Then I'll write Aunt Belle you're coming?"

He nodded. "Yes, tell her I will be pleased to come." He scraped his bowl to get the last drops of leben. "Sometime when I have more time." He took up the atlas again, making a pretense once more of hunting for Boston's place on the map, but banged the book shut, impatient with it and looked squarely at her. "I could not leave now," he said. "The Land needs its people. Children are people. Look at how much Asi and I can both do. Why, just now, on the way back from school—"

"I know." She choked up. "You were spies."

"We were spies." Teddy puffed his chest out. "You wait and see what we will find out." He rose, then, went to her side and with a softness unusual for him, stroked her arm and laid his hand on her cheek. "Today, we were reading Gideon in school," he said. "We were reading what God told him to tell the people before the big battle. *'Whoever is fearful and afraid let him depart.'*"

She circled his thin, wiry middle with both of her arms and hugged him and wanted to cry. Afterwards, she was not sure why she had been so disturbed. It was because Teddy would not leave, of that much she was certain. But whether it was his bravery or the innocence of his courage that had affected her, she was not sure. But she felt an irrational anger toward the Old Testament because an apt quotation had sealed her child's destiny.

IV

IN THE SECOND week of March Dinah came home. Gan Darom, being young and impetuous, concluded it need not wait for a convoy to fight its way through. Dan and Avrum could take the big lorry in with a load of potatoes, and bring back what had to be brought, along with the flour and the cattle fodder. An innocent load on an uncovered truck—there was logic in that—had a better chance than a string of slow moving, armored vans. The boys took along Dinah and her friend, Ketti, on the sound premises that the British never searched women and no driver in his right mind would try the road through Faluja without small arms, at least, in the truck.

They left before dawn, while the mustard landscape was shrouded in mist. At the roadblocks, sleepy sentries roweled the load of potatoes, found only what it was meant they should find, namely, nothing at all, gave a cursory glance at identity papers and let the lorry go on. Moreover, when it sped by the thatched huts of an Arab village, a sniper behind a hedge of tall, mud-splashed cactus aimed at the tires and barely missed. That encouraged Dan to step hard on the gas and keep his foot there, so that they entered Jerusalem before the city had rolled out of bed.

The morning was cold. The rising sun had brought gentle light but no warmth. The jouncing lorry rattled in vacant streets. Somewhere in the hills, a rifle spat and echoed.

Dan stopped in an alley near Zion Square. "We drop you here," he told Dinah. "Meet you here in an hour," and added, "Be on time. We won't wait." Dan's tone made the instant a crisis so that she stood irresolute, wondering whether she ought to run and catch up with the truck. Her stomach was quivering, a fluttering begun the instant she jumped from the lorry. It puzzled her. What am I afraid of? she wondered. Of meeting Imma and Abba? What can they do to me?

She climbed Ben Yehuda Street's slope and stopped, cold with shock. The wireless had said this had happened a fortnight ago, but hearing about has none of the impact of sight. Cold rage filled her chest. She turned into King George. Down below, the Old City's walls stood intact, rosy pearl, in the morning light. Intact. Only the New City, *our* houses wrecked. She ground her teeth. Only *our* walls!

When she passed the British light tank at the corner of her parents' street, she glared at the Tommies and remembered the revolver under her breasts.

These particular Tommies didn't personally merit her fury. They were runty young men from homes where there had seldom been enough to eat, and a hot bath was rarely bothered about, because who could buy fuel to warm water up? They served in His Majesty's forces abroad not from passion for glory of Empire but for devious reasons, one because he'd had a bellyful of the grime of coal pits and the whine of a nagging mother and the other because he had married at eighteen, out of ignorance and of guilt, a skinny slut who had said she was bearing his child. He'd given the baby his name all right and an allowance out of his pay, but he'd be damned if he would come home and keep house with the bloody whore. Nevertheless, they dreaded each sunset, were scared of the dark. The contempt in the faces of passers-by made them crawly and sick. A soldier's life wasn't worth a piastre in this bloody place. Lord, get us out of here fast, they would pray. Lord, keep us all in one piece till we get on a boat.

They scowled at the girl, yet pretended they hadn't seen her go by and after she'd passed wondered aloud whether they should have asked who she was. Just as well not to, they assured one another. Nasty, those bloody kids were. But why was she wearing an Ayrab's keffiah? And brown as an Ayrab, she was— No, none of *those* girls would be seen on the streets with indecent bare thighs. That young one was up to no good, you could jolly well bet. Yet the people who lived on this street had a good reputation. Oh, probably just a Girl Scout, they concluded, coming to visit a friend.

Udi saw her first. He was poking about to see what new blooms had popped overnight. He smelled Dinah before he saw her, cocked his clipped ears, shot down the path and hurled himself at her, all but knocking her down. His yelps woke up the block.

Jacob ran out to the balcony, shrieked, "Shalom, shalom," cried out to Edith, "Get up, hurry. Dinah is home." Edith's head, pillow-tousled, showed long enough to wave frantically and blow a quick kiss.

Up and down the street, people heard Udi barking and knowing he barked only for joy, asked themselves, "What is the best good thing that could happen to Udi? Why, Dinah, of course. Dinah Hirsch must be home." Some of them wondered how she had come, some of them wondered why. Yora Levine thought it too bad Udi had informed everyone.

Dinah took the steps two at a time.

"Hurry, hurry, hurry." Jacob was at the door, in pajamas, arms spread-eagled for her. As he crushed her to him, he felt the hard rod of the weapon beneath her soft breasts, and, without meaning to, scowled while he placed a long kiss on her mouth. "You look well," he said, stroking her hair. "The morning star is not lovelier."

"You look the same as you did." That was clumsy, not warm enough. "I'm glad," she tried to temper her gruffness. "I'm glad, Abba, you never change."

He held the door wide. "Enter, princess! Welcome home!"

The peculiar churning started again. I'm excited, the girl told herself, I'm overcome with my joy. Yet she stepped gingerly, pulled in two ways, as if eager to be home again and afraid to be. There! See the polished, carved woods, the thick, gleaming rugs, the iridescent glass, the shimmering copper, the elegances with which you once lived! Aren't they dazzling? Aren't you glad to be here? The sun's rays were tapping the living room windows, prodding the Roman glass, and streams of iris, mauve, green, and gold, criss-crossed and dappled the walls. Are you sure the funny feeling isn't you're sorry you've given up this?

She stood in the doorway, just looking, then whirled and ran to the steps.

"Imma!" she cried up the stairwell. Something electric swept through the house.

"Haviva! Haviva!" Edith took the steps running and held out her arms.

Dinah entered them edgewise, fretting a little in her mother's embrace. If she turns me around she may feel my revolver. She drew off, to stand facing, clasping her mother's hands, swinging the bridge of their arms.

My mother is thinner, Dinah said to herself. She looks worn out. She must be having a difficult time. They're not eating enough. There's nothing to eat. She's gotten older. She looks very old.

My daughter looks fine, Edith said to herself. Her bare arms, her legs, are full fleshed, muscle hard. She's browner. The white keffiah is dramatic against her dark skin and hair. Her blouse and shorts aren't clean. But her eyes are clear, lively, bright. She's changed. She has not. She has. It's subtle but there. She looks older, grown up. But not a woman. That isn't yet in her eyes.

"Well, say something," Jacob urged both of them.

They smiled at each other but they still could not speak.

Edith's first words welled up. How are you, dearest? How is everything? Dear, we have missed you so much. Are you thrilled to be home? How long will you stay? Are you happy there? (I half-hope you are not.) Perhaps, now, if we can discuss it at last—it's no disgrace that a Negev kibbutz was too much for you. . . . Start talking, say something, speak. . . . "You need a haircut," was all she managed to say.

"I do." Dinah frowned and tossed back her long hair. "There just isn't time."

Jacob looked disgusted. "Haircut. Is that all we can discuss? Haviva, how did you come?"

"We had a load of potatoes to bring. Flour and feed we take back."

Her parents exchanged glances but her father said merely, "I do not know whether to be sorry or glad you took this chance."

"Sorry?" The girl blinked at him.

He put an arm around her. "You are home. I am glad."

Teddy clumped down the staircase just then. He whooped, drew himself up, breathed, "Nylon!" advanced with dignity and shook his sister's hand. Udi, too long ignored, bumped her, nuzzling her legs, and they all swirled around, making a maypole of her, until Jacob cried, "It's enough. Edith, make breakfast. We have a guest."

"Let's see, haviva, what would you like?"

Teddy looked from his father to mother, and his quick glance revealed everything. Abba is playing big shot. What have they to offer? Why, Teddy is thin as a rail! He's saffron yellow. You can bet he's not eating enough.

"We have everything," Abba was boasting. "Believe me, you'll see, we don't lack one thing."

"Everything." Imma was backing him up, lying as stoutly as he.

Then why are you starving? You're not fooling me. Well, if you wish it this way—Dinah glanced at the watch on her wrist. "I would love your good breakfast but there isn't time." She smiled, shook her head. "I meet the lorry forty minutes from now."

They looked stricken, sensed she had seen their dismay and had to gloss over it rapidly. "How is your watch?" Jacob asked. "Still keeping time?" He'd bought it for her, for her sixteenth birthday, white metal cased in brown leather, the sturdy practical time-piece you buy for an active child. He made a business of examining it, as a pretext of holding her hand.

"Good watch," Dinah said. "It's all that has enough time."

They laughed again, more heartily than the mild joke deserved.

"Do you know, haviva?" Edith said shyly. "I went to a concert with Carmela Levine. They played Gershwin and I heard not one note. I was thinking of you the whole time."

The girl drew her mother to her. "I think of you, too, Imma. I think of all of you, all the time."

"Then why don't you write?"

"Imma, there's never time."

"Well, sit down," Jacob said. "If there's no time then talk fast. . . . Edith, make coffee at least for our guest."

This morning, for spite, the current was off. There was all the bother of getting the primus out of the cupboard, alcohol-priming it, adjusting the wick, pouring kerosene in. Feet in the kitchen, mind in the living room, Edith's hands were all thumbs, everything to be done over twice. The talk on the living room sofa was well under way before she dashed in. Teddy was hunched, elbows on his knees, knuckles dug into his chin. Jacob had his arm around Dinah's shoulders. Even Udi was within the circle, head on the girl's lap. "We have finished the dining hall, the children's house and the bathhouse," Dinah was saying. "We've had hot showers for two months."

"Yoffee!" Jacob crowed. "Such luxury!"

"And the water tower, of course," she went on. "And the pillbox. We still sleep in pre-fabs, understand. The girls do. The pre-fabs are good, really, very. They keep out the rain. The boys use the tents.

We hope to start building houses for our married people. They're beginning—" all at once, shy, she glanced at her brother—"to kick about no privacy." She shrugged, spreading her palms, "There just hasn't been time. With the fences, the water pipes and the fields. And we had to build a good barn for the cows. We have twenty-four cows."

"Terrific!" Jacob's head bobbed. "Such energy! And where is our coffee, my dear?"

"Like everything else, it takes time."

"Did you hear, Edith? They have twenty-four cows."

"Twenty-four cows." She went back to the kitchen. The prosaic words said themselves over while she poured boiling water through the drip cup. "Twenty-four cows." Not important, yet very important. My daughter's a farmer. It's important to her. What's important to her is important to us.

She spread a linen cloth on a tray, set out cups and saucers, took down the sugar bowl and peered in. Dinah will understand if we don't have sugar for her. No, no, she'll understand far too well. She remembered the yellow box of white cubes Belle had sent in December, along with tinned lobster, tinned mushrooms and S. S. Pierce soups—"the delicacies you once used to like"—and she pushed a chair into the pantry, stood on it to reach the top shelf. "Where are you, Imma?" she heard Dinah call.

"What's taking so long?" Jacob yelled.

She dumped sugar cubes into the bowl, stirred water into milk powder and hurried in with the tray. Teddy reached for a lump of sugar, popped it into his mouth, stretched his arm out again, and ducked when his father grabbed for the arm. "For Asi," he mumbled as though that made it right.

"You see," Jacob gestured expansively, "I told you, haviva, we have everything. Coffee. Good milk, the best powdered, lump sugar, too. We don't lack a thing. You're not to worry about us, you hear?"

The girl smiled. "I will not worry and I will worry," she said.

"Now tell me, haviva." Edith laid her gaunt hand on the girl's knee. "Tell me everything."

"I've already told—" Dinah looked at her wrist watch again.

Once more the reminder, time's running out, get everything said or not say it at all. "You've told Father, tell me."

"I've told Father we've had a fine six months. Two hundred

saplings—apples and plums—have been planted. We've had a good crop of barley, alfalfa." She spoke fast and with pride.

"And potatoes," her father put in.

"Potatoes. No lawns yet, no flowers," Dinah said.

"The water tower and the fences," Jacob helped her. "The dining hall and the showers and the barn for the cows."

In Edith's mind's eye, the picture grew—on sun-crisped earth of drab mustard color, monotonous, hideous, bleak—a huddle of pre-fabs and tents, inside a wire fence, in a vast emptiness, a water tower, concrete torso on stilts, the white walls and red roofs of dining hall, children's house, showers, the long, narrow barn, the groves of slim saplings, the grain fields bright green (no lawns, yet, no shade), sun beating down, baking earth, browning flesh, and the winter rains pelt-ing, roiling the ground into thick, clayey mud. A little place, just beginning, unbeautiful, lonely, helpless and brave . . . She drew her breath in, let it out. "What do *you* do there, my darling?"

"I?" Dinah stirred a sugar lump. "I worked in the fields. Now I'm in the kitchen."

"You!" Her father roared. "Isn't the life hard enough without making your comrades eat what you cook?"

They laughed loudly, too loudly, for that wasn't much of a joke.

"I don't cook," Dinah hurried to add. "Chava cooks. And Ilana. And Ketti sometimes. I peel the potatoes and wash dishes." She glanced down at her hands. Her mother looked too. The thumbs had criss-crossed paring-knife nicks; the nails were broken and grimed. Dinah drew them down in her lap. "Don't stare at my hands," she ordered.

"Tsck, tsck," Jacob mocked. "My poor baby's hands. . . Let's talk of something important. The Tegart Fortress is close?"

We can see their lights."

"And it is reassuring?"

"Perhaps."

He looked at her hard. "The Arabs?" he asked.

"They used to visit, drink coffee with us. They were friends."

"Yes," Jacob said. The word was a question, not an assent.

Edith set down her cup, unfinished, but Dinah took time, drain-ing hers, before she replied, in a matter-of-fact tone of voice, "They cut our pipe lines several times. They ambushed our truck two weeks ago. Zvi was killed. He was married, with a little child." Her lips thinned. "We started our cemetery. That we must have too."

Add to the mind's picture, a spot, apart, in a eucalyptus grove, possibly, a mound with a name-board, the first. No. No eucalyptus, there aren't trees, only the saplings set out. . . . My child speaks of death so off-handedly. Can she know what it means?

"Tell me," Teddy bent forward. "Have you killed anyone yet?"

Edith's hands gripped in her lap, bone pressing bone, and all of her focused to catch each nuance of the girl's expression and voice.

"No," Dinah said again in the business-like tone. "Not yet. Any day."

There was silence. Then Edith cried, "Talk about something else. Talk about anything."

Jacob stroked her arm. "Speak of something else," he commanded. "Of your comrades, your group."

The girl's face relaxed the least bit. "We're a mixture. All kinds. Good workers. Intelligent."

"Who are your friends?" Edith took her coffee cup up.

"Everybody. Imma, is there more coffee? Toda . . . Ketti sleeps next to me. I think you'd like Ketti, Abba. . . . She's very lively, makes jokes . . . and is the best marksman we have. . . . She came with us today . . . and Dan and Avrum. Dan drove the truck. You'd like Dan, I think. He was born and raised in kibbutz. He knows more than most of us do." She wrinkled her small nose. "He likes to give orders too much," she said.

"Is he married?"

Dinah shot a glance at her mother and laughed. "He, married? Why, he's a child. He still slaps and pushes the girls. He's only eighteen.

Jacob grinned. "And how old are you?"

"That's different. Girls always act older than boys." She tilted her head back and smiled at the ceiling. "I don't know which I like better, Dan who is rough with the girls or Avrum who's still scared of them."

"How old is *he?*"

She brushed back a strand of dark hair. "Oh, he's old. At least twenty-three."

"What's Avrum like?" Edith asked.

"What's he like? Why, he argues a lot. Too much. About everything. Principle. Theory." She frowned. "I know what you're think-ing. You're wondering which one of them will be a husband for me." Her long hair kept swinging into her eyes, and she stroked it back with an impatient gesture. "Don't worry, Imma, I'll take care of that when there is time."

"Time." Jacob thrust his lower lip out. "For that there must always be time."

"No." The girl dismissed it with a wave of her hand. "Not now. Too much else." She set down her cup. "Let me look at the house."

Her brown body cut the colored beams of sunlight through old glass as she moved through the long living room. She touched little things, picked them up, put them down, ran her hand sensuously over carved table tops. At the piano, she halted because she was puz-zled by her photograph. "Why am I here with the old folks, the dead ones?" she asked herself as she moved on, up two steps, to the dining room, strode all its length to the windows and stood looking out. "Some day," she said, "we're going to have flowers. Gan Darom will be like its name. Garden of the South. I'll plant them myself when there's time." She turned suddenly. "Imma, what is with Arieh I know, but did David come back?"

"No, haviva."

"When is he coming? He will miss everything." She glanced at her wrist watch again, made a sound of dismay, before she sprinted up-stairs to her old room. Udi padded beside her into the bedroom, sniff-ing curiously, knowing something important was happening, but not sure what it was. She crouched on the edge of the bed and cradled his neck. "Take care of Imma and Abba and Teddy, you hear me, Udi? Be a very good dog." Then she got up quickly, without even glancing at the surroundings which used to be hers.

Jacob was on the upstairs landing. "Here," he tried to sound non-chalant. "A present. You can use it."

She stared at what lay on his hand. "Can't you?" she asked.

"Yes." Their eyes met. "Take it," he said brusquely. "We'll manage somehow."

She turned from him, modest, and opened her blouse, to anchor his revolver with hers in her brassière.

"It's loaded," her father said, "with as much as I had. Be stingy. Don't waste." Then he asked. "How many guns do you have?"

"After today, we'll have more," she replied.

"Enough?"

"How much is enough?"

He tried to laugh. "If God is willing, a broom can shoot. Have you good marksmen?"

"They will be better. By day we are farmers. By night—" She left the sentence unfinished.

"When do you sleep?"

"We sleep." She shrugged. "Tell me about you," she demanded. "You drive to the hospital every day?"

"Certainly."

"Past Sheikh Jarrah?"

"How else? Haviva, don't worry, we will be safe." He linked his arm through hers. "The hospital belongs to Americans. If they dared to harm one single stone, Truman would come with his atom bomb."

"Abba," she said quietly, "you don't fool me. We have a wireless in Gan Darom. We know everything."

"Then why do you ask me?" he cried and all at once he clasped her to him, held her fast, kissed her eyes, lips and cheeks.

She clung to him for a moment before she wrenched herself free. "Abba, please!"

"Excuse me, haviva." He lowered his eyes. "Excuse me, and understand."

Edith was waiting at the bottom of the steps. She held the sugar box out. "Give your comrades a treat. American sugar with tea." She saw the glance, amused, secretive, pass between her husband and child. "You have fine presents," Jacob said.

They walked with her to the door. The girl kissed them quickly and they kissed her. "Haviva, one question, just one. Are you happy, my child?"

"Of course, Imma. How can you ask?" She put her arms around Udi again. "Hold him, Abba, don't let him run after me." She pecked Teddy's cheek. "If you're good, very good and do your homework, in the summer you'll come to us, milk the cows."

"Can I shoot your Sten when I come?"

"What Sten?" Her hand was on the stair rail, starting down.

"Our Scoutmaster shot a Spandau," Teddy called after her.

"I don't believe it," she said without looking back.

Teddy squirmed between his parents, out to the steps. "He's sixteen years old," he yelled after her. "He showed us the empty shell that he shot himself. Didn't you know there's a Spandau in—"

"Sheket." Jacob gripped the boy's collar. "Run upstairs and wash. It's time you were dressed."

Dinah stopped on the walk and knelt down, to pick two purple pansies and tuck them into her hair. She turned, blew a kiss and set off at a run.

"Be careful," Edith cried after her. "Take care of yourself." Careful, her mind kept repeating as she stood in the doorway, watching the brown, barelegged figure in the white keffiah run down the street.

"Well," Jacob leaned against the lintel. "Well." His face writhed. "Their crops are fine." His voice was thick. "Good crop of potatoes, barley, alfalfa. They've set out saplings. Fruit trees."

"And they have twenty-four cows."

"She's turned the corner." His arm encircled his wife. "Come into the house, little one!"

"You gave her something. What was it?"

"Something she may need." He stroked her shoulder. "Get dressed."

"So little, Jacob." She let her head rest on his shoulder. "For so long gone and so much to face." She drew away. "How fortunate," she said decisively, "there was not time for her to ask how things are with us."

Shifra came late because the bus from the quarter in which she lived was forced by snipers to take a roundabout route. She lamented loudly when she heard that Dinah had been and had left. "Was she well?"

"Very well."

"Is she happy?"

"I think she is, yes."

Shifra looked wistful. "She should be happy. She is a something, a something big. What am I? I am nothing. What do I do? I spongeh the floors, beat the rugs. Who considers me?" She picked up an armful of rugs for their daily shaking outdoors. "I would go, too, but my father would break all my bones. With a stick he would beat me, if he knew I think such a thing. Some day, you will see. . . . Please, G'veret Hirsch, take good care today."

When Edith came out of the door, Tamar Atani who lived in the house on the corner was just turning into the left-side path to Jacob's office, propelling on spindle legs the enormous melon of her unborn child, and Edith stopped to say "Shalom" and "How do you feel?"

"It is almost ready." Tamar touched her swollen stomach delicately. "It is so hard to wait. If I could already hold the little one in my arms." She hugged herself as though she were cradling the baby. Her thin brown face was tender and sweet. "Four weeks still, before the good Doctor will take me up." Her dark eyes clouded. "G'veret, Elia, my husband, says he would wish I have the baby here in the town. Is there a danger to go up the Hill?"

"Doctor Hirsch goes every day."

"You see!" Tamar's white teeth gleamed in her smile. "If it is safe for him, is it not safe for me?"

No, Edith thought, as she walked up the street, it is not safe for him and it is not safe for you, but why should I tell you the truth? The terror from Sheikh Jarrah on the Mount Scopus Road cannot last. It must be stopped. In another month things may all be otherwise. The Hill is the best place for Tamar. She is too thin, too narrow hips. In Yemenite children, born poor, growing up with too little to eat, there's so often rickets, a deformed pelvis. If Jacob has a Caesarian to do—

Thinking of Tamar, she remembered herself with Dinah, a thin woman, too, grotesque with the balloon of the foetus, yet light of step, as if walking in glory. She remembered how Jacob had chortled when he showed the new born to her. "Here! Here's your daughter! So much trouble for this!" Like a plucked chicken and with that red, wrinkled face. "It's the most beautiful child in the world." "Liar! Only a mother can deceive herself so." There, did I lie? Is she not beautiful? This morning with the flowers in her hair.

She was smiling as she went down Ben Yehuda, past the street's gaping wounds, and no one could have guessed, seeing her stepping smartly, in a clean cotton frock, that Edith Hirsch had just said good-bye to a daughter traveling back to the Negev in an open truck and was going downtown to risk her own life once more on Princess Mary's pavements.

V

YORA LEVINE, blanched-almond color and still somewhat queasy, left his house late. He ran into Jacob Hirsch on the street and they walked to the corner together.

"So Dinah was home," Yora said.

"How did you know?"

"Your dog informed everyone."

Jacob sucked his lip down. "And so? Who is there on this street who should not know?"

"An Englishman lives on this street," Yora said.

Jacob glanced back. "I had almost forgotten," he said. "He is no one to worry about. In a little while we shall no longer need even to lower our voices. That, too, will be a comfort."

"I shall tell Nathan the girl was here," Yora said. "If he does not already know."

Yora was in pain when he entered the office building downtown and he walked past Duncan's door to the end of the corridor to wait till the wretched quivering had ceased. Then he wheeled and came back and went into Duncan's office.

Duncan looked up. "One of your boys got a street lamp on Jaffa Road last night," he began. "I presume you know that."

"You are sure it was one of our boys?"

The man smiled, a mere lifting of gray-mustached lip. "Assume for the sake of argument. With all the lead flying about, naming names doesn't matter too much." He motioned Yora to take a seat. "What can I do for you?" he asked courteously.

"Is the fuel holding out?" Yora asked.

Duncan gave him a brief, speculative stare. "You know the situation as well as I do. We are supplying whatever current we can, an hour, two hours a night. Beyond that—" He spread his palms. "If

Jerusalem householders wish light and power, let them end the fighting on the Tel Aviv Road."

"Until they do—" I'm handling it well, Yora thought, taking my cue from him, affable, man to man, no hostility—"it has occurred to us—"

"Who is *us?*" Duncan asked.

He tightened. "Those of us who are responsible for the New City's welfare," he said carefully. "I believe you know whom I mean."

If Duncan knew, he chose to give no indication, but said merely, "Proceed. What has occurred to *us?*"

He drew a deep breath. He leaned toward the desk. He said, keeping his tone cool, business-like, "Power is scarce and power is precious. It is less important for a householder to hear his wireless set for an hour than for a hospital to have current all night. Therefore, why should not whatever there is be distributed only to essential places?"

Duncan frowned. "That would require special cables."

Yora nodded. "We understand. We are prepared to assume the additional cost." He hitched closer to the desk. "We are in a war, Duncan, make no mistake. Whatever may happen elsewhere, in the New City there is order and planning." He paused, eyed the dapper, gray-haired, gray-clad man across the desk. "I speak to you as a business man." He licked his dry lips. "I speak to you frankly, because I have known you for years. You are a man I believe I can trust."

The man nodded gravely, "I appreciate that," but his forehead creased and he sat looking off toward the street maps and charts on the opposite wall with a queer, preoccupied gaze, as though, while Yora spoke, his own thoughts were traveling elsewhere.

Yora took a paper out of his pocket, laid it on the desk. "These are the essential places. We have made up a list. Hospitals, bakeries, synagogues, schools; you can see."

"Yes, a list." Duncan brought his wandering thoughts back. He barely glanced at the sheet. "It's as good a plan as any," he said finally. "As long as the bills are paid." He wheeled in his chair and turned to his clerk. "This is the essential list," he said carelessly.

"If there is a change in the list, I shall let you know. A school may shut down, an emergency clinic be opened up. Things change, you know."

Duncan passed his hand over his forehead. "I know only too well,"
he said.

"Very good. Then it is arranged, for this emergency—" Easily done,
Yora thought. Why was I worried? He is a business man. And unimaginative. He took out his cigarette packet, a red and white box
of Craven A, becoming daily harder to get. He extended the box. The
man at the desk smiled at him and held out a packet of his own. "One
of mine, Levine? My source of supply is still—" He marked Yora's
frown. "An even trade," he said smoothly. "I from you, you from me.
What could be fairer?"

VI

Dan decided to take the camel tracks home. By full daylight it was sheer foolhardiness to travel the road through Hebron and Faluja. The decision would have been excellent if the lorry had not been so heavy and if the winter rains had not rutted the trail.

The load looked lighter than it actually was because its top layer was feed for the cows, grown in Australia and pressed into compact small squares. Under the fodder were flour sacks, rye flour to bake into Gan Darom's bread, but a flour sack which conceals a rifle is heavier than a flour sack which holds merely flour. Because of the load, the axles moaned when the truck struggled through wadis and the motor hiccuped up every slope. Each time that occurred, Dan ground his teeth and Avrum, in back with Dinah, tightened his jaw and peered anxiously both sides of the track.

Dan was grim, but then Dan usually was, no laughter in him at all. He behaved, Dinah thought now and then, as though he alone had to bear the full weight of the Land. This morning only Ketti was gay, but so Ketti usually was. She sat up with Dan and jabbered and clowned. The stenciled black letters on the sides of the bales had delighted her. "So far to send for food for our cows. Are they worth so much trouble? Yes, they are very good cows. Would we send so far for breakfast for us? No. Is a kibbutznick worth as much as his cow? Certainly not. A cow costs money. How many hours must each of us work to earn Gan Darom the price of a cow?" Nobody answered. She didn't expect a reply. "Come." She nudged Dan. "Drive me to Australia. We have the lorry. Let us go on a holiday, all four of us."

That was Ketti. "Come let us laugh," she would say. "I like to laugh. I have cried enough in my life." Yet looking at her, you'd conclude she had never known any except happy days. Her hips swung, half dancing, as she strode along. She glowed with health, and when she laughed, there were fetching dimples in her round cheeks. Her eyes were sea blue, almost green, her hair yellow golden and long. She wore it in braids, a crown above a freckled face. Ketti's freckles were monstrous, her arms covered with splotches of rust. An Aryan type, pure Aryan sufficiently, everyone said, to have passed without danger when *that* trouble came. But that hadn't been so. She was the only one of her family remaining alive and she had the numerals on her forearm. Those were her problem these days.

She slept next to Dinah, adjoining cots in the pre-fab, and night after night, Ketti brought up the matter of the numbers. She had read or had heard that doctors knew how to take off that brand by grafting skin from one's backside or thigh and she swung in debate with herself over whether that should be done. "If I take it off, Dinah, I will be like everyone else and that is what I wish to be. Here I am home, no longer a stranger, outcast. So why should I keep what used to set us apart?" She was right. Dinah agreed and said when there was money and time, Ketti should go to Jerusalem, see a skin specialist and take her brand off. "They gave it to you as a badge of shame; why should you be marked with that shame? My father will bring you to the right man. It will be done. Now let's go to sleep. It's almost tomorrow and tomorrow's a hard working day."

Then Ketti would start all over again. "Badge of shame? No. In time it may be a mark of honor, of pride. If I do not keep it, I may forget. If we forget what happened there, we are forever lost."

That was right too. Yes, this is right; yes, that is right. How can two opposites both be right? For Dinah Hirsch, in her eighteen years, there had never been division of right. This is right, understand, only this, the straight line. This way we must live; this and this we must do. Build the Land. Defend the Land. Therefore I am Palmach. If I am Palmach, I must be where I am needed the most. That is the Negev. I am Palmach and in the Negev. There are no problems. Then, why this heaviness, this depression today? It might have been better not to have visited them. A short visit teases; leaves one full of regrets for what there isn't time to say or to do. They had felt that as well, especially Imma. She had said foolish things, like you need a haircut and which boy am I interested in? and kept harping on how many cows, and the last foolish question she asked, Am I happy here? Maybe (the notion stunned and dismayed her) she was waiting to hear I am not. That must be it. Last year, she accepted the fact of my going away and now she regrets. She wants me home, to treat me like a child. Mothers can't understand you have to live your own life. Even our Palestine mothers. They ought to know better. They don't. Mothers are the same everywhere.

Avrum slid over the tops of the bales. "How did you find your family?" he asked diffidently. Avrum's father, long since turned to ashes in the Treblinka ovens, had been a shoemaker in Lodz—a manual worker, revering learning, who had worked long, eaten little, to send his son to school. His parents had made another great sacrifice. They had sent Avrum away from Poland in time to be safe. What he remembered most clearly of both the parents he'd lost was his mother, bringing a slice of bread, smeared with chicken grease while he sat with his books, telling him, "Avrum, study, learn!" and his father, coming in from the bench, untying his apron, carefully washing his hands, before he picked up his son's book. As the twig is bent, so it grows. On his wanderings, a miserable, lonely hegira, over land, over sea, from Poland to Teheran, to Palestine, Avrum had been one of the few who gathered around the older boys of the group and memorized scraps of the history, algebra, geography those others once had learned from books. Here was Dinah, a daughter of culture, with a father a doctor, a mother who once had taught school. Be respectful to her, offer awe.

But she answered him briefly, "My family is well."

"They were glad to see you?"

"What else?"

He edged off, "Did they tell you how everything is?"

"In those few minutes?"

The fault must be mine, he thought unhappily. She finds me insensitive. "I don't wish to worry you but I understand the food situation is critical, and if we do not soon take the Castel, Latrun, it will be much worse."

"Don't you think I know that?"

I am tactless, he thought. She is distressed and I make it worse. He made a fresh start. "The flowers are nice in your hair."

She did not reply. He tried again. "The sugar is an excellent present."

"My father gave me a better one." She glanced down at her blouse.

He didn't grasp what she meant, for he averted his eyes, not wishing to seem so forward as to stare at her breasts. "They have many luxuries in America," he said. "I used to think I would like to go there some day."

"Sheket," Dan cried.

Avrum flushed and fell silent, convinced he'd been talking too much.

Over the rattle of the lorry, they heard the motor's wheeze. It coughed once or twice and went dead. The truck stopped. Dan jerked up the brake. He turned the ignition off. "Ketti!" he barked.

Ketti dipped to her bosom, brought a pistol out.

"Dinah!" The girl took out her father's small gun and gave it to Avrum. "My father's present," she said and brought out her own revolver, scrambled across the truck and stood scanning the drab horizon.

Dan had the motor hood up. The feedline, he called back, was clogged, bad petrol or dirt from the road. "Ketti, hand me the wrench. Do you have a hairpin?"

"How long?" Avrum asked.

"Who knows?" Dan replied.

They stood rigid under the searing aluminium sky, revolvers cocked, at the ready, while Dan sweated over the motor.

It was Ketti who saw the round of a white keffiah coming over a rise up ahead, a man tall on a horse and sunlight glinting on the rifle he raised. Ketti fired. The noise was like a cannon in the vast emptiness. The Arab rolled from his horse. The riderless beast charged toward them, suddenly veered and raced toward the plain. Ketti took aim. "No," Avrum cried. "No bullets to spare for a horse." He leaped from the truck, ran forward to the wounded man, on the ground.

"Get his rifle," Dan said without looking up.

Dinah saw the second rider and fired. The horse neighed with panic and reared as the man in the saddle struggled to stay in his seat. Ketti fired again. The rider rolled slowly, dripping bright blood through his robes to the dust.

Dan slammed down the hood and sprang into the lorry. He clicked the ignition, scraped his gear into reverse. Avrum leaped in. Dan pushed down the throttle. The engine hiccuped, turned over at last.

Dan shoved the gas feed to the floor and backed down the road.

At the place where two rutted tracks came together, he swung toward the highway and slowed the car down. The girls turned around modestly and slipped their revolvers beneath their breasts. Avrum gave back Jacob's gun. "A useful present," he said. "It works very well. I no longer need it. I have a British gun."

"Give me the rifle," Dan ordered. Avrum passed it up.

Dan brought the truck to a halt, ran his fingers lovingly over the weapon, but made as if to throw it away. Ketti snatched it out of his hand.

"Fool!" he shouted at her. "Would you like them to find a new English rifle in a kibbutz lorry?"

"Let them try to take it from me." She put it behind her, beneath her buttocks. "Their fingers will burn before they take this away."

No one tried. Their luck held up to the moment when the yellow stone oblong of the Tegart Fortress on the rise above Gan Darom loomed in front of the truck. Astraddle the road, blocking it, was a light armored car.

Dan pulled up the brake.

A Corporal climbed out of the armored car. "Let's have a look at your lorry." He kept his hand on his holster. Two men stepped out after him, with their guns drawn.

"We are from Gan Darom," Ketti said smoothly. "Bringing feed for our cows and flour for our bakery."

The Corporal gave her a rapid glance and a flicker, of recognition or interest, passed over his countenance. His sunburned forehead creased.

"Are you not the one—" Ketti's voice was like honey—"who stopped by our kibbutz three weeks ago?" Dimples dipped into her cheeks. "I know you. I sewed on your buttons for you."

He did not answer but furious crimson deepened his tan as he motioned the men to climb into the truck. They kicked the feed bales, stamped on the flour bags. One took out his knife. Avrum and Dinah held themselves taut while the man slit open a sack. Gray flour dribbled out. Not this one, fortunately . . . The next? . . . The man moved to another sack. Ketti clutched at his arm. "Is that nice? Waste our good flour." Her green eyes flashed at the Corporal. "Shame! After what I did for you."

He cleared his throat but did not reply.

"Have a sweet, sir?" One of the soldiers held out Dinah's present of sugar.

"That the best you can find?" the Corporal growled.

"We can open 'em all, sir—"

"Don't bother." He crooked his finger. The men jumped down. They climbed into the car. It backed, swung around. The Corporal waved the lorry on.

"Come see us again," Ketti called out to him as the truck rattled past.

The guard in the water tower saw the lorry approaching, sent word and Gershon, who was the settlement's chief, ran out to the gates.

"Hakol b'seder," Dan said. "All okay. A little trouble but we managed well."

VII

THE GROCER WAS SWEATING. "Women, stop!" He was all but in tears. "You will drive me insane." He cowered behind the counter, his hands over his face. "If I have nothing to sell, I have nothing to sell. . . . Go away. Go."

"My children are crying from hunger." A young woman in a white linen turban pounded the counter. "A crust of dry bread they have, nothing more."

The grocer let his hands down. He was a pudgy man, pasty-faced under his black skull cap. "So you kill me, will that give eggs and milk?" He lifted a can from a shelf, banged it down. "Here, Australian asparagus soup. You want, buy!" He showered a handful of small oval tins. "Spanish anchovy paste. You want, buy."

Leah Malkoff pushed forward. "My whole life I struggled and suffered for a Homeland. Now, this you give us to eat! For *that* I give *this*." She sucked in her cheeks, pursed her mouth and spat in his face. A hiss, part indignation, partly applause, swirled through the crowd as she elbowed her way, high pompadour quivering, out of the shop.

"Stay out of my store," the grocer remembered to scream after her. "Go send your son to open the road." He squatted on a box behind his counter and mopped his face with the flat of his hand. There were tears in his eyes. "Someone must do something," he moaned, "or the women will tear me apart. . . . Not you, G'veret Levine, not you G'veret Goldstein. For you there is always enough. These . . . These . . ." He glowered at the woman in the linen turban. "These wild animals! These jackals!"

The words were ripped out of his mouth. A blast rocked the store. It flung the women against one another, rained glass confetti on them. In the aftermath, a half-minute of deathly stillness, the women stared at each other, sheet-white. The blast had been near, in this neighborhood. . . . Where?

"The school!" Carmela Levine gasped. "Our children!"

"Our children!" the women screamed and like sheep, pushed each other and ran from the shop.

Sirens were wailing; whistles blown shrill. Keren Kayemeth Street was full of broken glass and racing people. They seemed to Carmela to be running the wrong way, not toward the school up the street but toward the opposite corner where the Jewish Agency's buildings were. She clutched a passer-by's arm. "The school! The children!" she panted at him.

"Not the school." He wrenched loose. "Worse. They have blown up the Agency."

A man at a corner roadblock was flailing his arms and shouting something one could not believe. "The Americans. The American flag. The American car."

Carmela shook him frantically. "What are you screaming? Not the Americans?"

"Why not, G'veret?" he snarled. "Are *they* our friends? Have we any friends? *They blew up the Agency*"

The man at the roadblock was wrong. The United States Consulate blushed. Yes, one of its Arab chauffeurs had taken a Consulate car, with its American flag, had used that to deceive the Agency guards. The Consulate apologized fervently. We should have checked on our drivers more carefully. Believe us, we deeply regret—

Friendliness engenders friendliness, especially when one craves above all to believe one has friends. The Agency apologized too. The fault is half ours. Our guards should have asked for the driver's papers and mission, not so readily let him go through. It is a pity, both parties agreed; lives were lost, a building wrecked, through carelessness. But the important factor remains, our mutual friendliness.

There was further proof of it later that week when Jewish Palestine's leader, Chaim Weizmann, had an affable visit with Harry Truman.

Thus, what occurred on the nineteenth of March was an unbelievable shock. On that afternoon, the American delegate to the United Nations told the Assembly that the United States had changed its mind about favoring the creation of a Jewish State, for which it had voted last November. The military actions, the united hostility of the Arab world which had followed the partition vote, had convinced his country, Warren Austin declared, that Great Britain and the Arabs were right. Division of Palestine was unworkable. A new plan for the Holy Land's future, he said, a trusteeship, perhaps, must be devised. The State was dead before it was born. Mr. Austin had declared it so.

The time difference between Jerusalem and Flushing, New York, is seven hours and therefore most of Rehavia's residents had gone to bed before the wireless could flash them the news. Since the next day was Shabbat, a good many failed to get up in time to hear the morning broadcast.

Shabbat in Jerusalem is what God ordained it to be, a day of rest. Everyone save the old and devout who require weekly prayer, and those who must man defense posts, starts the Shabbat the same way, by sleeping late. No shops are open; the newspapers don't publish; the buses don't run, and the housemaids, like everyone else, take a day off. A few who sit behind desks all week long and need exercise, put on their shorts, take their racquets and go out to the Rehavia Club's tennis courts.

Jacob woke around half past ten. Edith was still asleep when he went downstairs to put coffee on. Teddy heard him and surmised his father might require his help. The two dropped pots in the kitchen, banged doors. Teddy stepped on Udi's paw and the dog yelped. Edith woke, put on her robe and went down to see what the disturbance was.

By that time, Jacob was singing and Teddy struggling to accompany him on the flute. The song was a haunting Oriental lilt, in a minor key, a song of love for a strip of land. A great many people were singing and whistling that "Song of the Negev" these days. One heard it on the streets, in the buses, through open windows, a dreamy melody, pleasing to sing or to hear, regardless of whether one's child's residence was on that parched earth.

"Oh, Imma!" Teddy stopped puffing his flute. "You spoiled our surprise."

"We were going to treat you like a lady, bring you coffee in bed," Jacob said.

It was already eleven o'clock, a good excuse for skipping one meal and lolling around the living room. None of them was dressed when Nathan rang the doorbell.

Jacob went to the door. "What is it?" he cried out. "I heard no explosion. Where do they bomb us today?"

Nathan wasn't amused. "You have heard the broadcast?"

"Come in," Jacob said. "I have only just got out of bed." He shut the front door. "Well, tell." He glanced over his shoulder, as if the news he was about to receive might not be for his family's ears.

"The United States has abandoned us," Nathan said.

Jacob stared at him blankly. "Talk sense," he barked.

"It was on the wireless. Cairo is ringing victory bells." A spasm of coughing seized the man. He covered his mouth with his one hand.

"Sit down," Jacob said. "We will have coffee and look into this." There was something else he did not understand. If this is true, he asked himself, why has Nathan come to see me? Am I a statesman? Am I a diplomat?

Edith heard them in the hall, hurried back to the kitchen to boil water again, looked into the coffee tin, resolutely divided the remaining few grams, added them to the damp grounds in the drip cup, before she ran upstairs to dress.

Nathan entered the living room shyly. He took the plainest chair, straight-backed, frowning as though he disapproved of the Hirsch luxury. "I came to you, Jacob—" he hawked again—"to find out what this means."

"Me?" Jacob wagged his eyebrows. "I am Jacob, not Joseph. Can I interpret dreams?"

"You are an American," Nathan persisted. "You are the only American on this block."

"I beg to correct you. I was." His own words gave him pause. I was also a Russian, he said to himself. That was my mother country. I left. America gave me my schooling, my passport to here. This is my choice. This is my country. But this is no nation, not yet. Then what am I? I am a Jew. A Jew is a transient, a person in transit between nationalities. A man on his way. He felt confused and therefore, he had to shout. "So I lived in America! So I took a citizen oath! Must I understand a crazy country? Bevin plays a tune and they dance. Nathan, I swear to you—" he laid his hand on his chest—"I have no more idea than my young son." He broke off. "Wait, excuse me. I see our good Judge on the walk." He flung open the door. "Shalom, Henry. Have you also come here because an American lives in this house?"

Judge Winkleman nodded. "Precisely. I felt when I heard the wireless today, I wished to be with Americans. Frankly, I felt sorry for them."

"You have come to the wrong house. Jews live here, Palestinian Jews, not Americans. . . . Edith," he bawled up the stairs, "come down. Give me help. . . . Go in, Henry, sit."

Henry Winkleman entered, said a hearty "Shalom" to Nathan, spread his coattails on the sofa, and put on a long face. "Your country has made a disastrous blunder," he said.

"*My* country, *my* country." Jacob tugged at his pajama collar. "Marshall decides, Truman decides. Jacob Hirsch in Rehavia must apologize." He stopped suddenly. "Exactly what have they done?"

Judge Winkleman bent forward, weaving his long fingers together. "They have rejected Partition. They have given in to the British Empire and the Arab League. No Nation, no State. Let us try something else. They suggest trusteeship perhaps." He sat back. "Well, Jacob, what do you make out of that?"

He stood in the center of the room, an absurd pot-bellied shape in baggy, striped cotton pajamas and he scratched the side of his unshaven jaw. "What do I make? What can I make?" he fumed. "What is there to make?" He saw Edith and stretched his arms out. "Little one, thank God you are here. I am persecuted. Rescue me. You are intelligent. Understand, if you can, your country, the land of your birth, the wise, liberal democracy has decided we cannot have a State."

His wife was so used to her husband's excesses of vocal expression she merely lifted her brows, nodded "Shalom" to her guests, and answered mildly, "Jacob, why not run up and dress?"

"Run up and dress! Women! On the day of betrayal, the day of crisis—"

She looked from one to the other. "Tell me," she begged.

"Tell you? Tell? I told you. The United States has rejected Partition. The Arabs and England have won."

Nathan coughed, freeing his throat. "If we are to have a Nation," he said quietly, "we must win it ourselves. With our naked hands. We now stand alone."

She looked at him. She said, softly, "Alone is a terrible word. The worst word I know."

"You hear what she says?" Her husband jigged up and down. "'Alone is a terrible word.' . . . Do you know what alone is? I know. Let me tell you. One time when I was a boy in Russia, my father sent me on an errand, on a winter day. He was a *felsher*. You understand what that is? A doctor who is not a doctor. He puts on leeches, pulls out bad teeth. He sent me to bring back the leeches from an old woman whose bronchitis he cured. It started to snow, a blizzard, high winds. I could not see. I was lost. I stood alone, at the end of the road, and I heard the howling of wolves."

"Did they eat you up?" Yora Levine asked from the threshold. He had come in with Asi, without ringing the bell.

"Another wise man!" Jacob slapped his thighs. "The Rehavia Senate is meeting. Levine, take your chair."

Yora nodded at Edith and Nathan before he sat down. "Proceed, Hirsch," he said. "The wolves were howling."

Jacob glowered at him. "You can hear them today from Beersheba to Dan."

No one laughed.

"What is your defense of the action at the U.N.?" Yora asked.

Jacob plucked at his hair. "What defense? No defense. My wife said it. We are alone. What we must do, we must do alone."

Yora's face creased into deep furrows. "Can we?" he asked.

"You should know better than I. You know what we have."

"That's why I asked."

Nathan slid back in his chair and crossed his knees. "What choice have we?"

There was a long, profound silence. The woman, the children shattered it first. Edith left to go out to the kitchen for the coffee and Teddy and Asi turned back the piano lid and commenced to finger the keys.

"Can we win a war against six Arab nations without American help?" Jacob yelled over the racket the pianists made. "No," he answered himself. "Will the Soviet Union still stand with us? Only so long as it suits them to stand. Dare we then risk going on with our plans for a State? No." He hitched up his pajama belt. "It is against all logic for us to do this." A deep breath expanded his chest. "But we will manage somehow."

Edith came in with her coffee tray and he caught his breath while she passed the cups. Yora refused, and instead offered his cigarettes. Nathan took one. "I should not smoke," he apologized. "It is bad for my cough. But good for everything else." He waited while Yora gave him a light and Edith moved a small table over to hold his cup. He inhaled and exhaled gratefully, put the cigarette down on the saucer's edge. "And so," he began, "if we proceed against their wishes, it is conceivable we may fight American armies, on Palestine soil."

"And suppose we do?" Jacob rasped.

"Don't talk like a fool," Yora said.

"The road to the coast—" Nathan drew once on the cigarette, mildly coughed. "Unless we capture Latrun, unless we hold the road, they can starve Jerusalem, cut the southern settlements off—"

Edith's hand covered her mouth. Her husband glanced at her swiftly.

"So we will fight," he blustered again.

"With what?" Nathan asked. He looked at Yora and Yora at him.

"With our hands. To the very last man." Jacob gestured widely, impressed with his words, and looked around the room. His heart sank. A fine bunch of fighters, he thought. Henry is dried up, bloodless. See how he sits, sipping coffee, with us, withdrawn, as though he were wrapped in private sorrow. Yora has an ulcer. He is nervous. He sits smoking and drumming the chair. Nathan is brave, but he has only one arm. And I, big talker, great man, could I fire a shot, even in anger? His glance moved on, and came to Edith. Her gaze was riveted on the contents of her cup, as if it held tea leaves, not coffee, in which the future might be read. My beloved wife, my little one. She is too timid even to carry the pomegranate. She would rather perish than inflict a hurt, endure rather than kill. The children . . . The two on the piano bench were picking out, note by note, the "Hatikvah," with the loud pedal on. The children, he thought again, our sabras. They'll fight for us. They have no doubts, no inhibiting fears. Emotion made phlegm in his chest. "Sheket, *yeladim*," he shouted as much to ease himself as to silence them. Then he said,

"There have been miracles before in this Land. They will come again. We have no choice."

Nathan shook a long cigarette ash into his saucer. "No choice. That is for Yora and me to say, not for you. Henry and you have a choice. The United States and South Africa will take you again. We have no other place. Suppose we run? Where can we stop our running? At the sea. We will drown. Suppose, well, suppose, we find a ship. It brings us where? To Mauritius, to Cyprus? To another hellhole of tin huts and barbed wire? No, we have been running too many years. Now, we stand." He planted his shoes on the rug. "Here we stand. If it is war, it is war. If it is death, it is death. Every man must be ten; every gun a whole arsenal. We have no choice."

Edith put down her coffee cup. "I am afraid of only one thing." Her voice trembled. "I am afraid of being afraid."

The words stood separate, filling the room, for a long minute until Jacob rose, moved to her, and kissed her forehead.

Henry Winkleman smiled at them, coming to life. "I am reminded," he began, in a measured, almost painful drawl, "of a Zionist orator we used to have in Capetown. The gentleman wished to be considered literary as well as eloquent, but there was one error he made time after time, a mistake so amusing—and in its way right— that no one would call his attention to it and audiences came merely to see if he would say it again. You will forgive me—" he glanced at Edith—"if I tell it in the presence of a lady and children. Whenever he spoke of our pogroms, our disasters, our miseries, invariably he ended with the same line. 'Our people,' he would say in a voice like thunder, 'are forever between the devil and the W.C.'" He paused, bobbed his head to acknowledge the burst of laughter and then rose to go. "That is precisely where we stand today." He threw a smile, tinged with triumph, at Yora Levine, as he went toward the door.

"You know," Jacob said thoughtfully, when the men had all gone. "I have misjudged the Judge. He is human. I am convinced he came in today to tell us his old Capetown joke."

She did not reply because her mind was too full. She was thinking of Belle, her sister, of her family and one-time friends in the States, of people she knew, and did not know, wondering whether they also had gathered, in dismay and the need to comfort each other, on this

Shabbat, and what *they* would do. They too were betrayed, their country's honor, its word, for men of good will everywhere had rejoiced when U.N. had created the State. We know what we must do, she thought. We have thrown our lives and our children's, into the gamble for nationhood. But what will *they* do?

VIII

MANY OF THOSE in the States who read of the Partition reversal laid their newspapers down, took their hats and coats and went out to a double feature at the neighborhood movie house, but one young man did a definite, positive thing about the event at U.N.

His name was Al Brody. He lived in New York and he valued his life very much. He had had several opportunities to learn how precious it was to him, twenty-four different occasions when he had raced against fire-spitting Messerschmitts back to a base in the British Isles and once, when he had parachuted out of a blazing B-17, onto enemy soil and, lame and bleeding, had fought off, in desperate personal combat, a horde of Germans with sticks and stones in their hard-knuckled hands; and for eleven long months after that, while he wallowed in filth, in mud, in daily despair, behind the barbed wire of a prisoner of war camp, watching flesh dwindle, grow tight on his bones, nursing the sores of scurvy, hoarding his physical motions like jewels, wondering whether his family would ever find out how he'd died. He knew that he wished to stay living, though he was not entirely sure why. When freedom came and he tottered down a leafy Bavarian road, he felt he had just been reborn. From here in, he was starting to live, and by God, it had better be good. What had happened to human beings in this last decade was not going to happen again. He'd personally attend to that.

After Al left the hospital, he didn't speak about what had happened to him. He didn't discuss it, simply because no one cared to listen to him. The war was thoroughly over by the time the medics had brought his blood count to normal and his weight to par and stories like his were ten cents a dozen with the medals tossed in. The first night he was back in the railroad flat on Washington Heights, which was home, when he made an attempt to get some of it off his chest, his Old Lady put her hand on her heart as if she were about to have an attack and panted, "My, my, to think you faced all that!" His Old Man said thickly, "You don't have to tell me what you been through. I understand." The funny thing was he did understand. You could count on the Old Man to understand.

Al's Old Man was an intellectual type who drove a hack in the smoke and soot-filled five boroughs of Greater New York, because a doctor had once advised him to do outdoor work. His poor health had been merely a rundown condition, with chronic cough, from bad air and stooped posture at a pressing machine but it had frightened the Old Man into thinking he might be getting t-b. He had been educated, in a way, by Yeshivas in the Old Country, night school and free lectures at Labor Temple and Cooper Union, by reading books and newspapers and by just listening to the people who ride taxicabs. He was short and stubbed and seemed fat, from the layers of old sweaters he wore.

Al was ashamed of how his father looked and what he worked at and he spent a good deal of time dreaming about getting rich, so that the Old Man might buy a couple of suits and stop driving a hack.

Al had a girl, Paula. She became his girl while he was a Sophomore at C.C.N.Y. She was cute-looking, dressed well and was eager in bed, and they got along fine until he decided to get the jump on the draft and enlist in the Air Corps. Then Paula wept and suggested they ought to get married but he was too smart. She wrote him often, as long as he had an A.P.O. number, sent him candy and cake. He remembered occasionally to write her thanks, but he found the girls in England as eager as Paula and as dull afterwards.

Paula didn't listen, either, when he tried to tell her. She said, "Forget it, lover boy. Just kiss me and forget everything. It never happened." But it had happened and it was extremely important and it should have been told. He toyed with the notion of writing a book and thought, hell, no, don't be a sucker, who wants to read books about war? For that matter who wants to read about anything which really matters to the human race?

He spent a good deal of time by himself, at first, in the railroad flat in New York, reading, listening to WQXR on the radio, and teasing his mother's goldfish while the Old Lady cooked noodle soup, potato pancakes, pot roast, and all kinds of greasy and starchy stuff, on the supposition that fatten Al up and he'll be okay. He used to

listen to quiz shows a lot, was surprised at how many of the answers
he knew and wished he was there at the studio to take a jackpot and
make the family rich. It was a shame the Old Man had to be out in
all kinds of weather, time his fat, lazy son started bringing a few
simoleons home. He wished he had pep enough to know what he
really wanted to do. He still saw Paula, occasionally, because she was
pretty good horizontal and because it was too much bother to build
up new relationships but he usually waited until she called him and
he never called her.

He hung around like that for six months. Then he and the Old
Man decided that since there was that G.I. bill, Al should go back
to college and get his degree, maybe try for a Master's, as well. The
Old Man said it was okay with him to go on driving the hack and
what he made and what Al got from the Government was plenty
for just three of them. He added that Al had served his country and
helped to get rid of the monster who had all but destroyed his own
people and between him and the Government, they owed it to Al to
look after him.

The Old Man was wonderful, no doubt about that. There was only
one thing on which he and Al did not see eye to eye. The Old Man
was a Zionist, had always been, going to meetings whenever he could,
and paying his *shekel* regularly. He had one of those little blue and
white boxes with the six-pointed star, on a shelf in the kitchen, and
whenever the Old Lady wasn't around, he dumped his tips into that,
to help to buy Palestine land.

When they talked about it, Al made his own position plain. "Pop,
that's not going to solve our problem," he said. "Not one little bit.
All we get is another small country to make a new reason for war.
Nah, Pop, let's fight for justice, for all minorities, all over the world,
not just for one little spot of our own. Yeh, I know what happened in
Germany. Wasn't I there? But a state of our own ain't going to
change it. Don't kid yourself, Pop. The anti-Semites will be tickled
to death if they get us all in one spot. Kill us quicker that way. One
atom bomb, poof! No, Pop, it's education we need, teaching people
that people are people. Maybe the U.N. will work and maybe it
won't. But let's give it a chance. It's U.N. or else."

Whenever he dared to cut class, he used to go out to Lake Success
or Flushing. He often found himself wishing Al Brody of New York

could get himself made a delegate, too; delegate-at-large, from humanity. Once he mentioned to Paula that he had been out at U.N. and she said, "Lover boy, why do you waste your time? Everybody knows that's only talk."

Even when the U.N. sent a commission to Palestine and began to argue about the problem, the Old Man still couldn't make first base with Al. He respected his son too much to get tough in an argument, and in any case, he never had words for what was deep in his heart. But he knew Al would understand how he felt on that night when the U.N. finally voted to partition Palestine and set up the State. He came home around two in the morning, walked into Al's bedroom and put on the lights, woke his son up and made him come into the living room for a glass of schnapps. "I am a short man," Al's father said. "But tonight I feel six feet tall." It turned out that the Old Man had been at Flushing all day, had been sitting right there when the roll call was taken and he had had to work late to bring home a few bucks.

When he went to sleep finally, Al thought, Jeezus, I didn't lift one little finger, but by Jeezus, it's here and I'm proud.

One night, a month or so after that, the Old Man had some passengers in his hack, two men and two women whom he had picked up near Sixtieth Street and Madison Avenue. They gave him the address of a Chinese restaurant on Mott. One of the men and one of the women, he gathered, were foreigners, out seeing the sights, and after a while, he realized they were from Palestine, and what they were talking about, sometimes in English, sometimes in Hebrew, which he understood a little from his old books of prayer, interested him very much. He saw their faces in the reflector over his wheel and he liked their looks.

After he'd pulled to the curb at the Chinatown joint, he said, without turning around, "I have a son who may wish to enlist in your air force. Can you tell me where he should go?" He heard a buzz-buzz in Hebrew in back and saw by the mirror they were studying the card which held his photograph and his name. Brody, he thought, that could be a Mick and he thought, if they need proof I'll show them my shekel receipt.

They got out of the cab. One of the men gave him a dollar and change, including exactly ten percent for the tip. The other walked around until he could look the Old Man square in the face. He must have been reassured for he gave him a name and address. "Thanks," the Old Man said. "Shalom," the other man said.

When they had gone into the chop suey place, the Old Man wrote down the name and address, put the paper away, behind his license. He didn't mention to Al that he had it. He merely kept it, in case.

On Friday, the nineteenth of March, one of Al's friends proposed they cut classes and ride out to Flushing to the U.N. He had heard Warren Austin was going to have something important to say. Austin said it, all right, and as Al listened, he found himself clenching his fists and muttering under his breath, "The dirty bastards! It's a sell-out! A deal!" He looked down at the British delegates and at the Moslems in their fancy robes, and choked up with rage. They can't do this, his mind kept muttering. My country I almost died for, it can't run out on them.

"I'm ashamed of my country," he said to his friend in the subway, going home. "They're selling us out. To Arab gangsters. To Arabian oil." Out of his mind went all the memories of all the friendships he had made in the British Isles. He said he thought it was time someone taught England a lesson they'd never forget.

"Who'll teach 'em? You?" his friend inquired.

"Me and a million just like me," Al said. "Remember what happened in Spain?"

"Yeah, remember," his friend replied.

"This'll be different," Al said. "I'll take care of this, in person, Al Brody, myself."

He realized he might lose his citizenship if he went over there to fight in a war and he told himself he didn't care, if they could do that to us, my country I fought for, I almost died for, could go back on its word, who wants to be a citizen of a country like that?

He told the Old Man that night how he felt and the Old Man took out the scrap of paper with the name and address. "I think you should go have a talk with them," the Old Man said and slapped Al on the back. They decided not to tell Mama, in case something came out of this, her heart wasn't good, and she'd start worrying. The best thing to tell her was Al was giving up college and going out of town on a job.

It was far from easy to get to see the man whose name was on the slip. A number of bright-eyed, close-mouthed secretaries looked Al over and let him do the talking, before they passed him on, to several young men who did the same thing, and he began to think, Nuts to this! until he suddenly realized the tale he was telling was quite a dilly, his Old Man getting an address in a taxicab in Chinatown. He stopped explaining, and simply said, "Look, if you're going to have a war, I want to fly planes for you. Here's my record. Am I good enough?"

After that, a young man in rimless eyeglasses, who spoke with a foreign accent, led him down a long corridor, twisting and turning so much he knew he would never find his way there alone, all very hush-hush, like a spy melodrama, and he took him into a little room where two young men sat, smoking and studying the carpet. He told Al to wait while he knocked on a door and went in.

Al eyed the two other men. They looked like Micks. "Flyer?" he sent one questioning word toward both of them.

"Uh huh," the one guy said.

"You waiting to see—?" Al mentioned the name.

Both guys grinned. "We *saw* Joe," the other guy said.

"We're all fixed up," the first guy said.

"Say, look, you won't mind, I'm just curious, are you two Hebes?"

They both grinned. "Patrick O'Cohen," one of them said.

"Then what the—"

The young man with the glasses opened the door and summoned Al and a man behind a desk let Al walk all the way to the edge of his desk before he said, "Shalom." He was a good-looking guy, the sort of profile you might want to put on a postage stamp, clean-cut and strong, sun-bronzed, wide awake, about thirty-five, with a build that could pretty well take care of itself. He was carefully dressed in a good business suit, a conservative tie. His expression was open and friendly, yet giving you nothing at all.

"I understand you want to fly for us." The man spoke with an accent which might have been British. "Please sit down," he said.

Al sat. He slapped his discharge papers down on the desk. "Here's the record," he said. "Am I good enough?"

The man read the papers thoroughly, as if he had plenty of time. "You were captured," he said.

"Is that good or bad?" Al asked. A hell of a note, he thought, if they hold that against me.

"We're paying flyers one thousand a month," the man answered him.

He whistled. "You don't need to give me that kind of dough," he protested. "I'm doing this because I feel it here." He slapped his left breast.

The man smiled. You couldn't tell from his smile whether that pleased him or not. "That's the scale," he said. "If you're as good as your record, you will be worth it to us." There was the merest twinkle in his eyes.

"I get it," Al said. "You need flyers bad." He corrected himself. "Badly," he said. It seemed at the moment important to appear to be at least as well educated as the other man was. This is illegal stuff, he said to himself, pay enough and you get what you need.

"What have you flown?" the man asked.

"B-17s, B-24s," and he added, "I could handle a B-29."

The man smiled again. "You won't have the chance. We have a small country. Before a B-29 could take off, it would be over the border, in Trans-Jordan at least. . . . You'll use what we have. Ever flown a Piper Cub?"

Al's eyelashes flapped. "Will you have anything better?" he asked.

"We hope," the man said. "Can you leave right away? I mean tomorrow, not three weeks from now. We have some men going out."

"The Micks?"

The man grinned broadly this time. "They are good flyers," he said. "That is what we need, in a war."

It's going to be one hell of a war, Al thought, Micks fighting Arabs out of Piper Cubs.

He was in such a hurry for the next twenty-four hours there wasn't a minute to ring Paula and tell her he was leaving town.

Part Three: April

I

BEFORE DAWN, on Easter morning, a long convoy set out from Jerusalem to bring essential supplies to a bloc of settlements near Hebron. It found the road clear. That was fine. The Mandatory appeared to be keeping its word that supply routes would remain open and would be patrolled.

The convoy started back after sunup on a highway between fields of daisies and anemones and fragrant with blooming of almond and peach. It passed Bethlehem, heard the Easter bells ringing, and the intermittent crackle of guns. Then it found its road blocked. The patrols, it was plain, were now busy elsewhere.

Since most of Jerusalem's armored vehicles were in that convoy as well as two hundred and fifty brave men and girls, it had, at all costs, to get through. The drivers plowed on, knocking over the cans filled with sand, plunging through wooden barriers spanning the road. Eight roadblocks were passed.

The snipers kept nibbling. Lead pellets bounced off the sides of the trucks. At the ninth roadblock, the lead lorry skidded into a ditch. Its motor went dead. The men in the vehicle behind it jumped out to try to lift the car up. The convoy had to stop. While it was stalled, Arabs streamed down from the hills and opened fire with rifles and small machine guns. All the cars but the first swung around and sped back. They left the disabled vehicle blazing down in the ditch.

At Nebi Danyial, just beyond Bethlehem, there was an abandoned stone sheep house. The trucks halted there. They encircled the building, bumper to bumper. Behind that stockade, they prepared for battle. They had a few Stens. They had some grenades. They had little water or food. They had a wireless. They had fifteen minutes to plan strategy.

The sheep house lay in a valley in a bowl of hills. Down those hillsides the enemy swarmed, wave after wave, howling, *"Aleyhoum,"* and pouring lead. Now and then a grenade's explosion shattered the rhythm of machine-gun rat-a-tat. The Bethlehem bells were drowned out. At intervals, a voice bellowed in English for the beleaguered trucks to give up.

Within the house, a walkie-talkie let Jerusalem know the plight the convoy was in. In many places, short-wave wireless sets picked up the battle, heard, shot by shot, how gallant young men fought through a day and a night for their lives and their vehicles.

Gershon, at Gan Darom, in the Negev, let Dinah listen a while on the short-wave set in the pillbox under the settlement's water tower. He watched her face, puckered up. "The voice." She seemed puzzled. "This sounds like Arieh, Arieh Goldstein who lived on our block. Can he be a battle commander?"

She sounded so awed Gershon had to laugh. "One commands a battle when one has a battle to command. For Haganah, one needs no diploma from St. Cyr or West Point."

"Wait, listen!" The girl held up her hand. "Hear what he says: 'This way, *zipora*. . . . Down, zipora. . . . Thank you, zipora. . . . Thanks.' 'Zipora' is a bird. Gershon, listen, see, if Arieh is crazy that he talks to the birds."

She leaned over the table, lips parted, while he put the ear-phones on. He listened and roared with laughter. "He calls an airplane 'Zipora.' Our planes are in action at Nebi Danyial. *Our planes!"*

"Our planes!" Her eyes bugged. "Eisen beton!" she shouted, exactly the way her brother might have.

Al thought he was handling the Piper Cub just as he had seen the other flyer do, but battle smoke was so dense he could barely make out the swirling mass of the enemy on the ground. A weird howl rose from the earth, prolonged and shrill, like an Indian war whoop. His spine tingled. It's war all right, kids. . . . Primitive. Savages, red skins . . . Cowboy, ride . . . He pulled out the pin, drew his arm back, and hurled the grenade. He heard an explosion. The tiny plane bounced, like a dory on a rough sea. Smoke spread a tarpaulin over treetops and fields. He couldn't be sure what had been hit. *"Lo, zipora!"* His radio head-set was crackling, but what it said meant nothing to him. He flung another grenade *"Lo, zipora, lo!"* The voice sounded urgent. He got the impression it was shouting at him. He started to sweat. "Zipora, you speak English, perhaps?" He means me. Go ahead, buster, talk. "Listen, you bloody fool, on which side are you? Take your plane in. . . . *Take your plane in. . . . Take your plane in.*"

He swung the Piper around, tight-lipped, faintly sick, and headed back to the base.

The so-called Commander at the so-called airfield had apparently heard the score on his own walkie-talkie, because he greeted Al with a disgusted shrug and waved a boy in faded fatigues into the Piper's cockpit.

One of the Micks who was lounging out on the field came over to Al. "What kind of a deal is it, bud?" he wanted to know.

"Nuts!" Al spat. "If all they wanted was pitchers why didn't they hire the St. Louis Cards?"

Ida Goldstein saw the crowd in the Agency courtyard when she ran to the drugstore and she paused long enough to ask the man who stood near the steel and stone stumps of the road barrier, "For what do they wait?"

"The British are bringing them in. Those who lost the battle at Nebi Danyial."

She wondered whether she also should wait. How do I know Arieh was in that convoy? And how do I know he was not? No, she decided, five are waiting at home for me, I cannot stand here to wait for one. Yet when she came up King George Avenue, going home, she could not resist and ran across, to stand on the rim of the crowd. On tiptoe she barely could see the tops of the heads of the dusty, bloodied men and girls who sprang from the lorries into the arms of parents and wives. Not one was red-haired and tall. You see, she said to herself, I was right. My heart would have told me, as it told all of them, if my child had been at Nebi Danyial.

Gordon Leake was in Colonel Bromley's office next morning on business which had to do with arrangements for safe conduct and transport for those of his department who still were in town, when a sergeant major dropped by to make a report on the events at Nebi Danyial. The Sergeant Major's conference was in a lower echelon but since there had already been acrimonious criticism of the extraordinary timing of the Army's arrival, just as the battle was lost, and of its delivery of the loser's trucks to the enemy, the Lieutenant with whom the Sergeant Major conferred brought him to the Colonel himself.

The Sergeant Major made his formal report, voiced his conviction the gun-running bastards had got what was coming to them, and finding receptive ears, went into details. He had been one of those who had come up to the house on the road in time to make sure the surrender was orderly and complete. He'd arrived as the sun was starting to drop, and in the center lorry, in point-blank range of the most withering fire, he had seen a tall youth standing up. The lorry was full of fighters, but this lad was taller than all the rest and he had carrot hair and spectacles which caught the lowering glint of the sun.

Since all this was no skin off his back, Gordon had paid no attention until that description ticked from his ear to his brain. Tall, lean, spectacled, carrot-topped. That fitted the Goldstein lad to a "t."

"Did you, by chance, learn his name?" Gordon ventured to ask.

" 'Is name?" The Sergeant Major scratched the side of his head. " 'Ow would I know 'is name?"

The Colonel's aide chuckled. "I can tell you his name. Goldstein, if it matters at all. We had him in milit'ry court, running guns, six weeks ago. He stood up and made us a speech. That's how I knew who it was. I heard that same voice on the wireless, giving the battle orders. We had his number, all right."

Colonel Bromley raised his eyebrows. "Very good, sir," he said to his aide and, "Go on, Sergeant."

The Sergeant Major went on. The red-headed lad, Goldstein or whoever it was, he reported, had had a Sten and was pumping the thing for all it was worth, a natural target, up there where the sun could kindle his hair. In shorts and no shirt. No proper soldier at all. "A fightin' fool, if I ever saw one," he said, with a trace of respect.

"Trouble with these bloody bastards is they're too brave."

The Colonel coughed lightly, a hint. The Sergeant Major took it. "What I mean, sir, is they've got no common, ordn'ry soldiers' good sense. What I mean," he floundered, "is part of good soldiering is to know 'ow and when to look out for yourself. But these bloody fools stand square to fight. You'd think 'twas a 'oly disgrace to get 'it any-wheres but the chest or the 'ead. Now you take an' Ayrab, 'e is no coward, but 'e is no fool. When the goin' gets rough, 'e yanks off 'is shoes an' lights out for 'ome. But you take this red-'eaded idjit, 'e stands up there bangin' away with 'is Sten. A good shot, 'e was, that I can testify to, but comes the minute, 'e's pulled 'is trigger one time too many. An' what does 'e do? Chucks down 'is gun and starts throwin' stones, throwin' stones, mind, as if they was 'and grenades. That's when they got 'im. . . . I saw the blood gush down the side of 'is fice. But does 'e quit? 'E does not. 'E stands there throwin' the stones till they 'it 'im again. Square in the chest. . . . Then some of 'is buddies, they carted 'im off and that was the last we see of 'im."

The Colonel asked, "Mister Leake, are you ill?" and "Sergeant, is that all?"

The Sergeant Major wiped his brow. "That's all, sir." He turned to go out. "They'll never get nowheres," he said before he left, "till they learn 'ow to duck."

The Colonel grimaced. One might have taken the twitch of his mouth for a smile. "I shall not be unhappy," he said, "if they never learn."

Gordon's chief, Henderson, had a pile of papers before him and was systematically tearing them up, tossing the shreds into a paper carton. "Oh, it's you," he said absently when Gordon entered. "What dates has Bromley given us?"

"Beginning the eighteenth. He gives us a fortnight. We're to make every effort to limit the luggage for all personnel. The men are to sell all they can and not shop. Lorry and ship space, you know."

Henderson leaned over the stack of papers to make a note of the date. "Don't be so glum. Sing, man! Rejoice." He turned around in his swivel chair. Through the dusty windowpanes, he could see spirals of smoke, drifting up from the courtyard, melting into the blue of a brilliant spring day. "Professionally," he mused, "I deeply regret to see the labors of thirty years go up in smoke. Personally—" his voice crisped as he swung back—"departure cannot come too soon for me. Astonishing—" he rubbed the index finger of one hand with the thumb of the other—"and I find it hard to believe, that it is no longer safe or respectable to be an Englishman in Palestine."

The restaurant was all but empty when Gordon got there. A press correspondent and a girl secretary from the Public Information Office were on the stools at the bar and a girl and a man at a corner table. The restaurant's plate-glass windows had been blown out when Ben Yehuda was bombed, and weren't replaced, merely beaverboards spanned across, so that the room was painfully dark with inside-a-tomb gloom. Candles flickered in beer bottles at both ends of the bar.

In the bad light, Gordon didn't discover at first that the girl at the table was Millie. The man who was with her rose promptly when Gordon came over, and he guessed she had told him she had a date. He knew who the man was, knew he was friendly with an unsavory crowd, the crowd generally credited with setting the Hasollel and Ben Yehuda Street bombs, and therefore he glanced guiltily back toward the bar, hoping the P.I.O. girl had not recognized *him*. The man with Millie, however, greeted him by his name, loudly enough for the girl to hear if she cared, and he had to respond. "I'll be running along," the man said. "Leave you two to your fun. Cheerio."

Millie didn't reply, not "see you again," or "glad to have run into you," and Gordon concluded, as he seated himself in the chair which still was warm from another man's buttocks, that as far as she was involved, the tête-à-tête had been nothing more than another male Englishman, suffering from scarcity. He and I, he thought—a fine situation when we two are in competition for *her*.

"You were late," Millie sulked.

"I'm sorry. You weren't lonely."

"Oh, that one!" Millie shrugged.

"Draw the line somewhere, will you?"

"Don't be nasty," she answered. She stuck her leg out and said, "See!" It was a shapely leg, one of her two perfect features, and she dressed it well, always in nylon or silk. The stocking had a run. "It happened just now," she pouted. "When I came to meet you. My last pair."

He said that was a shame. Her ways and her wiles were so transparent, and that had amused him sometimes. Now it did not. He was tired; he'd exhausted himself in a fruitless debate within his own head. He found himself wondering why he had bothered to meet Millie at all.

"Gordon." Millie drew her leg under the table. "If you were a very nice boy—" she smiled at him pointedly—"you would say, 'I go buy you another pair.'"

He shook his head, "You know as well as I do what's to be bought."

"That is not so. If I had the money, I know a shop."

"A pound or is it two?" He again shook his head.

She pouted. "I cannot imagine why I meet you," she said.

"I can't imagine myself."

It was all too true and it cut two ways.

Of all the girls he had in Jerusalem, Millie was the dullest by far, dull and demanding, always a pitiful story about something she just had to have. Whatever of food or of drink she was offered was never quite right yet she pretended to be very big, self-sacrificing, when she consumed with a good appetite whatever was served. Vertical, she was a nag and a bore.

It was simply the situation of no choice. Years ago, when he had first come out, he had had a Yemenite, Penina, the maid in the place where he lived, a thin, exquisite, olive-skinned child with sparkling black eyes. The affair had lasted until he went on a holiday home. Then, it was she who had said, "It is best to end it, haviv. You could not marry with me. My father would never consent. It would hurt both of us." It was she who had said, "You have taught me the meaning of love. A beautiful thing is never a sin. I thank you very much."

It had occurred to him that he had said nothing, during the affair, or at its end, of marriage or love, not even verbalized in his thoughts what her passion and beauty had meant to him, and when, on the ship back to England, he recalled her words, he was a little afraid. And so, on that leave home, he had married Veronica, telling himself, there now, I'm safe, safe from consuming passion, from gossip, from folly, safe with my kind, with an Englishwoman, adequate, cool, yet clinging, admiring her male, triumphant in having attained the status of Mrs., proper in manners and speech, a woman to introduce to superiors and friends. I am safe with the right sort of wife.

All that was enough to persuade him Penina meant nothing to him. In a city as small as Jerusalem, there remained, however, a passing chance that somehow he might encounter the girl, or meet someone who might mention her, and he wondered half-heartedly whether to ask for transfer to another country.

One day, on Jaffa Road, he ran into the woman who had owned the house where he had lodged and she offered the news that Penina was dead, blown to bits in a bus which had run over a mine set by Arab terrorists. For a moment or so, he was blind with rage, and for days was profoundly depressed; on every Arab he passed, he turned the cold stare of loathing. You did this to her. Murderers! Yet in time he knew an odd sort of relief because the mere thought that she might have married, had a dozen babies, grown withered, weary and old, would have been even worse than her death. For him alone, and for eternity, was the memory of that brown body against his fair one, of her tiny hands, fluttering like swallows, over his belly, his armpits and loins.

After that, he had a few furtive affairs, with a Sephardi, dark like Penina, with a lush Egyptian (and took a bit of joshing about his taste for dark meat), with a Russian, a Pole, but there was always a risk in a gossipy city like this. The best of them, Rosa, the black-haired Russian, who worked for Broadcasting and had a flat of her own, had talked to him about other men who visited her and left him no doubt she would talk to them about him.

After Veronica went back to England last year with the rest of the British wives, pickings were lean. Which of them, even the fat, ugly ones, would take up with an Englishman? Yet a man needs a woman and in many ways—across a table, in an armchair in the same room, as well as in bed. He needs someone to whom to tell what happened today at the office, what I said to him and he said to me, to ask, what do you think I should do about that or this? Desperately needed, more than ever in these terrifying last days.

Millie was pretty, though not nearly as pretty as she thought she was, but she looked and smelled clean. Her bobbed fair hair was thoroughly brushed. When she wished to be, she was witty, her accent charming. Her age was indefinite, like her antecedents. She was flotsam of Europe's debacle, washed up on this shore. Sometimes she claimed to be Viennese, sometimes French. She worked in a consulate, as a secretary. That was the one certain fact that was known about her. The rest was all rumor, which she never affirmed or denied, for instance, that she had an Arab husband, was abandoned by him, that she knew where he was and was in touch with him, that she didn't know where he was and was sad about that, and that she didn't know, didn't care, good riddance to very bad rubbish, indeed; that she worked for Intelligence of one side or another, and that she merely was one of those who knew how to use the single cash-bringing asset given to women to insure their survival in a hazardous world.

Gordon signaled a waiter. "What will you drink?"

She thought wheesky would be excellent but presumed there was none. The waiter agreed. "Then brandy and soda. Why do you ask if there is no choice?"

There was a choice, brandy or beer or local wine. He requested beer for himself, and asked how the chances were for a meal. Slight, the waiter conceded, some sausage, potatoes, grits and tea, no sugar, lemon, or cream.

"Gordon," Millie asked when the waiter had gone, "what will become of us?" She planted her elbows on the table, rested her chin on her hands. "Gordon, take me with you," she said.

"Where to?"

"To England."

It startled a smile out of him. "Where'd you get the notion there's food in England?"

"Who speaks of food?"

The waiter brought their drinks, heard Gordon ask, "Scared?" and hung around the table, fussing about wiping the wood, but she waited until he had departed, before she replied, "Who would not be?"

I don't know, he thought. I do know, he thought. "My neighbors," he said.

Millie wrinkled her nose. "And you believe that?" She shook her head vigorously. "There is not one woman, there is not one man in Jerusalem who is not scared. Believe me, I know." She looked peaked and all at once, old, he thought, and he found himself recalling some of the things he had heard about her. Dangerous game, he thought dully, me out with her. It doesn't matter, really does not, in three weeks, I'll be clearing out. Then, why, he asked himself, should I fret over whether to tell Ida Goldstein her son is dead? Must this be my last act, to bring her bad news?

"Gordon," Millie started again. "When do you leave?"

Oh no, he thought, no information, not out of me. Now, does that matter? he reconsidered. Shout from the rooftops we're in retreat. He finished his beer. He said, in a bored, level tone, "We'll be cleared out before the end of this month."

She licked her lips as if they were dry. *"Après moi, le déluge."*

"Finish your drink," he replied. "The fizz is all out."

She sipped slowly, making a face, set down her glass. "Amusing," she said, "to see Englishmen running away."

He flushed. "We're not running away. We're finished, you know." And told to clear out. You've funked your job, Sons of Empire, pack up and go. It's not fair, not just. I've done a good job. My child was born here. My whole career has been in this place. I've been happy here. Then why am I running away? *Lord Jim,* he thought, and he felt himself growing hot.

"Gordon." Millie kicked his leg under the table. "Tell him to hurry, hurry up with our food."

In the street, Millie linked her arm into his. "Do we go to your flat or mine?" she asked.

"To yours," he said quickly. Each time in the past, when she'd asked, he had had to pause, to get over a hump. There was something that didn't smell right about taking a girl to Veronica's flat—stripped, but still Veronica's flat. Yet he knew, when he came down to it, it was not that at all. Someone would know and everyone know, he had brought home a girl of doubtful repute. The night the *Post* was blown up, it had been the worst kind of luck to be walking along with Millie when Miriam Goldstein ran out of her house. Why do I stay there? he wondered. Why don't I move into a Zone? His head started to ache. He wished he were at home, by himself, in bed. Yet he walked with Millie down Jaffa Road in the soft mildness of the spring night, aware of the scent of her hair, her arm's pressure against his ribs and knew he was grateful for that.

Once, she remarked, gaily, when a fireworks show lit up the sky,

"There's target practice in the Old City tonight," and when he didn't respond, said in a way that was half inquiry, "I have heard the Arab Legion has already moved in from Trans-Jordan." He answered, "Oh, God!" and, lest she give undue weight to his expletive, hurried to add, "Oh God, your chatter bores me."

Her tongue clacked angrily. She kept silent for half a block, then said again, "Gordon, take me with you when you go."

"Of course not," he said.

"I will die here."

His lip curled. "So will many others."

"Don't you love me, Gordon?"

"No," he replied.

She drew her arm quickly out, moved ahead of him. He let her go, and came to a halt where he was. "Good night," he sang out.

She came back a step. "You are leaving me?"

He said, "Yes, you've not far to go. You'll be safe."

"You do not come to my flat?"

"I'm too tired. I wouldn't be any good."

"And I have wasted the evening for you!" Her voice was shrill, no charm in the accent at all. "I have torn my last stockings for you."

"I'm sorry." He bent dutifully to kiss her but she drew away.

"Damned Englishman!" It was as if she had spat.

You, too, he thought, even the whores. . . . He wheeled and began to walk fast. "You will be sorry," she called after him.

I shall, he thought miserably, and he knew that someway, somehow, he would crawl and make this up to her. It would cost a pair of nylons, at least.

The concertina on the corner was making a hideous noise, and through the closed, shuttered windows along the street Gordon could hear the faint hums of talk and of battery radios. No one was abroad in his street. He paused outside his own house, to stand awhile in the scented dark. I can't go in, he thought. I can't face it, yet. He thought of going back downtown again, to the King David bar, and decided not. He considered going in to Ida's at once, getting it all over with, while the Sergeant Major's story was fresh in his mind, and he stared at her drawn window blinds. There were pin-pricks of light. They're up; it's too early for bed. They're sitting around Max's couch. Talking about Arieh, perhaps, wondering where Arieh is.

Arieh. Why, he was only a shaver when I came here. I taught him to read. I did that. I taught him English from my own books. . . . And that pretty sister. We were all so pleased when I found Deborah that job. Ida baked a *dobosch torte* and brought it up.

A chill seized him. He hunched his shoulders, walked softly upstairs and lit a candle. The flat was empty, all but. Most of what remained was canvas-wrapped, roped. When Veronica and Betty had left, the sofa, the armchair, the lamps, the dining table, the corner cupboard and chairs, the dishes, the comfortable bed, had traveled home, too; to wait till another outpost of Empire provided the Leakes a few rooms of their own. But Gordon had kept the Rehavia flat because it was rent-fixed and cheap and because it was home. Home! Naked rooms with an Army cot, a ragged chair borrowed from a requisitioned flat, a wireless set and a bottle of brandy.

He carried the candle into the bedroom. If there were only some light, he thought. There's an omen in this. No electricity. It ends in darkness. We have turned back the clock.

He set his brandy bottle on the floor next to the bed, undressed, crawled between dingy sheets, poured himself a drink and lay, arms under head, staring up at the ceiling. "Veronica," he asked the emptiness, "what shall I do?"

"Why need you tell Ida?" Veronica might have replied.

"She has to know. She deserves to know."

"I'm not sure. You've always gone a bit out of your way to be palsey with those people down there. You're leaving the country. Stay out of their business now."

The grotesque dance of the shadows upon his ceiling disturbed him; the room seemed too hot. He rose, blew out the candle, pulled up the blind and leaned on the sill. I love this city, he said to himself. Jerusalem's deep in my bones. . . . Like Penina, the Yemenite . . . Here, I was loved. Greatly loved. Here, the happiest time of my life . . . Here, I belong. . . . Why must I go?

I shall miss Jerusalem's nights, the stars so clear and so close. It's easy to understand how the Nativity was tied in men's minds to the gleam of a star in this sky. He thought he saw a star moving and peered intently. It was a flashbeam, beyond the pines. On a roof. On whose roof? He turned from the window. I'd rather not know.

One of the children was wailing downstairs. Cry, little one, you've something to cry about now. And tomorrow when I bring you the news . . .

Ida doesn't cry. She's a lady. Great lady. Incongruity hit him. The little woman who bakes cookies and strudels to earn coarse gray bread, a great lady? Now, now, don't put it on. But she does not weep. She has fortitude. He groped for his brandy bottle, hit it unexpectedly, so that it almost fell to the stones and terrified he might lose this one comfort, he lighted his candle again, poured a tumbler half full and drank it down fast. His eyelids grew heavy. He forgot to blow out his candle before he fell asleep.

He awoke feeling loggy, splashed himself with cold water to come all awake, stood scratching his head at the basin, trying to recall what it was he intended to tell to someone today. He dressed painfully in yesterday's unfresh underwear. While he was dressing, he heard a brief spasm of gunfire. Then he heard the grandchildren, singing a play game in the yard, and what it was he had to tell someone soon, came back to him. But still he waited, pacing the room, before he found courage to open his door.

Ida answered his knock. "Shalom, Gordon."

"Shalom."

"Come in. Have you had coffee yet? Come, have it with me."

"Thank you, no. I'm not feeling right."

"Too much schnapps?" Her eyes twinkled. "Black coffee will help."

"Later I shall have my tea."

He stood in the passageway, twisting his hat. She was a bit of a thing, this mother of Arieh, always was, but she'd gotten thinner, and now she seemed like a wraith. Her rust-colored hair was coming in white. She was in house dress and apron, neat as a pin, but her naked big toe stuck out through a ragged gray felt slipper. When he saw that big toe and torn shoe, pity exploded inside him and color drained from his face.

"What is it, Gordon?" she cried, seeing him. "Have you something to tell?"

He nodded, but couldn't yet speak.

She glanced toward her living room. "Max is in bed. You will not mind if we go in the kitchen. The rooms are not made. My daughter-in-law is running around to try to buy candles and a few tins." She led the way. "Sit down, please."

He sat at her table while she poured the lees of her coffee pot into a cup. "Drink it. I am sorry I cannot offer bread." She stood over him. "What is it?" she asked. She seemed anxious but not too greatly distressed.

He began cautiously, "Do you know where Arieh is?"

Her face, beneath its paprika freckles, turned tallow-white. "If I knew would I tell?"

"Ida." He pushed back the cup. "Did you know?—Please sit down—" He waited until she had drawn up a stool. "Had you heard he was in the Easter convoy to Kfar Etzion?"

"That he would never tell even me." Her eyes bulged. "Tell me," she demanded. "Did you hear that he was?"

He stared at the scrubbed stones of her floor, sickening with distress. Then, stammering a little, he said that a member of the relieving forces had seen in the action a young man of Arieh's description. He did not say more, but bowed his head, listening for what might come from her. He heard only the sounds of the children outside, and Max, two rooms away, clearing night mucus out of his throat.

Then she made a small choking noise and he forced himself to look up. She was sitting on the stool twisting her apron between her work-roughened fingers, rubbing a piece of the cloth as though she had to wear it away. The rubbing made him nervous. He covered one hand of hers with his own to make her stop.

She drew her hand out. "Gordon, the man the Sergeant Major saw was *gingy?*" She touched her own hair.

He nodded.

"And spectacles?" She touched her eyes.

He nodded again.

"He was tall, thin?" Her fingers ran down her ribs. "Gingy, tall, thin, spectacles—" Her face was working. "Tell me more. What happened to him?"

He answered by lowering his head.

"No!" she cried. "No!" and hid her face with her hands. "God in heaven," she moaned, "I am a small woman. What do You want of me?"

He saw nothing else but her hands on her face, freckled, ridged hands, with swollen joints and a worn gold wedding band, stared at her hands, as though he meant to retain a mind's photograph of how Ida Goldstein had covered her face to stifle the first cry of anguish in all of her life.

Finally he rose and stood back of her, unsure of himself. He put both his hands on her shoulders. She pulled away. "Go," he heard her moan. "Go." But he stood, stubbornly trying to think of something to do or to say to express how he felt. He could think of nothing. Without another word, he went out of the room and the house.

On the path to the road, it occurred to him she hadn't asked about Veronica and his child, and he tried to make something of his annoyance, for the sake of his pride, but could not, for he knew what it was. She somehow thinks it's my fault, he said to himself. I'm not Gordon Leake. I'm the bloody Empire.

I can't go back to that house, he decided as he passed the roadblock. I can't go back to that street. I'll send for my things, move into a Zone. I dare not go back to that place. They hate me there.

He was sad, since this quiet street in Rehavia for so many years had been home.

II

NUMBNESS CRAWLED UP Ida Goldstein's limbs. She fought against it, whispering, as though that were a talisman to drive the rigor away, her youngest son's name. She heard Max calling beyond the wall, "Who was here, Imma?" and she stirred at the sound of his voice but could not answer him.

"Was it the Britisher?"

She let her hands down. The room was black. What has happened? It was morning; now it is night. Have I been sitting here a whole day?

"What did he want?" Max was demanding.

What did he want? What did he want? She stared straight ahead and saw nothing. I am blind, she thought with heart-constricting panic. I am blind, like Max.

"Imma," Max called, "Imma, are you there?"

She struggled to find a voice to call back to him. "Wait, my son. Wait, I will come."

The black was gray now. Table, stove, sink took on shape. She sat awhile longer until the way to the door was visible. Then she slid off the stool and groping along the passageway, stumbled into the crowded small room she shared with the two little girls. Half-blind still, but with fingers that flew, she took off her apron, put on her hat and her gloves as she always did when she went out.

She went in to Max. The sick man sat painfully up. He had not yet put on his dark glasses and his raw, red eye socket gaped into her face. "Put on your glasses." She gave them to him.

"Who was here, Imma?" Max asked.

"Gordon."

"What did he want?"

"A cup of coffee."

"You are lying to me. He would not come here for that."

"He wished to tell me he had a letter from Veronica and the child."

"Were you glad?" he asked acidly.

"I'm going out," she replied. "I will send Shlomo in, in case you need anything."

She sent the child to his father, then ran out to the road and there she stood, looking one way, the other, undecided to whom to go. Finally, she ran down the street to the apartment house in which Nathan lived.

When he opened the door and saw her, he said at once, "Yes, it is true."

She tottered. He thought she was going to fall. "Please, come in, sit," he said quickly, but she did not move. He took her hand. "Ida, believe me, we will not forget," he said; but she drew away and gripping the stair rail, made her way to the street.

The sunny morning was gray as ashes; the flowers had lost their fragrance. The gunfire was like a baby's rattle. In the warm spring sunlight, her teeth chattered, knees shook. Why she went, how she went, she did not know, but she found herself standing in the hall of Edith's house, saying to her, "Arieh is dead."

The metal something Edith had in her hand clanged to the stones. "No," she cried out, "No. NO," before she took Ida Goldstein and held her, like a child, in her arms.

Shifra, passing through, saw them there, locked together exclaimed, "What happened, G'veret? What is it now?"

Edith's lips formed the words, soundlessly. "Arieh. Her son."

"The poor woman! Can I bring her coffee? Can I give her something?"

Ida heard her. She stirred. "Thank you," she said. "You are good."

"I cannot bear it." Shifra's voice cracked. "I must hide myself."

Ida moved out of the gentle embrace. "I must go." But she did not go, and stood, wringing her black-gloved hands. "Edith," she faltered, "Edith, my friend." Her frail body swayed. Edith caught her, led her into the living room and they sat close, on the couch. Ida shut her eyes. "Another child," she rocked back and forth. "I have given another child to give us a State."

A tremor ran through Edith Hirsch. She laced her fingers together tightly.

"I am a small woman. It is a big price for me. Deborah. Then Max. Now Arieh."

It was unbearable. Stop it, stop her. "Sheket," Edith had to cry out.

Black-gloved talons clutched both her hands. "Give me the chance to talk once," Ida pleaded. "Only once this luxury. To you I can speak, my neighbor, my friend. Someone else will be angry with me. . . . All my life, since I can remember, I dreamed of one thing, a Nation, a State. You, too, like me." Her voice gentled. "You, too, have offered a beautiful child." There was compassion in her ravaged face.

Edith bit her lips and felt pain.

"Excuse me, forgive me, my friend. I must talk. You will understand when I tell you what I have felt. Edith, many times, when Arieh was away, when I did not see him a very long time, I have lain awake. In the night, in the dark, when no one could see, I have said to myself, we will give our children to create a State. Correct. And who will thank us for that?"

The pulse in Edith's throat beat hard. Her nerves drew and ached like a boil. She pulled her hands free, covered her mouth.

"This time will pass. People will start to forget. They will become busy with everyday things, with cooking the meals, going to work, quarreling with neighbors over some trifling matter. People forget very fast. It is hard to remember very big things, because we are small. Small things are big things to us. . . . Edith, will someone remember, when that time comes, that Ida Goldstein, the Hungarian gingy who lives in Rehavia with a blind son, once had another son and a daughter?" Her voice dropped, faint, no more than a whisper. "No one will remember but me."

She looked up. She saw Edith's face. "Forgive me," she begged again. "I make you pain. Your heart is like mine. . . . See, Edith, you understand. They will be happy with their sons and daughters. They will say to the little ones, 'In 1948, we made a Nation, we made a great history.' Only I—" she was whispering again— "only I will remember once on a time, I had a beautiful daughter and a brilliant son. It will not count to them that I gave my children to make the State. But to me nothing will count except my loss to me."

I, too, a child. No, please God, no, Edith prayed desperately. It *is* too much to offer Dinah as the price of a State. Too high a cost. These glorious children of ours. She clenched her fists, pressed them into her jaws. Which do you want? Edith Hirsch. Your whole life, you had an ideal, a purpose, a dream. Now which, your living child or this State?

The question stood in her mind, stark, glaring, as if in bright lights.

Ida stood up suddenly. "Why am I talking so much?" She began to smooth down her skirt, caught a glimpse of her ragged slippers and protruding toe and made a sound of dismay. "Without shoes, I run. Like a crazy woman, I run. Like a crazy woman, I talk. Edith, I beg you, forget all I said." She gave her feet another shocked glance. "My dishes are still in the sink. And it is time to put on the beans."

"Haviva," Jacob murmured. "Try to sleep. Shall I mix you something to quiet your nerves?"

She said no.

"You're hungry. You don't eat enough."

"But I do. Oh, I do."

"Is there a piece of bread in the kitchen? I'll get it for you."

"Please, I dont want it. Please, Jacob, sleep."

"After you." He propped himself up. "What's the matter with you?"

"Nothing. Nothing special."

"Are you worrying about my trips up the Hill?"

She said no. He didn't believe her. "I tell you it's nothing to worry about. If they're not shooting, there's nothing to worry about and if they are shooting, we travel so fast, there's no time to worry."

"Do you have to treat everything as a joke?"

"Do you know a better way? If I laugh, I can sleep."

"Then why don't you?"

"After you, G'veret."

"Must I sleep? Is it a rule?"

"Yes, you must." He flipped on his side. "Are you worried you won't have a State? Ben Gurion promised today. He is reliable. We have gone so far, there is no going back. See, haviva, we are destiny's children. . . ."

"Stop, please, stop," she cried out.

He sat up. She knew he was watching her. "Talk. Talk to me," he insisted.

"I can't."

"Why not? Big secret or big foolishness?"

She pushed him away. "Please don't nag. I'll lie down in Dinah's room and let you sleep."

The blinds were drawn there and she had to grope to locate the cot. She sat on its edge, hugging herself against the room's musty chill before she stretched full length on top of the spread. The coarse woven cloth scratched her bare shoulders and arms. She tossed, uncomfortable, finally rose and crouched at the window, on the chest which held Dinah's old books and toys. She pulled the blind up.

The night was luminous. The star-spangled curtain swung low, above black silhouettes. The cypress trees at the edge of the lawn raised their jagged teeth.

At night Jerusalem takes your breath, she said to herself. Peace, holiness, sacred beauty. In beauty, she sleeps. "Sleep, city, sleep." Her mind tried to set it to music. "Sleep, city, sleep, sleep while you may." That wasn't right. A rhyme was missing, the rhyme for sleep. . . . Leap, heap, keep. "Sleep, city, sleep, your peace you will keep." She frowned, tantalized because the words and the tune didn't mesh. My error. "Play, gypsy, play while you may." That's what belongs to that tune. The old Victor Herbert. Or was it Friml? Our radio's so highbrow, we rarely get light tunes like those.

Down below where the Old City was, something rose in the sky. There was a shower of pinpoints of light. A Roman candle. Fireworks. The Fourth of July. Belle and I never had fireworks on the Fourth of July. Father wouldn't spend money that way. Waste it on Chinese gunpowder when it should be dropped into the blue and white can! To buy land. His obsession, buy land. Yet Father, you never saw it. Like Moses, all your life yearning for the Promised Land, and dying too soon. But your work was done. Through me. Through Jacob and me and our children.

There was another flash in the sky, another shower of bright sparks. Signals. Are they ours or theirs? It's the Old City. Theirs. What do they signal to whom? She heard a sharp rat-tat-tat and after a moment, answering spatters of noise. Disturbances. Let's not be foolish. It's war, the real sounds of real war. No fooling. Not Fourth of July. She heard a deep boom. A mortar. Are they using shells? The machine guns barked at each other again. And again. Tonight is especially noisy. Has full-scale attack already begun? What do you do? Do you run, stand, or sit?

It occurred to her the shooting might have waked Teddy up and she crossed the hall. Teddy sprawled, sound asleep, one outflung arm holding a tin. When she tried to remove it, he gripped it more tightly, without waking up. She ran her hand over his brow. It was damp with sweat. Yet she pulled his light blanket to his armpits, tucked it around, and caressed his hair. He ground his teeth. A bad dream? Does he fight while he sleeps?

Udi's cold snout touched her leg. She gave him a pat, aware of his naked ribs as her hand stroked his side. She stopped at her own bedroom door, considering whether to return to bed, and she heard Jacob's snores. How they sleep, my menfolk, the sleep of good conscience and honest fatigue!

She went back to the chest by the window and looked out again. Quiet now and lighted by stars, Jerusalem sleeps, undisturbed by impudent noises which imitate war. The cypress trees sway. The pines rustle. We sit at a window, holding our breaths. We are destiny's children. So frightening and lonely to be destiny's child. The street seems lonely. Jerusalem's lonely. Cut off from the world. By the hills, by Arab steel. Do they know, outside, how lonely we are? Do they know what is happening in this city of peace? Peace? With unmarked fresh graves?

In the hills, on the Bethlehem Road, Arieh lies in a fresh grave. Arieh.

Frightening and full, the dilemma came flooding. The same thing can happen to us. Which do I want, my child or a State? Always, I have wanted this Homeland, this Nation, this State. Must I buy the State at the cost of my child?

I am not alone. Every mother whose child ever served in a war, asked that question as well. Yes, I wish the world safe for democracy. But do I wish more the living child of my flesh? Yes, I want Hitler and all he stood for wiped off the earth. I love freedom, but I love my child.

One leg beneath her, felt numb. She stretched it out and the blood circulating again, made it tingle with pain. She rubbed the bare leg, impatient with it, asking herself, Do I have a choice? Do any of us have a choice?

We have not. History has forced this upon us.

That is not so. We who are American born have a choice. We can leave; we can run. If we wish.

We haven't the choice any longer. If the last ten years have taught us a thing, they've taught us just this, our choice is either to fight or to die. To fight as they did in the ghetto at Warsaw, on the long chance some may survive as free men.

That is not so. The choice is simpler. Lillie Gross had it. And took it. She kept David safe. She'll regret it, all of them will, who ran away. They'll be the lepers, outcasts.

Better a live coward than a dead lion.

No.

She clenched her fist, opened it.

Yes and no.

If I lose my child and gain a State, is it worth the great price? And if I lose my child and gain nothing, nothing at all? That too may come out of this.

The riddles were drawing her taut, like a coiled spring. We're gamblers, playing a reckless game with the lives of those who haven't yet lived. But they have. Don't you think this is living? This is life at its crest, the war for dignity, liberty, for nationhood. But war's not for children. They should be going to school, learning skills, the skills of construction, of peace. They should be learning love, trying love, finding love. That's what belongs to their years.

God, take me instead. If you require blood sacrifice for this State, take the old, not the young. The old. Jacob? No, good God, no . . . I mean a useless old woman like me. I've done my job. I've given a boy and a girl to the Land. Take me, God, and let the young live. Abraham laid his dearly loved son on the altar, an offering to God. And God spared the child, took the willingness for the deed. There's an omen. If we offer our children, willingly, on the altar, they will be spared. . . .

She rested her head on the cool windowpane. Must there be a choice? My child or a State? We'll have both, thank you, please. Wait, you will see, we'll have luck. They won't let it happen. The statesmen will talk, pass resolutions, debate, but when the time comes, they won't permit war on our soil. This is holy. Holy City and Holy Land. We'll be safe. Rest assured, we'll be safe. A little hunger, a little fear. Disturbances. We're so used to that. Patience. Firmness. We'll have our State. The State, too, is our child. We've lived for it all these years. It's as dear to me as my life. If it demands a life, then take mine. She found herself arching her throat, as if for a sacrificial blade. I have no fear for myself. Only for those whom I love.

She felt strong and brave and relaxed. She threw back the spread on the cot, lay down and all at once, Dinah seemed here and close, and she stretched her arms out, as if to draw Dinah in, circled them on their own emptiness and fell asleep, her arms rounded as though she held the girl there.

III

SHIFRA DIDN'T COME in the next day, nor the one after that, but in the morning of the third day, a bedraggled woman, with bare feet and three chins, an unfettered bosom and hips, a trailing scarf on her head and jangling silver chains, hung with amulets, rapped on the front door.

Shifra's mother, the woman announced, and God should have stricken her dumb before He made her reveal that shameful fact. She had suffered much in her time, borne many children, struggled to rear them in piety, sometimes the food was lacking but never the discipline, and why had God punished her now? His ways were inscrutable, dared anyone question too much? Yet the G'veret might very well ask— This was G'veret Hirsch, was it not?

When Edith said that it was, Shifra's mother marched into the hall. A fine house, she observed, and that proved that Shifra was out of her head. Would a girl, if she had her good sense, leave a place like this? She waddled into the living room, ran her hands over the fabric of chairs, sighed and plumped down on the couch. She was weary, she said, she had walked all the way and not sleeping last night. Her husband had made her feel she was somehow to blame. Yet, as God was her witness, she had tried her best.

"What happened to Shifra?" Edith managed to break in to ask.

What happened? What should have happened? The worst. Consider her dead, Shifra's father had said. If she ever dared to come home, her father would leave her a cripple for life.

The woman's dialect was difficult. Her emotion made it even harder to understand what she said. "What has happened to Shifra? What? Tell me what?"

What? Does one admit one's own daughter is crazy? Or wicked? A young man turned the girl's head. Not to marriage. No, no. God would have been merciful to grant us that. . . . The woman rolled her eyes piously. . . . Shifra had sworn she was still intact and there was no young man. I want to be a soldier, I must be a soldier, the girl had said. G'veret, can a sane person talk such nonsense?

It began to come clear. Shifra had joined Haganah. Edith moved toward the woman, warming with sympathy. "Be calm," she said. She used the Arabic *"shvue-shvue."* "Take it easy. Your daughter has done what all the children are doing. We have women in our Army, you know."

Shifra's mother smiled with closed lips. "You cannot fool me. We have no Army," she said.

Teddy was due from school any moment and would be wanting lunch and so Edith said briefly she was sorry to lose a good maid, but since Shifra had gone to the Army, the least she could do was clean her own house. She thanked the woman for coming to tell her and said "Shalom."

Shifra's mother didn't get up. Instead, she settled herself more firmly on the sofa, and remarked it was a pity to leave G'veret Hirsch. (Such a small woman, she probably did not eat enough. Certain ladies, she had been told, considered it beautiful to be thin. She herself disagreed. A woman was not a woman unless she had flesh.) It was a pity to leave a delicate woman with a big house like this, no one to spongeh her floors, shake her rugs. If the G'veret wished—the good God knew she herself had plenty of work with eight little ones, yet she might manage two days a week.

"Shalom," Edith said in despair. "Thank you for coming. Please, I am busy. Please, go."

The woman savored the rug with her calloused big toe before she pulled herself up. "G'veret, you forget." She stretched out her hand.

"Baksheesh? You come for baksheesh?"

Shifra's mother thrust her lower lip out. "I come for the wages," she said.

"Of course." Pay and be done. She took a tentative step toward upstairs, where her purse was, and stopped, remembering how little cash there was in the house. "We will bring it to you. My husband will bring it out to your house. He will take care of it."

She counted her coins; a two-piastre piece, a shilling, a ten-piastre, a one. Seventeen piastres, not even a half pound. In all my life, Edith told herself, with a sharp sense of shock, I've never had so little cash in my house. And how will I get any more? No one is paying medical bills. No one can get to the bank. Too much sniping in town. What will happen to our Sterling deposits. The pound is still currency, but should we draw it out, hide it under the mattress? . . . I must ask about this. Someone should know what to do.

What do you do when you are about to start a State? This hasn't happened to us in two thousand years. What are the rules? Do you merely tend to your knitting and let history make itself?

How do you get what you need? Petrol for Jacob's car? That isn't a problem. We have no car. They've commandeered it. Jacob walks or rides in the convoy up to the Hill. Fuel for the primus? Jacob said he'd try to bring home D.D.T. It has a paraffin base. It will burn. It's better than nothing at all.

There's no electricity and candles more precious than rubies are. Our radio is dead.

They're not delivering the mail. They're not collecting the mail. The red box on Keren Kayemeth is stuffed so full, you can't get an envelope in. I should write to Belle, cable her to send money, send food. How? Can we get to the post office, buy a stamp, send a wireless off?

Civilization is falling apart, all the familiar props. Everything ends before it starts fresh.

Shifra has left. I won't find another maid. The young and strong have other duties. They should. Margalit stopped weeks ago, said the bus trip was too hard, but to Shifra admitted the truth. She's afraid to leave her children alone, they'll run in the street and be shot. Can I wash clothes, spongeh floors, stand in queues to find that the grocer has nothing to sell, race about, track down rumors of food? And do what I'm assigned to do? . . . Somehow, we'll manage. We must. We have no choice.

She heard the door bang. "Imma!" Teddy was home. "Where are you?"

She scooped the coins into her purse, thrust the bag back in a dresser drawer, and laughed at herself. When I had money enough,

I left my purse lying about. Now my seventeen piastres have to be hid.

"Imma, I'm starved." Teddy came up the steps.

"Wash your hands."

"What's for lunch?"

"Margarine and bread."

"Is that all?"

Can you answer, "That's all," when the boy's eyes are sunk in their sockets and his shorts skid off his hips? "Wait, darling, be patient, one of these days—"

"Imma, can you remember way back, when I had my party?"

As she measured kerosene frugally into her primus to heat water for tea, she felt dizzy and had to brace herself with one hand on the wall. I'll be better, she thought, when I've had my tea.

Teddy bit into his slice of bread. In four bites, it was gone. "I hate the bakers," he grumbled. "Why do they make this taste so good you want more and more? When there is none, they should make it taste bad."

She broke her slice, passed half of it over to him. He pushed it back. "Take it, darling. I am not hungry. I never am."

He looked at her, disbelieving. "Mothers never are. That's what they say."

"It's true. We don't run and jump all the time. We don't have to grow." She put the half-slice on his palm. "Eat it, please do."

He looked at it and at her, inching the bread toward his mouth. He munched slowly, trying to make each morsel last. "Imma, this is the wing of a chicken. It is a salad with tomatoes. It is a big apple. If you think hard enough, do you know? you can make it taste like whatever you would like to eat."

IV

THE BOYS BUZZED about it all morning at school. In fact, all Jerusalem buzzed about nothing else. The Lechi had captured the village of Deir Yassin, near the city's outskirts. The Lechi commander maintained he'd had word the place would be used as springboard for an Arab attack upon Jerusalem. Good, capture a village. But must you massacre women and children? Must you stack corpses and burn them like wood?

Asi tried to bluster. "They would do it to us if they got the chance."

"They would not," Teddy said.

"And why not?"

That stumped him. He tried evasion. "Because we wouldn't give them the chance."

Asi shoved him. "Listen to him. He talks like a baby. Leib, show him the book."

Leib, who was one of the older boys, looked around to make certain teacher wasn't in sight before he drew the picture album out of his blouse. His father, he hastened to inform the boys, didn't know he had borrowed the book. His father didn't want it known he had it, for people might wonder why he had ventured into the Y.M.C.A. Compound where Arabs hung about, or how he had induced an Arab vendor to sell the album to him.

The boys huddled close and goggled at the pictures. They were photographs of male cadavers, stretched on the ground or stacked in heaps, naked and slashed, testicles ripped away, crammed into sockets where eyes were gouged out, or into dead mouths. Men in Arab attire, with fixed bayonets, stood grinning alongside the dead.

The boys shivered and hugged themselves.

"You see!" Asi gloated, pointing down on a page. "Now you believe?"

"It's a fake," Teddy maintained stubbornly.

"A fake, huh, a fake! Just you run fast so they never catch you. Just you stay away from the Old City gates. . . . You see, now, you see! That's why the Lechi had to do what they did. Give them their own medicine."

There was a crowd on King George, lining both curbs when the boys left the school yard. Teddy poked his head between two men. "What is it?" he asked. "A parade?"

"The Deir Yassin captives," the man told him.

He reached back for Asi and pulled him through. "We're in luck," he whispered. "In time to see them."

Asi rolled his blue eyes. "Remember to jeer and to hiss," he said.

The lead truck moved tortoise pace up the wide avenue. Armed Lechi soldiers marched alongside, alert, sharp-eyed for danger, remote but still present, from a sudden attack by the Mandatory's dwindling police force.

In the front of the truck, behind the driver, Deir Yassin's *Muktar* stood, a tall, robust, handsome man. His arms were raised. He stared forward, jawline set hard. No muscle quivered in his swarthy face. At his side stood a boy of ten or twelve. The boy's arms were lifted but he did not look ahead. Left and right, he turned tear-glistening eyes. The eyes met Teddy's. There was in them such hatred that Teddy felt himself growing hot. "Let's get out of here." He yanked Asi's sleeve. "Let's get out of here fast."

"Coward! They can't hurt you. They're tied."

"I have to go, Asi. I'm going to be sick."

Imma wasn't home. He watched for her from the balcony, and when he saw her come up the street, he ran down. "Imma, why were you so long? I needed you. I was sick. . . . I saw something, Imma. It made me sick."

By the look on his face, by the tone of his voice, she knew but she said, quietly, "Tell me, Teddy," and waited for him.

"I saw the prisoners. Lechi's prisoners, from Deir Yassin. They were on trucks. Like animals." He burrowed his head on her belly and started to sob. "Imma, was that a fair thing to do?"

"It's war, son. In war—"

He turned his face up. "Imma, can that happen to us?"

Can you answer that? Can you say, Yes, son, it *has* happened to us? That is where this began. It's nearly two thousand years since Titus dragged us to Rome, in chains. Will that once more be the end of this perilous road? She averted her eyes while she answered, "If God is not on our side, it can also happen to us."

He clenched his dirty fists. "He will be on our side. Where else can He be?" Then he asked, "Do you think they will be afraid of us now and will stop this war?"

"I cannot say."

"Will they be even worse, Imma? Will this make them better or worse enemies?"

He was doing, she realized, what all Jerusalem was doing this day, trying to calculate what the Deir Yassin massacre might eventually cost.

She sat him down. "Teddy, darling," she said. "You are a boy and you are also a man. Today you've learned something very important, a thing many people never learn about war. It is cruel. It hurts him who inflicts injury as well as him who receives. When you are cruel, you hurt your own self, down deep, where no enemy can possibly reach."

He listened, his eyes enormous, watching her face. He nodded, agreeing with her, but she wasn't quite sure he understood or believed. How can he? she thought. I hardly believe my own words, and when he had gone upstairs, she found herself wondering what bitter fruit would spring from Deir Yassin.

V

Tamar Atani's time had arrived and Tamar insisted that Doctor Hirsch must deliver her child in the Hadassah Hospital on the Hill. It was no mere whim. There was a good reason. She had been one of eight children. They had all slept on the floor in one miserable room and at night had covered themselves with rags. Once, as a girl, she had gone to visit a friend who was sick in the hospital on the Hill and the wards, the row after row of white beds, had appeared like heaven to her. Her friend, a poor Yemenite, too, lay like a queen on white sheets, on a beautiful bed.

True, Tamar now had a bed in her three room flat and she owned four bed sheets. But that was not equal to that dazzling row on row, in the palace up on the Hill.

Tamar's husband and Doctor both tried to alter her mind.

"I, too, have wished," Elia Atani said, "our child to be born in the finest hospital in this land, but the risk is too great. You will be far and if I cannot come to you—"

"You will come. If Doctor Hirsch can travel each day—"

"He returns, to sleep in his house. But if they should some night—" He regretted his words and left them unfinished because it was bad to alarm a woman about to give birth. As it was, life was trying for Tamar, the standing in queues, with her heavy belly, the little to eat, the less than ever to pay for what one ate since the jewelry shop had been boarded up when the front line in the war which was not a war, moved up to its street. If Tamar had not enough to eat, how would she have strength for the birth and to nurse the new-born? Elia made believe he lacked appetite, so that his wife might consume what he left on his plate. He invented a game, feeding her with a spoon. "I must practice," he said, "to know how to care for my son."

"My son," Tamar said, like a stubborn child, "must be born in the hospital on the Hill."

"We are making a hospital here," the Doctor told her. "On the Street of the Prophets. If you do not rush us, we will have it in time for your son."

"Is it as large as the one on the Hill?"

"No, it is not."

"Is it as fine?"

"Not as fine. But good. Good enough."

"Not good enough for my son."

"It will be easier for me if you have the child here, in town."

Tears sprang to her eyes. "You go up the Hill for others. Why not for me?"

One dare not dwell on the danger in travel up past the Grand Mufti's house at Sheikh Jarrah, nor on the continual shelling of the hospital. One dare not frighten a woman about to give birth. Yet she herself mentioned it. Whenever she saw Dr. Hirsch, she asked, "Was there shooting on the Mount Scopus Road this last night?" and when he answered no, whether the convoy had been fired at or not, she replied gleefully, "Then what have we to worry about?"

What, indeed? Her narrow, crooked pelvis was one thing to worry about. And her lack of vitality. It would be a long labor and a difficult birth. Dr. Hirsch sighed and told himself every day, they have promised to keep open the hospital road. That is one promise they will surely keep.

Just before dawn, on the thirteenth, Elia came running to tell the Doctor that Tamar's water had broken. Dr. Hirsch dressed and ran down the cool, scented street to the corner house. The labor pains had barely begun, merely a pinch now and then. Elia made coffee; the Doctor drank it, waited an hour, said, "There is enough time. I shall send the ambulance." He came home, shaved, had more coffee and kvacker with Edith and Teddy, kissed them, said, "L'hitra'ot." For no reason whatever, he turned around on the steps and came back to the kitchen. "Don't worry." He raised his wife's chin and kissed her again. "Be a good girl," he said. "Tonight we will go to the cinema. The Eden has an American film. Cowboys, I believe."

The convoy for the hospital and the university formed at a clinic in town, ten vehicles, a lead car, swathed with thin metal sheets, its windshield latticed, flying the Red Cross; then an ambulance, metal-sheathed, with a hole to see through to drive, a small car again, two buses, a second ambulance, and motor cars in the rear, a slow-moving procession, freighted with precious cargo. In one of the ambulances rode a world-famous doctor who had devoted himself to conquest of trachoma, in another a young cancer specialist, driven from Europe by Hitler, already acquiring world fame; in the buses, a talented psychologist and a brilliant physicist, working on problems of light. There were teachers, students, nurses, technicians, as well as women who scrubbed the hospital wards. There was an old man in a grimy kaftan who had cataracts which required surgery, a woman with painful gall stones, a boy with a fractured leg and hip, Tamar who was giving birth to a child, and the drivers, of course, whose lives were as valuable as anyone else's. While the convoy was turning a corner, those in the last car saw Professor Gross running, stopped to let him in, and raced to catch up to the convoy.

Tamar and the boy with the fractured hip each had the supine position in an ambulance. With Tamar rode Dr. Hirsch and Dr. Ginsberg, the eye specialist, his wife, and Dr. Kaufman, two nurses and the old man with cataracts. The ambulance was jammed and Dr. Kaufman being Yecke and therefore conspicuously polite, apologized to the Frau Doktor for crushing her dress. *"En davar,"* she answered tartly. "No matter. I can bear even that." Nevertheless, he still fussed, and finally asked one of the nurses, an elderly woman who sat beside Dr. Hirsch, to change seats with him. Dr. Hirsch grinned. "Good. Now all is arranged. That insures a safe trip."

Dr. Kaufman resented his tone. "I wished only to make the Frau Doktor comfortable."

"How do you know the Frau Doktor would not enjoy a handsome young man next to her? It has been long, I wager, since—"

The Frau Doktor who was gray-haired, blushed agreeably.

"One makes the most of opportunities in times like these," Jacob said. "Her old man has deserted her—see—"

Dr. Ginsberg was up front with the driver. All one could see of him was silver-white hair, so thinned that the pink of his scalp showed through.

On the stretcher, Tamar lay swaddled in blankets as gray as her face, but with a faint smile on her lips. She kept her eyes shut as the doctor had ordered her to, but she wasn't asleep. Instead, she kept thinking, How long will it take? This pain is so little, nothing at all, for such an important thing as a child.

Dr. Hirsch held her hand. His finger tips ran now and then to her wrist, to make sure of her pulse. She opened her eyes, her lips moved, but she could not be heard above the car's noise and he had to bend to her mouth. "You will let Elia know," she was saying. "As soon as you can. It is a pity he could not come too."

"Why do we need him? He finished his job nine months ago." He patted the mound of her stomach. One of the nurses, who was young and blond, flushed and giggled. Jacob tscked. "No laughing matter. You will find out, if you have not."

"Jacob, if your wife knew how you carry on—" the Frau Doktor said.

"She'd applaud me," he said.

The old man with the cataracts tugged at the young nurse's sleeve. "Sister," he quavered, "will the operation hurt me?"

"It hurts!" Tamar cried suddenly. "Doctor, a very bad pain!"

"Hold my hand. Hold it tight." He watched her face convulse, lips drawn away from clenched teeth, breath hiss, and slowly abate. "Doctor, why? Why must it hurt so?"

"*En braira.* No choice. How else would you get rid of that?" He chortled with spurious gaiety. "Now and then a foolish woman comes in to me. She thinks maybe it is not practical to have the child. Times are hard, money scarce. Can she change her mind? Please, Doctor, have you a pill or powder or maybe an amulet to dissolve this melon?" He waited for someone to laugh but no one did, and he said to himself, Hirsch, clown, be serious, once in your life. Here lies a symbol. The Land is with child. There must be agony and blood will flow before it is born.

A blast rocked the ambulance. It rose in the air, dropped with a crash. Those inside it slid together, in a heap. The elderly nurse flung an arm over Tamar to hold her fast. "We have hit a mine," the driver cried. They heard Dr. Ginsberg say, without excitement or fear, "We are trapped." They drew in their breaths. No one spoke. No one could. The old man with the cataracts started to pray. *"Shema Yisroel, Adonai Elohenu, Adonai Echod—"* He could barely be heard through the rattle of bullets against all sides of the ambulance.

"I've been hit," Dr. Ginsberg said quietly. His wife struggled out of the heap on the floor. "Come back," she cried. "In here with us."

"Leave the driver?" His head turned, so that in the profile, they could see half a smile. "Give me a bandage. It is nothing. A scratch on my leg."

"They're coming!" The driver yelled. A grenade flashed near his head. He ducked down in the seat. Gasoline flared against the windshield.

"We'll be burned!" The blond nurse screamed. "God, oh God, we'll be burned!" She skittered, jackrabbit fashion, toward the back of the ambulance, where the door was. The Frau Doktor held her arm. "Discipline," she said, sternly. "Discipline, Sister."

"Doctor," Tamar cried again. "The bad pain!"

He gripped her hand, gave a quick glance at her gray, delicate face, and at the watch on his wrist, then at the tops of the heads of the men in the front of the ambulance and he felt himself being made useless by too many happenings at once. This is not the moment for active labor, he thought irrationally. This is no time for a child to be born. And all at once, he thought, we may die, I may die, and was stunned, and then angry and after that deeply sad. It occurred to him that all those who were with him must be thinking the very same things. I must brace them, he said to himself. I must give them courage. It is up to me. "Wait!" he said heartily. "Help will come. The British will save us. Their post is a few yards away."

Through chattering teeth, the blond nurse said, "The bus behind us is burning. The bus is on fire."

Tamar struggled to sit. "Doctor, I cannot bear it. Help me, Doctor!"

He groped on the floor for his bag. While he was opening it up, hunting his morphine and sterilized needle, shrapnel ripped through the side of the car. Dr. Kaufman cried out with the sting of pain and the old man once more prayed. Yet Jacob held Tamar's arm, plunged in the needle, and gently forced her to lie down. One thing, he said to himself, one thing at a time. Put her to sleep, then take care of my colleague's wound.

Dr. Ginsberg turned around. "They are coming in numbers," he said in a voice unhurried, unraised. "It will not be long. Let us say 'Shalom.' . . . Beloved, kiss me." The Frau Doktor clambered over the huddle on the floor, put her arms around his neck, and her lips on his. "Shalom. Shalom, shalom!" she cried.

Inside the ambulance, each one shook hands with every other and said, "Shalom" and almost immediately there was a difference. Struggle to live and resentment of death tapered off. This was a thing accepted. There was nothing to do now but wait.

Lead hailed against the car: there were yells and explosions outside. That was periphery, a world detáched from this small, darkened van, this island where men and women huddled, resigned to death.

Tamar slept. The old man prayed until his head started to nod. He made snorting sounds. Dr. Hirsch busied himself trying to stop the flow of blood from Dr. Kaufman's arm. The blond nurse helped him. Together they managed a tidy bandage. The young Doctor thanked them, said no, it did not hurt much. He declined a morphine injection but swallowed two sulfa pills. Jacob slid back to the side of the stretcher and felt Tamar's pulse. It was shallow, too fast. Timing the beat, he noticed that it was close to noon. We must get moving, he thought. I have a woman in labor, about to give birth. He crooked his finger for the elderly nurse, asked her to make a screen with her skirts, turned down the blanket, rolled up Tamar's gown and put his stethoscope to the swollen flesh. The banging of grenades, the crackle of bullets made so much noise he could barely discern the unborn's heart beat. "The child is in position, alive," he said.

"How shall we prepare for the birth?" the nurse asked.

His glance met hers. She was an old-timer, gray-haired, and used to hardships. Her face was pale but there was serenity in her eyes. "There is time," he said. "Still much time. When it comes, somehow we will manage, you know."

"I know." She stayed, squatting alongside the stretcher, with him. The firing quieted somewhat and hope of rescue began to mount.

They shifted positions, rearranged themselves inside the wrecked ambulance. The driver cried out that, through the peephole, he could see Army cars turning into a road a few hundred yards off. Dr. Ginsberg raised the shield over the glass, took out his white handkerchief, waved it, and shouted, "Help, help."

The storm of metal came before he had even time to pull down the shield. The driver clapped his hand to his cheek. Blood gushed over his hand. The blond nurse moved to give him a wad of gauze. She tripped against the stretcher. Tamar stirred, opened her eyes and started to scream.

"Sheket!" Dr. Hirsch found himself yelling at her. "Sheket, donkey!" The elderly nurse put her hand on Tamar's mouth. The young woman struggled to rise, then collapsed and fell moaning, tossing her head from side to side.

"Bachayeye," the driver shouted. "I will not sit here and wait for my death." He sprang from his seat and began to run. "He has fallen. They shot him," Dr. Ginsberg reported to the inside of the car.

There was a crash, like a blow from a giant's fist. The silvery head in the front seat sank slowly, disappeared. The Frau Doktor screamed once, clapped her hand on her mouth, stumbled forward. The elderly nurse barred her way. "You must not see," she said and held the Frau Doktor in her arms. Tamar moaned; the old man prayed louder. The others heard without hearing, the moans and the prayers.

Time blurred; hours ran into each other. The Frau Doktor sobbed softly while the elderly nurse held her, stroked her hair, like a child. Dr. Kaufman sat staring, as if in catalepsy. The blond nurse buried her pretty face in her hands. The old man again fell asleep.

Jacob glanced at his watch dial again. The time was past two o'clock. I should be hungry, he told himself. Why am I not famished? The body has stopped wanting, it is ready for death. He thought of how sad his family would be when they learned of his death and the thought of their sadness distressed him. I must leave a message. My colleague said, "Shalom" to his wife. I must leave a last word. He said, loudly, "Whoever of you stays alive, please, I beg you, go to Edith, my wife—"

The elderly nurse glanced up. "She will understand what you wished to say, without telling her."

That did not satisfy him. He managed to take out his prescription pad and fountain pen. *"Edith,"* he wrote, the lines slanting crazily. *"I bequeath you my hopes and send you my love. Take care of the children. Shalom,"* and signed his name. He tried to reread it but could not because his eyes were glazed and so he recalled the words and repeated them to himself. They were cold, he felt, yet adequate. Be sparing with words. They have an enduring effect. Say merely the name of the loved one and the "Shalom." Then he unstrapped his wrist watch, took out his wallet and placed it, with the prescription pad with the note, into a clean handkerchief, tied the ends of the cloth together to make a package. He wedged it into the space between the stretcher and the ambulance wall. As he did that, he thought, this car may catch fire and then what I have done is useless. Yet, he reconsidered, if it does not burn altogether, this still may be found and taken to her. He thought what a fearful thing it was to be burned to death and then said to himself, others have died in fire before me and the agony will not be endless. Perhaps there will be a swift bullet before. Let it come, come quickly now. But so unjust, so cruel, that we, who sought only to serve, must die thus. They have paid us for Deir Yassin and it is not fair.

Tamar's hand, flailing in agony, struck his cheek. Stupid girl, he thought, if you had not been so insistent, we'd not have been bothered with you. And it occurred to him that if Tamar had agreed to have her accouchement in town, he would not be here. And my children would not be orphans, he thought. Then he was ashamed of himself and he bent over the stretcher and wiped the sweat from her face. He felt her pulse again, took his stethoscope out for her heartbeat and her child's, and thought, the infant's sounds stronger than hers. He began to fret. We shall lose them both, mother and child, if we do not act right away. Then he remembered where he was, and thought, does it matter, two more?

He saw his young colleague with the injured arm rise and inch toward the back of the ambulance and start to open the door. "Where are you going?" he cried out to him.

"I cannot sit and wait, I must try," the man said, without looking back. The blond nurse stood up, looked around with a kind of sadness. "Shalom," she said. "Shalom, *Haverim*. I must try, too."

The elderly nurse shook her head. "You and I, Doctor, we are of the old school. We stay with the sick."

"At our posts, we two fools."

The Frau Doktor wriggled out of the nurse's arms. "I, too," she said. "This is what he would have wished me to do."

It struck Jacob strangely, the "he would have wished me to do." He is dead, my colleague is dead, and now she is a seer. She looks into his mind. How does she know what he would wish her to do? When I am gone, Edith will speak just this way. Jacob would wish me to do this or that. How does she know? I don't know myself, what I would wish her to do. I'd wish her to be safe. Her and Teddy and Dinah. More than all else. To be safe. Well. Alive. I know what a precious thing every life is. I know, now, at this moment, that more than all else, I want to live. Thinking and breathing and feeling. I. Me. A person. Not a heap of bloodied flesh like that one up front. That is the instinct. To live. Man gives himself grandiose notions, ideals, a Homeland, a State, when the need, the wish above all, is to live, be alive, on whatever terms.

"Doctor Hirsch," the Frau Doktor said, "let me sit by your patient. It will comfort us both." She moved to the side of the stretcher, and began to stroke Tamar's sweat-damp face. "How can we help her, Doctor? It is too hard for her."

At four o'clock two inches of metal ended Tamar Atani's ordeal. The bullet crashed through the wall and entered her side, a few moments before an armored car reached the ambulance. Her pulse was still faintly flickering when a British voice called, "You in there!" An officer pulled open the rear door and said, amazed, "Why, there's a whole crowd in here, alive."

"Quick," Jacob shouted at him. "Move her quickly. All speed. We must save the child."

The rear cars of the convoy had seen what had happened up front, and immediately their drivers swung around and raced back to town.

At noon Professor Gross returned to Rehavia. He spoke with Nathan for several minutes before he went up the street to his house. He felt exceedingly tired and wondered why that should be. Nothing happened to me, he reflected, our car returned, one instant of terror should not weary me so. I am tired with anxiety, with strain, with age. Yet when he glimpsed Jacob's house down the street, he felt that he understood why he was tired, and argued with himself. I do not make these conditions. I accept them as they are. I was in the last car. I ran after the car to get in, go along. Is that my fault? In a way, he knew that it was, yet he could not admit to himself that he had tried to be late, to miss the dangerous convoy.

When he told Lillie about the ambush she said, "We must go to Edith at once."

"No," he answered.

"Yes," she said. "Whatever is, we have been friends. If she is in trouble, we must go to her."

The front door stood ajar. They knocked on the door frame and entered, heard footsteps, and Edith's voice, calling from upstairs, "Who's there?"

Lillie Gross pressed her hand on her thumping heart.

Edith came down the staircase, stood, without speaking, holding the rail. Lillie Gross stretched her arms out. "We came," she faltered and could not go on. She dropped her hands.

"Yes?" Like an icicle, the one word was.

The Professor cleared his throat. "The convoy," he managed to say.

A chill ran through Edith. Jacob, my husband! She cried out his name.

Lillie Gross took a step forward and again stretched her arms. "Edith, my friend—"

"What is it? What happened?" Her head pivoted like a mechanical toy.

Professor Gross looked down at the carpet. "They are under attack, at Sheikh Jarrah."

"You saw? You were there?"

He nodded, unable to meet her eyes.

"And you are safe? You are always safe." She turned and ran up the stairs. They stood watching until they heard the slam of a door. Their shoulders drooped. They went out, feeling shrunken, defeated and old.

She had been making beds when her neighbors came and so slow is the human reflex in its acceptance of shock, that at first she tried to go on with the job, but found she could not, and dropped into a chair. Teddy came home. Faintly, she heard him calling "Imma." She thought, I must go down, and started to move toward the steps. Her knees buckled. She fell in a faint.

When she woke, it took a long while to recall why she lay on the floor. Then, painfully, she dragged herself up the narrow steps to the roof and stood, rooted and impotent, watching the smoke over the Sheikh Jarrah Road, hearing explosions and shots.

Teddy had hunted for her, had run to Carmela Levine. He and Carmela found her, stood with her through the afternoon, holding one another, not daring to speak.

Gershon, in the pillbox at Gan Darom's wireless set, heard the news of the convoy attack and was at first undecided whether to let Dinah know, but at suppertime, in the dining hall, he told her quietly, "You will hear it from others, then hear it from me." He saw her blanch. "They have given some names. Not Doctor Hirsch." He laid his huge hand on her head. "Havera, you must be strong."

The others with whom the girl worked and lived seemed to draw off, making a circle around her, as if her grief were a sickness which might contaminate. It was Ketti who spoke to her first. "Eat, Dinah," she said.

"How can I eat?"

Ketti shut her eyes, opened them. "Eat." She thrust the soup spoon into Dinah's hand. "If he is dead, you must be strong. And if he is not, you must be."

Jacob came in at suppertime, swinging his bag. His face was ashen, but his manner, as always, was gay. "Mazel tov," he said. "A boy. Three kilos and a half." Edith flung herself at him, her hands searching his features, his arms and chest for affirmation that he was alive. "Is it you?" she said over and over. "Are you truly alive?"

"What else? I promised to take you to the cinema. I am a man of my word."

It was Teddy who clamored for all the details while his mother could do nothing more than stare at Abba as though she had never seen him before.

Abba was in it, trapped in an ambulance, shot at and grenaded from ten in the morning to four o'clock. Many people were killed, but Abba not a scratch. That's how one expects it to be. *They* are killed—*people*—but not one's father. Abba takes care of himself. He has a personal angel, perched on his shoulder. "Tell me everything, Abba. . . . What happened, then?"

Jacob held the boy clamped between his knees, kept stroking his hair. "Don't make something of nothing. I sat and they shot. Does this make me a hero? Certainly not."

She clung to him and did not try to talk. Nor did he. And he clung to her. Her thin hands caressed his torso, his face and his loins. Her mouth lay on his, thirstily, as though she could not drink enough of the living warmth. Afterwards, locked in each other's arms, they both slept.

Edith woke first, tried gently to disentangle herself but her light movements roused him. He moaned, rubbed his eyes and sat up. "Where am I? I keep hearing sounds. Firing, screams." He sighed deeply, waking. "I remember." His arms closed, like a vise, around her again.

"It was dreadful?" she whispered to him.

"Haviva, it was."

"Were you frightened?"

"Nachon. Am I stone?"

"Did you pray?"

"Haviva, I?"

"What did you do?"

"Do? Nothing. It is dull waiting for death. I watched Tamar. Poor child. And kept thinking."

"What did you think about?"

"What does a person think about? All sorts of things." He laughed. "I thought about the day we first came. Do you remember how rough the sea was? The tender in Jaffa harbor. You stood on the ship's ladder and screeched, 'I can't, I can't, I'll be drowned.' And the big Arab porter picked you up like a sack of potatoes. Your mouth popped open, surprised. . . ."

She squeezed his hand, nestled her head into his shoulder. He laughed again. "I thought of what trouble you had with Ivrith. You mixed up the sexes always. *Mah sh'lom'ach* when you meant *Mah shlom'ha*. And of the day you burned your hand on the primus, and stormed around our flat. 'Take me back. Take me home, where there's a gas range.' And I sang you 'Home on the Range.' "

She put her hand over his mouth. "Stop! If all you remembered were my foolish moments, don't tell me, don't talk to me."

"As you wish." He started to roll on his side. She drew him back, stroked his cheek. "Didn't you think of our children at all?"

He was silent a moment or so, then he said, "Yes, I thought of them, too. I thought of the last time I spanked Teddy. And I thought, I was wrong, it wasn't his fault, it was Asi's. I should have apologized to my son. I must do that as soon as I see him again."

She laughed softly and asked, "And Dinah? Did you think of Dinah as well?"

He waited again before he replied, "I tried not to think of Dinah. To think of Dinah meant to know fear again." He felt her fingers tightening on his. "So I tried to think of Dinah, years past, the day she was born. I wished to name her Sophie, after your mother, but you said, 'No. Dinah is the daughter of Jacob. Dinah is her name.' And I said, 'Jacob also had a dozen sons. Can you fill the rest of the bargain, madame?' And you—I was surprised at you, really, that day—you said, 'Twelve sons and one daughter, by two wives and two concubines. Are you prepared to fill the rest of the bargain, sir?' "

"I believe you could have," she said.

"What's wrong with the one wife I have? What was missing to-night?"

She did not answer. He spoke for her. "This was the first time in how many weeks? We forget, almost, how to be normal. . . . It took death, coming near—" He broke off, because his throat filled.

Neither talked for a while, then she said, "Haviv, while I stood on the roof, I thought of two things. How can I live without you and how can I tell our children? How can you give so much hurt to a child?"

There was silence again, before he said, "Haviva, difficult days are ahead. If either of us—"

"No." The instinctual denial. "No."

He went on, firmly. "If I should die, I wish you to know just one thing, I have always loved you very much."

She touched his hand. "And I you."

"Whatever comes, the knowledge of love gives us strength."

"Jacob," she said, "the children. We can be spared. But they must not die."

"Nachon, they will not die." There was silence again and she thought he was drifting to sleep until he asked, "Haviva, were you afraid today?"

"I am ashamed to tell you. I was weak, hysterical. I think I fainted."

"Poor little one." He stroked her hair. "Edith," he said, "fear is a personal thing. No one can say to another, don't be afraid."

"The fear is not for me, believe me, Jacob. One is never afraid for oneself, only for those whom one loves. I try not to think of Dinah, because I am afraid for her all the time. And for Teddy and you."

He propped himself up on an elbow. "Do you know," he said carefully, as though he were making a formal statement, "I am very lucky."

"All of us, we all are. . . ."

"Not just today, that I lived. Always. I am lucky that I married you. A clever man, to have found the right wife." He bent over and kissed her lips, a long, intense kiss. "I am tired," he said. "Let us sleep." And turned on his side.

She lay awake, wondering why that good-night kiss was so strange, like a last farewell, as on a death bed.

In the morning, he said, "Today, you need not worry. I do not think we will try to go up the Hill. Edith, go in to Elia Atani. Comfort him. He is young to know such sorrow and loss." Then he added, "We must help his son to live. God only knows how. Corn flour and water is poor substitute for his mother's milk."

VI

FOOD WAS THE most critical problem. True, sniping was constant and the Arab mortars had begun to hurl shells into the New City's congested quarters. But a bullet strikes only once out of many and hunger hits all alike. Women braved the gunfire to rake over gardens, abandoned by Arabs, for shreds of withering lettuce, and they picked nettles in the open fields.

The grocer on Keren Kayemeth acquired a few boxes of kvacker and doled them out among families with children to feed. Jacob and Teddy were in the kitchen when Edith opened the box. They heard her disgusted outcry, ran to see what there was. Fat white worms wriggled on top of the grain.

Teddy made a retching noise. "Quick, Imma, throw it out."

"I will not." She hugged the box to her. "It is good food."

Jacob glanced at her and shrugged. He slapped his son on the back. "Fat and protein," he said. "Just what we lack."

"I won't eat it." Teddy shuddered and made a fearful face.

"If I will, you will," his mother said. "Whatever we have, we eat."

When she brought the porridge in, he was still truculent and he watched sullenly, lips sealed, arms folded on his chest while his mother dipped her spoon into her bowl. His eyes were riveted on her spoon as she raised it up, into her mouth. He saw her throat muscles ripple when the kvacker went down. She didn't grimace; her face was serene. He was flabbergasted. His mother, that dainty lady from Boston, in the United States; his mother, that fussy lady, who was always saying, "Teddy wash your hands; you'll get sick," was eating kvacker *with worms*. "That settles it." He flung down his spoon. "Never, never, never, as long as I live, will I make a State again."

Udi was afraid of outdoors. He had to be forced to go out and then, lacking energy to come in, found a sunny spot, stretched there and slept. Once a day, Edith brought him a bowl, pushed a few spoonfuls of kvacker or water soaked crusts under his snout and turned away quickly from his reproachful, lustreless eyes.

Udi envied the neighborhood cats. They dashed about, finding mice, and looked sleek. Asleep, he thrashed about because his stomach hurt. The trip up a staircase exhausted him. His family was aware of his trouble, he knew. They tried to make up in affection what they failed him in nourishment. Teddy helped him up, into the bed, not alongside. "What will become of Udi?" he wailed. "If we can't feed him, he'll die."

Edith made up her mind. One morning, she went into Jacob's office, while he was packing his bag. She said, "I want chloroform."

He gaped. "Have you gone out of your mind? Who will you kill, you or me?"

"Udi. We can't feed the dog. He's suffering too much. Dinah would agree, it's more merciful so." Her voice was ineffably sad.

He blew his nose, wiped his eyes. "No, little one. Every drug we have is too precious to use on a dog."

"Then shoot him. You have a pistol."

"I gave it to Dinah, last month, when she was here."

"Oh!" She gave herself an instant to recall, comprehend. "Then go to Nathan. Tell him to send someone to shoot our dog."

"Can he spare a bullet? A bullet is a precious thing." He took both her hands between his. "Haviva, Nathan crawls along our lines, and pleads, 'Children, dont shoot. Don't waste a bullet. We have none to spare.' No, haviva, Udi will have to suffer, to starve, like everyone else. There can be no special favors for Dinah's dog."

He let go her hands, went on packing his kit. "Remember," he said, "no one is more important than anyone else. If we starve, we all starve. If we die, we all die. If we succeed, we all do." He said, "L'hitra'ot," kissed her forehead and left.

But by the time the housework was finished, she had decided what she had to do. She walked down to the Security Zone on King George Avenue, glancing over her shoulder, to make certain no one she knew was around, and said, in her best Bostonese, to the

Tommies at the Zone gate, "Good morning, could you do a favor for me?"

"Eh? What's that?" They looked at her hands, felt for their side-arms. She smiled crookedly. "I'd like one of you to come down to my house and shoot my dog."

Somewhere in this was a dirty dig or a trap, they were sure. The woman looked and spoke like a lady, and she seemed flat, but how could you know she hadn't concealed the grenade somewhere else? "We can't feed our dog," she was saying. "He's suffering and grow-ing weak. It's rather frightful to see." The way she said that, with quiet dignity, made them a little ashamed. They could not guess she, too, was ashamed because she had begged a favor from English-men. They whispered to one another before one of them touched her sleeve. She pulled back, instinctively. He was gallant enough not to take note of that. "Ma'am—" he was red as a beet— "don't kill your dog. We'll feed 'im for you. . . . Which 'ouse is it, ma'am? D'you mind if we bring a packet for 'im tonight?"

The package they left on the bottom steps was large. It held greasy fragments of meat, white bread crusts which once had sopped gravy and two large beef bones. And it held a tin of sardines.

Udi gobbled the meat scraps and bread. Jacob said, at supper that night, "Are you a magician, Edith? How did you conjure up a tin of sardines?" She left the room, pretending she hadn't heard.

Teddy said at noon, "The bean soup is yoffee, Imma. It tastes as if it had meat." He asked for and got a second plateful. "Imma, have we won the Road that we have such good food?"

Udi tried his teeth on the bones. He hadn't the strength to dig in but he hugged them against his swollen stomach. Life was good once more; he had bones and he had tasted meat.

The next package contained two eggs, the one after that four bananas, and then an unopened tin of bully beef. Should one rejoice or be covered with shame? It was shame Edith felt and some dread. Udi will betray us, give me away by looking healthy. Last night, Jacob said, "Didn't I tell you not to worry for him? Dogs somehow survive." Teddy asked, "Imma, why do you tie Udi up in the kitchen at night? He won't run away.

Udi had to be tied. He'd sniff the soldiers bringing the packet and he'd bark for joy.

She got the habit of fluttering around the front window and door, to snatch up the bundle the instant it was placed on the steps. Everyone surely saw those Tommies come up the walk. All Rehavia would ask, "Why do British soldiers go to Hirsch's house?" Yet Teddy's eyes glistened when he saw the boiled egg. Wait till he sees the banana! And tomorrow, we'll have a banquet on their bully beef.

If I tell my menfolk where it comes from, they may elect to starve. Yes, they would, even Teddy, even Udi perhaps. They'll gag, be afraid they're being poisoned. Yet this is human and kind. Shall I deny to a stranger who chances to be my enemy, the right to be merciful?

She told Jacob that evening where the food had come from. Teddy heard what she said to his father. He glared at her, then looked at his dog, and burst into tears. "Only make them do it at night," he pleaded. "If anyone sees English soldiers come up our walk, they'll be sure we are spies." But her husband said merely, "Interesting! Our dog feeds us, not we him," and afterwards, "A man who is not realistic is a fool. If we eat we have strength. If we have strength, we can work. Let the matter stand there. Nevertheless, a man may be pardoned, if in these circumstances, he has a poor appetite."

Madame Malkoff heard by the grapevine, which all Jerusalem was, that in the Mea Shearim quarter there was a shop which had lemons to sell. Madame had now and again thought of lemons in this famished April, not, however, with the fervor with which she hunted sugar or cigarettes or meat. But if lemons are to be bought, should one miss the chance?

Mea Shearim was far, the bus service catch-as-catch-can. She considered sending Ephraim and decided not. They will tell him they have no lemons. Everyone else will march out with lemons and the idiot will take a shopkeeper's word. God, why did you punish me so, to give me a fool for a son?

She saw little of Ephraim these days. He was away from the house all day long, sometimes until late at night. She suspected a girl, God forbid, a Galician or even Sephardi, perhaps. Yet his face and neck were sunburned, his hands were blistered. He must be working. She asked him point-blank, got no reply, and she guessed. In the wadi, opposite the new burial place, many men were leveling a field. "Jerusalem must indeed be badly off," she said sharply to him, "if they put you to work."

She stopped by to ask Nathan what Ephraim was occupied with.

"With what he needs to be," Nathan said.

That was no answer to give an old Zionist. "Haver," she told him forcefully, "I have been in the confidence of far more important men than you will ever be. All our leaders drank tea at my table. I cherished more secrets than you will ever hear."

"Madame," he answered, "I am busy. Please go away."

She inhaled and exhaled. "Upstart! Galician!" she bellowed at him.

She thought of going to Yora Levine but remembered in time that Yora had, long before, shown her the door. He is a snake, that one, she thought. A silent snake. Who would trust him?

Yet without Ephraim to go on small errands and the maid disappeared, as all the maids in Rehavia had, life was difficult. Her bulk did not travel easily, and the fact was she was old. But she made her way along King George Avenue to Chancellor Road, and down to Mea Shearim, stopping now and again in strangers' doorways, to wait out a spasm of cross-fire and gossip a bit. She haggled with a shopkeeper who had never seen her before, would never again, carried off a prize, a wizened small lemon and a tin of tomato paste. She strolled a bit on Chancellor, reading with interest the Etzel warnings of doom to the British, which were painted on walls, studying the posters glued up, and thought how lively this neighborhood was. They ran a war the way a war should be run, with slogans, with threats, with the spirit of violence, not with the tight-lipped starvation and discipline of the Rehavia district.

She insulted a filthy beggar squatting on the steps of the Bikur Cholim Hospital where the mortuary was, but before he could answer in kind, she dropped a piastre into his palm, pleased with the adroitness with which she had circumvented a possibly potent curse.

It was mid-afternoon before she came back along the hump of King George. Since she was tired, her bulk and white hair moved ponderously across the open space at the crest of the Gardens. It made an excellent target for a sniper on a roof part way down the slope. She heard nothing and felt no pain, merely dropped in a heap. A machine gunner, perched near the sniper's hide-out, poured a fusillade into the street, for the sport, and to keep help from quickly reaching her side. Tommies, on guard at the wire of the Zone up the street, heard the shots, and sensibly stayed where they were.

Madame was thoroughly dead by the time the ambulance came. Mortar shelling had concentrated around Chancellor Road by then, and the ambulance driver concluded it made no difference to the dead, was more safe for the living, to take Madame to her own house.

There was something ironic about it, some people said, this old Zionist dying before the State was attained, on a ridge overlooking Jerusalem's hills. It was a warning, other ones said, more cogently, that the open space on King George must be walled up. A few practical people found themselves thinking that in case the son gave up the flat, they might make a deal.

There were no tears for Madame, merely a few nostalgic sighs, as for an era attaining its end.

Lillie Gross took two candles from her meager hoard and went down, as was seemly for the closest neighbor, to cover the mirrors, light candles and receive the mourners.

Though Madame had been a free thinker, in death they made her Orthodox. Two old women, white shawls on shaved heads, crept through the perilous streets to the house to strip off the bloodied garments, wash the body, shroud it in linen, stretch it out on the bedroom floor. Two old men came to sit near the corpse and pray for its soul. The bearded men with the gold-headed canes and the women with the dust-sweeping skirts came down the street as they used to do on Shabbat. Isaac Winkleman saw them going and nagged his daughters. "Hurry, Maida and Jenneh. Come to Malkoff's. What kind of neighbors are you? Everyone will be there before us." He was in a dither of excitement, since Madame's misfortune, was in a way, his good luck, at long last a chance to sit at a table with these old Zionists.

Of all the neighbors, only Max Goldstein, Gordon Leake, and Yora Levine could not come, each one for personal good reasons. Carmela came early, left early. She was on night duty, driving a Haganah car. Henry Winkleman had time for no more than a handshake, a "how are you?" as she passed him, ending her condolence call as he entered for his. The Hirsches were late, because Jacob didn't get home until long after dark and they ran to the Malkoff house, through a night awesome with exploding shells.

On a massive sideboard of the taste of the century's turn, in a frowsy room, stifling with odors of kerosene, camphor and putrefying flesh, Lillie Gross' candles guttered in heavy brass sticks, threw fitful patches of light on a huge samovar, and on Madame's friends, surrounding the oak dining table. Isaac Winkleman found a place in the circle, sat there, ignored, but with a beatific smile on his face.

Ephraim crouched alone, on a stool, near the wall, his head in his hands.

Jacob touched his shoulder and Ephraim looked up. He had not been weeping though his eyes were red. "Is it true?" he asked. He seemed to be dazed.

"Whenever it happens, it still comes with shock," Jacob said. "When anyone dies, a world dies."

"A world dies." Ephraim repeated his words. "True, a world dies." He swayed, like a worshiper at prayer. "Doctor." He halted his rhythmic motion. "Then, now I begin a new world." He cringed, then, as though ashamed he had sounded glad. "What could they have had against her?" he cried. "An old woman like that!"

A man at the table looked up. "What could they have had against her!" The sharp spade of his beard jigged with emotion. "She was a prize, a great prize for them, an old Zionist, friend of the leaders. In the siege of Jerusalem she fell. It will be in history books. You can make a romance from that. An intellectual, an idealist, come to the—"

A woman's voice rose waspishly. "An idealist, you call her? I happen to know, personally, she came for another reason entirely. The man's name was Yasha and she was in love with him and he had a wife—"

"Sheket," someone cried out. "Is this the time—"

"Whatever the reason," the man retorted. "She came. She gave a son to the Land."

Heads pivoted. Ephraim felt their stares and lowered his face.

"The husband! Where is he now?" someone asked.

"Who knows and who cares?" someone replied. "I talked with him once. He said he could be patient with all of the others, but Sergei, that vulgarian, loud mouth—"

"But you see, she was clever. She chose correctly. Sergei left her the property when he died. He made her rich."

"Leah should never have married the *schlemiel,* Malkoff. Why did she marry with him?"

"Who else would marry with her?"

"Sheket!" A woman glanced over her shoulder, toward Ephraim. "What kind of talk in front of the poor orphaned son?"

"Doctor—" Ephraim pulled at Jacob's pants leg—"tell me, what was my mother?"

"She was your mother. That is enough."

"I wish to know," Ephraim said.

Jacob let his gaze slowly travel the table of ancient magpies, all hushed and attentive for what he would answer. "Your mother loved life," he said clearly and loudly. "That is the best eulogy I can give for her or for anyone."

Lillie Gross came from the bedroom just then. Always plump, she still had much flesh, but it flapped in loose folds and she walked mincingly on her tender feet. She saw Edith standing with Ida Goldstein and the Winkleman sisters, in a group near the door, and she took a step toward them. The circle of women closed as if tightening ranks.

The spade-bearded man at the table, plucked Lillie's sleeve. "G'veret, if you are not of the family, could you make me perhaps a glass of tea. I have walked far. I have far to walk."

She brightened. Her backward glance, toward the group at the door, seemed triumphant, saying, you see, I am wanted, by these others, if not by you. "Me also, G'veret," Isaac Winkleman's voice trembled with eagerness. "I should like once to drink tea with them."

"Ah, the times I have sat around Leah's samovar and drunk her tea," a man sighed. "It was like the old days in Moscow."

"A salon she had. There and here. Yes, she loved life, I heard that one say to the son, she loved life."

Ephraim looked up again. "What is life?" he muttered. "Struggling and suffering. Uncertainty. Pain. What is there to love?"

"A poem!" a woman cried. "See what our Leah created! A poet she gave to the Land."

Lillie Gross hobbled out with a tray of glasses of tea, set one before the spade-bearded man, one before Isaac Winkleman, and carried the other to where Ephraim sat. On Ephraim's saucer lay a sliver of lemon. He winced. "My inheritance," he said bitterly. "My mother gave up her life to get a lemon for me."

Jacob shook his head. "She gave up her life," he said stubbornly, "because this is a time when people die for no logic or sense. Our neighbors are leaving us one by one. Who will be next?

"Be patient," he answered himself. "In God's good time we shall know."

VII

On the morning of April eighteenth, a caravan entered the city, seventeen miles of convoy which had snaked through the hills. Watchers on rooftops saw its approach, spread the word, so that by the time the trucks had begun to roll through the New City's streets, thousands were waiting to cheer it and dance. There was food in the lorries, one thousand tons, and other things just as life-giving as bread. *"If I forget thee, O Jerusalem,"* was scrawled on the sides of the trucks. The miracle was, so secretly was it done that not a shot was fired at the convoy all through the night of its journey from Tel Aviv here.

Three days after that a new convoy arrived. It lost six lorries on the way. But here were flour, beans, coffee, grits, egg powder, milk powder, margarine, cheese, matzohs for Passover and even petrol.

You see, people said to each other, there are miracles, there is God. If you will it enough, it is no miracle, agnostics replied, this is our work, our Haganah.

There were only a few, however, who did not in those days believe in God and His miracles and speak freely of Him, just as there were a few who declined to partake of the food in the convoy because it had been transported on the Shabbat, and others, still huddled around the Wailing Wall, in the Old City, who told one another, "We will surely be saved, either by a miracle or a natural event," meaning by "natural event," Messiah's coming, and who in blind faith, continued to pray and declined to arm.

Ida Goldstein stopped by at Edith's to ask if the Hirsch family would make *Seder* with her. "Max is not religious. There is no man in my house to read the *Haggadah*." She did not say, Max is blind, he can no longer read. She did not say, Arieh is dead. She said, "Your husband, the Doctor has a fine voice. He would be like a *Hazan*.

My grandchildren are old enough now. I should like them to know how the Almighty God once before set us free. We will have matzohs and wine and I will make a good soup."

The New City felt a quickening of life. Isolation was ended. Jerusalem is not abandoned. Our brothers are here.

The streets swarmed with men and girls in khaki, openly carrying rifles and Stens, and the British, defied to attack or disarm, did nothing at all. Carpets of barbed wire lay in the streets before the Zones where the Mandatory waited, counting off its concluding days. The light tank withdrew from the corner. The Tommies stopped leaving bundles for Udi, but there was more kvacker, beans, grits which one might divide with a dog.

A poster appeared on the walls, a dramatic thing, an arm and clenched fist with English words, "It all depends upon you," and the Haganah symbol of the blue and white flag above the Old City walls. Everyone took these words as his own and worked feverishly, as though he alone were the one to defend Jerusalem. Bank clerks and bookkeepers mixed cement and helped to erect a high wall (with slots for rifles) on King George Avenue, where Madame had died. Near the wadi, the cleft in the hills on Rehavia's outskirts, girls skipped rope, hens cackled, blue passion flowers crawled along a garden fence, while boys and men—students, gravediggers, shop clerks—hacked the red earth to level an airstrip below the hillside where the casualties of each night's shelling and sniping lay in boxes of pine, patiently waiting their last resting place. The work went on even on the Shabbat. "It is permitted," the Chief Rabbi said. "Provided no one smokes on the field, or rides going to or coming from it." Outside the city, from Galilee to S'dom, battles raged, and some word of the struggle seeped in. The *Palestine Post* came out every day. Those who had battery sets heard the wireless, and mouth to mouth spread the news, Sheikh Jarrah taken, then lost; Katamon taken and held; Arab fugitives cluttering the roads. The streets were pitch dark, and only those who had urgent business went out into the shell-noisy nights.

There was a small crisis, a matter of installing a cable direct to a schoolhouse in whose basement, at night, rifles (brought up in flour sacks in the perilous convoys) had to be cleaned, oiled, assembled and doled out sparingly. The schoolhouse had been on the same line as a clinic which had had a direct, devastating shell hit. The power line had been cut.

It was a delicate mission, demanding finesse.

"Duncan," Yora started the conversation in an off-hand way, "you do not fail to inform me whenever our boys perform some mischief. I regret I must tell you that Brigadier Glubb's Legion marksmen have wrecked the line here—between this clinic and this schoolhouse." He pointed down to the addresses on his list.

Duncan clucked. "Too bad, too bad." Then he smiled, that mere lifting of upper lip. "Is it so important? Must your schools be open at night?"

An innocent question. Why, then, should sudden pain tweak Yora's bowels?

"I've wondered," Duncan said mildly. "Your schools and your synagogues. I wondered about those as well. . . . Do you people pray every night? I thought it was just once a week. As a matter of fact, I've been asked."

I've been asked. By whom? Who else sees this list? Who else knows? A clerk? An engineer? . . . Push back the pain. Pretend this means nothing at all. "We pray every night. These are times to send many prayers to our God."

Duncan's head bobbed, assenting. "You do well to pray." Then he shrugged. "School or synagogue or whatever. Really it doesn't matter to us to whom we sell power." He broke off, looking up. "What's up, man?" he asked crisply. "You're pale. You're white as a ghost. . . . What you need is a drink."

"Thank you, no." Yora backed off.

"Come, now." The man was up, on his feet. He had hold of Yora's arm. "Let's duck over to the King David bar. Do you good. . . . Bet you've not been there in months. . . . Don't say no. Good lord, man, you *need* that drink."

The bartender was new. He did not recognize Yora Levine and the handful of men in the dim, cool barroom where the drum-beat of near-by gunfire was faint, wore the uniforms of the British Army or the International Red Cross. There was no one whom Yora knew. One drink, quickly finished. Greater risk to be stubborn, refuse, than to drink, he told himself.

Duncan ordered brandy and soda for both. He raised his glass. "Cheerio." He touched it to Yora Levine's. "I suppose," he said amiably, "I'm to consider buying this drink as a sort of investment. If you people make this thing tick, it's well to be on your good side." He winked and touched Yora's arm. "We've got along up to now, haven't we?"

At that instant, a man entered the bar. Yora knew the man. He had done business with him. The man sold brushes and paint. Yora had bought paint from him for the walls of his house. He disliked the man because he was small, in stature and personal outlook, disagreeable, picayune.

The man was alone. He stood in the doorway, surveying the room with a cool insolence. When Yora's glance met his, he nodded, and came unbidden over to Duncan and him. He said, "Shalom." Yora answered, "Shalom," and Duncan removed his hand from Yora's arm. The paint dealer marked it and looked sharply at Yora. "I am surprised to see you here," he said, in Ivrith.

"I am surprised to see you," Yora answered him. He shifted uneasily. "Excuse me," he said. "This is a business conversation. Please do not interrupt."

Again, a rapier-sharp glance before the man nodded, said, "Slichah" and "Shalom," and left.

Duncan watched him go out of the bar. "You didn't introduce me to your friend," he said, in mild rebuke. "You looked frightened to death. . . . I can't figure you people out. . . . Is it already a crime for one of you to drink with an Englishman?"

"What is it, Yora?" Carmela demanded that night. "Why can you not sleep? You toss and you moan. . . . Have patience, in a few weeks—"

He stopped in to see Nathan next morning and caught the man as he was about to leave his house. "Nathan, there is something I must discuss with you."

"I am in a hurry. I am expected at—"

Yora flushed. "You could not spare a minute?"

"I could not." Nathan sighed. "Well, you are here. Then, speak up."

"This matter of the power—" he began.

Nathan pursed his lips. "You are managing well. I have heard no complaints."

"You will hear none, I hope." He mopped his forehead with a dingy handkerchief. He let his breath out. "It has merely become too hard for me." He saw Nathan draw himself taut.

"All of us do things these days which are too hard for us." Nathan said. Then he added, in a gentler tone, "I did not expect this from you." His glanced sharpened. "Hey!" There was a tic in Yora's cheek. "Are you losing your nerve?" he asked. "Of whom are you afraid? Go. Do your job."

Of whom afraid? Of everyone. Of myself. My nerves are tatters and shreds. What frightened me? A word. An inflection . . . "Are your schools always open at night?" "Do you pray every night?" And a paint merchant saying "Shalom" in the King David bar. . . . Who is he? Nobody. No one at all. So he saw me with Duncan, having a drink. So he will gossip and say Levine is friendly with Britishers. . . . Levine has always been. It is his business to be. . . . Nathan is right. I am losing my nerve. God, give me control and patience. In a few weeks this will end. . . .

VIII

THE JUDGE ADJOURNED the case.

Few cases came into the District Court, few litigants or counselors at law. For the few that ventured, adjournment was the most sensible course. Why decide by Mandatory law—that mumbo-jumbo of British, Moslem and Mosaic codes? Wait, in another few weeks, if we live, we shall have our own laws.

Most of the judges had ceased coming down to the Russian Compound where the courts sat. The neighborhood was too dangerous, too close to the front line which was not a front in the war which was not a war. Henry Winkleman, however, made the trip every day. If one does not do what one always did, he asked himself, how is one to fill the days? Sit in the sun, recklessly, as my father does?

Frequently, he was called for conference at the Agency headquarters, and now and then he dropped into the offices where he once practiced law. His erstwhile colleagues were busy, drawing up wills. Everyone seemed to be drawing a will. Human life is transitory but property lasts. It is important to provide for the future of the strip of land, the necklace, the diamond ring, the silver plate.

He took his own will from the office strong-box, read it through; Maida and Janet, share, share alike, provision for Father, if he outlives me. Why should he not? Stray bullets have not studied mortality tables. Once, when the Judge had emerged from the Agency buildings at sunset, a bullet had spattered against the wall, two inches over his head. This one missed. Will the next?

He read his will through. It was meager, barren, no "dearly beloved," no child. Suppose, he considered, I left her a small legacy, a gift to her and her son and her little girls? I should like her to know that for what she once was to me, I am grateful still. No, there would be gossip. I should be gone, deaf in death, it could not touch me. But a married woman's good name— He folded the papers and put the will back in the safe.

Gordon Leake hung around in the corridor near the courtroom until Judge Winkleman emerged. He stepped up and touched the robed arm. "I want to speak to you," he said.

The Judge looked around cautiously. "I thought you had just left us," he said.

Gordon moistened his lips. "I don't wish to go."

Judge Winkleman smiled. "Like us, you have no choice."

"I have a choice." Gordon swallowed his spittle. "I can stay if I wish."

"Stay or go." The Judge shrugged. "It is no concern of mine."

Gordon looked down at the timeworn stones of the hall. "I thought you might help me," he said.

A policeman, pacing by, glanced at them, and it occurred to Judge Winkleman that it was not wise for them to be seen here together. "Nature calls," he said quickly. "If you should have a similar need, at the end of this corridor—"

After Gordon came in, Judge Winkleman turned the lock in the door and went to the basin, to make a long ritual of washing his hands. The Englishman started to speak, found his words would not come. He strolled to the window and stared through the dirty small panes.

He seems an emotional sort, the Judge thought. That's odd, yet not odd. Practiced calm—who should know better than I?—is not lack of feeling, merely its mask. Does he think to atone, in his person, for others' blood guilt? He remembered the man had a wife and a child. The woman had been in his house, at one of his sisters' teas, a pleasant person, yet cloddish, without a spark. Was she the reason? To leave means go home, go home means to her. Many a man has accepted the onus of being a hero, to escape an unsatisfactory wife. He smiled to himself. How do I, a bachelor, understand matters like these?

One must weigh. The man might be useful. If he's to be trusted. How could one know if he were? The burden of proof is on him. He will need to be watched. He'll have to have rations; eat like the rest. And what can he learn that we cannot find out ourselves? Suppose this is a trick? Will we ever again trust a Britisher?

He dried his long fingers meticulously on the frayed embroidered towel, brought from home. Let's at least hear him out. "Leake—" he began.

Gordon veered from the window. "I've been watching the rain. Have you ever seen such April rain?"

"Symbolic?" The Judge lifted his brows. "The deluge."

"And high winds, cold winds. They're dampening our fires." He pointed. "We're burning records, files. Planned chaos. You know that, do you not?"

"I know that," the Judge said. He did not think it needful to mention that he knew, of personal knowledge, that each sheet of paper had been secretly copied on microfilm, hidden away, so that this chaos, so flagrantly planned, would not come about.

"Well, sir—" Gordon started and stopped. He had said "sir," like a schoolboy, or an inferior. He flushed, was irked with himself for both the word and the thought.

"You wish to stay," the Judge prodded him.

He nodded.

"Does anyone know of your plans?"

He shook his head.

"Will you tell anyone?"

"I don't know, sir." The "sir" again. Get used to it, he warned himself. In a fortnight or so, they'll be the top dogs, but keep your dignity, if not as an Englishman, then as a man. "I'd planned," he began again, "as far as I'd made any plans, to drop out of sight. Let them assume I've been kidnaped or killed." He smiled crookedly. "It has happened before."

"With headlines all over the world," the Judge said.

"I'm not that important."

"You're a Briton in Palestine, sir." Judge Winkleman smiled.

At the "sir," Gordon lifted his head and smiled into the other man's smile. "You make it hard for me, Henry," he said. "We have been neighbors for many years. There's no reason to fence with me now. Look here, don't you think I'm aware of what this means? I've been thinking it over for weeks. Lose my passport, be cut off from my daughter and wife, be killed here, perhaps. I know all that, I know it quite well. But I also know that I cannot leave." His voice and his face seemed to the Judge profoundly sad. "You may think me presumptuous." His solemn gaze was clear and direct. "But there was another Englishman who believed in your cause and who served you well. I refer to Orde Wingate, sir."

In spite of himself the Judge had to smile. "Forgive me," he murmured. "All due deference. You are no Wingate, you know."

Gordon's voice deepened. "I wish I were. But whatever little I have to give—" He laid his hand on his chest. "I cannot explain it, but Jerusalem and I belong together, I feel."

The Judge stepped away from the window, paced slowly across the small room. He turned at the basin, leaned on it. "Where will you stay? Not in Rehavia. No matter how you feel, we would never chance your living there."

"I haven't been in my flat for some weeks. I have a room." The blush seeped back into his face. He lowered his eyes. "With a woman," he said.

"Oh!" The Judge's eyes glittered. "I thought so," he said.

"She's not the reason. She's j-j-just a—" he was stuttering again— "c-c-convenience."

"They are sometimes called that, I believe. A discreet word for the Holy City. Officially, we have never had whores."

"Please, I beg you, please." He waited until he had steadied his voice. "Millie can be useful as well. More than she knows. Matter of fact, knowing her made me think— She works in a consulate, of a neutral country."

"There are no neutrals," the Judge said coldly. "If you are not for us, you are against us. When you do as much for our enemies as you do for us."

"That's the point," Gordon said. "That's just what I thought. She hears all sorts of things. She can be useful to *us*." I've said *"us,"* he realized. I have cast the die.

"If I understand you correctly—" the Judge spoke with care, as though he were examining the facts in a case—"what you are proposing to me is that you wish to serve in our Intelligence and you ask me to make proper contacts for you." He marked Gordon's quick nod and went on, "You ask me to vouch for you, is that it?"

Gordon's head rose. "If you will."

"Can you convince the woman—" Judge Winkleman made a small hut of the tips of his fingers and studied them thoughtfully—"that you have abandoned country and wife for love of her?"

Gordon smiled faintly. "I can try."

"And if you fail?"

Gordon drew a deep breath. "Any man who has lived in Palestine all these years is not afraid to die, sir," he said.

Part Four: May

I

"History is a great beast," Judge Winkleman drawled. "It feeds upon innocents. It alone in this country now has sufficient to eat."

"Good enough to put into a book," Maida said. "But may I ask, what prompted that?"

"Today's newspaper." The languor in his voice was due to no sleep. "In the last five months, since the United Nations voted to partition Palestine, more than five thousand Arabs and Jews and Britons have died and more than six thousand have been wounded."

Janet got up from the table. "As long as this shelling goes on, I shan't leave the house. I do not hanker to be a statistic," she said as she walked to the windows. "Henry, we should have sandbags, at an exposed corner like this." And we should have an able-bodied man in the house, Henry's no better than an old woman in emergencies, she decided, as she walked back. "If you were to ask me," she said. "Making history is a nuisance."

Maida stacked the cereal bowls. "I feel so sorry for you," she said tartly. "I'm the one who goes out. I'm the one who walked Princess Mary. I'm the one who monitors a switchboard. You'd have a different outlook, if you did some war work."

"War?" Henry Winkleman pushed back his chair. "We are not at war. It is not permitted, you know. The United Nations, which is very safe in the United States, has forbidden us to have a war. Or for that matter to have a State. What we hear all night and day, what we see, what we look forward to, is an illusion, contrary to fact." He got up to go. "Father," he raised his voice, "I have said it often, I repeat it now, I wish you would not go out."

"But I must," the old man answered. "It is my duty."

The world had grown small. It had come down to a street, any street, *this street,* through which one ran, crouching, an animal scuttling, to the grocer on Keren Kayemeth and back, to assigned tasks for defense, home again, through thoroughfares blanketed with broken glass, twisted, ripped wires, and freshly chewed stone, a glimpse, on the run, of the hellish nightmare of a beautiful city, deliberately, systematically being blasted apart.

There were new neighbors whom one never met, because no one went visiting, a middle-aged couple who had been blown out of a Ben Yehuda Street flat and were delighted to have Gordon Leake's rooms; and an elderly widow, whose three sons were in the Army, who was glad to get Madame's room in return for cleaning Ephraim's flat.

The world came down to a house, any house, *this* house, whose windows were plastered with netting against flying glass, whose doorway and basement entrance were sandbagged, close to whose gateposts lay a nasty small heap of garbage, where flies buzzed around and cats prowled, scavenging.

In Hirsch's yard, a woodfire smouldered in an oven Teddy had made out of stones and old tins. The geranium hedge blazed scarlet and roses bloomed, pink, yellow, crimson. The bougainvillea was purple tapestry on the wall. The white jasmine's fragrance competed with woodsmoke and rotting garbage.

The world came down to part of a house, one floor, on which the Hirsch family lived, ate and tried to sleep.

Teddy was delighted with the change in the house. No one else was. The change had been made during a morning while he was in school. Four young men and two girls in khaki took over upstairs. They helped Edith carry mattresses down, set them in a row on the living room floor, next to the unwindowed wall, and move the sofa to the opposite side.

When Teddy came home and saw what had happened, he almost went out of his mind with sheer joy. He wanted to run up at once to make friends with the soldiers. His mother said no. He wanted to dash over to Asi and tell him. Again, his mother said no.

After sunset and before the new moon was up, sandbags, several rickety cots and a wireless, with batteries, were carried upstairs and a something heavy and long was hauled to the roof. The young men spent most of their time on the roof, using binoculars, and cleaning and oiling and coddling a gun which they never fired.

They slept upstairs, too, but went for their meals to the Ben Yehuda Street mess. Edith, whose defense assignment was there, frequently ran into them and they pretended as she did, that she had never seen them before.

They promised to keep the rooms clean though no one expected they would and in time the second story sent down an acrid smell. Edith fretted about that, asked for permission to go up twice a week and scrub the rooms thoroughly. She found them a primus, a *finjan,* and a pot to boil water in, to make themselves coffee or tea. Her dressing table was their kitchenette. They let water boil over and seared the varnish off. "I will fix it, I will paint it myself," one of the soldiers declared.

"No matter. I can bear even that."

"G'veret, you are so kind to us, we must not do you harm."

In return for her kindness, the G'veret requested they let her run upstairs now and then, and ask, "Any word from the Negev settlements?"

The two girls who worked the battery set were usually agreeable but when the night had been noisy and their sleep broken up, they said curtly, "Please, G'veret, do not pester us. If there is news we will tell you. We have work to do." One of the girls was fat, with an oily, pimpled skin. The other was little and lithe and pretty. Her shorts were barely longer than a loin cloth. She wore baby-blue socks, and coming off or going on duty, an Australian bush hat, with a chin strap.

The girl soldiers slept in Dinah's room and set up their radio there. Edith liked that. "This is my daughter's room," she told them. "Dinah Hirsch. Do you, by chance, know her at all?"

They said they did not and asked where she was.

"In the Negev. Kibbutz Gan Darom."

They looked impressed. "Do you hear from her?" the fat girl asked.

"No," Edith said. "Not a word, all of April, by mail or by messenger." One could say, she supposed, no news is good. But Dinah, too, might be chafing at the lack of contact. The wireless must surely have told them what is going on here. Yet if she had heard the wireless, the girl, in any case, knew her father was not one of those who had died in the convoy ambush at Sheikh Jarrah.

Whenever he heard their footsteps, Teddy dashed to the hall to say "Shalom" to the soldiers on their way through. Occasionally, they gave him a pat on the head or a friendly shove. Now and again, he slipped upstairs and was permitted to sit on the floor and hear the wireless. What was said was in code, which he could not understand, although he pretended he did, and he gave Asi detailed accounts of what he believed he had heard. He hinted to the soldiers that he was a boy who might be trusted to go up to the roof—his own personal roof—but the soldiers smiled and said a firm no.

The neighborhood knew that the soldiers and their gun were on Hirsch's roof but when anyone went down the street, he averted his eyes from the Doctor's house lest he chance to see what he had better not know was up there.

The Army had use of the bathroom upstairs. The family used the small washroom in the corridor next to Jacob's office. It did not matter that there was no shower or tub. Water itself had grown scarce.

At night one candle did little good in the large living room. Edith saved the drippings, put them away in a tin, braided thread into a wick and a week's drippings made a whole candle again. The Roman glass was gone, swaddled in blankets, put away in a trunk. The piano, stripped of its covering and photographs, stayed in its place and sometimes, on the quieter evenings, Edith would play, by candlelight. Her fingers were stiff from housework and the music they made did not satisfy her. But when she played, one or two of the soldiers would come down and stand in the doorway to listen to her.

In the evenings when his mother had to be out of the house, and the shelling was near and was bad, Teddy and Udi squatted under the piano, though Teddy insisted he wasn't afraid of the shells. In the day time he was too busy to be. He and Asi ran messages, drilled and marched with the Scouts and worked, secretly, on high explosives. Film, ordinary photographic film, Teddy had somewhere found out, was made of glycerine, and if nitro-glycerine is not glycerine what else is it? Why could not Theodor Hirsch and Asaph

Levine serve their people in this emergency? They stole pelvic x-ray films from Jacob's files, set them to boil over the wood fire in the garden, until Edith caught them and made them quit.

Occasionally, afternoons, other boys came into the street, and there would be a fight between gangs who called themselves "Etzel" and "Lechi," and made weapons out of tins filled with sand. Ida Goldstein made them stop that because there was always the danger one of the toddlers would get in the way and be hurt.

With such incessant excitement, it was not surprising that the boy slept fitfully. When Jacob was out very late, as he was frequently, Teddy sometimes crept to his mother's mattress, and each time a shell went off, asked, "Do you think that was where Abba is?"

Abba was on the Street of the Prophets, in the temporary hospital, not merely delivering babies and tearing his hair over miscarriages brought on by shock, but operating on casualties. He came home exhausted each night, stretched out on his mattress and, immediately, fell asleep.

During one night, a small shell dropped in the garden. It woke no one, for the very good reason that no one had been able to sleep, and when this crash came, it was merely another loud boomp against which one pressed one's hands to one's ears, and hunched into a tighter knot. Not until morning was the household aware that there was a hole in the lawn and a cypress was sheared as though lightning had struck. The concussion, however, had blown out the tubes of the wireless upstairs and shattered windows in the room where the girl soldiers slept. "How fortunate Dinah wasn't there," Edith said.

"Teddy will drag the top of the tree to the cellar," Jacob ordered. "If he isn't lazy you'll have enough wood for your fire."

II

Yora Levine stared through the shimmering white heat of khamseen, at the freshly dug hole in his neighbor's yard and began to tremble as though he were cold. Carmela came down the hall from the bathroom, started to dress and to tell him something. She was puzzled, she said, driving last night, she'd caught a glimpse of a man coming out of a house near Mamillah Road and she could have sworn it was Gordon Leake. "He has left, I know that, but Yora, he lived on this block so many years, I could not make a mistake. Yora," her voice rose, edgy and thinned with fatigue, "could it be he?"

He forced himself to turn away from the window. "All Englishmen, like rats, look alike," he growled.

"Yora." She clung to him. "All Jerusalem suffers as much as you do. When I look at you, I wonder, will my husband die of sheer anxiety?"

"One way is as good as another."

"I beg you, haviv, for my sake, take care."

He did not answer. This is nerves, only nerves, he kept telling himself. Too much strain, the breaking point's edge. If I had something—a cigarette, even—to quiet this gnawing torment.

He remembered. At the back of the dresser drawer, a small brown box lay—local cigarettes of a brand which in better times, he would have rejected with scorn—cached like jewels for a moment of ultimate need. His manner was furtive when he opened the drawer and took the battered box out. Three left. Only three. His hand shook as he cut one in half. He locked himself into the W.C. and smoked until the red ember scorched his fingers.

He came to the office late. That did not matter. His going downtown was a futile gesture. There was no longer a chief of department. There was no longer a schedule of work. There was no longer a department, in fact. This was the fortnight of hiatus.

He sat at his desk and buried his head in his hands.

The shell dropped in our street last night. My neighbors, my family might have been killed. Our street is close to a school, to a synagogue. Their shelling is accurate. It is as if they have a map.

They *have* a map. I gave them a map. I gave Duncan a list. That is as good as a map.

This is nonsense. I torture myself.

Duncan would not give them the list. I know him. We are old friends. . . . But he is an Englishman. No. Not even an Englishman would be so perfidious. . . . He groaned. . . . The shelling is so accurate. Every place, every district where— No. . . . The Arabs never needed my list. They lived with us here, for so long. They know where our schools and our hospitals are, what buildings are large enough to serve our needs. There is nothing my list could tell them that they do not already know.

There is. "Why are your schools always open at night?" "Do you pray every night? I thought it was just once a week." Those innocent questions. Innocent?

Yes, it was a risk. It was from the first moment a risk. We should have worked out some other plan. Which other plan? Who has thought about this as much as I have and have I been able to work out another plan? For a fortnight, they still are masters, they control light and power. I have no choice. Why was I, of all men, selected for this? . . . Because I was friendly with them. . . .

Today, I must give Duncan a new list. . . . And tomorrow the shells will fall. . . . It is not to be borne.

He opened the drawer of his desk. His revolver lay in that drawer. He took out the gun. This is so simple, he thought. Why did I not think of this before?

He raised the revolver to his right temple. This goes quickly. Pull the trigger. Finished. Carmela, farewell, he thought; my children, farewell. The cold steel felt soothing against his flesh.

I must write a note, he told himself. I must let them know why. He laid the gun down, drew a sheet of paper toward him and started to write. The steadiness of his hand surprised him. *"I find myself in an impossible position,"* he wrote. *"Too great a burden has been placed upon me. I can no longer endure the uncertainty and strain. A moment comes when a man can no longer live with his agony."* He signed his name.

He read the note over. His long forehead creased. It is not clear. These are hysterical times. So a man thinks. So he writes. . . . It is hysterical. Let it stand. It will do.

He picked up the revolver again. Sweat had broken out all over him. He felt it soaking his clothes. He thought, why did I waste the half cigarette? I need it now, this moment. He thought, could there, by chance, by good luck, be a cigarette hidden in my desk? He put down the revolver and began a frantic search through the desk drawers.

There was nothing. He slammed the drawer shut. His eyes fell again on the note. He read it through, again carefully, and then snatched it up and crumpled it in his fist.

Fool! We distrust when no man betrays. Our nerves make cowards of us. Go on with your job, to the end.

He saw the revolver again, and he shuddered. My raw nerves would have made a coward of me, he thought as he put it back into his desk. My nerves would have left Carmela a widow and my children fatherless.

His step was firm and his back straight, shoulders up, when he carried the new list to Duncan's office.

III

At Gan Darom, there was a tipsy half-moon. By its light, they were building a wall, a foot thick, a man's height, cement filled with gravel, inside the wire fence on all the four sides of the settlement. Sweat drained down the naked torsos of men and stained the girls' shirts. Khamseen was here, draining, depressing heat. The night was gritty with blowing sand. It filled nostrils, parched throats, stuck to the sweat. When anyone tired, he lay on the ground. Someone else ran to work in his place.

In the potato field, Dinah and Dan and a new young man named Joshua, were laying mines. They worked by only the light of the moon without speaking to one another or looking at anything except their work, all except Joshua. Now and then, he glanced furtively toward the Tegart Fortress on the ridge. These stone barracks, commanding every strategic rise in the landscape, he still regarded with awe. The Union Jack fluttered over this one by day; after dark, its lights burned steadily, vigilant eyes, watching each move the settlement made, seeing, but giving no hint of whether, after the fifteenth of May, these might be the eyes of an enemy or of a friend. It was past his understanding that the others never so much as gave the Fortress a glance. Is their not-looking also a fear? he asked himself.

Dan tried to reassure him, in his own abrupt way. "We have learned, expect nothing; if they are friends, good—if not, we take care ourselves."

Dan liked Joshua. He was more patient with him than he was with anyone else. Joshua had a fragile air which made one want to shield him, though the facts said his fiber was tough. A boy separated from parents, who had found his own means of survival in Auschwitz, had run the borders, risked the illegal journey by ship, is no tender flower. Yet even Dan seemed to feel that he was, treated him like a younger brother—in his way, courting the man, telling the others he hoped Joshua would like Gan Darom well enough to remain.

Joshua wasn't sure. The reason why became explicit to him after Dinah ripped her hand on a wire. She hadn't been aware that she had, and when she stood up, she mopped her face with the flat of her hand and smeared it with blood. Joshua made a startled noise and Dan kicked him and he stayed quiet until they were back inside the settlement's fence. Then he tried to explain. "When I saw the blood, I thought you had been shot."

"If I were?" she replied.

"Were you?" Dan asked.

"Nothing. A scratch on my hand." She rubbed the hand on her grimy shorts.

"Let me see." Dan picked her hand up. "Get it bandaged."

"It's nothing, I tell you."

"*Malesh.*" He shrugged. "If it becomes infected, what good are you? Can we lose the use of your hand?" He pushed her rudely. "Go, donkey, I order you."

This roughness was what distressed Joshua. In his parents' house in Prague, people had spoken gently. The proper relation of man to man, he had been taught, is love your neighbor, show consideration lest you inadvertently hurt someone's feelings. To many, it seemed more than strange that a sensitive soul like this one had survived these last years. They did not know and he did not tell them that to survive, he had amused his Nazi masters, played the piano for them, and therefore they had let him live, long enough to be saved. He did not speak about that to anyone here, except to Ketti, who like himself had the brand, and she had smiled enigmatically, said, "It is good you decided to be a farmer, like me," and asked, "Will you play again?"

"In time. In time, I will give our comrades pleasure."

Ketti had smiled again, strangely, "I shall be surprised if you do."

His fingers were excellent for delicate work, like handling explosives, laying mines, making electrical contacts, repairs. He worked hard and was eager to please. They like me, he told himself. Dan has told me he hopes I will stay. Yet what sort of people are these?

They are hard, rough and crude. Perhaps it is the times. This isn't the hour for good manners. Afterwards, when we are a State . . .

Lights were on in the children's house, hidden by sacking spanned over the windows. The children were up; the playroom was stifling, but though it was long past bedtime, the babies were being remarkably good. The older ones sat erect on their nursery chairs, clutching small bundles of clothing and toys, not making a sound. They knew they were going somewhere, exactly where no one had said, nor, the eldest being no more than three, would they have understood why. The youngest, who was still being fed at the breast, lay in his white crib, his belly sated, gray eyes open and bright, waving his arms, cooing at personal delights.

The children were leaving tonight and Chaya, the mother of the nursling, was going with them. Gittel, the nurse, should have been the one to go but she could not be spared. Gittel was folding the diapers, packing them into a cardboard box when she saw Dinah across the room's width and she dropped her work. "Wash your face," she whispered. "The children may be frightened of you."

She went with Dinah into the shining, tiled nursery bathroom, glanced at the torn hand. "It's nothing," she said. "We can't spare a bandage for such a small thing." Gittel looked tired, as everyone did, drawn and gaunt, much older than her twenty-five years. She leaned against the washbasin and said quietly, "We shall be lonely after tonight." An eloquent glance passed between Dinah and her. One was sparing, more parsimonious than ever, with words in these days. Speech took one's strength, not merely of throat, but of heart. Who does not know what it means when you send the children away?

They went back to the playroom together. Something tiny and soft touched Dinah's leg. She bent down to Shoshanna, the daughter of Zvi, who had been killed in the raid months before. The tot was smiling at her, mouth smiling, but sleepy eyes grave.

"Kiss me good night, Dinah-minah," the little girl said. "I'm going for a ride. I'll be back tomorrow, Dinah."

"*Habubala.*" She got up quickly, wheeled around and stared at the brown sacking over the windows.

Dan came in. He said, "Ready!" Judith, Shoshanna's mother, darted over, picked up her child and pressed the little girl against her sweat-stained blouse. Gittel took the child from her, went first, holding Shoshanna's hand. Behind her was Amos, with a big boy's haircut, cropped to the scalp, waddling with what he thought was a mannish stride. His father, Reuven, stripped to the waist, tried to take his free hand. "No, Abba," Amos said, "I am a big boy. I walk alone." Gila, his mother, said, "Amos, please, be a good boy."

"I am a good boy," Amos said.

One of the two toddlers, who, heavy-lidded with sleep, dragged his feet, was Gershon's child. Gershon could not be there, but Hanna, his wife, held the boy's hand, and the little boy held the hand of a small girl, whose parents clung to each other and not to her. Chaya and her nursing baby and her husband, Shmuel, were at the end. It was hardest for Shmuel, they all understood. He was losing the comfort of both wife and child. Dan brought up the end of the line with the valise of diapers and the box of food.

The little procession picked its way carefully over hummocks of earth freshly dug for trenches inside the wall. When a child stumbled, one of his parents hurried to pick him up, for the chance to cuddle the warm flesh once more. From the ditches, from tents and pre-fabs, men and women streamed down to the gates.

A bus stood there, without lights. From it a rustling came, like a purring brook. The children of all the near-by kibbutzim were leaving tonight, in this bus, over roads that were possibly mined, away from sure peril, through possible danger, in the hope that they would be safe.

The mothers picked up their children, held them, one embrace more; the fathers lifted them into the bus. Dan carried Shoshanna in. One of the children, suddenly terrified, began to cry. They heard a voice in the bus, asking sleepily, "Why is that baby making a fuss?"

Chaya handed her infant to someone inside, turned and kissed her husband, whispered, "Shalom, l'hitra'ot," and picked up the crying child—it was Hanna's boy. "Sheket, habub. Chaya will take care of you."

The driver stepped on the starter. The motor roared. The bus moved. The huddle near the gates surged forward but no one made a sound. They stood watching the bus until its dark hulk merged with the plain. They heard a voice—it was the new immigrant, Joshua, the pianist, out of Prague, "So it was," he was saying, "when our own parents sent us away."

"Fool!" That was Avrum, answering him. "It is not the same. They go to our own. They will come back."

"I do not feel well," Gittel said. Her hand was at her eyes. "It must be khamseen."

Gershon was at the wireless set when his wife came in to him. He slipped his ear-phones back.

"The bus has gone," she said.

His hands dropped. "I did not say shalom to our child. He was afraid?"

"He was afraid," Hanna said.

He touched the back of her hand. "So am I," he said.

The box was buzzing importunately. He put his ear-phones on again. She waited until he was ready to speak with her again. "Jerusalem," he said briefly. "The Iraquis have cut their water pipe line at Ras-El-Ein. I would rather you did not tell Dinah, she worries too much." He frowned. "Somehow they will manage," he said. "Their help will come. And ours. It must be so."

IV

AL BRODY OF New York who three weeks ago had thought of himself as the person who had come to deliver that help, strolled along Hayarkon Street convinced he had been there before. Familiar, this waterfront was, Manhattan Beach on a Sunday, perhaps. All Tel Aviv struck him as somewhere he had lived all his life, upper Broadway in Washington Heights or West Fordham Road in the Bronx. That was okay. He liked the look of the place; he liked the bumptiousness of the crowds in the streets. But what bothered him as he walked down Hayarkon in his old U.S. Air Force uniform (markings removed) was that he wasn't sure the city liked him.

It gave no sign of affection. It did not even seem to know he was there. He knew from personal experience and from what he had heard and had read how a populace was expected to act when its liberators arrived. Pretty girls flung their arms around soldiers' necks, hung them with garlands, and said, "Take my lily white body, it's the least I can give." Not here. Hell, no, brother. The babes don't know you're alive and they do not care. When they give you the eye, it's as though they wonder why you're taking up valuable space. . . . See here, sister, he growled in his mind to a girl in khaki who swung along near the curb, don't you know I've come here at great personal risk, to give you a country and flag?

She doesn't know and she doesn't care, he answered himself gloomily. That's how they are. Stuck on themselves. Those bosomy babes with the sparkling eyes whom you saw in the streets looked so damned efficient. Too damned efficient, if you asked Albert Brody, in their slacks or their shorts. With their Stens. They carried those clumsy, homemade shooting irons as though they knew what Sten guns were for. And that isn't nice, he assured himself, a young girl toting a gun. Take a WAC or a WAVE, did she shoot? She did not. She knew her place. A girl in the U.S. Army, Navy, or even Marines was there to look snappy, answer the phone, type letters, do paper work, raise morale. Killing is not a trade for a girl. Put that on the record and underlined.

Okay, these babes have lousy legs. Chunky. Give me Paula's gams any time, even if she doesn't have brains and doesn't know how to shoot. (Damn good thing she doesn't know how to shoot!) And they carried themselves as though they were God knows who. Chesty. Stuck out. Stuck up. Don't bother me, Buster, I'm special. When God invented me, he broke the mold. Sabra. Cream of the crop! Okay, if that's how it is, that's how it is, but just give me a personal chance to find out what makes them tick. Don't try to tell *me* there's a healthy babe who doesn't care about sex.

The guys? Well, what do you make of that character, chewing the chin strap of a tricky bush hat, a blue and white kerchief around his throat, wearing sneakers and a big knife? Palmach! Look, kid, you're a big boy, cut out the cowboys-and-Indians stuff.

The older folks? Well, all right, they're like Pop and Mom but how are you going to converse with them? What language, I ask? I'm an American. I spik Eenglish, only. Oh, maybe a few words of German, of Yiddish and high school French. No Ivrith, very sorry, but that's how it is. Nope, not even Bar Mitzvah Hebrew. Don't ask me why. My Old Man didn't believe in that stuff.

And no Russian, no Polish, Bulgarian, Hungarian, Czech, Roumanian, Greek or Arabic. Babel, that's what they got. Babel and Ivrith. Why didn't that guy in New York tell me I'd have to speak Ivrith to get along here? Maybe I'd have thought about it twice. Maybe.

Also, the food was no good. Greasy, overcooked, insipid. Worse even than Mom's. And the local cigarettes cost a fortune and tasted like straw.

Boy, did I get into a deal!

The country, physically, hadn't impressed him—what he had seen of it, that is. He had arrived at an airfield and every airfield looks so much like the rest you can cure insomnia if you count them like sheep. From barracks to Tel Aviv, a bad macadam road, lined with small factories and jerry-built houses and crawling with beaten-up buses and trucks, the old Boston Post Road near Bridgeport, by God! Give me Old Jerusalem, beautiful Galilee, that Lake Kin-

nereth you sing songs about. Give me the Middle East flavor, give me
the biblical touch. Inspire me, kids; come on, give me fervor. That's
what I want.

The answer was that he was lonely and therefore he griped. No
buddies, no pals. Three weeks in a country and no social life. The
Micks who had flown over with him hadn't panned out for him.
A guy that's just in it for dough, he decided, isn't a teammate in
a deal like this. The two who had come on his plane were already
disgusted, the same business of not knowing the language and no
dice with the girls. "The trouble with all the babes around here,"
one of them said, "is you have to disarm 'em before you can lay
'em. They use hand grenades for falsies out here."

However he personally felt, Al had to take the other side of
the fence, try to explain and apologize, and he wasn't sure why he
did that. "They're human, too, why not?—but these babes just
have other things on their minds. A cause, bud, a war. Come back
some time when they aren't so busy making a State."

But what he personally needed was someone to whom he could
talk, someone to tell him the score.

Well, there was Saul. Saul was an interesting type but he was
far from sure he liked Saul. Saul had been on the Czech plane
which had flown them in, and Saul, in a way, was the boss. Saul
had a nutcracker face and perpetually angry eyes. He had owned
up to twenty-one years and not more than the equivalent of fifth
grade in school, but he left you no doubt he was the smartest guy
in the world. What he knew was what any man knows who has
won his Master's degree in concentration camps, guerrilla armies,
and on illegal ships—how to be ruthless, resourceful, and smart.
To the American flyers, Saul had been civil, but no more than that.

He hated Americans, he had confided to Al on the plane. "Coca-
Cola and chewngum and chazz, what else do they know?" He
spoke English, as he spoke every language, with a coarse guttural.
"They ride on subways so they think they are God knows what."

You never get anywhere when you argue with wise guys like
that. Nevertheless Al had tried. "What the hell do you know
about Americans anyway?" he had answered back.

Saul's smile had been nasty. "I saw them in Rome. I saw them
everywhere. I am never wrong."

Look at me, he wanted to say. I'm an American. I didn't have to be here. I'm not in this for the dough, believe me, I'm not. I didn't ask you to pay me a thousand a month. I'd have come for peanuts, I told the guy that. I had it tough in the last war, as tough as you, pal. The Nazis threw the book at me, too, and if I hadn't had luck, just like you, I wouldn't be here. I gave up a good bed in New York, and college and plenty to eat. I'm risking my life to give you a country and flag. But all he ever said to Saul was, "Give us a chance, bud, to show what we've got."

Yeah, give us action, if you can't give us polite time of day. Not that screwy deal you gave me on the Bethlehem Road. Look, bud, I pilot aircraft. That's my business. You put a B-17 pilot into a Piper Cub and tell him to get a hot ball over the plate.

"The trouble with an American," Saul had said, "is he thinks because he is an American, he knows how to do everything better than everyone else."

Okay, Buster, okay, but don't take it out on me for that dud. Don't keep me sitting in a crummy barracks that isn't a barracks, a shack with mattresses tossed on the floor. That drives a guy nuts. Give us some officers who've seen the inside of a plane and speak a language you can understand. And give us planes. Not Austers. Not Piper Cubs. You won't get nowhere with those. Look, maybe you don't know how an Air Force should be run but I have some idea. One good medium bomber and we'll have Cairo wiped off the map.

"Wait," Saul had said. "When we get planes. When we get fuel . . . You think it is easy for a poor country to run a war? Why did you let your America embargo matériel? Why don't you Americans send us what we need? We are poor, you are rich."

Rich! Let us laugh. Al Brody's Old Man scratches a living, driving a hack. "You foreigners think all Americans are millionaires," he had told Saul.

"Foreigners!" Saul had bucked at the word and made that grimace he used for a smile. "Who is the foreigner? You or me?"

"We'll talk that over some day, us two," he had replied. "Over a drink." That was another thing he needed someone to make clear to him, what he, a Jew, born and raised in the United States, meant to himself and to anyone else around here, where he fitted in if he wasn't a Zionist or a refugee.

They used Saul for a kind of nursemaid, Haganah liaison, if you wished to be posh, for the imported airmen, and Saul dropped around at the camp, to try in his sarcastic way to keep them pepped up. Saul had fixed him up for the leave, and said, meet him for a drink, at the Park Hotel, Tel Aviv. Leave-town, Tel Aviv. When you go into wars you meet a lot of funny leave-towns. And funny wars. Is this a war? If you ask Brody, it looks like tiddlywinks.

The sun and the afternoon were unreasonably hot. Khamseen, they called it. A draining, dusty heat, which set your nerves on edge. His throat and nostrils felt like an old blotter. His hair, usually curly and crisp, lay flat on his skull, the oils all sucked out by dry heat. Even the weather to annoy you, by God. Not even a breeze from the sea, to waft you the wholesome aromas of hamburgers, pop corn, hot dogs and beer.

Gat Rimmon. Kaete Dan. Call those hotels? They'd be second-class bathhouses at Long Branch, N.J. . . . Take it easy, Brody, don't be such a louse.

Okay, here's the Park. At least it *looks* modern. There's a bar and it's cool.

Saul was waiting on a bar stool. He and the bartender were the only ones in the bar lounge. "Shalom," Saul said. He did not get up but he put out his hand.

Al answered "Shalom" self-consciously. This "Shalom" which everyone said, the bus drivers, cabdrivers, waiters, whomever you met, was, if you asked him a ridiculous way to say both "hello" and "goodbye." Shalom . . . Peace . . . Talking themselves into peace, when there was no peace.

Saul had a glass before him. "What do you drink?" he inquired.

Al thought he'd like a cold beer, but he glanced at Saul's glass. "Lemon squash," Saul explained.

Al made a face. "Nix. Got beer? Any beer? Local beer?"

The bartender leaned over the wood. "Take his advice," he said in adequate English. "In khamseen, no alcohol."

"Okay, I'm the sucker. Let me have lemon squash." He took a sip. This sickening sweet sour, roiled up with charged water, was no beverage. It was citrate of magnesia and he didn't need that. He pushed back the glass. "Give me a Coke."

Saul flared. "You see! Whatever American is, is the only thing any good."

"Listen, bud, one more crack like that out of you and I'll think I picked the wrong enemy. I came here to fight Arabs, not you."

He saw the bartender wink at Saul, guessed they were ganging up, and he half rose to land the first blow. Abruptly, he sat down again. Take it easy, he warned himself. These are my own.

Saul was grinning at him. That also got his back up. "You came here to learn," Saul was saying. "You have much to learn. Lesson one, in khamseen, drink lemon squash."

He didn't reply nor touch his drink, but sat on the stool, staring at nothing, with a sour taste in his mouth and bitterness in his heart. To come this far, with his purpose and sentiment, and only find arrogance and dislike. I'll go back, he told himself. I'll tell everyone, write in the papers, scream everywhere, they don't want us, they hate us. They make you a foreigner here, treat you like dirt, because they came first. "Listen, bud," he said painfully to Saul, "what makes you, not just you, everyone, so goddam unfriendly to us?"

Saul winked at the bartender and shrugged. "I invite a man to drink at the Park. Is that unfriendly to him? The bartender, the management, they should be insulted, perhaps, that you consider this an unfriendly act."

Whatever you say, you're always wrong. He scuffed his shoes on the stool. "Cut out the horsing around," he muttered. "Give me some work. That's all I ask, what I came for, to give you a flag and a country. . . ."

He saw the bartender and Saul start toward him and he ducked off the stool. He heard Saul ask, coldly, "What do you think we have been doing here ourselves all this time?"

He stalked out and stood on the hotel's stone terrace, feeling the sun sear his flesh. He thought, wretchedly, I can't call one single shot, whatever I say, what I do turns out to be wrong. Hell with it, hell with it all. Let them get me transportation and call the deal off. . . . And if they don't give it? . . . Golly, I'm stuck. . . . Why, these bastards might bump me off. . . .

He heard his name called and did not turn around, but waited till Saul came up to him.

"Leave me alone," he muttered. "Let's call it quits."

"Quits?" Either the guy did not understand or didn't want to. "We did not talk," Saul said.

"We talked, brother, plenty, too much."

"We had something important to talk," Saul said. "There is a big job you will do for us."

His attention sharpened, but he still would not let Saul catch on that this mattered to him. "Who, me?" he said. "I'm the American dope. Give me the carfare and let me go home."

"You will stay," Saul was saying. "You will help us get a country and flag. You have come. You are with us. And perhaps, when you have seen how much we need you, you will stay after that."

"Who, me?" he said again. "Just let me finish this show and get the hell back to where I belong."

V

In Jerusalem there was also khamseen, but no lemon squash, only a pailful of water, per person, per day for drinking, for bathing, for washing the clothes, spongehing the floors, watering the garden and flushing the W.C., not a glassful to spare for a refreshing drink. It was hard to keep in mind not to waste, to plan in advance what uses to make of each day's ration: today, we wash out a change of underwear for each of us in the water with which we have already sponge-bathed and scrubbed our teeth, and, tomorrow, we use our bath water to spongeh the floor, and no matter how black the pail's leavings are, don't throw it away. There's also the garden and the W.C.

The soap-scummed residue of personal, dish, clothes and floor ablutions stood in a bucket alongside each W.C., with a tin for a dipper, less than a pailful of waste water for a family for each day. In the morning, the Hirsch family, went, consecutively, in turn, to the little washroom so that a single bowl rinsing might do for all three.

A foul stench pervaded everyone's house. The housewives were ashamed. Civilization is utterly lost when you can no longer pull the "Best Niagara's" chain.

Only the children were pleased, the older children, that is. They were no longer nagged about taking showers or even washing their hands, but the babies, with just one sponging a day and no wet sheets hung in the bedroom to moisten the air of khamseen, fretted, got sick.

A cart with a tank and a hose came up every street once a day. The youngsters screamed, *"Myim, myim,"* and the women ran out with pails, jerry cans, the baby's bathtub, the dishpan.

When Teddy was home, he helped his mother carry her water pails in or the soldiers assisted, if one of them chanced to be free.

When the water carts came, one moved fast, for bullets whooshed through the trees while one stood at the curb and there was always the chance a shell might drop on the queue. It had happened, and more than once, in many parts of the town. Stand in the doorway, until the cart came, then run, stagger back with the pails, the weight of the water all but ripping one's arms from their sockets.

On the first day when the cart came around Edith held her water ration books up to be punched and saw Professor Gross. He still wore his stiff-collared white shirt and little bow tie, and his salt and pepper goatee was, as always, carefully trimmed. He stood beside the water cart, handling the long water hose clumsily, and he felt he had to explain. "Even if there were students, even if we could go up the Hill, this is not the time to teach philosophy." His eyes twinkled behind his gold-rimmed eyeglasses. "All my life, I have wished to do something—" he fumbled for his word, brought out, "practical," and then turned pink, as though being thought brave was an embarrassment. He clamped off the hose, lifted it carefully from Edith's pail, letting the last of her quota drip in, and turned to punch Carmela Levine's ration book.

While Edith was hefting her pails, she heard him ask Yora's wife, "Would you see, would you ask, if someone will help my wife carry our water pails in? She is not very strong," and it struck her that this was a penance of his and pitiful, that he needed to humble himself because his only son had not returned. It was on the tip of her tongue to say, "I'll help her after I bring mine in," but she found herself hardening as she went up her path. "Lillie does not deserve it," she said to herself.

Until the fourteenth of May, no one in Jerusalem was sure of what would occur. While the last of the sand grains were running out of the glass, a vote was being taken at Lake Success, on, of all things, the old, long-discarded, discredited Trusteeship plan for the future of the Holy Land. Statesmen were talking furiously, pontifically into a whirlwind. In the tired, lonely, broken city in the Judean hills, there was speculation and dread. Lorries and jeeps, with new tires, roared through the streets and Tommies laughed, waving goodbye. The Mandatory was departing and from the Old City the Arab Legion was hurling shells.

An Englishman, David Courtney by by-line, wrote in his *Column One* of the *Palestine Post,* one morning of that ominous May, *"If the Powers have not the will to raise their shield before the Holy City, there is nothing left for the people but to fight for their lives in the streets.*

"In the omissions of the Powers who have the means to end this defilement of body and place, is the real and unforgivable sacrilege. Until that is acknowledged what is left for a man in the streets of Jerusalem but to pick up his gun and go forth in anger?"

Pick up his gun! Ephraim Malkoff, the poet, trudging off to stand guard at an empty airfield with his Sten, his newspaper or book. Nathan, with the one arm, crawling through warrens of wrecked shops and dwellings, pleading, "Children, don't shoot." Benjamin, the Egged bus driver, deciding how handfuls of men and girls should be moved here and there, hunched at a wheel, night after night, on roads honeycombed with lethal mines; the soldiers on Jacob Hirsch's roof, nursing an unfired machine gun, husbanding its cartridges against the hour when the enemy might storm this ridge; Yora Levine, racked with the pain of his ulcer, doling out rifles each night in the schoolhouse basement, hearing the ping of shrapnel against its stone walls; Jacob racing down King George and the Street of the Prophets, delivering babies by carbide lantern light, in a room rocked by shells, doing surgery, too, on ghastly wounds of chest and of head, amputating arms and legs, refreshing himself with cold noodles and tea, and a third of a cigarette; Carmela Levine, driving through winding alleys and stony hill roads, shuddering against the spatter of lead on the windshield and sides of the car and wondering whether her children were safe; Professor Gross, on the water cart in the shell-riddled streets; Edith handing out bread at an Army mess, keeping eyes lowered, not to see the disappointment of hungry soldiers who received only one slice.

Bakers running at night to their ovens, shopkeepers racing at dawn for fresh bread, housewives debating each morning whether to risk the trip to the store or let the children go hungry today. (Bread or a mother, which do they need more?) Printers running to get the newspaper out, doctors and nurses racing to hospitals and cellar shelters. Running. Everyone running to cheat the guns and the shells, barking and crashing from behind the gray walls where Glubb's Arab Legion waited as conquerors, poised to reduce all Jerusalem to its will.

Pick up his gun and go forth in anger! Rather in great weariness. It was a singular tiredness. It stemmed as much from loneliness as from lack of vitality.

VI

EARLY ON THE morning of the fourteenth, the pretty girl soldier came downstairs to say, "Come up, if you like. Sir Alan is starting to speak."

Jacob spat. "Who wishes to hear—" he began. Edith cut him short with a look and he reddened as if caught in conduct unbecoming an intelligent man. Edith rose and took Teddy's hand. "Come," she said. "The end of an era. That we must not miss."

The correct English voice, flowing out of the wireless in Dinah's bedroom, sounded rueful and sad, and when it ceased, they found themselves holding their breaths. "Come up to the roof," a soldier said. He led the way up.

They passed the binoculars. Here was history in a tiny circle of glass. It went rapidly. The Union Jack dropped from the flagstaff on Government House, a black Rolls Royce moved away. A flag rose, the white-grounded Red Cross, unfurled in the hushed, sunny air, no nation's flag, merely the symbol of prayer for mercy.

An extraordinary stillness seemed to rest on the shimmering rose-colored roofs, the city holding its breath. The skirl of a bagpipe came, faint, eerie, like a child's wail in the night. Then, in the hills, a machine gun barked. "Finished," Jacob rubbed his hands. "Done." Yet no one moved until they saw the planes rise, three small white birds, circling briefly, until they were lost in the blue firmament.

People were in and out of the Doctor's house all day long, because the wireless was there. They excused themselves, this has not happened in two thousand years; the enemy stands behind the Old City gates; we must know whether we fight as a Nation or as a rabble, defending our lives.

Out of habit, Judge Winkleman walked down to the Russian Compound though he knew court would not be in session today. He saw new policemen in the same blue with silver caps as the old.

They said "Shalom" to him. He said "Shalom" to them. He watched them parting the barbed wire of a Security Zone, diffidently, as though they were not quite sure that they dared, and he stood for a moment or two, regarding the litter within the barbed wire: scraps of paper, rubber and cloth, empty cartridges, brown cartridge belts, an old shoe, a few playing cards, a cracked looking glass, bits of rope. Rubbish, he thought, our legacy.

He walked back. His sister Janet served him a slice of bread and his tea. Then he and his sisters and father dressed, as for Shabbat, and strolled up the street to the Doctor's house. Teddy was home alone. They asked if he'd mind if they stayed. He said no, but after Maida Winkleman asked, "Which one of you was it who started the fight in the road yesterday?" he edged out of the room and sat on the stairs. Edith came back from duty, and shortly after, Max Goldstein was led in by his wife. Ten minutes later Ida appeared with the three little ones, scrubbed up and dressed in freshly ironed clothes. Teddy ran across the street to fetch Asi and magnanimously told Asi's sisters they could come too. Asi's parents were out, off on duty somewhere. The widow who lived in Ephraim's flat knocked on the front door and came in. Word spread that the Doctor's house had a battery wireless, and people streamed in from the house on the corner as well; Benjamin's wife, the Pole who taught school and his wife, the two Yecke sisters and their old mother, Herr Prinz, with his upholstered wife and his mother-in-law. When Herr Prinz arrived, Teddy and Asi moved into the hall, whispered together and scowled portentously. Those who could find places sat. The rest stood, in a silence through which one could hear the incessant chatter of guns. Udi crept out of the square of warm sunlight where he usually toasted his ribs, loped through the lower floor, sniffing at everyone's shoes until he found Edith and pushed his snout up to ask, What is this?

The girl soldiers moved the radio to the head of the staircase and turned the loudspeaker up. A man was talking, describing a dais set up in a Tel Aviv museum room, no splendid trappings, a modest, functional room, with a microphone and a picture of Theodor Herzl behind the speaker's stand. He was giving the names of the people assembled. His voice was excited and awed.

The smallest children sat on the stairs. Teddy and Asi bustled past them importantly, to the wireless and ran relays to tell the living room what was being said.

Jacob arrived around half-past three. Ten minutes later, Carmela Levine came hunting her children. She was full of news. "We have moved into the Generali Building without firing a shot. We have moved into all of the Zones." Carmela said everyone down in town kept asking everyone else had it happened yet? And wondering whether it would. There were rumors there might be a change. Marshall, the American Secretary of State, had sent word to delay. It had provoked a confusion; no one was sure of what to do next. The town was hectic, she said, and a strange sensation to walk through the Security Zones. But frightening, at the first look, to see the new police, with the old British caps. A store of them had been found in a basement in the Russian Compound. Why buy new? There's enough to spend money on. "Their ghosts will be with us for a long time," she said.

Five minutes before four o'clock, the wireless girl cried, "Here it comes!" They stood up, even old Isaac Winkleman who could not hear and Max Goldstein who could not see, and pressed forward to mass in the hall at the foot of the steps.

Carmela craned her neck for her children, made them duck under legs and come to her side. "Pay attention, yeladim," she whispered. "This you must remember as long as you live." Ida Goldstein edged through the crowd to Edith's side.

"*Kol od baleivav, pnee ma.*" In that museum room in Tel Aviv, they were singing the anthem of hope. This singing in this freighted hour was making a new song of it, a chant of fulfillment, a national anthem.

Behind the wireless the soldiers stood on the landing, grimy knees rigid, heads up. Shouldn't they be at attention? Salute? Jacob chuckled to himself. "Such an army! We haven't even a salute."

"*Nefesh, Yehudi, homiyah . . .*"

Jacob took up the song. The children joined. Max Goldstein hummed the melody. Edith and Benjamin's wife and Carmela Levine sang the words, in clear sopranos.

The song ended. A man started to speak. "*The land of Israel was the birthplace of the Jewish people.*"

"Ben-Gurion!" Judge Winkleman cried.

"Listen, everyone. Ben-Gurion!" Jacob echoed him.

There was a brief rustle and crackle as they moved forward and closer together.

"*Here their spiritual, religious and national identity was formed. Here they achieved independence and created a culture of national and universal significance. Here they wrote and gave the Bible to the world. . . .*

"*Exiled from Palestine, the Jewish people remained faithful to it in all the countries of their dispersion, never ceasing to pray and hope for their return and the restoration of the national freedom. . . .*"

Edith raised her eyes, up the stairwell, toward the voice. Warmth coursed through her blood. She felt her throat, her heart swelling as if they would burst. Simple words! Clear, understandable. Some day they would be literature, taught, memorized from school books. Words written by men, men in dark business suits, white shirts, printed neckties, not by prophets or sages or seers. "Mother, tell me," some child in some future would ask, "what sort of people were those who wrote our Declaration of Independence?" "Well, Ben-Gurion was short and squat, with a face like a rosy apple, they say, and a ruffle of snow-white hair around a bald spot, and Shertok was handsome and dark with a black mustache and a charming smile. They were people like us, ordinary men." She let her eyes wander, circling the faces. She saw old Isaac Winkleman's joyous smile.

"*Accordingly we, the members of the National Council, representing the Jewish people in Palestine, and the Zionist movement of the world, met together in solemn assembly by virtue of the natural and historic right of the Jewish people and of the resolution of the General Assembly of the United Nations . . .*

"*Hereby proclaim the establishment of a Jewish State in Palestine, to be called Israel. . . .*"

Israel! Jacob exulted silently. My name. Jacob means Israel. "Mazel tov!" he cried. "Mazel tov! Mazel tov!"

"Mazel tov," Teddy and Asi cried after him.

Ida Goldstein wheeled blindly and buried her head in Edith's shoulder.

"*We hereby declare that as from the termination of the mandate at midnight this night of the fourteenth to the fifteenth of May, 1948, and until the setting up of duly elected bodies of State . . .*"

Teddy gasped, squirmed through the crowd and fled toward the passage which led to his father's office.

"*The State of Israel will promote the development of the country for the benefit of all its inhabitants; will be based on precepts of liberty, justice and peace, taught by the Hebrew prophets; will uphold the full, social and political equality of all its citizens without distinction of race, creed or sex, will guarantee full religious freedom of conscience, worship, education and culture; will safeguard the sanctity and inviolability of shrines and holy places of all religions; and will dedicate itself to the principles of the Charter of the United Nations. . . ."*

The sun, dropping while Ben-Gurion spoke in Tel Aviv, struck the west window upstairs, streamed through, cutting diagonally and gilding the heads massed below. Judge Winkleman noticed it and found himself wondering, Is this an omen, does this act automatically make us all saints?

"*With trust in Almighty God, we set our hands to this declaration at this session of the Provisional State Council in the city of Tel Aviv, this Sabbath Eve, the fifth day of Iyar, the fourteenth of May, 1948. . . ."*

The wireless box squawked once or twice and was still. So was the house. No one uttered a word. No one knew what to say or to do.

The soldiers picked up the radio box, yelled down, "Shalom! Shalom!" moved off the landing back to their rooms. The women on the fringe of the huddle began to stir. There was movement, shifting, preparation, but no words yet. Jacob made his way to his wife, began gently to thrust her and Ida Goldstein apart, thought better of it and embraced both of them. He kissed Edith's cheek, tasted salt. "With joy and with terror," he said solemnly. "I embrace both of you on this day."

"I am happy!" A husky voice rose, that of the Pole with the concentration camp brand on his arm. "For the first time in my life I know happiness." His wife pushed through to him and took him in her arms. The blond sisters and their mother slid toward the couple. Herr Prinz and his wife and her mother elbowed through. That group stood a little off from the others as if, to them, what had happened today was a special thing.

Herr Prinz shook his head ponderously. "But I'm afraid. They will not permit—"

"Who is they?" Jacob turned to inquire.

"They, the Great Powers." Herr Prinz grew red. "The United States. Britain . . . They have not given permission. We go against them. I do not know if we have the right."

"Yecke!" Benjamin's wife hissed at him.

Herr Prinz's neck swelled, his face purpled. "You will see. I have judged it correctly. Ben-Gurion makes himself a hero, with our blood and our lives."

"Teddy," Asi screamed. "Teddy, where are you? Come, listen to him. . . ."

Everyone started to talk at once, shouting answers at Prinz. No one could make out a word of what anyone said. Jacob clapped his hands. No one minded him. He raised the piano lid, banged an octave of keys. It brought a gradual hush. "Henry, you are the eloquent one," Jacob said. "Henry, speak."

Henry Winkleman wormed his way into the center of the room, while the others moved off, as if to make a dais for him. His glance circled the room. A smile spread on his hollow face.

"Shalom, Maccabees!" he began. "A new *Hanukah!*" He smiled again, pleased with himself. "The grandchildren of these little ones in this house will celebrate this historic event. They will read of the people who rose from the ashes of death camps and began to go home, the indestructible people who stole across borders, who, in leaking, unseaworthy ships, defied Britain's naval might, the people beaten and starved, bludgeoned with hoses and clubs, tortured, degraded, brutalized." His voice rose. He saw by the shine in Carmela's eyes, by the parted lips of his sisters, that he was an orator, perhaps for the first and last time in his life, finding and saying the words which the others had in their hearts. His chest swelled. "The greatest Powers, those whom they trusted with the Mandate of Homeland, with the cause of Democracy, abandoned them. They stood with their backs to the sea. A handful, without arms, without food, with naked courage and faith, humble men, clerks and printers, farmers and laborers, doctors and lawyers and students and teachers. *Ourselves.* They proclaimed a Nation, to fight, and, God willing, to live as free men." His voice shook. "Or to die, in dignity. If we do not survive—we here in this room—at least we have lived. We have lived to a glorious—" He stopped; his words hung unfinished. He meant to go on but did not, because Yora Levine had come in.

Yora looked younger by years, a man who had dropped a great weight. He carried two bottles of wine. "Yora!" Carmela cried. "You are late. Henry has just made a beautiful speech."

Yora smiled. "I can bear even that," he said.

"Just in time," Jacob took the bottle from Yora. "A *l'haim* to the State . . . Edith! Edith, where are you? Get our wine out."

Two bottles of port, wadded in cotton wool, came from the sideboard. All the glasses and cups in the house were brought out. Jacob's hand shook as he poured the wine. "First, the soldiers, our best guests, upstairs." The blond sisters ran up with the wine for the soldiers and remained there to drink. "Everyone," Jacob shouted. "Even the babies get drunk today."

They raised their glasses together. "L'haim!" Yora cried. Judge Winkleman lifted his hand. "We are a sovereign State now. The first toast, to Israel, our State. May it prosper and flourish and bring the world peace!"

Yora's mouth twisted wryly. "We have a simple State, Judge. L'haim is enough."

Ida's blind son held a cup to his little boy's lips. "Drink, Shlomele. Never forget. You and I, we have both lived to this day."

Jacob squeezed the man's arm. "Never forget one thing else, what it cost. Six million in Europe . . ."

"And Arieh!" Ida cried out.

There was through the room, indrawn breath and silence again until Henry Winkleman spoke. "I wonder, if any of us had been asked, any of us who today are jubilant, which will you choose, six million dead or a State? would anyone have wished for this State at *that* price?"

"Stop!" the Pole shouted. "You cannot ask that. My whole family was of the six million who died."

The awkward silence settled once more until Jacob laughed. "Well, in our lifetime we have it, what we prayed for for two thousand years. When things go wrong—we shall have no one to whom to complain but ourselves. We have not made *Gan Eden,* only a State. I do not know whether I shall like that at all. Meanwhile—" He set down his wine glass. "I left a woman in labor on the Street of the Prophets. I must run, introduce a new Israeli to our new State."

In the evening, before Jacob was back from the hospital, Ephraim came in with a poem. He had written in Ivrith, he wished it to be printed at once, and since the *Post,* the only newspaper regularly printed in town, was in English, he hoped G'veret Hirsch would kindly translate.

Edith thought the poem remarkable, remarkable for Ephraim, that is,

> *Today we have a State*
> *And I who was always hunchbacked*
> *Now walk straight*
> *And feel I am tall.*
> *A giant.*
> *With strength in my arms, in my loins.*
> *A man among men I have become today.*

"It is beautiful!" she said.

He gripped both her hands. His eyes met hers. He bent forward and kissed her lips. He grew scarlet. "Forgive me, G'veret, I forgot myself."

She laughed softly. *"En davar.* No matter. Is it every day, we have a State?"

Late that night, Teddy crept to his mother's side. "Imma," he whispered. "Are you ashamed of me?"

"Ashamed of you, haviv? Why should I be ashamed?"

"Because I wet my pants."

She ruffled his bristly head. "We won't tell a soul," and she said, as she had to Ephraim, "After all, is it every day, we have a State?"

He nestled toward her, quiet a moment, then asked, "Imma, do you think Dinah knows that we have a State?"

When Jacob came in, long after midnight, the pretty girl soldier tiptoed down the staircase to him. "I have wonderful news for you," she said. "I have just heard on the wireless, your country has recognized our State."

"My country!" His eyebrows wagged at her. "What other country have I but this? I am Israel."

"Ezra," Lillie Gross said to her husband. "I cannot bear it. I will not bear it. I will die of lonesomeness. Why could we not be with the others today? Are we lepers? Are we criminals? We did not tell him not to come home."

"Nor did we tell him to come," her husband said.

In the morning, as he always did, Isaac Winkleman walked to Keren Kayemeth Street and regretted to find that nothing had changed.

Two women in white shorts were playing tennis on the courts of the Rehavia Club, as they frequently did. The courts were in bad shape, and there was the danger from bullets and shells, but those who had the habit of tennis, persisted in playing their game. The morning-glories back of the courts were wide awake, an iris tapestry. The trees held their heads up, presented their various greens, the fig its ragged, large leaves, the olive its misty silver, the cypress its dark, pointed fronds. The sky was blue and clear, the sun warm and bright. There at the corner was the Mandatory's scarlet post box, with its crown and "G.R."—George Rex. He chortled. "Ex-Rex."

It was pleasant, delightful, as usual. Yet he felt a profound disappointment. Here is the first day of our State. And nothing has changed. The sky should have been a more glorious blue, the sun a diamond blaze, and in the firmament, cherubim, seraphim, should have been riding in fiery chariots and blowing trumpets. I have waited so long, and this is a day, like the rest. I shall ask them at the café, he said to himself, perhaps, one of them has seen something more, a burning bush, a sign in the sky.

He crossed Keren Kayemeth, and paused and leaned on his cane, puzzled because the café was shut, its blinds down, its tables inside, its door locked. He stood wondering, stroking his beard. "Is it a new law, now we have a State that cafés must be closed?" People ran by, keeping close to the building walls, but neatly dressed as if for a holiday or Shabbat. A Shabbat. He chuckled aloud. "I have been so excited over this State, I forget this was the Shabbat. I must run, too, and thank our God."

VII

At Gan Darom, they had just sat down to dinner on the first Shabbat of the State when a messenger came running from the water tower to yell that enemy planes had been seen. There was no time to scatter. Gershon stood up, as if to tell them what they had to do. Those nearest saw him tower above the long dining table for a matter of seconds before a bomb crashed through the roof, and another bomb after that. Then there were screams and moans. Those who were whole dragged themselves from the debris of plaster, dishes and wood and started to run.

There was no hiding place. Spitfires circled low, scattering lead. A bomber brooded over the settlement. Dan was close to the cowshed where the guns were, when the plane dropped its lethal egg. A volcano of stones and dirt spouted and covered him. The fearful noise of cattle in panic and pain made a weird cacophony with the roar of plane motors and the bark of guns. Reuven and Dinah were racing toward the pillbox beneath the water tower when they saw another bomb drop, the tower rock and spew its liquid in a heartbreaking gush.

To the trenches, everyone, to cower behind the wall, behind wire, behind a breastwork of earth. Time slipped by, hours or minutes, no one could be sure, until all at once they were aware that firing had stopped. There was no sound whatever except the pitiful mooing of animals in pain.

They climbed out of the dirt, staggered back. The water tower stood, a wounded torso on tipsy legs. At its feet the lost water had made a small lake and the parched ground was lapping it up. The sky was bare, without cloud or bird or enemy plane, merely the disk of fierce sun. It beat on the jagged roof of the smashed dining hall.

There they ran first, moved by one thought, and with frantic hands raked the bloody debris. Chava screamed. Her husband lay dead on the floor, his skull crushed. Avrum crawled toward them, dragging a shattered leg. Yona who had warned of the bomber had a gory hole in her face. And Gershon had been blown to bits. His wife saw his head, blown clear of his body, before Gittel led her away.

They stood stunned. Some, men and women both, sat down in the rubble and wept.

"*Haverim!*" That was Dan's voice. It shook with passion. "Will you trust me? Will you listen to me?" No one answered because no one knew what to say. "We cannot sit. Not a minute. We need one thousand hands for all we must do. Schmuel, Levi, secure the water pipe line. Save what we can."

He was right, they said to each other, if we do not have water, we will die in this desert of thirst.

"Joshua and I will work on the dynamos. Gittel and Judith, move the wounded into the children's house. In another hour it may be gone, but now, while we have the place. . . . Avrum, take the wireless." He bit his lip, remembering. "I shall take the wireless myself. You know your posts, but there must be changes, you understand. Ketti and Saul take pillbox one . . . Moshe and Dinah pillbox three. Reuven will have the Piat. Everyone to the trenches. Get your weapons. There will be an infantry attack after this, I am sure. Stand. Waste no ammunition. Every bullet must count."

As they raced to their posts, all of them thought the same thing, though no one said it aloud, since if they had talked of it now, common sense would have surely said no. We have a new leader. But Dan is too young.

The sun tormented their flesh while they stood at their posts, with rifles and Stens, Molotov cocktails and hand grenades, one Piat gun with only ten shells, one Bren with a half dozen rounds. Salt caked on their faces and armpits. They grew thirsty, hungry, tired and suffered with desperate desire to relieve bladder and bowels. But no one stirred from his post.

The enemy infantry did not attack.

After sundown, a girl runner slid through the trenches, calling this one and that to come to the children's house for instructions from Dan. The dead still lay in the dining hall. The floor was stained with their blood and the sickish sweet stench of putrefaction tainted the air. Buzzards wheeled in the sky.

In the children's house, Dan held an electric torch, pointed down, shaded with his dirty hand. Beyond the periphery of light, his face was gray. Yet he stood, shoulders back, a grown man.

"Tonight we start to dig bunkers." His voice was deep and strong. "We will use the wood of the dining room tables for bunks on which our wounded will lie. We will milk our cows. Ten are still living. Every night, I shall name two who can be spared to milk cows. Whatever we have to do, we do at night. By day, we stand guard.

"We will bury our dead, now, tonight.

"There will be no help for us yet. Kfar Etzion has fallen. We must hold out." His voice was calm, almost matter-of-fact. "Everyone may now have a drink. One cup of water for each. There is bread. There is soup. You will have your bread and your soup. Then back to your posts. Relieve the others for bread and water and soup. After that, we will work."

Shelling from the Tegart Fortress on the hill began that night and in its lulls, they heard jackals howling beyond the gravel-filled wall.

Edith and Teddy were alone in the house, waiting together for Jacob, when the fat girl soldier came down the steps. "I have news," she said bluntly. "Kfar Etzion is lost." She hestitated before she went on, since she had to go on, to explain. "That means gravest danger to all the settlements in the South."

"Yes . . . Yes . . . What else?" Edith managed to ask.

"What else?" The girl paused again, remembering first that she was a woman, and then that she was a soldier, as well. "Gan Darom has been attacked from the air," she said. "Egyptian planes. Bombed, machine-gunned. Their wireless has called for help."

Teddy glanced at his mother. They rose together, moved toward the girl soldier as though walking in sleep. "And what else?" Edith breathed.

"What else do you need?" The girl didn't mean to sound cross but she was tired, too, for not even a soldier can sleep when mortar shells bang all day and night.

"Details?" Edith forced the questioning words. "Names?"

The girl backed away, feeling sorry for her and for herself, too, because she was the one delivering bad news. "They report six dead. Four wounded. No names." When she saw Teddy moving close, gripping his mother's hand, her face softened somewhat. "You must continue to hope," she said before she went back to Dinah's bedroom.

When she had gone, they sat down again and Teddy burrowed his head in his mother's shoulder and she held him against her. The boomp of a shell, dropping near, shook the house. Teddy shivered, clung tighter and closed his eyes. "Where's Abba? Why isn't Abba here?"

Why isn't he here? her mind repeated, adding its own urgency. We have to share it. I cannot bear this alone. This you cannot share with a child. She pushed Teddy a little way off until she could raise his chin with her thumb. "Dinah is safe, you will see," she said stoutly to him. But if not yet, she thought, tomorrow, next day. Dear God, please God, if you please, God. Then she said, "Teddy, undress, go to sleep."

"I can't sleep, Imma."

"Go, try."

"Imma, was that last boomp where Abba is?"

"No, haviv, in another quarter entirely."

"Imma, why isn't he home?"

"He'll be home. He has much to do."

"Imma, when will he come?"

"When he is finished. Many people are sick."

"Wounded, you mean." Teddy's voice had a flatness. He sounded as he looked, like an old man.

"Go to sleep, dear. I have clean pajamas for you. I washed them this morning. Put them on now. They'll make you feel good."

"Imma, I don't like to leave you till Abba comes."

"The soldiers are here. We are safe."

"But you are sad. You are thinking. . . . It is not good to sit alone, thinking sad things."

"Go to bed," she said so harshly that he looked up, dismayed, but obediently began to take off his shorts and his shirt. Please, go to sleep, Teddy, her mind begged, lie down, turn away, so that I may have the luxury of being afraid and shedding tears.

He pulled on his pajamas, came over to her, kissed her cheek. "Lila tov," he said sweetly, "Sweet dreams," stretched out on his mattress and turned his face from the chair where she sat. She saw his shoulders heave, heard him snuffle, as though he were trying not to cry himself to sleep. She sat thinking dully, has the price been exacted from us? We have the State. Have we already paid the high fee? Will we know, will we even be told, if our loved daughter is taken from us?

The pain, long forgotten, suddenly slashed at her belly and back, so severe that she had to creep to her mattress and lie down, doubled up.

VIII

THE EXPLOSIONS WERE over toward Mea Shearim, a considerable distance away, when Edith left the Ben Yehuda Street mess the next night and she said to Joan who was working there, too, "If we run, we can be in Rehavia before the shelling gets there." The Legion gunners seemed to work on timetable, rotating their shots systematically. You could practically clock yourself for whatever trip had to be made.

"Then let's run," Joan said. "I hate to leave Dovidl after dark. Our children will all be nervous wrecks. Shirley's lucky she's in Tel Aviv. I wish I was. Let someone else be a hero. I yield the privilege."

They had reached King George and, spent with running uphill, slowed their pace. The arch of night sky was dappled with stars and fantastic with bursting shells. Behind them, an explosion went off, not too distant, probably near Chancellor Road.

"They're swinging," Joan cried. "We're next. Shalom."

"L'hitra'ot," Edith gasped and ran on alone. At her corner, she had to slow down because her breath failed, and she stopped, panting with sharp pain in her lungs.

The shells came, a dreadful procession, whistling and whooshing, a long slow, ominous whine. There was a fearful crash. The road quivered under her feet and she staggered drunkenly. Stones flew in every direction, rained all around, peppered her like small shot. A mushroom of dust arose, as though the earth itself opened up. Young Mussolini—the irrelevancy ran through her mind—the unfolding rose. Then she realized her own house had been struck, where her child was, and the scream which was starting froze in her throat.

She heard Udi howling and Teddy's plaintive "Imma, Imma, where are you?" as she flew up the path. The stench of sewage and choking dust of white fog filled her throat.

"I'm here. . . . Teddy, where are you? *Teddy!*"

He was beneath the piano, cowering, knees up, head down, in the foetus position. When he crawled out to her, he lay gasping. "I was alone, Imma. I was alone," was all he could say.

"You weren't alone. The soldiers—"

"I was alone, Imma. You weren't here."

When the plaster fog finally lifted, they saw that the office wing of the house had been struck.

Jacob found both of them standing, kalsomined with dust, like marble statues in the rubble.

"En davar," he said listlessly. "No matter. Let's go to bed. Tomorrow we'll look." He lay down on his mattress, utterly spent, and almost at once fell asleep.

Edith slept fitfully, and with the dawn rose, threw on her clothes and ran out to see what had been done to her house. The shell had dropped just outside the office entrance. The outer wall had collapsed, fallen in on the waiting room. The office beyond was untouched but the washroom was wrecked, a shambles of porcelain shards, flushbowl and basin, and twisted torn pipes. The nastiness out of the pipes was so foul she had to run out to the lawn. The hibiscus was flat, crushed by falling stone, and there was a pit in the lawn. She stood staring at it. *My* house, *my* garden. This could not happen to us, she assured herself, even while she saw that it had.

Teddy ran out, half-dressed, while she was there, dashed into the wreckage, scooted out, pinching his nose. "What will we do now, Imma?" he asked. "No W.C. What will we do?"

"Do? Use the upstairs till we get a plumber. That's what you do. Be practical. Don't stand wringing your hands."

Teddy scooped up chunks of metal. "A twenty-five pounder," he crowed.

She struck the shell fragments from his hand. "Don't touch it."

He looked at her curiously. "What's the matter with you? This can't hurt me."

"Pick up the wood. At least we'll have that to cook with."

Jacob came out while she was in the yard, boiling kvacker and coffee over a fire out of his waiting room chairs. He recognized the charred slats, and he shrugged and said as he had last night, "En davar. If we live we can always get new."

"If we live," she repeated.

"We will live." He picked up the pot of porridge, carried it into the house.

At breakfast he said, "A second hit. They seem to have chosen us for a target. We may have to leave. Pack a valise, Edith, the few little things we need most. If we become homeless refugees—" His mobile face worked pitifully. "A change of clothing, a little cash, that's all we will need." He finished his coffee. "Teddy, come help me. We will carry my instruments down to the cellar, to the safest place. If we live, we will need to start earning a living again. That is all we will need."

When he had left for the hospital, she packed a suitcase, a change of underclothing for all three of them, socks, stockings, shoes, a shirt apiece for Jacob and Teddy, a dress for herself, a small packet of Sterling paper which Jacob had managed to get from his vault at the bank, a bag of her few bits of good jewelry. On top of the garments, she placed Dinah's silver-framed photograph.

She carried the suitcase out to the hall, to be ready and waiting, and walked back through her house, seeing her chairs and tables, her piano, her bookshelves, the unmade mattress beds, in the sandbag-darkened room. The plaster dust coated each polished surface, and Jacob's painting of storm clouds had been knocked from the wall. She picked it up, put it down. En davar, she said to herself. It does not matter. Nothing matters now except to remain alive. And does even that matter much? Death means relief from this endless, heart-curdling terror. Kind, generous death.

She scraped the kvacker pot and the breakfast bowls into Udi's dish and got herself ready to run to the store for the day's ration of bread. Nathan came over just as she was setting out and inspected the damage. "Twice at this spot," he observed thoughtfully. "Very strange." He went up to the roof and quickly came down. "You will have your second floor to yourself, G'veret," he said. "A gun is too valuable to risk."

The soldiers moved out during the day and the house seemed like a hollow rind, missing the pounding of shoes and the radio's gabble. The soldiers asked courteously did she wish her mattresses carried upstairs. "En davar," she said. "We are used to living like this."

When they were gone, she went up. Boards spanned the windows in Dinah's room and it was pitch dark. The furniture was nicked, scarred and blanched. The bathtub and basin were filthy; the bath-room stank. Cigarette butts, fruit rinds, newspapers littered the floors. All soldiers are pigs. Even ours.

She started down to get water to begin to scrub up, but instead sat down on the steps with her head in her hands. It doesn't matter, she thought. If we live, we will fix up our house. If we live . . . There's one good thing. The W.C. upstairs is available.

It was not easy to find a new location for the machine gun. By late afternoon, when Yora stopped by, Army headquarters was still arguing. *This* building was too near a clinic; *that* had too weak a roof, another was in a location visible to numerous passers-by.

It was Yora who suggested the place. That morning, riding about, spotting power lines which had been torn by last night's shelling, he had noticed a vacant house, on a rise, in a cul-de-sac, where trees were numerous and thick. It was out of Rehavia proper, away from its school and synagogue, yet close enough for the quarter's defense. The neighborhood formerly had been mixed, Arabs and Jews, side by side, but the Arab owners of this large, sturdy house had locked windows and doors and had fled.

He drove over in a jeep with Nathan and several military men. Yes, it seemed to all of them excellent. The vicinity had had little damage from shells, and the reason was good. Scattered about, within a short range, were legations of several small countries, which both warring parties hoped to retain as their friends. And over the tree-tops towered the stone Madonna on Terra Sancta's dome. "Was she not one of us?" Yora asked. "Let us for once claim her pro-tection. They have not spared our houses of God, but Jesus and Mary they still respect."

After sundown, the locks on the front door were pried, the machine gun was hauled to the roof of the Arab dwelling behind the church, and the soldiers moved in.

The house dazzled them. Their shaded hand-torches picked up details, evidence that the man who had lived in this place had had a fortune to waste and had squandered his pounds to achieve a nightmare—wallpapers of crimson and emerald green, orange and pink, all flecked with gold, chandeliers of chrome and tortured blown glass, a barroom with the zodiac in gleaming gold on its ceiling arch.

The two girl soldiers chose luxurious beds with soft mattresses but the young men set up their austere canvas cots. All of them gathered around a mahogany table to drink tea from French china cups. "So—" One of the men put his feet up and lolled on two chairs. "We live like conquerors even before we have won."

"I liked the other place better," one of his comrades said. "It was more home-like, more friendly, in the Doctor's house. In the evenings when the G'veret sat down and played music for us . . ."

"The child will not pester us. It will be hard to fight this war without his advice but we will manage somehow." They were drinking tea when the first shell shook the house.

Around midnight, there had been a lull in the shelling of the town. Then, all at once, a single shell came screaming, swift and direct, as though a street address were tied to its nose. Another shell followed, another, another, pounding one place. It seemed not merely an act of war's destruction but of insolence.

At daybreak, a rescue crew dragged from the rubble of the gaudy house in the cul-de-sac behind Terra Sancta, the broken bodies of two girl soldiers and four young men, and the useless steel of a smashed machine gun. The plump girl soldier was still breathing but she died in the hospital.

The news flew through the city.

"One of our posts was wiped out last night. Everyone killed."

"The position was set up only a few hours before."

"Someone reported to them. There are spies!"

SPIES! A new fear! The sensation of sinking in quicksand. The horror of ears and eyes everywhere. Bewilderment. Confusion. Panic.

Yora, white as paper, ground his back teeth and ripped the flesh of his cheeks with his nails, asking himself, "How did it happen? It is impossible to believe. . . . This could not be a coincidence. . . . We were betrayed by someone."

Out of heart-sickness, because he had suggested the place, he avoided the Army headquarters, and even the flat of Nathan, his neighbor and friend. And Nathan avoided him, because he was racked by a guilt of his own. "I was careless," he thought. "I should have remembered the consulates. . . . But can we search and watch foreign legations for spies? We must trust someone. . . . Whom can we trust? When will we learn that we have no friends?"

When Edith heard about it, she mourned. "Yesterday, they were here, alive, in my house. . . . They seemed like children of mine." But Teddy ran about, spreading the gossip. "Spies told the Arabs where the post was moved."

Spies! Dread sweeping the town like a gasoline fire. Everyone searched every passer-by's face, asking himself, Was it he?

Yet in forty-eight hours the spy fever, the mourning were over, because events crowd each other when there is a war and time is lacking to mull, speculate or find out. On the before-dawn of May nineteenth, a shock troop of the Palmach achieved what no Jews had in almost nineteen hundred years. They smashed the Old City Wall. Fighting their way with grenades, they reached the beleaguered handful near the Wailing Wall, brought food, medicine and small arms.

They were counterattacked and forced to withdraw.

IX

WHAT BEGAN ON the night of the twentieth of May made the weeks before that seem pastoral. There was an unreality about the days and the nights, and a monotony. In the streets one did not see people, merely silhouettes racing through fogs of dust and hail of metal.

The unreality became the reality, yet it remained altogether unreal since we are human beings, God's children all, and this does not happen to people like us. It was fortunate, in a way, that lack of sleep numbed everyone's brain because if one had been able to sleep and to think afterwards, it would have been evident that this could not be borne by mere flesh and blood.

Sometimes, late at night, Jacob Hirsch took a candle and book, climbed up to the more dangerous second floor of his house, pulled the blinds down, and shut himself into the stifling, foul W.C. to read for an hour. "Allow me the luxury," he implored his wife. "A little privacy, a distraction. It gives me the illusion I am human still."

"Occasionally a hoarse boom was heard. That lifted hope. This is ours. This is the new Davidka. A homemade mortar of ours. It is powerful, they say. Powerful enough? Why does not help come to us? Why is no hand lifted to save Jerusalem? Why do *They* let the Legion rip the Holy City apart?

Courtney wrote in the *Palestine Post: "There is a new glory in the City. The golden shine of people who are brave and trusting, have an excuse to hate and don't hate. This is a proud day and a man is proud to be among them. A nation grows great. A city becomes holy, holier than any place, in the blood and spirit of its men and women."* Beautiful words, heartening words. Poetry. People read "Column One" in their smothering, candlelit rooms, were lifted a little, but not for long. When one is weary and dirty and hungry and much afraid, it is difficult to think of oneself as noble and holy and brave.

It was hard to say whose job was most hazardous, that of Professor Gross, who traveled with a water cart through flying steel all day long, or that of Yora Levine, who rode about all night, spotting power lines broken by shells, and directing the crews which spliced them together again, or that of Dr. Hirsch, who had to race down King George and Chancellor Road and the Street of the Prophets, day and night, operate by the sputtering light of a carbide lamp and run home through the shell-pitted streets in the dark, or the housewives who raced to the shop for three slices of bread every day, and the pitiful ration of cornflour, beans, margarine, the morsel of herring, the few grams of sugar, the tin of milk, the square of chocolate. Even at home, no person was safe, since any moment, the roof, the sheltering walls might crush him to death.

Yet if you had asked Ephraim Malkoff, he would have been quick to admit he had the easiest job. He guarded the gate to the airfield. He stood and sometimes sat at the gate with a Sten which he never fired. He was supposed to halt strangers without proper passes, keep them from entering the field, and his time was passed in angry debates with neighborhood boys with nascent earlocks, lured by the novelty of the field, with neighborhood housewives who also were curious, and old men to whom all the city belonged, because they had come there to die.

As a general thing, however, Ephraim's days were dull. He had time to read the two or four sheets of the daily newspaper through several times, though English was not the language he read most fluently. He had time to watch the funerals—the gray lorries carting yesterday's dead to the opposite hill—and to think about them. His own mother lay there with the rest. He sometimes thought about the world which had ended when she had died, not merely his personal world of bickerings, strains and sullen hatreds, mother and son endlessly guilty for all they had done to each other, but the world of Basle congresses, Zionist dialectic, of white bearded men and large-bosomed women, debating over glasses of tea.

How different the reality of nationhood was. It was a poet standing guard from dawn to dusk with a Sten, at an empty airfield.

Henry Winkleman was the only one whose life had not changed very much. He went to court every day. Litigation had taken a holiday but the Israeli police in the blue caps of the British police brought in black-out violators, women who, on very hot nights, simply had to pull up window blinds, or pious young men with long curly earlocks, charged with harassing soldiers on the Shabbat. It was dull to sit all day long and deafening, for the Russian Compound was near the front line.

Henry envied his father who was fortunate enough to be deaf. The old man did not think he was lucky. He chafed because his daughters wouldn't let him go out. "What are you afraid of? That I will be killed? I have lived long enough. I have seen the State born. Let me die in Jerusalem's streets. What good am I, lying here, on a mattress in a dark room?"

"No, Father," Janet shouted at him. "You'd be more of a nuisance if you got killed." She sighed and said to Maida, "Two thousand years we dreamed of this State, and, for spite, it had to happen in our lifetime."

Herr Prinz who lived on the corner and was well in his fifties, protested that he had a bad back and nervous disorders which unfitted him for war work, but he was ordered to dig trenches three hours every day. One morning, going on duty, he met Dr. Hirsch and they made their way up King George together. At the corner, where the Doctor went downhill toward Chancellor Road and Herr Prinz went up toward Agrippa's Way, they said "L'hitra'ot."

Dr. Hirsch heard an explosion and spun around in time to see the bloodied fragments of Herr Prinz's body come whirling down. He started to run toward the place where the shell had dropped, took a step forward, then a step back. "No, as long as I can, I must stay alive," he said to himself. "God wills it so."

Tamar Atani's son, born by Caesarian of a dead mother, was dying, lacking strength to fight for its life on cornflour and water. When the nurses saw he was moribund, they sent for Dr. Hirsch and he brought Elia Atani, and they sat together while the infant breathed its last, in a ward lantern-lit and tormented by shells. It was two in the morning when the Doctor's stethoscope could no longer find the faint beat of the heart and the scrawny body began to feel cold. Elia Atani stood beside the crib, his head lifted up, his profile beautiful, like a cameo. Dr. Hirsch and the nurse heard him speak. "The wheel will turn. For what you have done to my wife and my son, you will pay. For all of this you will pay."

Dr. Hirsch walked home with him, since they lived in the same neighborhood. The shelling was continuous and seemed to be all over town. Elia Atani would not run, would not take cover. He walked recklessly in the middle of the road.

After the child had been carried in a gray lorry from the mortuary to the cave in the hills opposite the airfield, Elia Atani locked his flat and asked for full-time army duty. The officer with whom he spoke told about it afterwards and described the man who stood before him as tall, a giant in fact. That puzzled everyone, for it was known that Elia Atani, like most Yemenites, was a little, thin man.

X

WHEN SAUL TOLD Al Brody the mission he was to fly, Al was pleased; in the evenings to the Negev, back to base by midnight, refuel and load up for the Jerusalem field, come in there at dawn, clear right out again. But when they showed him the plane, he almost packed up to go home. An Auster. Even Saul kidded about it. A primus, he called it, a rudimentary cookstove. "Sorry," he said. "Your Truman has sent us his best regards but not his Super-Forts."

The Jerusalem field, too, was a dilly, a postage stamp. A monastery blocked its approach through the hills. Not even the Auster could risk flying in before day. Al scooted, dropped his bag of shells, medicines, powdered milk, official mail, picked up a Haganah officer or V.I.P., traveling to Tel Aviv, and whirred, hell bent for leather, back before full sunrise. Often, in the few minutes he stayed on the field, he heard explosions and crackling shots and sometimes his passenger told him how bad the night had been.

The field in the Negev was better, not concrete, but it had space. The Negev had nothing but space. No one could have been more surprised than he was to find houses and human beings on that fearful wasteland. When he first saw the Negev, by day, on reconnaissance flight, the word which came into his mind was "Badlands." He had never seen the terrain referred to as the Badlands, and if pressed, couldn't have named the state it was in, but wherever they were, this should be the look the Badlands must have, forbidding, in sheer ugliness. His mind hunted for similes which might tell the folks back at home how it looked, mustard plaster left over night, or spoiled liverwurst. Unappetizing. And barren and parched, not a tree, not a shrub, except those which were planted by the settlements. How precious each tree must be! The Gyppos, the bastards, knew that, when they shelled the fruit groves and set them afire. As he flew, Al saw the bonfires below, grain fields and orchards burning, flames spreading, whipped by a breeze.

He swung in every night, dropped his supplies, and swung out. Occasionally he stayed long enough for a glass of water or cold tea at the dining hall near the field. The people at the base were pleased when he did. They slapped his shoulders, called him *"Haver"* and *"Hevraman,"* and though he did not understand most of what they were talking about, those two words he knew, "Comrade!" and "Brave guy!" He liked that. Okay. Later on, he knew, someone would come from the besieged settlements near the base, to pick up a handful of shells, a little penicillin, morphine, dried plasma and sulfa pills. He imagined them, shadows, crawling on bellies, through wadis, over hummocks, risking their lives to get what he brought. Someday, when I have time, he thought, I'll stay down, look around, meet the folks. Without a war, under the best circumstances, he felt, it took all kinds of guts and a little madness to want to come down to this land. He wondered what kind of people they were who chose to live in this forbidding place.

One night he knew. He had trouble with his feed line coming in and stayed to check. When a primus is half an air force, you can't risk cracking it up. The mechanics suggested he eat while they worked on the plane. They were good mechanics, they assured him. The R.A.F. had thought so.

Two people came into the dining hall while he was there. They were dirty and hot and looked beaten-up. They were offered a dish of salad, a cool drink and were pleased as kids. When he took a good look, he saw they were kids, only kids, and one of the kids was a girl, with black, almond-shaped eyes. With a bath, a haircut and the right clothes, she could have been quite a dish. He saw them talking with the woman who served them, saw them glancing at him, heard the word *"Amerikaner"* and guessed he was being discussed. The woman brought them over, and said, "Our comrades of Gan Darom wish to shake your hand."

Both the young man and the girl had strong masculine grips. They didn't say anything, but he sensed appreciation in their handshakes and he felt high as a kite. "Aw, it's nothing," he said. "This is my job."

Then the girl said in English, real English, but with a funny accent, "I understand you fly into Jerusalem. How is it there?"

"It's still there," he said grimly. "That's all I can say."

She had a deep frown between her eyebrows. He smiled at her. "You speak English," he said. "That's good."

"Is it?"

"You bet. You can't imagine what a treat it is to hear your mother tongue."

"Mother tongue? Why don't you speak Ivrith? That's our mother tongue."

She wasn't exerting herself to be pleasant. Your error, Brody; she's like the rest, putting a foreigner in his place. "I'm a stranger in town," he said amiably. "Haven't had time to learn. But I know a few words. Shalom. Toda . . ."

The girl nodded encouragingly.

"And—" He slipped his arm around her waist as he might have made a mild pass at a girl back at home. "I know haviva," he said.

She whirled away, swung around and slapped his face. "I'll teach you one more," she was in a fury, all but spitting at him. *"Blee yadayim!* Keep your hands off!"

He backed away, cheek stinging and dignity even more deeply hurt. "Okay, baby," he muttered, "you don't want to be pals. Okay with me."

He was climbing into the cockpit when she came up to him. She had washed her face, combed her hair and looked better, much.

"I am sorry," she began without preliminaries, "that I slapped your face."

"That's okay," he said. "I've been slapped before." He grinned. "No hard feelings. I don't hold a grudge."

She looked down at the ground. "I have made it difficult to ask what I wish," she said.

"Ask it," he growled. "But blee yadayim."

She laughed. Her teeth and her smile were nice, he thought. "You are clever and quick. That is good," she said. "Do something for me, please. A very big favor. When you come in to Jerusalem, please tell them at the field to get word, if they can, to my parents, that I am well. My father is Doctor Hirsch. He is well known. I am Dinah."

"Will do, Dinah." He touched his forehead in a kind of salute. "Shalom."

"Toda raba. Shalom," she replied. And she added a word he did not know. What she said sounded like "le hitrout." He memorized it as he flew back, in order to ask what it meant. He was surprised when he learned it meant "Hope to see you again."

The kvacker on the garden's woodstove was almost done when the Legion gunners swung to the range of the street and the sky overhead was alive with hurtling death. A shell dropped just beyond Levine's lawn and the spatter of shrapnel, dirt, stones, made Edith scurry for shelter in the kitchen doorway.

She was huddling there, fretful the porridge would burn, when she heard her name called. Across the lawn, Ephraim Malkoff came, zigzagging, hopping like a rabbit. "I ran all the way from the wadi." He laid his hand on his scraggle-haired, naked chest and glared at the noisy heavens. "G'veret—" his breath came hard—"I have a message. . . . A man, a flyer . . . He was in the Negev. . . . He saw Dinah last night."

She seized his hands. "Tell me. Tell me fast."

"She sent a message. She is well."

A strange thing happened. A phenomenon. The world moved closer. The June day sharpened. The heavens became a brighter blue. The metal shells racing across the azure were magnificent stars, gleaming suns. The cypresses were a fresh, brilliant green. In the rose beds each flower's hue glowed separately. "Thank God," Edith said again and again. "Thank God." Such triumph gleamed in her face that Ephraim covered his eyes, as though he had been staring into sunlight's hot blaze.

Neither of them saw the smoke rising on the little woodfire where the morning's porridge was burning, caked hard as tile to the pot.

XI

At first Millie had been greatly pleased. Can a woman receive greater flattery than a man's willingness to abandon wife, child and country to stay at her side? "I can't take you, my dear," Gordon had said after two pair of nylons had restored good relations. "Much as I might like to do it. But what I can do is stay here with you." But by the end of May, she had begun to be bored. As a lover, he was only sporadically ardent, as a conversationalist, no better than fair, and as a provider, nil. It was she who risked snipers' fire on Mamillah Road every day to get to the consulate where she worked, crawling on hands and knees, ripping her clothes on barbed wire, she who brought back the few grams of sugar or coffee, pilfered or begged from the consulate's stocks, she who ran for and shared her ration of bread, she who drew the day's water from the well in the yard, before she went to work, she who threw out the night slops. A high price for love, if love this might be. Frankly, if there had been at any moment another choice, Gordon Leake would have found himself homeless, in the violent streets. But in time of siege, a woman who likes a man in her bed, keeps what she has. It was comfort at night when lead and steel hailed on the roof to be able to stay close to him and hear his breathing in the fearful dark. If this house is hit, she often thought, at least I am not alone in the place.

In the mornings, she left him abed and how he passed the long day, she did not know. She knew merely that he did not leave the room, that he kept the blinds down, because he did not wish to be seen. The house lent itself to that rather well. It was an old Arab building which had been turned into flats. Millie's large room had a separate entrance. Arabs and Britons had lived in the place and had left and they occupied it alone.

When Gordon first came he had made clear that, above all things, no one was to learn he was here. While his compatriots still were in town, she could understand, let no one know a British administrator is deserting his family and country for love, and later on, when he said he thought it best that an Englishman should not be seen lest his presence be misunderstood, that made sense as well. She asked him, point-blank, whether his staying had something to do with a definite plan, secret work for his Government, and he had smiled and said, "No."

"But, Gordon, do you wish me to believe you want to stay here with *them?*"

"I want to stay here with you," he replied.

"And afterwards?"

"We will see."

"Gordon, have you stayed because you believe the Arabs are certain to win?"

"If I believed that, I should have gone to Amman. . . . Millie, can't you believe I stayed here for you?"

She asked, once or twice, in the softness of bed, whether it was part of his plans to make her his wife, but he said with a gentle evasiveness, "Remember, I still have a wife."

"Millie, I like you" was the most he would say and that had begun to be true, for a man does feel humbly grateful toward a woman who is generous and brave and does not interfere with his work.

During the day, he tidied the room, boiled the beans for supper on the primus, and read his Bible. Orde Wingate, who also had gone to *their* side, had been a biblical student, and out of the Scriptures had come his conviction that peace would enter the world only when Zion was free. And Gordon Leake, who had turned his back on wife, child, country and self, went, too, to the Scriptures, consciously imitating, to try to find for himself, a faith to justify what he had done.

The primitive shepherds, and tin-pot kings of the Book distressed and confused him. They were lustful and greedy, stubborn and eternally making wars. They tried God's own patience again and again and brought down His punishments. Yet this people, no better, no worse, no greater, no less, than all other people, had given the Western world what it knew as God. *"O Jerusalem that bringest good tidings, lift up thy voice with strength; lift it up, be not afraid, say unto the cities of Judah, Behold your God."*

Sometimes, late at night, he went out; for air, he told Millie. He was never gone long but until he returned she was frequently frightened and told herself, with surprise, that this dread, in his absence, meant she was fearful for him. A joke on you, Millie, to fall in love with a man without passport or money or influence.

What she did not know was that in the morning he wrote out carefully all she had told him, the gossip, the rumors which she had gleaned at the consulate where Red Cross and U.N. personnel, where Englishmen, French and even Arabs visited during the day, small bits, and not for him to decide whether these might be true or false, items such as "That new Haganah mortar, the Davidka, is terrifying the Legion on the other side of the wall. They are certain the Old City will be captured. The U.N. is working frantically to bring a truce before that occurs. Brigadier Glubb's face must be saved." "The Arabs are convinced the Hebrew University has made an atom bomb and that it will be dropped on them. Their propagandists abroad are being instructed to stress the violation of holy places by Israeli bombs." "The accuracy of the Legion shelling of the New City, some Arabs are boasting, is due to the fact that they have a list of the locations of all military objectives, munitions assembly and storage depots, and headquarters. They claim to have received the list from a man who got it from a Haganah officer named Levine before the Mandatory left." Gordon wondered about the name when he wrote it out. It can't be the Levine I know, he assured himself; a common name, there must be many called that.

When he delivered his reports, he, too, ran, toward an old Arab house near St. Louis Way where Intelligence headquarters were, and when his silhouette was seen in the shell-riddled streets, he seemed merely another man running to preserve his life.

It was an especially bad night when he brought the report on Levine, one of the worst nights, not merely because of the shrieking shells but because of a sickness of heart everywhere that the Jews in the Old City, racked with influenza and dysentery, and out of ammunition and food, had had to surrender. The Hurva, oldest synagogue in the world, was in ruins, and the Wailing Wall finally in Arab hands. Throughout the Arab world there was jubilance, and among Jerusalem's defenders the deepest despair.

When the men in the house near St. Louis Way read what Gordon had written they were so shocked at first they could do no more than pass the paper from hand to hand, incredulously. Then tensions, long held in, exploded and they began to pound the desk and to shout.

"Not *Yora* Levine!" one of them shouted. "We know Yora Levine."

"Who does not know Yora Levine?" someone yelled back.

"It cannot be Yora Levine."

"Why not? He was with the British a long time. He was friendly with them."

"Suppose he was friendly? He used them for us."

"And for himself. Who is an angel? A saint?"

"You are crazy. I saw him only a few nights ago. While the shells were falling, he rode through the streets. . . ."

When the officer who was in charge in this place eventually came, they showed the report to him. He was a man who once had sold brushes and paints and whose cunning, whose brashness, and personal connections among all elements had made him valuable to Intelligence. His face screwed itself into a tight, ugly knot. "It can be true," he said. "I saw him drinking with Duncan at the King David bar. He was anxious that day to get rid of me."

"Did he know who you were?"

"He knew *me.*"

"Did he know you were Intelligence?"

"Did any man know who was what one month ago? We were secret, were we not?"

The paint salesman sent for Nathan and showed him the Englishman's brief report, and through Nathan's mind flashed recollection of the morning when Yora had come to his house and he had noticed the nervous twitch in his jaw. Then he remembered that two shells had dropped at Hirsch's house while the machine gun had been on its roof and that Yora had been the one who had suggested the place behind Terra Sancta where the machine-gun post had been hit and wiped out. Remembering all that, he said, "I myself will bring Yora here."

Part Five: June

I

THEY RAPPED ON Yora Levine's door at two in the morning and at first, because of the cannonading, no one woke to the knock. In a brief lull between shells, Carmela heard the pounding on the door and thought, being too sleep-drugged to remember that that had been moved, They're firing the machine gun on Hirsch's roof. She sat up, petrified, convinced the gun had gone off because Arabs were storming this ridge.

Her husband hadn't awakened. He snored heavily.

She heard the rat-tat again. Someone *was* at this door. Heart thumping, she ran to open it up. "G'veret Levine." She was relieved to hear Nathan's voice, but cranky with her own weariness, she scolded, "Why do you come at this hour?"

"Is there a better time to find a man home?" Nathan stepped over the sill. Two soldiers were with him. "G'veret," he ordered, "wake Yora at once."

"What is it? My husband is tired. He has only just gone to sleep."

"An emergency." The soldiers followed him into the hall.

She shook Yora's shoulder.

"*Mazeh?*" he muttered from the depths of slumber. "What goes?"

"Nathan is here. An emergency."

He sprang up. He was rubbing his eyes and reeling with fatigue when he went to the hall. "Mazeh?" he asked again.

"Get dressed," Nathan answered.

"What is it?"

"You will learn in good time."

Something in Nathan's voice, a nuance of menace, constricted his throat. He fumbled with his underwear in the dark, thrust his foot

263

into the wrong leg of his shorts, almost fell as he pulled his foot out. I'm nervous, he thought—the knock on the door in the night. Why should it upset me? This is *our* country, Nathan is my friend.

Carmela buttoned his shirt. Her fingers were cold. "Don't be afraid," he whispered to her. "There is nothing to be afraid about." She knelt to help him on with his shoes and walked beside him, to the hall. "Go back to sleep," he said.

"Will you be long?"

Nathan answered for him. "That depends," he said.

"Shalom," she whispered.

"L'hitra'ot," her husband replied.

The children had not waked up.

In the dark, clamorous street, Nathan walked at his side with one of the soldiers ahead, one behind. "Why do they surround us?" Yora asked. "Are they afraid we'll escape?" He concluded that, with the boom of the shells, his questions had not been heard for no one had answered him.

A jeep stood before the house on the corner and they climbed in. Yora sat between the driver and Nathan in the front seat. The driver, he noticed, edged slightly away and he moved against Nathan, thinking he had crowded the other man. "What is it?" he asked Nathan again. "Is there new trouble on the Road?"

"No."

"Is it Sheikh Jarrah?"

"No."

"Is it trouble with Etzel or Lechi?"

"No."

"You have caught spies?"

There was a silence, but he caught a movement, freighted and tense. He nudged Nathan's thigh. "Tell me. To me you can talk."

The driver made a rasping noise. "We have talked to you too often," he said.

He sat back, away from both men and forced himself to laugh. "Yes," he said heartily. "Let no man speak to another. Silence is best. Seal your lips, lest one blame another for our defeats."

The jeep jerked forward, picked up speed, bounced on the rutted, shell-riddled pavements. It stopped in front of an old Arab house, near St. Louis Way. Yora knew the house. He wondered what urgent thing had come up that at this hour this headquarters needed to consult with him.

The soldiers began to climb out and he climbed out, without instruction or urging from them. He strode a step ahead, so much in a hurry to learn what all this was that he stumbled on a stone in the path. A soldier gripped his arm to prevent his fall. He wrenched the arm free, marched ahead. He himself raised and let fall the metal hand of the knocker—the Arab symbol of friendship which was still on the door—and to a dark slit and glittering gun barrel, gave the proper password.

The hall was pitch black but he strode ahead, direct to the door under which a white glimmer showed. The door swung at his touch on the knob and he stopped, amazed, since everything appeared so ready, so planned. Because he had stopped suddenly, those behind piled on him and it seemed to him they were forcing him into the room. He pivoted to growl at them before he strode in.

The white light of a carbide lamp flung shadows high on the vaulted chamber and drew a luminous circle around a flat desk. Behind the desk sat the man who used to sell brushes and paints. That startled him and the recollections of his old dislike and the moment's acute distress in the King David bar gushed like vomit into his throat. *He* is a big shot! Yora said to himself, God help Jerusalem!

To the right, near the desk, was a man who had run a garage. Near him a Yecke who wrote articles for the press. He knew both of those men.

He said to the room, "Shalom" and *"Ma yesh?"*

No one answered him.

"Speak," he cried out. "What gives here? Why have you taken me out of bed? I've been riding the streets for twelve hours. I've earned my rest."

"Then rest," the paint salesman said.

Someone pushed a chair toward him. "Sit down and please do not shout," the paint salesman said.

He sneered at the man. "You are also an officer? *You* give *me* commands?" He saw the man smile, unpleasantly.

A form bent toward a form. "He has cheek," he heard someone say. "I have never seen anything like it before."

Nor I, he thought, as he sat. The room was full. Beyond the light's circle, he recognized people he had known long and well. They were staring as though they had never seen him before. "What is it?" He pounded the desk edge. "Tell me," he cried.

There was a long silence, seconds in time, hours in his deep anxiety.

"Yora." The man back of the desk paused to let the name stand alone. "When did you last see the Englishman, Duncan?"

His bowels stabbed him fiercely. "I saw him last—" He tried to answer explicitly, fighting his pain. "On the day when he was last in Jerusalem. Either the twelfth or the thirteenth of May."

"You have not seen him since?"

"I have not," he said firmly and added, "Thank God."

Back in the shadows, someone tittered. Bristling, he glanced toward the sound.

"You have not been in touch with him?"

"I have not." He stood up. "By what right—" he was shouting— "do you question me?"

"Sit down," the paint salesman said. "We wish to know—" his breath hissed through his teeth—"when did you give him the list of locations of our headquarters?"

Yora gaped. "Who says I did that?"

The door was opened. A man came in. He saw, with amazement and shock, it was Gordon Leake who had lived on his street. Carmela had said she had seen him in town. It was so. *All Englishmen, like rats, look alike.* This is obscene, he thought wildly, an Englishman confronting me.

"Leake." The paint salesman's eyes were crafty, his little smile sly. "Repeat what you know."

Gordon came slowly to the side of the desk. His face, in the eerie white light, seemed sad and too pale. He did not look at Yora but kept his eyes down. "In the Old City, some Arabs are b-b-boasting—" The stammer was familiar. In my living room, in my house, it was to me, Yora thought, he had said he wished to remain. It occurred to him now that, possibly, on that day, he had been rude and this was a kind of revenge. Should I have altered my manners, for him? Why, I even gave him a cigarette. If I had that now— Listen. Pay attention. Hear what he has to say. "The p-p-pin -p-p-point accuracy of their sh-sh-shelling is because they know the l-l-locations of all m-m-military objectives in the New City. The l-l-list, they are b-b-boasting, was p-p-provided by a Hag-g-ganah Commander named—" he swallowed air—"L-L-Levine . . . That is all I know." The stammering voice faded. The room rustled and buzzed.

Yora's fists clenched. He remembered himself in his office, holding a gun to his head, and he thought, as he had thought that morning, "Carmela, farewell." But he moved so close to the desk its wood pressed his flesh. "Are you out of your minds?" he roared. "To make something of this?"

The paint salesman did not look at him but at Gordon Leake. "What is the source of your information?" he asked.

"I'd rather not say."

Yora clutched at a straw. "You see," he sneered, "unfounded gossip, rumor. What madness is on all of you? Peanuts, setting yourselves to judge me!"

The paint salesman looked at him, just the flicker of a glance, with eyebrows raised. "Toda," he said to Gordon. "Wait in the next room. We may wish to speak with you privately, later on."

"Thank you, sir," Gordon said and turned to go out.

Yora wheeled. "Come back," he shouted. "Look me in the face." He saw only the Englishman's retreating back. It struck him the fellow, oddly enough, appeared to slink.

A soldier opened the door, swung it shut.

In the hot silence of the shadowed room, Yora stood panting, unable to get back his breath.

The paint salesman bent forward. "Then you never gave Duncan a list?"

He evaded the question. "I have not seen Duncan since the thirteenth of May."

"After that, you never gave anyone a list to send to him?"

"I did not." The weight on his chest was stifling. "Someone open a window," he begged.

"You see!" the garage owner cried from the shadows. "He gives a signal. He calls to his friends."

He whirled on the man, furious. "Hysteric! Fool! You know who I am. All of you know who Yora Levine is, what he does. Tonight I was riding these streets—"

"That is beside the point." The paint salesman clasped his hands before him. "Did you or did you not," he asked, with dead-level calm, "drink with Duncan at the King David bar?"

The intestinal pain gripped him fiercely once more. "You know that I did," he rasped. "You saw me yourself." He drew a deep breath. "So that is it. I am dragged from my bed, questioned, humiliated, because I had brandy and soda with an Englishman."

"With his hand on your arm, best of friends . . ."

"Listen!" He sensed the peril in the insinuation and his voice rose to challenge it. "I had a favor to ask of him—"

"In return for the favor you did for him? How much did they pay you for that?"

"Pay me?" he snapped. "In your peanut brain nothing matters but money. . . ."

Nathan moved from the shadows to his side at the desk. "Before the thirteenth of May," his tired voice asked, "you were in contact with this Duncan, were you not?"

The room spun around. The pain in his belly was unbearable. His hands unclenched and dropped limp. "I had to tell someone where current was needed." His voice was so low they could barely hear what he said. He heard a hoarse whisper explaining, "You see, after the thirteenth, he did not need to give them more lists"; and he answered the unidentified voice, "Yes, of course. They were gone. We ourselves controlled the power. There was no further need to ask favors from them. Listen!" He began to shout. "I did not like it myself that I had to trust Duncan because I needed him. Nathan, you remember I came to you one day? I tried to tell you—"

"I remember," Nathan said coldly. "I remember how you spoke, how you looked. Very nervous, as if you had some secret guilt."

He tried to be calm, a reasonable man, disputing with sensible men. "Yes, even then, in April, my fears troubled me. This matter of letting them know where we had to have power. It had a danger. I was aware of that, too. Any man, even Duncan, he may be careless. A clerk, an engineer might chance to pick up the list. I tried to be careful, tactful, subtle. . . . Then I said to myself, it is foolish to worry. We have lived with Arabs many years. They know the New City like an open book. A hundred, a thousand could tell their gunners where likely targets might be. . . . And I also thought, surely Duncan would not deliberately do such a thing."

The paint salesman shook his head smiling, a smile like a sneer. "You have known Englishmen, Yora. Who should know better than you what an Englishman is?"

"Listen!" He bent forward, emphatic, earnest. "This job was given to me in February because I was friendly with them. I chose with the greatest care a man I believed reliable and without imagination. It was my duty, my simple assignment. I had to give him a list."

"You see!" The room was alive, a pit of snakes, hissing. "He confesses! You see!"

"Confesses!" He laughed, mirthlessly. "What have I to confess? I had no choice. If it is said today that my list served their purposes—" He stopped. He searched the faces in the shadowed circle, desperately hunting a sign of recognition of his meaning and worth. These were my friends and my comrades, he told himself. What more can I say? War makes men insane.

"There is something else." That was Nathan, standing beside him, face rigid and cold. "You will remember, Yora, there was a machine gun on Hirsch's roof?"

His gray eyes bulged. "I remember," he breathed.

"Two shells dropped there."

"I remember," he said painfully. "I remember well. It was across the street from my own house."

"The house of the Doctor was struck," Nathan went on. "Not the house of Levine."

His hands clenched. "Am I now being tortured for my family's good luck?"

"Yora!" The syllables of his name dropped as into a well, a bottomless darkness and depth. "The machine gun was removed. It was set up in another place. Who suggested that other place?"

He bowed his head. "I." He heard a voice whispering, "This we did not know."

"What happened there? Have you forgotten? That very night."

His head swirled; his stomach churned. The thick silences of the shadowed room seemed to envelop him. He could not breathe, speak or move.

"Was it not more than strange that that very night, we lost six soldiers and a machine gun in that place which Levine selected for us?

To whom did you tell that, Yora? Through whom did you work? Tell us, I beg you. Do this one last service for us, so we may save other lives."

He took a step forward. He raised his closed fist. "I should kill you for this," he cried out. "I should strike you dead."

The man behind the desk lifted his hand. A soldier, with several days' growth of beard, stepped forward and took Yora's arm. He struggled, cried, "Stop! What is this?" Then, all at once, he sagged and let the man lead him into a candlelit, white-washed room, small, like a cell. He sat down on a wooden bench, his head in his hands, and after a while, felt curiously at ease, as one does when a long festering sore is excised. He asked the soldier, "What will they do with me now?"

The man shrugged. "How do I know? We have not had traitors in two thousand years."

"I am not a traitor," he answered. "This is cruel nonsense."

The soldier backed away, to the door, shaking his head. Yora found himself wondering whether the doubt in that headshake was of him or of those inside who had sat in judgment.

"How long will I sit here?" he asked.

The man did not reply. Yora held his watch close to his face, the better to see in poor light. Four o'clock. Had Carmela gone back to sleep? Was she sitting up worrying? The children are with her. Their presence will comfort her, she will comfort them. I am tired. I, too, would like sleep.

He slid back on the bench to ease his spine against the wall and shut his eyes. Words tore at him. *"Traitor."* Me? How dare they? *"He has confessed!"* Confess what? That I arranged for power and light. That I drank at a bar with Duncan. I had to do that. . . . If not I, someone else would have had to do it. . . . No one else could have done what I did. . . . No one else was so friendly with them. . . . I saw the danger myself. What could I do? There was no choice. . . . Have we gone mad with the sufferings of siege that we call brothers traitors when something goes not according to plan? Have we created a Nation so that peanuts may play Hitler's role? . . . The paint salesman sits in judgment. He saw me with Duncan. . . . Did I know he was spying on me? That is ironic. We were so careful, so clever. No one knew who was what in our Haganah. Everyone kept his mouth shut. . . . He makes himself a big man. Not at my expense. No! For this there will be a day of reckoning. They dare not do this to me.

Was it not more than strange that that very night we lost six soldiers and a machine gun in that place Levine selected for us? What do you imply, my friend Nathan? That I ran with that news to our enemies? That is libel, base slander. And that is madness. Nathan, I too was appalled when that happened. I was fearful that in our wide city there were many spies. . . . But how can you be such a criminal fool? I, Yora Levine, who has given his years and his strength to our Haganah— Take one fact, add another, mix with coincidence, hysteria. . . . Furnish no proof. . . . Accuse, torture an innocent man. . . .

He felt acute discomfort and got up to go to relieve himself. The soldier stopped him at the door. "I must," he protested.

"You must wait," the man said. "You must wait in here."

He sat down, sweating profusely and loosened his blouse and belt. He squirmed on the bench.

At half-past four, Nathan entered alone and signaled the soldier to leave.

He stood up. "Get out! Why do you come here?" Violent anger flashed through his brain. And then it ebbed, became a dull weariness. "The other I understand," he murmured. "He is a fool. But you, Nathan . . ."

He saw the man's shoulders droop as though their burdens had become too great. "You accused me!" He raised his voice. "You dared to blame me!" He heard Nathan sigh.

"Yora." Nathan kept his eyes down. He is ashamed to look me in the eye, Yora thought. "Yora, I am not happy in what I must do. The sentence is passed. It pains me to tell this to you, my old neighbor and comrade and friend." His head rose. His jaw firmed. His eyes were like agates, bright, hard. "It is also a matter of private pain that you, my old neighbor and comrade and friend, have been guilty of treason, delivering military secrets to our enemies. Because of you and what you did, many have died these last weeks."

His spine braced itself. He stood soldier-straight. "Nathan," he answered clearly and firmly, "you are a liar and fool"; and when the man said nothing to that, sarcasm deepened his voice, "The machine gun post I dismiss because it is too nonsensical to discuss. Yes, Levine found the house. But you and several others agreed to the place. . . . But the matter of the lists—" He was gesturing widely, as though this were an everyday argument in which one reasonable man might convince a reasonable fellow. "That is something else. I knew there was risk. You remember, I came to your house. The thing worried me. You were too busy to listen. I tried to tell you. . . ."

Nathan passed his one hand across his forehead. He sighed again, before he said, sternly, "It was your responsibility, Yora, not mine. Each man had a personal responsibility for the security of the State. You were given this task. You were told *what* to do. You were not told *how*. It was your responsibility to find a way, without betraying us." His voice had grown sharp, penetrating, a prosecutor's tone. "It is a fact that the enemy's shelling has been accurate. It is a fact, you admitted yourself, that you gave Duncan lists. It is a fact that there has been boasting—" He looked down then, at his left side where there was no arm. "When I was in trouble—" his words came clearly, measured and spaced, "I found a way. Listen, Yora, you know how I lost my arm—"

"Yes, I know, I know, who does not know?"

"I was in a room in my flat," Nathan went on, as though Yora Levine was one who did not know a story, now all but legend, which a whole city knew. "I was teaching a group to use hand grenades. I saw a boy pull out the pin. I snatched it from him and held it away, through the open window. I could not drop it, not into our own quiet street, where children, your children, play. I held it, Yora. I held it in my hand and watched it blow off my arm." He raised his chin. "Do you think I wished to lose my arm? No. But better a thousand times, my left arm, my right arm, my eyes, my life, than the smallest harm come to Jerusalem through fault of mine."

His sense of injustice rose in full flood. "Then you are a saint and I am only a man who makes mistakes. It is a pity we cannot all be as brave and as holy as you." He shook his head with violence. "Sometimes," he went on to say, "I grow bored with these heroics of ours. A man must be more than a man. He must be a giant, a hero, an angel. Nothing he does dare go wrong. He tries his best. It is not enough, never enough. . . . You ask too much. . . ."

"The times ask it," Nathan answered. "And they will accept nothing less. Each man we trusted must fulfill his trust."

"I fulfilled my trust," Yora said obstinately.

No answer came. Instead there was a protracted silence, a pregnant hush, pent in the narrow white room, beyond whose thick walls the mortars' pounding was like a muffled drum beat. Two men who had known one another for years looked into each other's face in the pale candlelight, one haggard, beseeching mercy, the other grave and deeply sad.

"Yora," Nathan said, "because you have been our comrade, and for the sake of your children, to spare them disgrace, we give you a choice. We will tell a lie for your children's sake." He opened the holster at his hip and took out his own revolver, "Accidents can happen," he said. "If you are wise, you will accept this choice." He laid the pistol on the bench.

Yora glanced at the gun and then at Nathan's face. He drew back his shoulders. "A bad joke," he said stiffly. "I do you a favor, I laugh."

"Fifteen minutes." Nathan replied. "That is time enough to make your peace."

He stood motionless. "You have gone mad," he said. "You will be ashamed of this night's work."

He was still incredulous when they led him to the courtyard of the house just as day was beginning to break. While he stood there, between two soldiers with rifles, he heard himself being discussed and peculiar things asked, whether a bandage should be worn and how far off to stand. His mouth curled with contempt. *Purim spielers*, acting a play, they do not even know the gestures to make. This could not be true and it could not be happening to Yora Levine. Of all the monstrous things which have been done in this land none is more monstrous than this. Power corrupts, he thought; it goes to little men's heads. While *they* were here, someone needed to give them a list of where we required power and light. I was chosen for that. It was not easy for me. I sensed the dangers. I went through agony. I was even ready to take my own life but I did not because I had a job to do. I am no traitor. I am simply a man who had no choice. They prove my guilt with the coincidence of a house that was shelled. He thought all these things, thought them so clearly that he was sure he had said them aloud. The case was plain, a child could understand this. He wondered whether this was an ordeal of some kind, a medieval testing by fire of his courage and loyalty. If that were so, it was unjust, for Yora Levine had been wretched enough while the British were here. End the melodrama and let a suffering man go to the W.C.

When they led him to the end of the courtyard, elbowed him flush against a high wall, he would not turn around and the last thing he said, as the rifles were raised was, "Can we afford to waste bullets on this kind of sport?"

The shots were heard, of course, but they sounded exactly like the other noises of war.

It was a cool morning, before a very hot day.

II

THE ONLY ONES of the street who received direct reports, were Carmela and Judge Winkleman. The Judge received his report during the morning, at court. He had been lecturing a blackout violator, a new immigrant. "Suppose the enemy saw your small light and dropped a *pagaz,* a shell, on your house?"

"God forbid! But it was like a prison, hot, close. Five minutes to breathe."

"Which is more important, your comfort or the city's safety?"

He warned her against repeating the offense and fined her five pounds. There was no clerk and he had to write out the disposition in his own hand. He glanced up when he finished, to call the next case and a man in the doorway caught his eye, mouthed an urgent, "I must speak with you." He excused himself, left the bench and went with the man to a small room down the corridor.

"Your Englishman has proved his value," the man began as soon as the door had been shut. "He turned up the arch traitor for us."

Judge Winkleman nodded and smiled, but the smile congealed on his face, when he heard the man add, "It was one of our own, can you believe? It was Yora Levine."

"Are you sure?" His voice shook.

"Are you sick? Sit down. . . . Yes, he made a public confession. There is no doubt. He was cynical about the whole thing. He made a joke at the end."

Poor Carmela, he wanted to cry, poor children! But struggling to show nothing of what he felt, he asked with icy calm, "Did the traitor tell what motive he had?"

"No." The officer tried to be accurate. "I was there. I heard the whole thing. We assumed he was deep in their debt, for what they had done for him, his position, his rank. . . . And possibly what he expected afterwards."

He brought his hands together, studied his fingernails. "Where did the Englishman get his facts?" he asked.

The officer blushed. "From that woman with whom he lives." He grew even redder. "We brought him to headquarters and she disappeared. Into the Old City, perhaps."

"And the Englishman?"

"We are holding him."

"He confronted Levine?"

"He was there. He had little to add. We heard it from the traitor himself. He knew Duncan. He drank with him. He gave him lists. He admitted that openly."

"What defense?"

"No defense . . . What defense could there be? He knew what he was doing. He kept shouting he had no choice. Make what you will out of that. Nathan himself confronted him with important facts."

Judge Winkleman paced to the end of the room and came back. "It is inevitable, in confused times," he murmured, "that some men go mad." Then he asked, "Has she been told? Levine's wife?"

"She will be told. Whatever is convenient for her to be told."

"What will become of her and her children?"

The man shrugged. "He should have thought of that before he did what he did. An honorable man has regard for his family. Will you guarantee the woman herself is innocent?"

"I will," he said sharply. "I know that woman. I have known her most of my life."

The officer smiled sourly. "We knew him too, most of our lives. That is the greatest shock, that we were so tricked. It will be best for her and her children to go away as soon as they can. Our people may tear them limb from limb."

Judge Winkleman sat down abruptly. The officer stared at him. "Judge," he said, "go home. You are sick."

He sat staring ahead. Thus we begin, he said to himself, with treachery in our midst. And on my own street. Did Carmela know? She shared his bed, shared his life. She was happy with him. . . . *Was* she happy with him? Did he have another life, which she could not reach? . . . There was gossip, that much I know. Was he cruel to her? Was he mentally sick? Perhaps not even he understood what he did. Or why he did what he did . . . What will become of Carmela now? He was shaking. He could hardly sit still.

I did not plan it this way, he cried to himself. I am sure I did not.

Two officers came to Carmela's house at suppertime. When she saw them she felt a warning chill. "Has something happened to Yora?" she cried.

"Abba!" Asi took up her cue. "Abba has been killed!" The girls clung to her skirt and peered into her face.

The two men looked away. "Send the children out," one of them said.

"Yeladim, go to kitchen. Dish out your beans. Eat. I will come." They went, looking back, watching her walk ahead of the officers into the living room, her finger tips at her mouth. One soldier stayed in the hall, the other, a young man, younger than Yora, with a pleasant, sunburned face, followed her in and stood, ill at ease.

"My husband is dead," she said to him. Her hands flew from her lips to her breast.

"Who told you?" The man seemed disturbed.

"My heart told me."

He took a paper from his shirt pocket, unfolded the sheet, and as though he were speaking just to himself, he began to read, "Former Haganah Commander Yora Levine was at thirty minutes past five o'clock on the morning of June the second, executed by order of a military court in the City of Jerusalem for the crime of high treason against the State of Israel, imparting military secrets to the enemy."

She listened to him, her head cocked, her face drained of blood. For a moment the house heard no sounds except the boom and rattle of guns and the wall-muffled murmur of children's voices. Then she said hoarsely, "It is a lie."

The man folded the paper. He pivoted as if to leave. Carmela clutched at his arm. *"They* believed *this? You* believe *this?"*

He eased her hand off. "It is not for me to believe or not to believe. It is for me to bring you the fact."

"Fact! What fact?" Her voice rose, agonized. "Where is he? What have you done with him?"

"That has been taken care of," he said.

She felt her knees buckling and clung to the frame of a chair. "I am not to see him again?"

He edged toward the door. She ran after him, seized his hand, pleading, "Was there no message for me?"

"No message. He treated it as a jest. They told me his final words were 'Can we waste bullets on this kind of sport?'" His shoes scraped the floor, shifting nervously. "You will do well, G'veret," he said and his manner was kindly, "if you and the children leave Jerusalem as soon as you can. I hope it can be before people know." He put his hands on her shoulders. "Believe me, G'veret," he said, "I feel sorry for you."

She did not hear him go out because her knees melted. The swirling inside her head gave way to merciful blotting-out black. When the children had eaten their beans and came in, they saw her sprawled on the floor and started to howl because they thought she was dead. Nobody heard them, except their mother. Their wails came to her as in a dream. "Weep, children," she murmured from the cool stones of the floor. "Weep. Your beloved father is forever gone."

Henry Winkleman sat down near the candle, laid out Patience, and swept the cards together again. "You're nervous as a cat," Maida said. "A game would calm you. I'll get Janet. We can play three-handed bridge."

He pushed the double deck from him and rose. "I'm going for a walk."

"Now? Are you out of your mind?"

"I think so," he said.

He stood at Carmela's dry, dusty hedge. The house was dark. He told himself he heard sounds of sobbing within, but he knew he did not. A stream of bullets whizzed over his head. A tracer streaked through the sky, and for an instant, he knew the wild hope it might fall on him. He took a step up the path toward the house and stepped quickly back. "How much better," he said to himself, "if this had been razed by a shell."

It was a secret and therefore it traveled fast. Throughout the city, everyone knew, almost at once, that a traitor had been caught and executed. You see, people told one another, that's why we have been without water and food. We were betrayed. That's why we are shelled night and day. He is to blame, he and those on his side.

Neither the food nor the water situation nor the enemy's shellings had changed, but the traitor is caught and therefore things will get better at once.

Who was it? Very few knew the traitor's name, and so everyone ran down the roster of persons he personally disliked and selected a probable one. They were eliminated by sunset, when the name was known.

One of the printers on the newspaper made a trip that evening to visit Max Goldstein, a surprise, because even in far less dangerous days, his former colleagues had rarely had time to visit with Max. "Which house did the spy live in?" the man asked.

"Spy? What are you talking about?"

"Did you not know you had a spy on your block?"

"You're joking."

"I only wish that I were. The man was betraying us all along. For months we have been at his mercy. Thank God, he was caught, executed. Now, at last, we are safe."

"Who was it? Do you know the name?"

"Levine, the traitor's name was."

"Yora? I do not believe it. It cannot be true."

"Ah, it is, it is. Too true, unfortunately. What terrible things men will do, for British gold. . . . Did you know the man, personally, by any chance?"

"I knew him a little, not well. He was not a friendly man."

"You see, a typical spy. In their pay, avoiding his neighbors."

"That last is true," Max said finally and with decision. "I always suspected him."

When he told his mother she said, "It cannot be. It is a mistake. As soon as I can, I shall go to Carmela and learn how this evil gossip began."

Max told his wife, and through her it traveled the queue at the grocery store.

When Professor Gross and his wife spoke of it, the Professor tried to explain, "They say he did it for money, but I, for one do not believe that. Another factor is more probable. Flattery. They made him feel he was one of them. British charm is a potent and heady drug. It has seduced many men." He walked out on the balcony to gawk at his neighbor's house and when he came back, said to his wife, "Whatever her husband was, Carmela must be in great distress. Do you think you should go to her?"

"Are we only welcome when there is a death?" Lillie Gross asked.

The man who had moved into Gordon's flat caught up with Jacob on Keren Kayemeth. "Doctor," he began, while they scudded along, "have you heard about the spy on our street?"

Jacob stopped. "Who?"

"The man with the blond mustache. I did not know him very well. Levine, I believe the name was."

Jacob laughed raucously. "Why don't you say Hirsch? Jacob Hirsch. That's just as logical."

The man shrugged and walked on. "Believe me or not believe me, I tell you the truth. He confessed and they shot him at once, I am happy to say."

"The siege has gone to your head." Jacob fell into step beside him. "There is a well-known hysteria which comes from anxiety, from lack of sleep. Men begin to have fantasies. They distrust one another, accuse one another of things. A temporary insanity, actually . . ."

"Insanity? All of us should be as sane as those who caught him. What I cannot understand is how one of us could do such a thing."

"One of us!" He could no longer be lucid or calm. "Why should not one of us do this or that?" he yelled. "Have we not the right to have sons of bitches? Where is it written that we must all be saints?" He had lost his breath shouting and hurrying, and he kept quiet until he had caught it again. "Anyhow," he said, "I do not believe one word of it." Yet as he ran on, he remembered himself in the April convoy, in desperate danger, thinking the need is to live, on whatever terms, and he wondered, did Yora sell us out to save himself because he was sure we will lose? One gambles always, he thought. There is in every man's soul, in time of crisis, an instant of wavering. How can I judge Yora Levine?

Edith learned it from the grocer. "G'veret Levine has not picked up her ration," he said. "Although her husband was a British spy and was shot, I do not think her children should starve. Perhaps I am wrong but that is how I feel."

"What are you telling me?"

"G'veret Hirsch, I swear it is true. How does it come you do not know? That's how it is. We do not see what is under our nose. There are some who say she was in it with him. They did for money. They always lived high, you know. Before, when I had merchandise, she always bought my most expensive tins. I should not speak so, I profited, too. . . . Others say he owed the British money and they forced him to do what he did. . . . I am a plain man. It is hard for me to understand how one of us—" He spread his palms. "Yet, sometimes when a man is squeezed to the wall . . ."

"It is not true," she said stubbornly. "She is sick. Her children are sick. That's why she has not come to the store."

"Then you will bring her rations to her? You could leave the food on the steps if you do not wish to go in."

"She is my friend. Give me her rations. I'll bring you the coupons tomorrow."

He leaned over the counter. "G'veret, it is not for me to give you advice, but in your place—" he wagged his forefinger—"I should be careful how I use the word 'friend.' There is much anger over this thing."

"Give me the rations," Edith said. "I will bring them to my friend."

Preposterous, she thought as she ran up the street. Yora's away on a mission, and this fantastic story has gotten about. That's war. Believe nothing, unless you have seen it yourself. She ran up the path to Levine's house before she went to her own. No one was in the yard, but she heard the children inside. Asi came to the door. He opened it just a slit and peered out. She pushed but he held it against her. "Asi, I have brought your rations. You will bring the coupons to the store." She took the bread and groceries from her shopping bag. He opened the door a few inches wider and stretched his hands out. He looked wasted and yellow, with hollows under his eyes.

"Are you sick, Asi?"

"No. Imma won't let us go out."

"She's right. It's too dangerous. Where's Imma?" She pushed the door.

He pushed it back. "Imma won't see anyone. Give me the ration."

"What is it, Asi? What has happened?"

"I do not know. I only know Abba went away in the night and Imma says he will not come home." He gulped. "It is what sometimes happens to soldiers, that's all she said to us."

She did not tell Teddy, merely said, "There is sickness at Asi's. Don't go over there yet," and she waited until she heard Teddy's regular breathing in sleep before she spoke to Jacob of it.

"I knew," he told her. "I did not tell you because I did not believe it was true."

"Is it true?"

He faced her, his forehead knotted. "Edith, I have asked myself that one hundred times, since I heard. How can you be a man's friend for so many years and not know what he is? Then, I said to myself, come to the point, how much does any of us understand about anyone else? We do not understand our own selves. How can we know someone else?"

"We knew Yora. We knew him as well as ourselves."

"Nachon. So we thought. But, Edith, remember, he was with the British a very long while. Could he have remained with them if they were not sure of his loyalty? Perhaps he owed them money. Perhaps he was in debt and needed their Judas gold. Perhaps he merely pretended and never believed we could win this war, and he gambled on their victory. . . . Don't interrupt, little one, he may have believed exactly that. Mind, I do not say I believe these things. I merely try to be rational about an irrational circumstance. . . . The pity is we shall never know the real truth. Perhaps they knew of some wrong in his past and they had him in their power. And perhaps, this to me seems most logical, our friend was insane, a madman, unsuspected. . . ."

"And perhaps," she broke in, stubborn still, "it was not true."

He shrugged his hands. "Would they have taken the life of a father of children if they did not have proof? Could we at this time waste one single life, especially a man who was skillful and brave? No, little one, I fear it is true. I pity Carmela with all my heart. It is a dreadful burden for her. I believe he loved her very much. Therefore, I am sure he was insane."

After a moment, he added, "If not he, then those who accused him . . . War breeds madness, you know."

Later, he asked. "Will you go to her, Edith?"

"I went. She would not see me."

"I, too. She would not see me."

"I will try again."

"I, too," he said. "Whatever happened, she and the children are innocent."

Teddy learned about it the next afternoon.

In the morning his Scoutmaster came to his house to inform him that at four o'clock there would be a special meeting of the Scout troop in the school yard.

"I don't know if Asi can come," Teddy said. "I think he is sick."

The Scoutmaster smiled knowingly. "He'd better not come. The meeting is about him."

"About Asi? What has he done?"

"Don't *you* know? Well then, come find out." He wheeled on the steps. "Don't tell your parents," he said. "They might keep you home. Too dangerous."

Teddy hoped to get there early but, at the last moment, Imma had a job for him, a nasty job, burning the soiled papers from the wastebasket alongside the W.C. By the time he arrived, ten boys in khaki blouses and shorts and Ata blue scarves already stood in a semi-circle in the school yard, close to the wall. Teddy took the end of the line.

"Stand at attention, heads up." The Scoutmaster was a lanky sixteen with large nose, thick-lensed spectacles, and a drillmaster's air. "No giggling, no whispering . . . Teddy Hirsch, I mean you . . . Moreover, if I give the signal you will all march in orderly fashion, no pushing, please, into the shelter." He scanned the sky, as though he might judge from one gaze when, from what direction, shells would be likely to fall. Then he cleared his throat and puffed out his chest.

"Scouts," he began, "I have called this meeting to discuss a matter concerning a member of this troop."

One or two of the boys looked at each other and smiled in a superior way. What are they smiling about? Teddy wondered. "What is the mystery about Asi?" he whispered to the boy next to him.

"Look at him." The boy's elbow nudged the lad on his other side. "Teddy makes believe he doesn't know."

"Maybe he's in it, too," the other said.

"Yeladim, sheket!" the Scoutmaster cried. He hawked again. "It has been decided you are to hear the true facts, so you can decide what is to be done." He glanced at the sky and began to speak fast. "Three days ago, it was learned that a man of this city had served as spy for the enemy." There was considerable clatter of gunfire that instant. He took a few steps forward, into the semi-circle, and the boys flattened themselves against the wall. When the fusillade ended, he started once more, pointing upwards dramatically. "That same enemy whose guns you just heard. Who is destroying our city, who is—" He gulped. "Well, the traitor was caught," he went on. "He confessed. He was shot."

Teddy jumped up and down. Wait till I tell Asi. He hasn't heard this. Then he fretted. The Scoutmaster said this meeting was about him. What has Asi to do with this?

"The traitor, it is my duty to tell you," the Scoutmaster's voice dropped to a stage whisper, "was the father of Scout Asaph Levine."

He could not believe it. He would not believe it. Not Asi's father. Not Asi, *my* Asi. Tears spurted into his eyes. "It is not true," Teddy yelled. "Asi is my friend."

The boy next to him snickered. "Asi is his friend." The boys were all nudging each other, tittering, whispering, "Asi is his friend."

He felt himself getting sick. He was aware of tears rolling down. Angry, he brushed them away.

"Sheket, yeladim!" The Scoutmaster clapped his hands again. "Come to order. We have a decision to make. What shall we do about Scout Asaph Levine? Speak one at a time. Raise your hands."

A tow-headed eleven year old had his hand up first. "I think he should be expelled from the troop," he lisped.

How could he do this to me? Teddy thought savagely—to me, his best friend? How could he shame me before the whole troop?

The Scouts were chattering; the Scouts were squawking and shouting. "Expel him," they were yelling. "Expel the traitor's son. . . . Throw Asi out."

Louder than all the rest, Teddy found himself shouting, "Expel him. Throw Asi out." Suddenly, he clapped his hand on his mouth and stood in stark terror, thinking, What do I say?

"We will take a vote." The semi-circle braced itself and grew quiet.

"All those in favor of expelling the son of the traitor, Yora Levine, will say *Ken;* those opposed will say *Lo* when I call your names out. . . . Shimon Ben Aaron . . ."

"Ken."

"Yoram Dalidansky."

"Ken."

"Dov Gruenbaum."

"Ken."

"Theodor Hirsch."

The eyes were on him. He wanted to run, he wanted to cry. He went hot and cold and he shook. He gulped. He heard his voice trembling as he shouted, "Ken."

Another name, another "ken," another, another. There was no need to count. No one had voted for Asi Levine.

The boys jumped up and down, slapped each other's backs. A good job done. Teddy Hirsch stood motionless, alone. Shame, like a fog, smothered him. His tears dripped, unchecked. I voted against Asi, my friend, he kept thinking. *Suppose he finds out.*

The Scoutmaster clapped for silence again. "It is no use to expel a Scout," he said, "unless the Scout knows he has been expelled. Who will notify Asi he has been expelled?"

"Write him a letter," somebody shouted.

"And who will deliver it?" the Scoutmaster asked.

The murmurs, the jabber began; the eyes pivoted. Teddy felt them as stabs in his flesh. He tried desperately to hold down his lunch.

"I vote Teddy tells him," somebody cried. "Teddy is his best friend."

The boys drew off. He stood alone. Panic raced through him. Animals, he thought. They want to tear me to pieces because I was his friend. What do they want of me now? I voted against him. What else must I do?

"I'll tell him," he shouted. A sob rose in his throat. "Now leave me alone."

The other boys ran home in groups and left him to go by himself.

He walked home slowly, although his instructions were always to run. He took the long way around, up King George, past the Agency buildings, one of the most dangerous corners which his father had specifically ordered him to avoid. He kept muttering, "Hit me, bullet. Hit me, shell," and kept thinking, "How could he do this to me?" and tried not to think, "How could I do this to him?" although that kept rising to cancel the other question out. He knew he hated himself and he knew he hated Asi for making it necessary for him to hate himself.

When he came at last to his own street, he remembered the day he and Asi had tried to be spies and had climbed into the tank. His feet dragged. He scuffed up the dust in the road. His toe hit a fragment of shell. He picked it up, held it clenched in his fist. He walked up the path to Asi's house and boldly banged on the door. Asi pulled it open a crack. He opened it wider when he saw Teddy and, wanly, he smiled.

"You are out of the troop," Teddy bellowed at him. "We expelled you just now." He backed up, hurled the shrapnel, and fled. He was at the foot of the path when he felt a sting in the calf of his leg and knew that Asi had flung the metal back at him.

He remembered to take off his Scout scarf before he entered his house. He was late for supper. His mother said, "I worried. Where have you been?"

She had made scrambled eggs of the egg powder on this week's ration, a treat. He tried but the eggs stuck in his throat and he gagged. She didn't force him. She had marked his flushed face, glazed eyes and slight limp. She put the scrambled egg away for Jacob and stuck a thermometer into Teddy's mouth. He had no fever but there was always the chance, she reasoned, he might be coming down with the flu. He lay down on his mattress.

"You're exhausted. Where were you this afternoon?" she persisted.

He did not reply and she thought he might not have heard what she asked. She repeated the question.

"At a meeting," he growled.

"A meeting? What kind of a meeting?"

"The Scouts."

"The Scouts!" She was certain then he had been somewhere he should not have been. "The Scouts haven't met in more than a month."

"We had a meeting today."

"Why didn't you tell me? Why didn't you ask permission?"

"It was secret."

"Oh, come now, come, come, what sort of *chisbat* is this? A secret meeting of the Boy Scouts! Let me hear. What's this all about?"

He sat up, his eyes wild. "Don't ask me."

"Teddy, don't be stubborn," she said.

"Don't ask me, I said."

She moved toward him, angered. "Master Hirsch, you're getting too big for your breeches. Even a sabra owes his mother respect."

He leaped up, his face livid, contorted with hatred, and swung wildly at her. She felt the lash of his hand on her cheek. Then he fled, out the door, stood in the middle of the heat-seared lawn, watching the exploding shells and the tracers light up the sky, and he prayed again, Hit me, bullet. Shell, come down on me, and kept asking himself, How could Asi do this to me? How will I bear this disgrace?

Within the house, Edith sat with her hand to her cheek. We have reached the breaking point, she thought. Flesh and blood can take only so much. Our nerves are bare. Even our child has begun to crack.

Udi, lean and dispirited after weeks on leavings of kvacker and beans, smelled Teddy in the yard and crept out to him, though he himself was terrified of this noisy dark. The boy put his arms around the dog's neck. "Udi, my friend," he whispered. "You are the only friend I have in the world." They walked slowly together as far as the old fig tree, lay down on the parched, prickly grass. His leg pained where the shrapnel had hit. I am crippled, he thought. The monster crippled me, and he said to his dog, "Udi, why should you and I live in a bad world like this? Let us lie here and die."

"Teddy, where are you?" He heard his mother. "Come in, right away."

"We won't go in." He hugged the dog. "I hit her. She'll punish me. Udi, why did I hit my mother? You know why, Udi. She asks questions. Too many questions. Too many questions," he sobbed. "Too many questions. Mothers haven't the right to ask so many questions. . . . I hate her. . . . I hate all the grown-up people. It's all their fault."

"Teddy!" She was out in the garden, darting about, under the rocket-lit sky, a ghost in her light summer dress.

Let her find me, he thought. Let her look and look. Maybe she'll be killed out here too. Good for her. She asks too many questions. This will teach her not to ask children questions. He squeezed the dog passionately. Udi wriggled and gave a protesting yelp.

Edith heard it. She stood, trying to decide from which direction the sound had come. "Udi!" she cried. He barked to reply. She ran toward the fig tree. Teddy sprang to his feet. In the instant of his indecision over which way to run, she caught him. "Son," she said gently, as she led him back to the house, "don't do this again, promise me."

He said nothing. He kept his eyes from her eyes. "Teddy, you're sick, dear. Lie down, go to bed. When Abba comes we'll find out what's the matter with you."

He undressed and stretched out. He squirmed to the edge of his mattress, farthest from her, shut his eyes, pretended to sleep. When his father came, he heard them beside his mattress; he felt his father's hand on his forehead but he did not open his eyes. "He is warm. He may have a fever. I would not wake him. Sleep is his best medicine." His parents undressed, snuffed out the candle, got into bed. He heard them talking in muffled voices for a short while and then heard their breathing in sleep.

Now I must do it, he thought. I will get a tin of petrol and burn down their house. I'll make a grenade, a Molotov cocktail. I know how to do it. I know exactly how. We can't have the house of a traitor on our own street. Yes, I will burn them all up, Asi and even Aviva and even Shoshanna, too. . . . Yes, and their mother . . . They are all the same thing. . . . That's what I'll do. I'll burn them all up. . . . No one will know I did it. People will think it was set on fire by a bomb. They will think they were punished for what they did. The sword they set against us was turned against them. People will think a miracle happened. They will never know it was me.

Where will I get the petrol? From the primus, of course. We have no petrol in the primus. Imma has to cook in the yard. Where can I get petrol? If the soldiers were here, they would tell me where to get petrol.

The soldiers went away. They went away because this house was hit twice. I know why. I know why our house was hit. The traitor told them the gun and the soldiers were here. I told Asi. I introduced the soldiers to him. I took him upstairs to hear the wireless. He heard everything and he told his father and his father told them. See! . . . See! . . . He rocked back and forth with his grief. . . . They were all traitors. . . . They got me into this, too. . . . How could he do this to me?

His stomach began to cramp and immediately a feasible plan became clear and complete. He pushed Udi away from his toes, breathed into his ear, "Lie still. Sleep. I have to go to the W.C." He padded upstairs and rummaged in his old chest of toys. The playthings clanked and he stood quaking, listening to learn whether his parents had heard. I'm lucky, he thought. The big explosions hide my little noise. He moved his things stealthily. I'm lucky again. The bully beef tin is still here. *He* wanted it. I'll give it back to him. I'll give it back. In a way he will never forget.

He tiptoed into the W.C. and after that down the stairs, through the hall, noiselessly opened and shut the front door. I'll give it to him, he kept telling himself as he ran across the road and up Levine's path. Oh, will I give it to him!

He raised his right arm, flung the tin of offal. He heard the crash of the glass, a mild tinkle in the furious din of the shells, before he fled back to his house. He threw himself on his mattress, buried his head in his pillow, sobbing like a madman.

Jacob woke and came to his side. "Teddy, Teddy! What's wrong?"

"Leave me alone."

He was aware of his father's hand on his body. "Son, don't feel so badly. We understand, Imma and I. Sometimes a child is tired, too. Imma understands why you did that to her. She forgives you. Don't feel so bad."

Teddy had a little fever in the morning. He vomited and would not take his breakfast tea. He had a large purple bruise on his leg. "How did you get that, son?" Jacob asked.

"I don't know." Teddy rolled over to hide his face.

"Keep him in bed," Jacob said. "Don't let Asi or anyone in."

As he went upstairs, heavy-hearted, to wash and to shave in a tumbler of water, he kept thinking, this may be typhoid or it may be the start of the flu. It's no less than a miracle we've not had epidemics. I wish I knew where the boy has been. He kept his fears to himself. "The boy will be all right. War nerves," he said to his wife.

She had to go out. The few slices of musty, dark bread must be brought from the store. When she got ready to go, Teddy sat up.

"Don't leave me." His eyes were wild.

"Just for a minute, son. I have to run for the bread."

He sprang from his mattress, clung to her skirt. "Don't go, Imma. I beg you, don't go."

"Teddy, I must. We'll have nothing to eat."

"No, Imma, please, Imma. You will get killed. Imma, the shells will kill you. Imma, please. I need my mother more than I need bread."

She stroked his face, tried to calm his hysteria and she did not leave the house. It's come, she thought. The siege has wrecked my child. If we do not have a truce soon, not one of us will be left sane or alive.

Next morning, his mood was changed. "What kind of a mother are you?" Teddy said, with the petulance of invalids. "Not a slice of bread in the house. You want me to starve? You want me to die?"

The night had been one of the worst and no one had been able to sleep, and the morning as bad as the night, a steady procession of screaming shells across the blazing sky. She stood in the doorway. "Stop," she cried vainly to the heavens. "Stop. Do you hear me, stop!" Steadily, with hopeless malice, they came, and in the lulls, she heard the Goldstein babies, screaming, as they always did, with sheer fright. It is impossible, I cannot go for the bread. Which does my child need more, a living mother or a slice of bread? I'm tired of dilemmas, sick of questions. . . . If the bakers have courage to come out to bake, if the grocers have courage to open their shops, if Jacob has courage to get to the hospital every day, dare I lack the courage to run for the bread?

She held her hands pressed to her skull, to shut out the din, and she ran through the hailstorm of metal to Keren Kayemeth Street.

She took Carmela's ration too, though the grocer protested "G'veret, I am not sure they will be allowed ration books."

"Then I will give you my own tickets."

She ran to Carmela's house before she went to her own. She rapped on the door. No one answered her knock. She called Carmela's name. She heard no sound. They have gone away, like thieves in the night, she thought. But she left the bread on the step.

"Where were you so long?" Teddy asked suspiciously. "Imma,

did you go to that house?"

"Be quiet, rest," she said. "No one is there."

Yet they were. By noon, the bread had been taken in but the house was silent and shuttered still.

When Carmela knocked on Winkleman's door, she was wearing a shawl and Maida at first did not know who this was, but after Carmela had named herself, Maida asked, freezing up, "And what do *you* wish?"

"Your brother," Carmela faltered. "I wish to speak with him."

"He's asleep. He is tired. You have no right to come late as this."

"When should I come, except late as this?"

"What is it, Maida?" Henry called from inside. "Who is in the hall?"

Maida's arm barred the way. "Stay here. I'll tell him." She hesitated. "Did anyone see you come in here?" she asked.

"Carmela!" He spoke with dismay and surprise, yet he was not surprised. Her coming was inevitable, part of the terrible sequence he had himself set in motion one afternoon last April. I was in this at the start, he thought. I must stay to the end. But, hurriedly, lest his sister try to surmise what went through his mind, he asked, "Did she say what she wants?"

"Shall I send her away?"

"Certainly not. Whatever has happened, she still has the right to come to my house."

He picked up a candlestick and went out to the hall. When he saw her, he put out his free hand and took her fingers, clammy and limp. "Do you wish to see me alone?" he asked.

"If you will."

"We'll go to my study," he said.

He set the candlestick down on his desk and motioned her to a chair. He went to the door, opened it, said firmly, "Maida, I wish privacy. Don't argue, please," shut the door and came back.

She was all but lost in the depths of his black leather chair, a slender woman in black. She had thrown off her scarf. By the candle's frail beam, he saw her chalk-white face and burning eyes.

Her hair was disordered as though she had not combed it all week, and her features seemed smaller, cruel, pinched. She was so beautiful, he thought. Where has it all gone?

It rocked him to see her so altered and to find his composure, he fussed with the blinds, making sure the slats were all closed, and heard her voice asking, with strained bitterness, "You would rather nobody sees I am here?"

He pulled a chair to her chair, straddled it. "That is not true. In my house, you are always a welcome guest."

Her hand reached to him. He saw her eyes fill. "Then you do not know," she said.

"I? But I do."

Gratitude softened her face. "I always knew you were just and good," she said.

He felt uncomfortable, blamed his straddling the chair and got up to change his position. "Henry," she began again, her voice tight, "this week a tin of offal was thrown into our house."

He started up but sat down abruptly and covered his eyes with his hands. She touched the back of his hand. It sent a shudder through him. "Henry, help me," she said. "Not for what I was once to you. For what I am now."

"What can I do? What can I do?" he murmured into the palms of his hands.

She did not seem to have heard. "The widow of an innocent man," she went on. "The victim of a tragic mistake."

He let his hands down. "Carmela, I pity you," he said earnestly. "But you must know he was tried."

"What kind of a trial?" she cried. "They took him away in the middle of the night, his own friends in whom he had trust. Like the German Gestapo. No chance to plead for himself."

"Carmela," he tried to say. "He confessed."

"Confessed what? What had he to confess?" Her voice rose. He looked over his shoulder, wondering whether Maida had her ear to the door. "Confess what he did not do? Confess he had always been loyal, devoted and brave. Confess these last weeks he ran, like a demon, here, everywhere, while the pagazim fell."

"Carmela." He took her hand. "A man's conscience drives him sometimes to do very brave things out of guilt." He was rather surprised to hear himself speaking these words, for he had never thought this before.

She took a word from his mouth. "Whose guilt?" she flung back at him.

"He confessed, Carmela," he said again.

"When they beat him, they tortured him."

He drew away from her, indignant. "You are speaking of us, Carmela. We do not do this."

"They were men, whoever they were, those who judged my husband, and said he confessed. Men and not God. Being men, they have made a fearful mistake."

"Carmela, they did their duty as soldiers, for the security of our State."

"And so I am a widow and my children are fatherless. Henry—" All at once, she began to cry. Large tears drained from her sunken eyes. She used her scarf to wipe them away. "Henry, help me, for my children's sake."

His arm went around her shoulders and she seemed grateful, for she moved against him and her sobs subsided somewhat. He stared into the flickering candle flame, raised his eyes to the shelves of his books. The law was there, precedent, rule and a little of human wisdom. Whatever Henry Winkleman, in dilemma, had needed to know had been in those books. Give me an answer, he begged his books. . . . How can I help? he asked himself. Why should I help?

It occurred to him then that there are no accidents in this world. There is a design, a fate, an inescapable thread, and whatever we do, consciously or unconsciously, is part of the inevitable pattern of our lives. On an afternoon in April, in the courts building in the Russian Compound, Henry Winkleman had set in motion a chain of events, from an Englishman and a stateless harlot to Yora Levine, because without knowing he wished it, he wished Carmela's husband dead.

He took his hand off her shoulder, sat gripped by the realization of the appalling thing which had been buried so deep in his mind and his heart. He tried to debate with himself. If I had not listened to Gordon Leake, had not brought him into our service, he would have gone to someone else. And am I to blame for what Gordon found out? . . . No, my guilt is only that I envied and hated Yora Levine. . . . She must not guess this, he warned himself. She must never find it out.

She was braiding her nervous fingers, this woman in black, made ugly by sorrow. "Henry." Her voice seemed stronger, composed. "I am a Jerusalem woman. Jerusalem women do not weep for their dead. It can happen to everyone here. We know this is the price we must pay for a Nation. . . . But I cry, Henry. Did you see that I cried? Do you know why I cried? I cried because I have not the right not to cry." She unclasped her hands, held them out. "I ask only to be like the rest, to have the right to be proud of my husband's death." She rose then, placed her hands on his arms, looked into his troubled, pale face. "Henry, help me," she said, again.

He took her hands off his arms, and held them. "Carmela, I promise," he said solemnly, "if we have made a mistake, I shall find it out, and that, too, the whole world will know." His own words —words he had said to her a few minutes back—ran through his head: A man's conscience drives him sometimes to do very brave things out of guilt.

III

THE MAN AT the top of the shaking water tower at Gan Darom had seen the tanks start from the Tegart Fortress on the slope and snake across the dun plain. He sent a runner to Dan and Dan sent the runner through all the trenches, warning them to be ready, it comes.

Be ready! With what? With gasoline in beer bottles, one Piat anti-tank gun, ten Piat shells, one machine gun, a dozen rifles and fourteen Stens. Be ready! meant merely, thrust aside weariness and forget fear. Defend or die. Die defending, rather than merely die.

Around the feet of those who stood in the trenches, swirled the foul sewage from broken drain pipes. Buzzards swooped overhead.

There was a rush and a roar. Silver birds with the green star and crescent drove the buzzards away. The earth rocked and quivered. In the deep bunkers, the wounded had to cling to their narrow wood shelves. Ketti swung the machine gun to her broad shoulder and fired at the sky. A thin stream of smoke oozed out of a plane; an engine spat fire. "I think I hit him," she told Dan with excusable pride.

"Don't waste ammunition." The exploding bombs made so much noise she could not hear what he said, and she fired again.

Dan looked older, much. He had grown a beard, a red bush surrounding his jaw. His cheeks were sunken, his eyes scarlet pools. Dan never slept, at least no one knew when he did. Day and night, you could find him, in the trenches, in a pillbox, at the wireless, hearing the headquarters ask, "Must you abandon the position or can you hold out?" answering, "We are holding out, but send us help," receiving the answer, "As soon as we can. Hold out!"

Hold out! Reuven had a wound in his shoulder, his left luckily, but he stood in a trench, for a man can hurl a grenade with his right arm. Reuven was weak from loss of blood, lack of food, and occasionally he had to rest against the wall of the trench. Avrum's shattered leg was in a crude cast, and the pain was so great that without morphine, he could not sleep, but a man with a cast can sit at a wireless set. Shmuel manned the Piat. Dinah had her Sten, and three bottles of gasoline at her feet.

"Don't fire until you must," Dan told the runner to say. "Don't waste a bullet. They are using the planes to soften us up. Then tanks. Then infantry. Save all you can for the infantry."

The measured clank could be heard in the trenches, the long gray metal snake, rolling over the hummocks, across the crisped fields where barley and alfalfa had grown. They heard the crunch as the first tank ripped the wire of the perimeter fence and the crash as it breached the gravel-filled wall. Through the gap in the wall they saw the steel nose. Shmuel fired the Piat. The shell pinged against the tank's side. It did not explode. The tank lumbered ahead toward the trench. Its guns spat. Dinah picked up a gasoline bottle and hurled it into the treads. Fire flashed. They heard an agonized scream within the tank. Then it stopped. The turret opened. Dinah hurled another bottle at the open vent. Soldiers leaped out. She could see rolling whites of eyes, a fear-contorted face, upflung, pleading arms. She fired her Sten. A soldier sank to his knees, then fell flat. Half of his body hung over the edge of the trench. His blood dripped, reddening the sewage at the bottom of the ditch.

Two other Egyptians began to run.

Now there was incessant firing, a melee of noise on both sides of the wall—Shmuel, banging the Piat; Yigal, the baker, a bull-necked, impetuous man, wallowing through the trench with a rifle, pulling the trigger again and again; Dinah hurling another bottle at the second tank and the tanks inexorably rolling ahead. Shmuel's Piat was finding the range, his shells exploding against tank after tank.

All of a sudden, the second tank halted almost at the tail of the crippled lead; it backed, swung around. Behind it the other tanks turned, away, retreating, in flight. Two wounded men blindly crawled through the field where mines had been laid. In the trench, they heard an explosion, saw one Egyptian flung high, come down scattered in death, the other roll over, lie flat.

Shmuel caught his breath. Then he yelled, "They are running. The tanks are running away."

The man in the watch tower saw the distant infantry, moving like a field of wind-blown wheat, halt, reverse, and begin to run back. We have a secret weapon, he gloated, their cowardice.

Yet they remained in their trenches, waiting for the infantry attack. The abandoned tank, reeking of burned flesh, stood before their eyes. Shmuel rolled the dead Egyptian over, out of the way. "Your man, Dinah." The swarthy face looked relaxed, its agony smoothed, almost as though the Egyptian were glad of his death. I was right, Dinah thought, as she looked at him, death is nothing of which to be afraid.

At nightfall, Dan sent the runner once more. "They will come again," he said. "You and you may have water now and your soup and chocolate. You and you may now sleep."

IV

ON THE ELEVENTH of June, firing stopped on both sides. Kauwkiji's Irregulars, dragooned from the alleys and bazaars of Damascus, Cairo and Beirut, had failed to reduce the settlements in the North. Arab Jaffa had fallen to Israel and Tel Aviv was secure. Haifa was safely within the State. Haganah was an army, resourceful, daring, disciplined and equipped with weapons, illegally purchased (defying U.N.'s embargo) or captured in combat from the British-armed foe. Stubborn Jerusalem, shelled day and night for a month, with little water and food, had raised no white flags. The settlements in the South had burrowed like moles into earth, had fired hand grenades from their trenches and turned Egypt back. Contrary to logic and prophecy all of this was. For the Arabs it looked critical. Accordingly, they agreed to a truce. Count Bernadotte boarded a plane for the battlefield, to try, under the United Nations' pale blue and white flag, to bring permanent peace.

For days before, no one in Jerusalem spoke of anything except The Truce and the last night no one slept even an hour, since from behind their stone battlements, the Arab gunners were firing with blood-lusting fury, as though, now or never, they must empty their arsenals. The sky was so crowded with bursting shells the stars could not be seen.

"Wait," Jacob said to his wife in the morning. "Don't go yet for the bread. Ten o'clock is the hour. Be hungry a little while more, but be safe." Yet he himself ran out at his usual time, for he knew that the wards on the Street of the Prophets would be filled with the casualties of the furious night.

At his corner, he met the two Viennese sisters who had once been dressmakers' apprentices and now were soldiers in olive drab, and he flung at them, while he ran, "Why do you go now? Wait. Wait for ten o'clock, for the truce," and they, running too, shouted at him, "Truce or no truce, we report for duty." They ran beside him, down King George Avenue, but being younger, ran faster than he, dodging and weaving through the metal hailstorm.

They were a half-block ahead, at the Ben Yehuda Street corner, and had just caught up with other young soldiers when a shell crashed. By the time Dr. Hirsch reached the corner, five persons were dead, including the two Viennese blondes.

While he knelt beside those who were still breathing, the firing suddenly ceased, as though a time clock had flung a switch, and an unnatural stillness settled upon the throbbing town.

"Believe it or not," Janet Winkleman said to the grocer at half-past ten. "On my way here, I heard a bird sing."

Janet told her father the café was putting out its tables and chairs and he shuffled to Keren Kayemeth, beaming congratulations at everyone he met on his way. Four people began playing tennis, two sprawled on the grass at the court, waiting turns. By eleven, Ida's grandchildren were chasing each other in the middle of the road, discovering the pits dug by bombs, the shrapnel nicks in house walls, collecting new toys; spent bullets and fragments of shells.

Carmela's children came out as far as their hedge, watched the children in the road until their mother instructed them to play in the yard. Teddy saw them from his balcony and went back into his house.

After she had finished marketing, Edith dropped in at Goldstein's to see how Max had been getting along. Maida Winkleman called to her when she left Ida's house, and she stopped there as well. The Winkleman sisters were gaunt, haggard, pale as dawn mist. Edith wasn't aware that when they looked at her, similar adjectives went through their heads. The ladies, however, were chipper, with renewed life.

"Edith, let me fix you a lemon squash. Once in four weeks, we can spare a glass of water for a friend."

"Bring me the glorious day," Janet said, "when we can pull a chain. The house reeks like a sty."

"I don't ask such luxury," Edith said. "Only clean, running water for my toothbrush."

They laughed and stopped laughing to stare at each other. "Why, we're normal!" Edith said. "We're laughing again."

Yes, laughing again, human beings, making calls, gossiping, Edith thought as she strolled slowly home. It's over, it's over. We're no longer imprisoned by flying death, but moving freely, upright, in the sunshine of a June day.

Our Rehavia's aroma is urine and dung and woodsmoke, not jasmine and roses and pine. But that too will pass. Our gardens are dusty and sere. We'll tend them again. We shall have good food and water, even to bathe, and sound sleep at night, in a bed, and this pleasantness of walking erect, with dignity, not running and crouching close to the walls.

The fatigue which had been like an aching boil had vanished, and she felt light; almost floating along.

Little Nommie was parading with her small brother, hand in hand in the middle of the road. A white cloth covered her pigtails. She was singing. "I have a white veil," she sang. "I am a bride. I am a beautiful bride." She looked up at Edith, gravely announced, "I am a bride. We are bride and groom." Jacob would have answered, "May you have many children," but his wife merely laughed, gave the children a hug and went on.

Lillie Gross was spreading pillows to air on her balcony. She waved, Edith waved back at her. Yet when she heard her name called, she remembered and she walked on.

How good this quiet is, she said to herself. It is to be savored in sips, like lemonade on the tongue and relished in all the senses, in the very marrow of bones.

Quiet! Children—her mind addressed itself to the little ones in the road—do you realize what quiet is? It's an ointment, spread on raw nerves, a featherbed for tired limbs. It's Isaac Winkleman, tranquil in the sun. It's Ephraim's housekeeper, watching a blue butterfly circling a hibiscus bush. It is the privilege of choosing your favorite sounds, music and laughter, yes, even church bells. . . . I've missed the bells. Perhaps now we shall have them once more. . . . It's wide open spaces in which to think. Of important things . . . How is my daughter? When shall we see her again? . . . How is my sister, my family in the States? Do they think of us, too? Do they know all that happened to us? And do they believe it? Will we believe it ourselves, in a month, in a year? Think! Four weeks of day and night shelling. People don't live through such things. The human constitution isn't built to endure so much noise, such continuous fear. A pail of water a day, for all purposes, and khamseen, besides. Will my refined relatives in the States believe that Edith Hirsch got along without bathing for more than a month? And ate porridge and beans and musty bread? . . . Yet, somehow we managed. We did our work. We kept our houses, ourselves, fairly clean. How we did it, I can't understand. We were dazed, drugged, in a trance. But we did it, that is the thing. We didn't run. We didn't cry, "Stop! That's enough!" We took it. Staying here, going on, pretending to live normal lives, we *are* here, in our Jerusalem.

But will anyone ever believe how boring it was, always to hide and to dodge, to sit, to lie in the dark, hearing only the whoosh and thunder of shells, no privacy, except our few moments in the W.C.? An hour of glory, indeed! They were difficult days, degrading, and if you want the whole truth, in their way, very dull.

Now we have time for excitement, elation, time to remember we have a State. That's funny. For almost a month, since it happened, no one here has had a chance to remember that we are Israel, a State.

Carmela, in black, came out of her house, with her shopping net, going to the store. They started toward one another. "Shalom," Edith said and held out her hand. Before Carmela's head turned away, she saw the flash of tears. She will not have me, Edith thought. My pity's too painful to her.

As soon as she entered her house, she took the suitcase from the corner of the hall where it had stood these last weeks, and began to unpack. She held the small bundle of Sterling paper, wondering, what is this worth? What shall we buy? She was pleased with the fresh underwear. I'll not need to use water for laundry today. She put Dinah's photograph back in its place on the piano lid, called to Teddy to help carry the mattresses up. "We're sleeping upstairs tonight. In beds."

He ran down, lifted an end of a mattress with his old energy. He's recovered, his mother said to herself. Then it was true that the bombardment had made him ill. "Well, son." She cupped his pointed chin in her hand. "Now we have truce, you can go out and play."

He squirmed off. "I don't want to," he said.

"Why not?"

He looked down at his shoes. "No one to play with."

"What's the matter with Asi?"

"I won't play with Asi," he said.

"That's silly." Her mind paused. Is that what has made Teddy sick? If it has, we must take care of this.

"Asi won't play with me either," Teddy said.

"Have you asked him?"

"I won't ever ask him. I won't ever go to his house."

After she had made up the beds, she said, "Teddy, I'm going to visit Carmela. I want you to come."

His face went ashen. He seized her hand, as though at all costs he had to stop her. "Don't do that! Imma. Don't go to that house!"

"Why not? Carmela's my friend."

He shuddered.

"Are you getting sick all over again?" she asked anxiously.

"Yes," he answered, promptly and with relief.

"Go out in the sunshine. It will do you good."

"I don't want to go out."

"Very well, sit here. I'm going across the road."

He flung himself at her, pommeling, clawing, screaming in frenzy. "Don't go there. Don't go. I'll get sick and die. I'll kill myself if anyone from this house goes over there."

She stopped talking about it and went to fix his lunch, watching him while he nibbled his olives and bread, sipped his weak tea and milk. I won't go yet, she decided. It isn't yet time; Carmela can't bear it and my boy's really sick. I can't risk upsetting him. "Go out on the balcony and get sun," she said before she left for duty at the Army mess.

Ida Goldstein put on her ancient straw hat and went down the street to Carmela's house. She knocked on the door, and when no one answered, she tried the knob. The door was locked. From the yard, she heard a flute and the sounds of children. She went around back. The children were under the olive tree. Asi was playing his flute and the girls making small heaps of stones and angrily knocking them down. "Shalom, yeladim," she said. "Isn't your mother home?"

Asi took the flute out of his mouth. "She's home," he said. "Where would she be?"

How badly the children look, Ida thought, neglected, sick. Asi's eyes are lost in his head. They have wasted away with hunger and grief. What can I cook for them? What have I to spare?

"Your mother did not answer the door," she said.

Shoshanna glanced up. "She doesn't want to see anyone."

"You're not welcome here." Aviva stuck out her tongue.

"We don't need anyone," Asi said.

"That is not so, Asi." She went to him, put her hand on his head. It pained her to see how he shrank from her touch. It's good I came, she thought. It's time I came. She opened the kitchen door, without knocking, and went in.

Carmela was in the kitchen, washing dishes. The room was fearfully dirty, as Carmela's kitchen had never been. Poor Carmela, Ida said to herself, she has been in trouble and no one to help with her work. What kind of a neighbor have I been? Should I have let the shells keep me home?

"Shalom," she said, and went toward Carmela with her arms outstretched.

Carmela's eyes flashed. "Who sent for you?" She drew back, out of reach.

"No one. I came to do something for you."

"Do something for *me!*" Carmela laughed, with bitterness.

"I would have come sooner," Ida said gently. "Only we did not dare to go out. I came as soon as I could. I know, too, what it is to lose a husband one loves."

"You do not know. No one else has ever known a tragedy like what has happened to me."

"My friend, you are not the only woman whose husband has died for this State."

"Died for this State?" The eyes glittered again. Misery twisted Carmela's mouth.

"Let me sit down," Ida said quietly. "I find these days I often need to sit down." She drew up a stool. "Sit, too, Carmela," she coaxed. "You, too, need more rest."

"Rest!" Carmela was mocking her with every word. "How shall I rest with the weight on my heart?"

"When I heard of it, I thought at once. it must be a mistake."

"And what else is it? A mistake of madmen." Her face was writhing. When she found she could not control it, she turned swiftly, dipped her hands into her dishpan and pretended to be at work.

"A mistake." Ida Goldstein folded her hands in her lap. "A mistake, too, is part of making a State," she said thoughtfully. "Understand, Carmela, child, see. I have thought a little about these matters." She spoke with care, for she wished very much to make Carmela comprehend what she was trying to say. "People die in many ways when a Nation is made. They die by courage, in battle, as my Arieh did. They die by malice, or by stupidity, like my Deborah. They die by accident, like Leah Malkoff. And they die by mistake as Yora did."

The back of the woman at the sink altered perceptibly, the merest head rise of arrested attention. Ida went on. "Every death serves the State in its way. Yes, first the stupidity, the malice, for it made us understand what the British were. Yes, even the accident. It made us hurry to build the wall on King George. It is a hard thing to understand, and sometimes, I, even myself, believed it was cruel and unjust to ask so much of small people like us. When I heard about Arieh, I cried out to God. But I know, I know clearly now, it is right. This is big. We are small, grains of sand. A big house is built out of small grains of sand."

The spine of the woman at the sink had grown rigid, the head lifted up. The dishcloth dropped from her hands. But Carmela Levine was not finished, not yet, with her bitterness. "You are done? Thank you very much for the speech, G'veret. Now, go away. I am busy. Some other time we will sit over coffee and talk theory."

"Give me your towel." Ida got up. "I will help."

"I need no help."

"But you do." She found a soiled towel, redolent of weeks of porridge and beans. She dried a saucer, a cup.

"Tell me," Carmela blurted. "If you are so wise, how was the State served by this mistake? By this mistake which left my children fatherless and in shame?"

Ida put down the towel, laid her arm across Carmela's shoulders.

"It is sad that it happened to you. With all my heart, I pity you. But if it was a mistake, then it will serve our Nation. Men will learn from it. They will learn to be careful and patient and just. This is all new to us. For two thousand years we dreamed of a State. But we have had it not even one month. We have much to learn. We will make other mistakes, many more. I wish it would not be so, but we are only people, and we make mistakes. From every mistake we will learn. And in time our Nation will be wise and just."

The water cart came late, not needing to hurry today. Two people watched it from their balconies. When the women all had their pails filled, Teddy dashed out for his family's ration and when he was carrying his pails up the path, Asi Levine came out, the last, alone, to get his.

Jacob was home early. "A wonderful day," he exulted. "Not a single new casualty this afternoon. . . . Little one, the Vienna Café and the cinema will be open tonight. We shall go, all of us."

He strolled leisurely through the lower floor of his house. The rubble dust film lay everywhere, on the dining table, the piano, the bookshelves, the books. The sandbags and netted glass panes made the rooms dismally dark. The wall where the mattresses had lain, now stood bare, waiting for the sofa to be pushed into place. The pictures, the hangings, the rugs, the nicknacks, the things which make house into home, were all gone.

He examined the ruins of his waiting room. Tomorrow, I shall look for a plumber and plasterer, he told himself. It is time to fix up our house. First we must find a glazier for Dinah's windows. He rooted around in the cellar, brought out his paint box and a strip of canvas, took a chair out to the yard. When Edith glanced over his shoulder, she saw he was painting the shattered cypress, the raw, reproachful arrow of broken trunk, pointing up toward the sky. "A souvenir," he said blithely, "of unbelievable times."

By evening Teddy appeared fully recovered. He held his father's hand tightly until they reached the end of their block. "Listen," he said at the corner. "That fool is playing his concertina again. He thinks he knows how to play the 'Song of the Negev.' I should have my flute and show him how to play that."

"The siege, unquestionably," Jacob whispered to Edith. "I must, when I have a chance, discuss this with pediatricians—the effects of prolonged excitement and terror on a growing boy. . . . Say nothing, act unaware, but watch the boy. He may not be as well as he thinks. Sometimes these things have lasting effects."

It seemed as if the whole city were out in the streets. Soldiers were dancing *horas* on the pavements, in the litter of broken stone, glass and ripped wire. Strangers yelled, "Shalom! Shalom!" to each other as though they were life-long friends. The Vienna Café was a family reunion. People greeted each other with "So you, too, are alive! I thought I was the only one."

As they walked home, under clean starlight, Jacob said to his wife, "Yes, we are alive. We are strong as lions. We have lived through Jerusalem's siege."

She linked her arm into his and pressed into his side, nestling to him. "Jacob, suppose—" He caught a tremor in her voice. "Suppose this truce ends and war starts again, have we the strength to go through this twice?"

He tapped her cheek lightly. "Women! Worrying women! When the first baby is born, 'Doctor, dear Doctor, must I go through the same pain the next time? Doctor, I couldn't stand it again.' . . . Twice, three times, ten, as many as needed, we will go through this, and more."

Before next morning's sunrise, one man of the street was no longer alive. Isaac Winkleman died in his sleep. "He went upstairs, last night, to his old room," Janet mourned. "The first time in a month. Do you think the exertion was too much for him?"

"He walked to the café and sat in the sun," Maida said. "In all the heat. Was that what killed him?"

"Why, no, it was the siege, I am sure," Henry answered. "We could hardly expect a man of his age to come through that alive."

"Yes," Dr. Hirsch agreed. "It was the siege, in a way. He did his duty. He served Jerusalem well." And he spoke the old man's epitaph. "I loved the Afrikaander," he said. "He was God's first gentleman."

His daughters and son felt that the Doctor was putting it on a bit thick, since, after all, he had had no more than a nodding acquaintance with the old man.

V

On the morning of truce, the guns of the Tegart Fortress were still lobbing shells toward Gan Darom and planes swooped, spraying lead, although the wireless had given both sides the "cease-fire." An incendiary caught the barley field's stubble and filled the trenches ' with strangling black smoke.

"We cease and they fire," Ketti grumbled. "That's what they mean by cease-fire."

But by noon there was silence, so sudden and strange that in the trenches they stood waiting, not sure of what you did in a truce. Dan himself made the rounds and told all but a handful they now might climb out. Unsteadily, they walked across their own land, not yet convinced one could stand and walk slowly, upright. Like visitors, they tramped their torn earth, goggled the rubble of dining hall, children's house, bathhouse and barns, the smoke-blackened, shell-pitted, slanting, empty water tank. Everyone's eyes were moist. That was from smoke, they assured each other, not the heartbreak of planted fields charred and the pitiful stumps of fruit trees.

"The fire will burn itself out," Dan said. "It will stop when it gets to the wall. We will work first on the sheds and see if our lorries can be repaired. And we will go to the base for a shower. Four can be spared at one time. Those who wish to go first will walk. I have arranged, they will drive you back, with supplies for us."

Dinah saw the plane at the base before she entered the bathhouse and left Ketti to ask a mechanic whether the American had come on this flight. "Yes," he answered, "the flyer is here. I'm busy, don't bother me. Look for him yourself."

"Ask him to wait, I must see him," she said and went for her shower.

The water ran tepid, merely warmed by the sun, but it was velvet on her arid flesh. She soaped legs and armpits, her feet, each toe separate; Ketti and she scrubbed each other's backs. She held her eyes open under the shower to watch the glistening stream run down her belly and thighs.

They did not dry themselves, but stood dripping, savoring the luxury of clean water on clean skin. They shook their wet hair like puppies, grinned with delight. Each of them said just one word to the other, the word "clean."

"A girl wants to see you," the mechanic told Al.

"About time some local babe took notice of me," he replied.

He was watching the mechanic at work on the engine of the old plane, admiring his skill, when girls came up to him, not one girl, two, a brunette and a blonde and both properly stacked. "Shalom," they said.

He answered, "Shalom," and gave the brunette an additional glance. "We've met before," he chortled. "Sure, we're old pals. You slapped my face."

He had the satisfaction of seeing her blush. "I would prefer you would forget that," she said.

"Think nothing of it. It's not the first time." He put out his hand. "Dinah Hirsch," he said. "Father, Jacob. Jerusalem. Correct?"

She took his hand, shook it forthrightly, dropped it at once. "Correct. I was grateful to you."

He waved his hand airily. "Nothing at all, any time, any time." Then he added, "You've lost some weight since I saw you last." And her skin was bad, broken out with mean sores, he noticed, but did not mention that.

"We've had a war."

"So I've heard."

"And now we have truce. And a bath." Her friend nudged her, wanting to be introduced. "Oh! This is Ketti, my comrade," she hurried to say.

The blonde smiled at him. He smiled back at her. She had lovely dimples and of the two was handsomer, yet in some subtle way, too obvious. Embarrassed for no reason he could explain, he sketched an arc on the ground with his shoe. "So you girls made the trip for a bath?"

"Our first in four weeks," Dinah said.

"Sissies! Try doing without for ten months. Boy, do you stink!"

"I know very well," the blonde said. She spoke English, too, that was fine, but with a foreign inflection, book taught, and unlike the other's accent. Dinah's English had the local accent, part thick guttural, part British Mandate.

"Now, how would a nice girl like you—?" he began to ask.

"This is how." Ketti swung her arm up and out, a casual and graceful gesture, but he saw her blue numerals and his manner changed. "Me, too," he said eagerly. "The bastards had me back of barbed wire. Prisoner of war."

Ketti's lower lip curled. "We had no Geneva Convention."

"You win." His hand touched his brow in a kind of salute. "You always will win. Whatever lousiness the future may hold for the human race, you'll still top the bill."

She scowled at him. "I do not understand."

"Skip it," he said. His slang was beyond them, he realized.

It was more than that. At this moment, they preferred a different conversational line. "What's your name?" Ketti asked.

"Al . . . Al Brody . . . from New York."

"From New York!"

He liked the way they mouthed it together, something special to have come from New York.

"Do you know Boston also?" Dinah asked.

He said he'd been there, big city but nothing compared to New York.

"Then it is just as well I did not go there," Dinah said. "My parents talked sometimes of sending me there. They once lived in Boston. I have an aunt, in a quarter near there."

Ketti looked bored. "What do you think of our country?" she asked.

"Well—" He jerked up his slacks. "I haven't seen much." He saw by their eyes they wanted a rave and he did his best. "Tel Aviv. Well, it's all right. Busy place. Modern, clean. Nothing to get excited about. And from the air you don't see a lot. And this—" His arm and glance circled the landscape. "You have to be nuts to think the Negev is worth looking at."

Dinah stared at him coldly. "We think it is worth looking at."

Her tone was more than reproving, it was arrogant. "We think it is even worth dying for."

"Take it easy, sister." He touched her arm. "Don't make me a speech."

She drew back from both his words and his touch. "Excuse me," she said, still faintly superior. "I forget. You are a foreigner, you cannot understand."

His blood pressure rose as it used to when Saul handed out the same line. "A foreigner, hey? Risking my life, running an airlift for you in a sardine can. A foreigner. When do I start to belong?" The girls were ashamed of themselves, he was pleased to observe. After a moment, Dinah tried a new line. "You go to Jerusalem still?"

"It's on my route. I'm the postman."

She frowned, not certain she knew what he meant. "You mean you do?"

"I do. Okay. Sure. You bet."

Ketti laughed. She had a lovely laugh, he took note. "I have learned something. Okay, sure, you bet." Feeling friendly, he took a step toward her, but she moved back, keeping her distance, making it clear she expected he'd do the same.

"How is it in Jerusalem?" Dinah wanted to know.

"It's still there. What more can you ask? Things are going to get better when—" He stopped himself. That was a secret an airman might learn as he flew. No, he decided, they may be the most tried and trusted, but they will not hear it from me. "I'll be going to Jerusalem for a while, at least," he said.

"You will take a message for me again?"

"Okay, sure, you bet. What do you want me to say?"

"The same as before. You saw me. I am well. And if you can, bring back a message from my parents to me."

"Will do. You girls staying here?"

"No." Dinah seemed to be doing the talking for both. "Soon, they drive us back in the jeep. Leave the message here. Someone will bring it to me."

He shook his head, smiling. "Is that hospitable, sister? What you should say is come up and see me some time."

She gave him a neat nod of agreement. "Some time. Not now. Now you will see nothing but bunkers and trenches and ruins."

"They shelled us," Ketti felt she had to explain. "From the Tegart Fortress up on the hill. They bombed us with planes overhead. They attacked us with tanks. They killed our cattle, burned all our fields, destroyed every building and house. We have slept when we slept, these four weeks, like animals, in holes in the ground. We have had three cups of water a day. We have had soup and chocolate and bread. Nothing more. We had twenty killed, fifteen wounded." She raised her chin with a soldier's pride. "We are still there," she said.

"Good going!" He clapped his hand on her shoulder. "What did you chicks do with yourselves while the excitement was on?"

"Ketti had the machine gun," Dinah said. "She used it one day for anti-aircraft. She hit one of their planes."

His eyebrow rose, skeptically.

"Dinah stopped the tanks," Ketti said. "With Molotov cocktails and a Sten. And all the tanks turned around and left us alone."

Both his eyebrows jumped up and he laughed out loud. This was a country of heroes, all right, but did they have to go around making things up? They've got a word for this in these parts. "Chisbat," he scoffed.

Ketti flared like a boxful of matches. "Chisbat, you call this! You see, Dinah, no one will believe it. Like in Germany, it was something you could not believe."

Dinah smiled tightly. "It is nothing to talk about. Only to do." She looked weary, he thought, fed up with this. "When you leave the message for my mother and father," she went on to say, "tell them, please, only that I am well."

"Will do." His hand dropped lightly on her arm. She ducked back. He forced a laugh to put her at ease. "Take it easy, sister. Who's been briefing you on American wolves?"

She looked at him blankly.

"Okay, skip it," he said. "Sometime when I have more time, I'll come down and explain."

"Come," she said eagerly. "Come when we are farmers again."

He grimaced. "Nah, I'll not be around here that long." He glanced at his watch and whistled. "Excuse me, kids. Here I stand chewing the fat, American Express has to be on its way."

They shook hands with him, said, "Shalom." When he climbed

into his cockpit, he saw them talking together and nodding toward him. They stood at the rim of the field, waving while he took off, and he thought, Success! Good luck, Al. At last you know a few local babes. Too bad they live out of town.

He veered from his route to fly low above Gan Darom, though the anti-aircraft at the Tegart made that a foolhardy sport, and he caught a swift glimpse of a wall, a water tower, leaning askew, and bashed-in roofs. Home, sweet home, he thought. Those poor babes.

He thought of them all the way in. The blonde seemed older and looked as if she knew what it was all about, though she wouldn't give it a chance, but he couldn't decide about the Hirsch girl. That one was no icebox, not with her bosom, her eyes. A handsome broad, even in her raggedy shorts and blouse. But she treated a man like another man, no making with the eyes, with the toss of the head. She stuck out her paw, shake, brother, pal. Like a man. And why not? If they're telling the truth, and why should they kid someone like me? she's killed like a man. That's a thing to tell the boys in the back room, back home. A beautiful babe throws a Molotov cocktail and stops a row of tanks. Think nothing of it, talk about something else.

What had impressed him most, he decided, was the cool casualness of their bravery.

"He is nice," Ketti said in the jeep, going home. "I did not think Americans were as nice as this. There is something—" she gestured vaguely, not sure of her word—"cheerful about them."

"But superficial," Dinah added.

"Naturally, superficial. He is a child."

Dinah shifted to defense. "He was a prisoner of war."

"And what was that? No gas chambers were waiting for him. He knows nothing still." Ketti spread her hands, shrugging. "He flies to the Negev. He flies back, like a bird. What does he see? What does he know? We tell him two little things. He answers, 'Chisbat.'" She ground her teeth. "If he comes back, I will teach him," she said.

"Ketti, do you hope he will come?"

Ketti's glance probed but failed to find what it sought. "Certainly, I hope he will come. He is charming and interesting, in his way."

She brooded a moment. "Yes, he is nice," she said. "I hope he comes again." She did not add what lay at the tip of her tongue, "To see me."

The jeep turned in at the Gan Darom road, threading warily. In the field where potatoes had been harvested before mines were sown, a scarecrow sprawled, the garments and shoes of an Egyptian soldier, bones picked bare by buzzards, bleached white by sun, the skull without lips where teeth seemed to grin.

Ketti pointed and shrugged. "That one knows what it is about. Too bad he cannot go back and tell them in Cairo, when you make war on Israel, you can become very dead."

"I killed him, too," Dinah said. "Dan and Joshua and I laid the mines in that field."

Ketti pinched her arm. "For a young girl, you do very well."

VI

Two days before the truce, a miracle occurred, as great as that other miracle in biblical times, when the Red Sea divided to let the Israelites through. A road was completed, hacked out in darkness under the very sights of the Arab guns at Latrun, hewed by bull-dozers and a thousand hands. Jerusalem was linked to the coast by an all-but-impassible road. With the cessation of fighting, trucks commenced to waddle through gullies, up steep inclines, bringing flour, fresh vegetables, oranges, fish, margarine, a chicken for the Shabbat, sugar, two fresh eggs a week for each child. And fuel for the dynamos, so that one might turn electricity on, read a book, sew, hear the wireless, *Kol Yisroel,* the voice of a State, bringing news from the desert, the hills, the outside world. The heavy trucks also brought other things. Now break the truce, Jerusalem at last could declare, and we give you genuine war.

The little plane, however, continued to come, carrying mail, and transporting to Tel Aviv and return officials of the new government or Army officers but it was merely a convenience now, not the life-saving thread. Infrequently, too, a bus or a limousine with a power-ful motor made the trip on the powdered talc of the brutal road and carried passengers back. Nathan was one of those who traveled. A government post was waiting for him in Ha' Kirya, the village out-side Tel Aviv, which was the new capital.

Henry Winkleman suggested to Carmela one evening that since traffic moved on the road, he would attempt to get passage for the children and her. He made the proposal in her house, not his. Maida and Janet still bristled because she had once come to him. "You have a brother, Carmela," he said. "Take your children and go to him."

"I have no brother," she answered.

314

He scratched his jaw, puzzled. "Levi Benatar. I remember clearly. Your only brother."

"He is no brother." Her throat was tight, for it is hard to admit my brother has rejected me. "I sent a message to him in February. He did not even reply. I have tried many years to make friends with him. He will not have me." Her sunken eyes sought Henry Winkleman's face. "He is a snobbish man, my brother, and arrogant. He forbade me to marry Yora." The tip of her tongue moistened her lips and she looked at him, thinking, it is ironic that Henry sits here. My brother and I had our quarrel because of him. "Levi never forgives," she said and smiled a small, sad smile. "Would he take us? No, it is as impossible for us, as for him. We all have pride."

He waited, then said, "Go to Haifa, to anywhere, where you are not well known. . . . This is too cruel for your children."

She gripped her fleshless, nail-bitten fingers. "They have lost a father. That is even more cruel," and rose to prowl nervously around her living room. She came back to stand near his chair. "No, Henry, you mean well for us, but for me there is no hiding place. Once—you may still remember, my friend—I was considered a beautiful woman." She laughed, a bitter sound. "No matter," she said. "No, Henry, I am a Jerusalem woman. This is my home. Here we remain, all of us, until justice is done." She moved around to face him. "Henry, I ask this not only for us, nor just for Yora's memory. I ask what I ask for the State."

He tried to break in, but she went on, her voice rising, "Henry, a fearful mistake has been made. I do not know why they did what they did. No one will speak. They have locked the details of that night, as in a tomb. I tried to see Nathan, to ask them of him. He would not see me. And now he is gone. . . . Has he run away?"

"Run away? Why should he—?"

She swept on. "Henry, we dare not leave this so, buried in silence. It is important to know. It was a mistake. Who made that mistake? Why was it made? Until those who murdered my husband are made to understand what they did, there will not be justice here. Our State is young, like a small child. It, too, must be punished when it does wrong. Otherwise how will it learn what is right?"

He was astonished and pleased. "I would never have thought of it this way," he murmured.

The sad smile again curved her lips. "You may be sure I did not think of it by myself. A woman told it to me, a simple woman of Jerusalem, like all of us." She laid her hand on her breast. "Henry, find justice for us. And a clean conscience for the State."

He slept little that night for a plan was maturing in his mind. I can go to Tel Aviv. To the Kirya. To the Prime Minister. I know him. He is a just and good man. He will listen to me. I will ask him to drag the full truth to light. . . . Why should I do this? For Carmela, of course . . . And for myself . . . And for our Nation, especially.

VII

"WHILE THE BOYS are being good boys," Al proposed at his base, "Do you think the Auster and I might spend this Shabbat in the Negev? I'd like to get a close look at that part of your State. It interests me very much."

He was surprised, most agreeably, when the officer, within the hour, returned with a leave chit. He hung around the Negev base in June's furnace heat until late afternoon Friday when a jeep departed for the direction of Gan Darom and he climbed into it with a heavy musette.

The driver was curious about why he was making the trip. "To see some babes," Al told him.

"There are no babies in Gan Darom. They were all gone before the bad fighting commenced."

"Not these babes," he said. "They're tough."

"So then what kind of babies?"

Al made an "O" with thumb and mid-finger. "Let you know tomorrow," he said. "Hope for the best."

"You are crazy," the driver said cordially. "All the Americans are."

They approached a cluster of huts made out of mud and dung, thatched with straw, fenced by a cactus hedge, man-high, and hung with black-peppered, pink fruit. Sabras, Al remembered, the fruit named after the local kids. Other way around, *they* took the name. Rough outside, sweet within. That sweet, I've still got to see, he told himself.

The jeep veered to the side of the road and stopped at the Arab village. Al thought the place was deserted until he saw a man with a Sten step from behind the cactus. "Two kilometers. Go straight," the jeep driver said. "One turn left. I would take you, only I have more important use for petrol."

He kept to the middle of the rutted, baked clay path and tried to walk fast because the sun had started to sink behind the distant brown Hebron hills. Plodding along in the sunset, in the endlessly stretching wastelands, he saw not a person or jeep, nor a camel or donkey, nothing except the black buzzards overhead. He felt like the last man on earth.

The only sound was a mournful baying, like a dog's but thinner and in an eerie way, menacing. Jackals, he realized. That made him quicken his steps. He peered sharply, certain he saw skulking forms around the mustard hummocks. No dice, he vowed to the emptiness, no supper off me. He started to run. The musette dug into his shoulder and he had to slow down.

The track was a rubber band, stretching, not two kilometers, make it at least three or four, before he reached the dirt thread which was the left turn. After he turned, he saw a yellow stone Tegart Fortress up on a rise, and straight ahead, a pitted wall, the blackened top of a water tower and fields in which grain had been charred. In the field near the wall, a skeleton in the rags of a uniform, leered up at him. There was wire around the field where the man lay. He tried to decipher markings on the garments. "Poor bastard. A hell of a way to be left. Will his folks ever know what happened to him?" he thought before he walked on.

Ahead of him, faintly gilded by the last of the sun, was a high wall, and in a breach in the wall, an abandoned tank. A man with a Sten, bare to the waist, with fleshless ribs, sprang out of a trench behind the wall and challenged him, in Ivrith. He answered, "Shalom," and took his chit out. Because he could not remember the other girl's name, he said, "I came to see Dinah Hirsch."

"In the kitchen bunker. That is where she should be."

He jumped the trench. The place was a ruin, earth torn up and criss-crossed by wire and foul-smelling damp ditches, stone rubble heaps and earth mounds. Nobody lives here, he thought, no one can live in this dump. Then he saw a woman walking, literally out of a hole in the ground, and he tried to keep incredulity out of his voice, long enough to inquire whether she knew where Dinah might be. The woman pointed into the ground. "In the kitchen," was what she said.

A ramp, with steps hacked in earth, led down to an oval chamber, hewn out of clay. A carbide lamp gave it light. It stank of kerosene, sweat, boiling soup. But in that fetid hole, a trestle table was up and because it was eve of Shabbat, two young women in shorts were laying a white tablecloth. They took no notice of him, went on with their work, until he asked for Dinah again, and then they pointed, a step deeper down into earth.

A deadening heat floated out of the cave. Primus stoves hissed in the hole, two of them holding kettles of soup. There was a tin oven, and girls barelegged, in very short shorts and hair bound up in scarves, were bustling about, trying to keep out of each other's way in a narrow space. Dinah, on a wooden bench, was peeling potatoes, dropping them into a pail, doing K.P.—he was past astonishment—in the bowels of the earth.

When she saw him, she plopped her knife and a half-pared potato into the pail, got up at once, wiping her hands on her shorts, "Shalom, shalom!" she cried. She looked and sounded pleased. "How did you get here?"

"A jeep part way and walked."

"You are wonderful!" She shook his hand, in her man-to-man way.

"If this was the States," he apologized."I'd have called on the phone, made a date." He grinned. "Quite a set-up you have."

She called the other girls over, said a few words in rapid Ivrith, which he guessed was summing him up, mentioned their names, "Chava . . . Ilana . . . Rima . . ." and his. They nodded amiably and went back to their work. "My parents?" she asked. "You brought my message?"

"I told a guy at the field. He knows your family, he said. Lives on their street. Ephraim, I think his name was—"

Her laughter rang out. "God help Jerusalem, if its defense depends upon him." Then she sat down, fished the knife and potato out of the pail, said, "Excuse me, I must go on with my work. You do not mind if I work while we talk?"

He swung the musette off his shoulder. "I'll unpack," he said, took out cognac, cigarettes and chocolate, set them near her on the bench. "I brought a few items for you and your friend." The other girls darted over, looked from him to his presents and beamed. "Cigarettes!" Dinah crowed. "The men will be pleased." One of the girls said something to her and she translated for him. "Chava says we celebrate tonight. Truce and cognac for Shabbat."

He began to repeat, "I brought it for you and your friend," but before his words had got out, he had figured it up, nothing's for anyone personally here, you divide what there is, and he merely asked, craning his neck, "Where's your blonde pal?"

"Ketti? Oh, Ketti is sick."

He said it was too bad. "Nothing serious, I hope."

"*Shil-shul.*" Dinah smiled. "Our national disease."

He answered her smile. "I knew it well."

"Go see her." She dropped the potato into the pail. "In the hospital. I will come for you there. Bring her cigarettes. She will be very pleased." She smiled again, this time with eyes as well as lips. "The hospital is next bunker to this."

Night was almost complete, just enough gray in the sky to help him find the next cave. He went underground. His eyes popped. There were wooden bunks, with clean mattresses, on which bandaged men lay, comfortable and neat. He asked for Ketti. A man motioned beyond and he went through a hollowed-out chamber, where packages of plasma and bandages and drugs and a clean sterilizer were stacked on immaculate wooden shelves and a table in the middle was scrubbed white. I'll be damned! he thought. How they did this, when they did this, no man will comprehend, but by God, they did it and you'll never lick them. Through that room, to another where he saw Ketti's bright hair.

She was lying down, nothing on but a loose slip, because it was fearfully hot. She sat up when she saw him and quickly folded her arms on her breasts.

"Take it easy," he hurried to say. "How do you feel?"

Ketti made a face. "Am I not stupid? In all the bad fighting, not one minute sick. But now we have truce—" She rocked her head in her hands. The half-moons of her bosom rose over the slip. When she saw he was staring at them an angry flush swept her face, throat and chest. "The hospital is not to visit," she snapped.

Funniest women I ever met, he said to himself. The only thing that upsets them is ordinary sex. This one's downright jumpy. Let's rule out the blonde. It's too hot to work hard. "Dinah told me to come visit with you," he tried to explain. "Till she finished her work."

Ketti wasn't appeased. "Oh, it is Dinah you come to see?"

"Why not?" He held the cigarettes out. "Brought a present for you."

That was better. She showed her dimples. *"Players!* Two tins! Enough for the whole hospital." She cradled the cigarette tins in her hands, admiring before she laid them down. "Well, now you have seen Gan Darom, do you still think we tell chisbat?" she asked.

"You're wonderful," he said sincerely. "You're the most amazing people on earth."

The right thing to say, her dimpled smile and her nod agreed. "Will they believe when you tell them in the States?"

"They never do." He found himself grinding his teeth. "What you haven't seen with your eyes, you never believe."

Dinah came in after that, with her hair combed, her face scrubbed, still in her tattered shorts and faded, sweat-stained blouse, but somehow looking as if she had dressed up. "What do you think, Ketti!" Her dark eyes shone. "He promised to come and he came."

Ketti looked at her hard. Her lips curled the least bit. "You are the lucky one, always," she said.

Success, Al thought, doing fine. The babes are tossing knives over me.

"Be careful," Dinah said as they emerged from the cave. "Here is a trench. Give me your hand." Her fingers coiled around his, hard, rough, strong fingers, a boy's, extended to help a comrade across a bad spot. His hand was in hers when they went down the rabbit hole.

A dozen men and women were jammed around the trestle table with the white cloth. The cognac bottle, he saw, was on the table and he was glad. There were stacks of sliced dark bread, metal cups, bowls. Dinah said something to one of the men, he spoke to the man next to him and they crowded closer to make room for Dinah and him. She introduced Al, calling out names: Dan, a kid with a scraggly red beard; Joshua, a blondish lad, next to Dan; Reuven, a heavy-set man with one arm in a sling; Yigal, stocky, thick-necked; Hanna, a handsome, older woman with sad blue eyes; Gittel, lean, getting gray; a half-dozen others whose names he didn't catch. They nodded, one or two said "Shalom." Then Dinah talked Ivrith again and the woman called Gittel began to speak English to him, with that local accent, saying thanks very much for flying plasma, morphine and penicillin to them. The cognac bottle was passed—Dinah told them it was his—and Reuven and Joshua said. "Toda raba." He noticed that each of them took no more than an eye-dropperful; either they weren't tipplers or they wished to make sure there would be enough for the rest.

The girls he had met in the kitchen brought in a steaming pot and Dinah stood up to ladle a thick mess of barley, beans and potatoes into metal bowls.

The food wasn't good, wasn't bad, and the most you could say for the bread was it was fresh. They all ate fast, as though they were starved or in a rush to get this over with, heads down, most of them slupping their soup, doubling their bread. Only Joshua and the girl at his side spooned daintily, showing that they'd been reared with the niceties of a well-mannered house. In the few moments between soup finished and tea to be brought, he stared around the table with frank interest.

There was no type, he decided. Their skin color was terra cotta, result of a desert sun, and most of them had unpleasant sores, but that was all in which they were similar. They were blond and dark and red-haired. It was hard to guess ages. If they were kids, they had matured fast. Some of the men had been growing beards, circular, like photographs Al had once seen in a schoolbook of Mormon elders out West. The Utah desert, the Negev desert, pioneers with identical beards. Remember to tell the folks this, how history repeats itself in beards. Joshua had a sensitive face but Dan seemed to carry the woes of the world on himself. Reuven had a classic profile you might print on a coin or a postage stamp. Yigal resembled Al's Old Man in the squatness, the set of the head. The women seemed older than the men did, no make-up, hair slicked back or tied in a scarf.

Tight-lipped, sweating, smelly, sunburned peasants and workmen, he added them up. No hero posing, no strut. Farmers, mechanics, housewives. Only the place where they gathered, under the desert floor around a white tablecloth in a room carved in earth made you certain new human dimensions had been achieved.

When they finished their tea they rose at once. Joshua and Gittel shook hands with Al, said "Shalom" to him, before they went out. Dinah began to stack empty tin cups. "I am on duty here tonight," she said. "Others will come very soon. It was good to see you. When do you leave?"

"Leave? I thought, I expected—" He laughed awkwardly. "I'm a dope. I imagined these places like a summer camp. Nothing fancy, but a transient can always find room in a tent."

"As we eat, so we sleep, underground."

He said he was willing but Dinah looked dubious. "You are an American. You are used to better than this."

"Weren't you?"

She shook her head. "That's different. This is my home." She hesitated a moment, then said, "Wait, we will see. First I must ask Chava if she will wash dishes tonight for me."

The dark was murmurous and Al knew there were people about, yet when he heard the baying of jackals he grew uneasy again. Dinah took his hand. "Be careful," she said. "A trench begins here. Jump." They jumped together. "I am used to this place," she said. "I will help you." On the horizon, he saw the orange arc of a rising full moon.

As they climbed over hummocks, she began speaking in the matter-of-fact way of a guide, "The first time they bombed us from the air, they hit the dining hall and the water tower. They killed our leader, Gershon. Dan became our leader. . . . He ate with us tonight."

"The boy with the beard?"

"Boy? He is nineteen years old. We have grown old very fast."

"Tell me what happened," he said, holding tight to her hand.

"They broke our water pipes. They wrecked our dynamo. They hit the cow barn. Half of our cows were killed the first day. By night, we worked digging bunkers. By day we stood in the trenches. Dan did not sleep and so we did not sleep. We milked our cows after dark. We were shelled every night but we did not worry so much because there was no danger then of infantry attack. Our enemy—" her voice lightened—"does not fight at night. He is afraid of the dark. . . . Be careful here. A bunker begins."

He did not require her comradely hand since the rising moon was making the hollows and humps plain enough, yet he let her lead while he studied her profile instead of the bumpy terrain.

"Afterwards, our cows were all killed," she went on, unaware of his interest in anything except local news. "That was bad, but in one way it was good. It is difficult to milk cows at night with shells falling around. And the cows were afraid. They made terrible noises, like people, crying. When they were all killed we did not have milk to drink any more. But we had the milk cans. We filled them with water from our long pipe. Dan led us to drink, like animals, three times a day, one glass every time."

"And to wash?"

"We did not wash, not ourselves, not our clothes." She laughed then. It was a low, pleasant sound, though it had an odd diffidence, as though laughing aloud were not the thing she did best. "The miracle was nobody got sick. We had no doctor, you see, just Gittel, our nurse—you met her—and one of our comrades who studied two years in a medical school. They did all they could for our wounded."

This is a girl, from a nice home, he found himself telling himself, fighting a war, living in hunger and peril and filth and speaking of it without melodrama, as if it were nothing at all, just a report on a term at boarding school.

"We never thought about being tired or sick," she continued. "We rested sometimes an hour. Then we worked again. Chava ran with the soup pot from the bunker, to all the trenches, when we could not leave our posts to get food."

Her speech fascinated him, the clipped sentences, bare bones of language, no color or flesh. What he could not know was that she was making an enormous concession by speaking to him in a language she'd always despised, and was doing what her own mother had all through her childhood begged her to do, extend to a guest the courtesy of making conversation easy for him by speaking his tongue. It was, in a way, her proof of trust and special interest in him.

"Jump," she ordered once more. "Here begins our second line."

On the other side of the trench, he halted. "Isn't there some place we can sit down and talk?" he asked.

"Talk? We are talking. Sit?" She drew her hand out of his. "There are two more bunkers. In these we sleep. That is no place to sit. . . . And the pillboxes, there I cannot take even you."

"Find a place," he said. "I want to watch the moon rise with you."

She answered him artlessly as a child, "That would be very nice," and again took his hand. "I will find a good place," she promised. "The best."

He saw a rubble heap up ahead, a crushed roof, jagged, etched by moonlight. "We will sit here," she said. "It was the children's house. It was the nicest place."

He lowered his head. "And they were all killed?"

"Killed? Certainly not. We sent them away. Children must always be safe. That is the important thing."

He faced her, put his hands on her shoulders. "Hear you talk! What are you but a child?"

"I am a farmer and soldier." She drew away, stood very straight. "Sit down," she said abruptly. "Here we can watch the moon rise." She sat on the ground, her back against a standing height of rough plaster wall and he crouched next to her, as close as he felt she'd allow. "I like to come here," she said softly. "We all like to come, now and then, to remember the children. We were very sad when they went away." She flexed her knees, wrapped her arms around.

The moon was a half-orange in a pinkish sky. The jackals howled. The weird light and sound made him jittery and he began to take his cigarettes out. "No." She touched his hand. "I am sorry. There is truce, but if a sniper should see that small light—"

"Okey-doke." He put his cigarettes back and clasped his hands on his knees. "I can see better now," he said. "I can see your trenches."

She sighed. "It is too bad you make us your first visit now. You should have seen this before. It was beautiful. We did everything, quickly and well, with our own hands."

He stirred restlessly, inched nearer, and not knowing how she'd respond, said, "Baby, I don't like you with your back to the wall. Come, sit here, against my knees. More comfortable."

Her head turned toward him, searching his face, before she scrabbled up. He glimpsed the profile of her full breasts beneath the taut cloth as she moved in front of him, and squatted again, her spine against his knees, her legs tucked under her. "This is better," she said. "Do you like this?"

"Better," he said. "Very much." Tentatively, he raised his hands to the sides of her head and buried his fingers in her soft hair. She straightened her long, naked legs, sliding back until her head touched his chest, like a little girl still, naively trusting, and she sighed as a child does when it is weary and has found place to rest. The quality of her innocence came to him all at once and he was deeply moved. He stroked her hair, brushing it lightly, as though the very tips of his fingers knew how precious was this which he held.

"I have been talking," she said. "And you have not. Now you talk to me."

"What shall I say?"

"Whatever you wish."

"Well—" He fumbled for words. "I think you're marvelous people," he started lamely. "I never knew there were people like you."

She wriggled as if in protest. "Why do you say *you*? Are you not one of us?"

He lowered his hands to her shoulders. "Me, I'm an American, here for a war."

"Do you come to every war?"

He chuckled. "When I believe in it, baby, I guess I do."

"Then you believe in this, so you are one of us."

He cleared his throat. "Not exactly. You see, it was like this, one day, I got sore. I was out at U.N.—"

"You saw the U.N.?" There was a new note in her voice, a quickened interest.

"On that day in March—"

"The nineteenth. When the Americans abandoned us."

He squeezed her arm. "Good memory."

She laughed. "We read. We have wireless. We are not ignorant."

"Did I say you were?" His hands rose again, caressing her hair. "Tell me." His voice had roughened. "Tell me, baby, what are you?"

"We . . . we are all kinds of people . . ."

"You." He prodded her arm. "You, I mean. Talk about you."

"There is nothing to talk." There was a trace of impatience in her tone. "I am a sabra. I was born in Jerusalem. I have very good parents whom I love very much." Her voice seemed husky, with emotion, he guessed. "And a small brother, Teddy, whom I love, too. And a dog, a big boxer dog. His name is Udi."

"Udi!" He chortled. "Silly name for a dog."

"A good name. A good dog."

"Okay, don't get sore." He ran his hand down her arm. "Go on.

Give me all the facts."

"Facts?" Her profile slanted obliquely. "I went to school. Then, I went into Palmach. Then I came here. That is all."

He took his hands off. Once, he thought, I laughed at a Palmach kid, on Hayarkon Street, in Tel Aviv. I know better now. But he couldn't quite get through his head that this girl with shining, soft hair was a shock trooper, deserving a fellow soldier's highest respect.

Her voice went on evenly, "We came here last October, our group. One hundred people. We had been all summer in another kibbutz, what we call the mother kibbutz, in the North, working together—" she laughed lightly again—"to learn if we liked one another. We were all kinds, you see, and from many countries. Some of us from the D.P. camps, some from the Youth Aliyah. Dan was born and raised in a kibbutz. That is why he knows what to do. Some of us sabras like me. Others from Poland, Germany, Czecho, Roumania. Some of us married—"

"Your friend, Ketti, what's she?"

"From the camps. From Germany."

He sensed a constraint.

"I know that. What else?"

She hunched forward. "Ketti is a wonderful girl. A wonderful friend. And sometimes a strange person. It is what she went through." She leaned back again. "I do not like to speak about Ketti because I do not understand her very well. What I like to speak about is what I understand." She drew up her knees, clasped her hands on them. "Like why we are here, all of us, because this is the thing we believe. If we are to have a State we must secure and make productive this Negev of ours."

He wasn't sure why, but she sounded stuffy, and he was irked with himself because thinking that seemed almost treachery.

"We must build up the Land," she went on. "We must defend the Negev with our blood."

Out of her intonation as much as her words, he caught a whiff, an echo of the meetings on which he had been weaned at C.C.N.Y., where the kids all delivered an indoctrinated line. Anger rose in him, not toward the girl, toward himself. You don't know the score, Brody, he lectured himself, you haven't got background to understand this.

"This is a good life for us," she continued, earnestly, a shade too much so, he thought. "This is the best life for us and our State, to work together, comrades, sharing with one another, to build up our kibbutz and our Land. The Nation, that is the important thing."

He tried not to comment at once, for what she had said and the way she had said it were almost as though the words weren't hers, rather the grandiloquent sentiments once uttered by somebody else, which you learn for recitations at school. He shifted uneasily on the ground. "You believe in it," he murmured. "That's all that matters."

Her face bent confidently near. "Don't you?" she asked.

He scratched a spot on his palm which did not itch. "Darned if I know. I'm not kidding, I can't make up my mind if all this is going to work out. Too many problems, a small state in a hostile world, this expecting human nature to change—I dunno."

She had drawn away and in the growing moonlight he could see indignation ruffling her brow. "It will work. It does work," she said with emphasis.

He pulled her back against him. "Let's not fight, baby. What I think don't matter, what you think—" He stopped because a man was coming toward them across the dirt heaps. "Uh, uh, company," he said.

"Joshua!" She jumped up. He thought she had been embarrassed to be found sitting here with him but she sang out, "Do you need me?"

The young man glanced at Al on the ground before he said, politely. "Dan asked me to tell you he gives you his bunk. He thinks it is better you do not leave Gan Darom tonight. If you got lost, wandered into Egyptian lines—"

Dinah cut him short with "Toda. Thanks."

Al scrambled up. "Tell him I appreciate that. But don't put himself out. I'll sleep here, on the ground."

"The Negev is cold, late at night." Joshua slid toward the wall, as though he, too, meant to sit down.

"Toda," Dinah said again, pointedly.

The man retreated a step. "I hope I will see you again." He sounded reluctant to leave. "Dinah—" he waved his hand graciously—"please resume your seat."

She waited until he was out of sight before she sat down again in front of Al.

"Mister Buttinski," he said.

"Joshua Perlzweig," she corrected him. "He is not one of us yet, but we would like to keep him. He knows how to handle explosives and he plays the piano."

"A fine combination." He laughed.

"The country needs both," she said. "Dan likes him. I think he tries to protect him because he knows music so well." Then she giggled, a funny, small schoolgirlish titter. "Joshua is a nuisance sometimes. He is not used to our ways."

"What kind of ways do you mean?"

She rested her head on his chest. "That each one of us takes care of the others, but we also know how to take care of ourselves."

His chest expanded. "If you mean what I mean, baby . . ." he began.

"What do you mean?"

He did not reply. He was remembering another evening when this girl had slapped his face. What the hell *is* the score? he wondered. Is it they trust you so far, lead you on, let you think—and then the flat of the hand, the quick push, the kick in the groin. Are they human or not? How far do you go?

All of the moon was now above the low hills, flooding the landscape with amber. This is corny as hell, he said to himself, full moon over the Negev, and me with a beautiful babe. Make a song out of this. Al Jolson could sing it. Kate Smith . . . She has—"When the moo-oon comes over the mountain . . ." He could hear the soprano blaring out of the radio in his airshaft bedroom on Washington Heights. Sadness swept him suddenly, nostalgia for home. He drew Dinah's head to his cheek, as though her nearness might banish his homesickness.

"What is it?" she murmured. "What are you thinking about?"

He made himself laugh. "Something corny. Foolish, I mean. A song on our radio back home." He tried to tell her about Kate Smith and the popular music on the Hit Parade. She took it badly. "Jazz, always jazz," she scolded. "You have no culture, you American youth. That is true, is it not?"

"It is not," he said stoutly. And a fine situation, he thought, me defending American yuks. "I go to college. I read good books. I like good music and there's no lack of that. Not just me. Plenty of guys like what I like."

She was silent a moment before she said, with an air of distance,

"I apologize if I offended you."

He stroked her hair absently, remembering Saul, and the quarrels they'd had. She had said what Saul had said. Between them and us, he wondered, exactly what is the score? "What have all of you got against us, against Americans, I mean?" he asked.

"Against you? We have nothing against you." He caught a defensive note. She wasn't being honest, he realized.

"Every time I get in a conversation out here, someone jumps down my throat. I'm American, therefore, I'm scum . . . why, tell me why?"

"You deserted us," she said after a moment. "On the nineteenth of March."

"We recognized you," he replied stubbornly. "On the fourteenth of May."

She moved away from him, disturbed by the rancor she heard in his tone and she knotted her arms on her knees. It was a while before he heard her low laugh. "I have solved the problem. I have the answer worked out. We are angry with you because in a way we are jealous of you. Young people like you in the States have so much and so little responsibility. We have so little and so much responsibility."

His mind started to argue. So much, heh? Depression and war and scratch for a living, live and die insecure . . .

Her voice went on, a shade wistful, "So little physical comfort, so little time, to study, to enjoy, to think. So little chance to do for ourselves the personal things. Since we were born, we have had this country on our backs." It sounded as though she were pitying herself.

Tenderness surged up in him. He drew her back into his arms, whispered, "Poor babe," in her ear, stroked her hair, murmuring, "Poor little chick," and then slowly turned her around until he could see her full face. It seemed very young in the moonlight, sweet and gentle and delicate. A virginal beauty lay in the parted lips. "How old are you, Dinah?" he asked.

"Eighteen." She appeared surprised he had asked.

"The age of consent," he muttered under his breath.

"The age of consent," she repeated. "I do not understand. To what must I consent?"

"Don't ask me," he growled. "I might be tempted to say." He let her go and drew his knees up, making a fence of his legs.

"What is it?" Her face bent toward him. "Have I made you feel badly again?"

"On the contrary, baby." Then, hastily, he said, "Talk. Let's talk. I'm very much interested in these ideas you have about us. Every American is rich. And uncultured. Uncouth . . . We are not. My father, for instance, he drives a hack, a taxi cab. . . ."

"A worker, like us," she exulted and touched his hand.

"He also reads books, goes to lectures. And he's a Zionist from way back."

"Then he should be here with us. . . . And you, too." She ran her finger tips along the back of his hand. "To stay, I mean, here with us."

He stretched his legs out. "Some other time, baby," he said, "we'll talk about that," and once more, he drew her against his chest. She lay there, motionless. "Dinah," he asked suddenly, "were you ever in love?"

She made a small movement, the child nestling closer. "I do not think so," she said. Then she turned her face up to his and he saw only her mouth. He laid his lips on hers, drank her sweet warmth. His finger tips moved to the round of her breast.

She allowed him an instant, no more, before she jerked away. "Stop! Don't do that to me!" she cried out.

He thought she was going to haul off and hit him again and he curved his arm to fend the blow. Instead, he heard her saying, in a voice tremulous with uncertainty, "No one has ever done this to me before. Is this love?"

He tried to keep his tone light, "No, baby, that's sex," and heard his voice shaking, too. "It has something to do with love. But it isn't all."

She bowed her head to let a silence settle between them before she said softly, "Let it wait. This is not the time." And after another pause, "What you did frightened me," but she straightened her spine against his flexed knees. "Let us sit as we were and watch the moon. That was very good. Let us sit and not talk."

The round orb was over their heads, an angry red, promising searing heat the next day. By its light, they could see figures moving about.

"It is late. Do you wish to sleep?" Dinah asked.

"No," he answered. "Do you?"

"I like to sit here with you. I have not in all my life had an experience like this. It is beautiful."

He let his legs down and drew her once more into his arms. Her cheek lay on his. Her fingers ran the length of his forearms, playing their own melody. Her every gesture and movement and breath spoke tenderness and her sweetness and strength seemed to flow into him. He could not speak, but he thought, this may be it. It's restful. It's gentle. It's like coming home. This may be what is called love. I wouldn't know. . . . This is new. No girl has ever made me feel this way before.

She spoke first, in a bemused half-whisper, "When I was a young girl, I used to write poetry. I should like to write a poem again, about this night. The moon and our sitting together in the ruins of Gan Darom. About the dream in my mind, that when this place will again be beautiful, planted with trees and with grass, and roses and jasmine, you will come back and we will be together and there will be time and you will teach me love."

His mouth inched toward hers and drew back. "Not now," he told himself fiercely. "Leave it alone. Nothing crude and No SALESMANSHIP." He moved her gently up and away.

"What is it?" she asked. "You are not comfortable?"

"I'm not comfortable." He heard himself. He sounded grim. He wanted a cigarette desperately, reached toward his pocket, remembered her warning and ground his back teeth.

She shifted her body until the back of her head once more touched his chest. "This is better? More comfortable?" She twined her fingers with his and did not speak for such a long while that he believed she had fallen asleep until he heard her repeating his name and softly chuckling, "Al. A funny name, Al."

"Albert," he said. "Al's short for Albert."

"What would it be in Ivrith?"

"Abraham. Avrum . . . I was named Abraham."

"Why did you change it?"

"Oh, to be more Americanized. A Hebrew name in America, well, it sounds out of place. Snotty kids make fun of you."

"Anti-Semites." She spoke with that same cockiness which had irked him before. "They compel you to change your Hebrew name."

He sighed. "You've got the wrong idea, entirely. Nobody makes you do anything."

"It is not so. I've read how Jews are treated and even Negroes . . . Al." She squeezed his hand hard. "Stay here. Don't wait, like Ketti, like Joshua, to run because you must. They came to us but they came as sick people, with experiences they can never forget."

He laughed and patted her arm. "Don't worry about me. Don't worry about any of us in the States. If I ever come back, after this one is over, it'll be because I want to come back. Because there's somebody I want to see."

She nestled to him and stroked his cheek. "Dinah Hirsch," she said confidently.

"Smart chick." This was better, much, the boy and girl stuff. Keep it light; keep it clean. "Tell me about your name. *Dinah*. It belongs in Mississippi. In Alabama. In Carolina. Not in Israel."

"But it does. Read the Bible. Dinah was the daughter of Jacob. His only one. My father is Jacob also."

He said that was clever, darned cute. "Are you like the Bible's Dinah?"

"Oh no." She sat up. "You must not think that." She seemed so distressed that he had to ask, "What's the story? What kind of a person was she?"

She giggled, that schoolgirl's titter so suitable for her eighteen years. "You must read it sometime, when I am not here. All I will tell you is she was not very good."

His leg was beginning to cramp. He eased her out of his arms. "Let me stand."

She jumped up and gave him her hand to help him rise, and he walked a few steps to get the kink out of his leg.

"Look!" she said. "Is our Land not most beautiful?"

It was anything but. Bathed in the unearthly light of the strange moon, broken and scarred, it was a place for the buzzards, for the jackals howling beyond the fence, not for romance. "It seems lonely to me," he said quietly. "How do you bear this loneliness?"

"Lonely?" She linked her arm into his. "We are never lonely. Oh, I miss my family sometimes. I would like very much to see them. And I miss my comrades who are gone." She slipped her arm out, to point off to the distance. "Our cemetery. Twenty good comrades. Twenty-one. Zvi . . . he died before."

He said gruffly, "It's chilly, Dinah. Don't you think you should go to bed?"

She sighed. "If you wish. We are both soldiers. We need our rest." She led him to the bunker where he was to sleep, and she put her lips up. "Lila tov," she whispered. "Sweet dreams."

She could not sleep, but since she had to be on duty at daybreak, she squeezed her lids shut. Each word he had said, she had said, kept repeating itself. Her breast tingled with the memory of his touch. I am glad, I am proud this has happened to me, she kept telling herself. It is only too bad it has happened now, when there is no time.

As the dawn broke, she climbed out of the bunker, took her Sten and dropped into a trench. Al found her there. "Thank you for everything, Dinah," he said with formality, because others were around. "I'd like to do something for you. What can I do?"

"Do? For me?" She wrinkled her forehead. "If this truce lasts, would you fly me to Jerusalem when Gan Darom can spare me? I would like very much to see my parents. I will send word to the base if it is possible."

"It will be possible," he said. "And a pleasure to see you again."

"That is also what I meant," Dinah said.

Part Six: July

I

MORNING'S FIRST LIGHT striped the east when Al brought the plane through the cleft in the hills on July's first day. He flung the mail pouch over the side, planted a business-like kiss on Dinah's cheek. "Mighty nice spin," he said. "Five A.M. tomorrow, same place. Enjoy yourself. My regards to your folks."

She tossed the ends of her white keffiah around her throat before she smiled, said, "L'hitra'ot," and climbed down, padding rapidly toward the gate.

A pot-bellied, gray-haired man with a briefcase eyed her as they passed, he going toward, Dinah away from the plane. "Who is it?" he asked Al while he strapped himself into the seat.

"A great lady," Al answered.

"What is the name?"

"Dinah Hirsch."

The man frowned. "The name is not known to me."

Al saw a chance. "The greatest heroine of this war. Single-handed, this slip of a girl stopped a tank attack. With a Molotov cocktail, no less." He fenced his mouth with his hand and winked. "Chisbat," he added.

The light was poor and Ephraim was not sure he saw what he saw. This resembled the Doctor's daughter, the one who had sent messages. But it could not be. She was in a kibbutz in the South. . . . Yes, it was she. I must speak to her, he thought, and then thought, better not. If it is not she, this woman will think me bold.

She came up to him, grinning broadly. "Shalom, Ephraim. How are you?"

He juggled his Sten, all at once, nervous, swallowed his Adam's apple. "Bokar tov. Good morning," he managed to say. "I am well. How are you?"

"I am well."

He gulped, inflated his chest. "Out of the fiery furnace, you have returned to us."

"Your mother?" she asked. "How is she?"

"She is gone. A sniper on King George Avenue. In April."

She looked sympathetic. "I had not heard. We heard little from here, except the biggest news."

"They have been tearing Jerusalem apart, that you have heard?"

"That I have heard. What else shall I hear today?"

He sucked his lip. "The Afrikaaner. You remember him? He died in his sleep the first night of truce."

"He was old. His life was lived."

"Who would have objected if he lived a while longer? He was my very good friend. He is missed."

"No doubt." Her brows drew together. "The others? My family? Our friends?"

She caught hesitation before he replied, "Your family is well," and demanded, "What is it? What happened?"

He gulped again. I am talking too much, he told himself. "You will hear, you will know, you will judge." Then he drew himself up, hefted his Sten to a poor imitation of "present arms." "It is an honor for me to welcome you home. Shalom. Shalom."

In the cool, pearl-gray morning, leaves whispered, a rooster crowed, and birds in the trees made awakening sounds. Dinah ran fast. From the distance, her parents' street seemed as the street always was, green-hung and golden, but when she came near, she saw the scars on the honey-hued walls of the houses, sandbags at windows, rubble dust drenching the trees, the gardens limp, the bougainvillea hanging yellow and sere, and finally, the cypress, riven as though lightning had struck, and the rubble heap which had been the office wing of the house. They were hit, here in this sheltered street! Ephraim had said they were well. But he also had said, "You will see."

She flew up the steps and rapped hard on the door.

Udi heard her, tried to wake Teddy but being feeble beyond his years, could achieve nothing more than a twitch of his paw and a piteous rasp. "Sheket," Teddy muttered at him. "Let a sick man sleep."

The urgent pounding woke Edith first. She ran down. When she saw the lean, coppery figure, she went white, screamed for Jacob, and flew at the girl, babbling loving and wordless noises, her hands searching Dinah's face to make sure she was real. Soon Jacob was there, folding his daughter and his wife in his arms, breathing, "Thank God. Thank God," until Dinah broke from them, panting, to hold them at arms' length.

They were all skin and bones, she saw, even Abba who had always been plump. They were gray. They had aged.

"How did you get here? How did you come?" Jacob cried.

"An airplane." (Don't let them guess what you see.) She grinned. "I have *protectsia*," she said.

He chortled. "Listen to her. These Negev kibbutznicks! Protectsia! Did you hear, Edith, did you hear?"

"The American flyer brought me in our plane."

"*Our* plane! Listen to her, *our* plane!" That was good, better, normal, Abba's old zestful self.

"The flyer who brought us the messages?" Edith asked.

"The same one."

"He is our very good friend. I should like to meet him some day."

"You will, Imma, I promise you will."

"Come into the house," Jacob shouted. "Princess, welcome home!"

She strode ahead of them into the house, shoulders back, seeming taller in leanness. It was the same house, yet like the street it had become otherwise. It was barren and dark and it had the foul odor of the trenches at Gan Darom. Edith ran to the windows, pulled up the blinds, threw the casements wide. Morning light gushed and bared the room's nakedness. The passage to the office was boarded up. Dinah pointed and her father shrugged. "Nothing. A pagaz. Merely the waiting room and the W.C. No one hurt. . . . Sit down, Dinah, sit."

She sat down. "No office. How do you manage?" she asked.

"Somehow." He sat beside her and cradled her hand. "Life is simpler. Pregnant women cannot run in the streets. I go to them."

"Your car?"

"The Army has cars. Not private doctors. I am not a big shot."
He chucked her under the chin. "Like my daughter who travels in
planes."

He had kept his tone gay, but the truth must be met finally.
"Abba, you're skin and bones."

"Are you fat yourself?"

"That's no matter." She reached around her mother's waist, drew
her close. "You, Imma, too."

"Who puts on weight in the summer?" Jacob waved his hand to
be finished with that.

"Summer heat." Edith scoffed. "Let him blame summer heat.
Do you know, Dinah, darling, for weeks all we had were three
slices of bread for each for a day."

"Who needs any more? It's enough, you see, we're alive."

"My brother?" She glanced toward the staircase. "Why hasn't
Teddy come down?"

She saw her mother's quick downcast glance and recalled Ephraim's words. "What happened to him?"

"The boy is lazy," her father said.

She looked from one to the other and could read nothing at all in
their eyes. "And Udi? Is my dog alive?"

"Well and alive, but lazy too." Her father slid closer. "Begin,
talk," he commanded. "Tell us everything."

"Tell *me*," Dinah said. *"You* tell me everything."

"We?" He shook his head stoutly. "We have nothing to tell. We
ate. We slept. We worked. We ran. We survived." He raised his
shoulders, dismissing all that with a shrug. "You are from the Negev.
You have what to tell. . . . Shall we have coffee? No, coffee can
wait. Start. Begin. Everything."

"We had a difficult time," she began.

"We, too," her mother put in, quietly, and touched Dinah's hand.

They gasped when she told them about the first bombing, and
building the bunkers at night, hacking the earth while shells were
bursting around, and the constant shelling from the Tegart Fortress
and the air attacks, and then about Ketti and the machine gun and
how the tank attack had been stopped. She did not mention the part

she herself had had in the tank battle, yet pride and passion swelled in her voice and even she thought, as she told it, this is a remarkable tale. She was aware of how different it sounded now than it had on the night she had told it to Al. She had been calmer, then, reciting facts, and the alien language had constricted her. This was heart speaking to heart.

"Don't think you're so much," her father broke in. "We were bombed and shelled too."

The hint of jealousy in his tone made her glance at him, surprised, before she hurried to finish. "We did not weaken. We did not fall. We held the position."

Edith drew a long breath. "We, too," she said.

Then, for a minute or so, they sat without talking. How different this was, each of them thought separately, from that other homecoming, in March. She had been a child, struggling to keep her old ties, half here and half in the world she was making, and her parents had fumbled and groped for contact with that new world of hers. The girl had been nervous, sensing their dread for her. There had been nowhere to meet, except in their implicit love. They stood on other ground now and each of them tried to give it its name.

Age, Edith thought. Not calendar time, the maturing out of experience, down deep.

Survivors, Jacob said to himself. We know all of us, how good it is to be alive.

Equals, Dinah felt. Soldiers and citizens, who've fought a war. It's worn them out but it's made me strong.

"Edith, make coffee," Jacob suddenly shouted as though his wife were not here, at Dinah's side.

The girl laughed. "Abba, you never change. That's how you used to yell."

"Should I change? Should the smell of gunpowder make a man change?"

Edith got up. "A good breakfast this time, haviva, no make-believe. With the new road, the truce, we have oranges, eggs. . . ."

"See, it is over," her father bragged. "We are living and our daughter is home and any day, when workmen can spare us an hour, we shall even have an unbroken house."

After her mother had left the room, Dinah said, "Abba, you are hiding something. What is it with Teddy? Why isn't he down here with us?"

He looked over his shoulder, out toward the hall, and framed his lips with his hand. "Nothing much." He tried to sound nonchalant. "The shelling. Excitement. A nervous reaction. These high-strung children of ours."

"How long is he sick?"

"Since last month. Since just after Yora was shot."

"Yora killed too!"

He felt miserable. He shouldn't have told her, he knew, and he looked down at the stone blocks of the floor. "He was shot as a traitor," he said.

Silence stayed in the cool, dusty room, until Dinah said firmly and clearly, "I do not believe it. It cannot be true."

Her father stared at the stones. "Would they have executed him if it were not true?"

She felt all at once unsure, the rare confusion of right and wrong. "How did they find all this out?" she demanded of him.

He did not dare look at her yet. "The Englishman brought it to light, Gordon Leake, who used to live on this street."

Her eyebrows rose. "We use British informers against our own?"

"We have our share of fools," he burst out. Then he said, "Dinah, your mother and I have wished not to believe and have tried not to believe. It is a difficult thing to accept, either way. If it was true about our friend, then how can one ever trust any man? And if it was not so and an innocent man was done to death—out of hysteria, out of lust for power, out of I know not what—then how can we trust ourselves?"

She waited a short while, her forehead wrinkled in thought before she asked, "And Teddy has been sick with grief for his friends all this while?"

He shook his head gravely but did not reply.

"What has happened to Carmela and the children?"

"They are there, across the street."

"You go to them?"

"We did. She would not see us."

The uneasy silence again, until Jacob cried, "Enough. Speak

about something else. . . . Leah Malkoff was killed by a sniper."

"I know. I saw Ephraim at the field." Then she asked, "Has any-one heard from Arieh Goldstein?"

Again her father lowered his gaze. "He died, more than three months ago."

"I thought I heard his voice on the wireless, from Nebi Danyial."

"He died there."

"That I did not know." She braided her fingers. "Arieh brought me into Palmach," she said softly. "How sad for Ida." She waited a moment. "And David?" she asked.

His reply came through pinched lips. "He did not come back. No one speaks to his family these days."

She shook her head. "Much has changed in our street." She rose. "I'll go to my brother, see what is with him."

Teddy heard her on the staircase and squeezed his lids shut to pretend that he slept. Be sick, he ordered himself. You fooled your parents this very long while, well when you want to be well, sick when you need to be sick. Dinah isn't smarter than Abba. You can fool her, also.

Udi rolled off the cot when she entered the room, came toward her, sniffing, let out a modest yelp, the best he could do. She stroked his lean flanks before she went to the bed.

"Shalom."

Teddy opened his eyes reluctantly, muttered "Shalom," and turned his face toward the wall.

"Teddy, what is the matter with you?" she asked the back of his head.

Without turning, he mumbled, "I'm sick, can't you see?"

She touched his forehead. It was warm but not fever-hot. She said, "I don't believe you are sick."

He burrowed into his pillow. His muffled voice growled, "Let me be."

"Is this a time to be sick, when we have a State?"

"Let me alone. I want to be sick."

She gripped his shoulders, forced him to roll over and held him pinned. He stuck his tongue out. She tweaked his ear. He started to blubber. She was sorry, then, and she put her arm around him, and said, gently, "You can tell me, Teddy. You can talk to me. Why are you sick?"

"I feel bad," he sobbed. "Very bad. You made me feel worse."

She walked to the window, walked back. Abruptly, she asked, "Teddy, what bad thing did you do?"

"I threw a piece of shell at Asi," he told his pillow.

"Well! And what did he do?"

Teddy turned part way around. "He threw it back at me. He hurt my leg very much."

"You threw it at him. He threw it at you. So, you are even."

"No, I threw a tin of offal into his house."

She pursed her lips, made a whistling noise.

"In the middle of the night," Teddy said.

"And what did he do?"

"I did not see him after that."

"And you have been sick all this time?" Sick with guilt, sick with shame, she was sure, asking for coddling, worrying his parents, making them take care of him. "Get up," she commanded. "Get out of bed right away. You were a fool and a beast. If you'd told your mother and father, they would have whipped you, finished and done. . . . Get up. I am Palmach. I order you."

He sat up, hiding his face in the crook of his arm. "Will you beat me?"

"Of course. Get up." She shook his narrow shoulders. "You donkey, you little jackass. How could you be so stupid, so mean? Was Asi to blame for what happened? Don't you think he felt badly enough? . . . Get up, get dressed, come downstairs. You're going with me to his house, to beg pardon of him."

Edith watched her lead Teddy out of the house. Our girl acts like the head of this family, she said to herself.

Teddy clutched Dinah's hand. He held it all the way down the walk and only let go because sweat was gluing his palm to hers. He stayed close to her, shoulders squared, but inside he was jelly and he was sure he was going to throw up. He glanced at her once, sidewise, while they crossed the road, and wanted her hand again, but her stern face said no.

At the beginning of the path up to Asi's, his steps began to drag. "Dinah, let us first walk to the corner."

"Why shall we walk to the corner?"

He lowered his gaze from her unyielding eyes. "I want to buy him a present," he faltered.

"A present, eh? What kind of a present could you buy for Asi, here, now?"

He sucked his lip, scratched the heel of one hand, to gain a few seconds' reprieve. "Well, they have Penetro cough drops in boxes. Imma bought me cough drops. They taste like boiled sweets."

"Have you money?"

He dug into the pockets of his shorts. "I'll go back." His tone was hopeful. "I have two piastres in my other pants."

She nudged the small of his back. "March! You'll buy him cough drops some other time." She gripped his shoulder. "It's disgusting to find my own brother a coward," she said.

Yet it was she who rapped on the door, because at the final instant his courage oozed and he ducked behind her, ready to run, if she let his arm go.

Carmela opened the door, a Carmela, not merely gaunt, hollow-eyed but all gray-haired, gray-faced. Surprise lighted her eyes for a fleeting moment. "Dinah! Dinah Hirsch!" she exclaimed. But she made no move to open the door.

"Shalom. Teddy and I have come to see you." She thrust Teddy forward.

"We do not want to see him."

The boy cringed against her. She felt his moist hand on her leg. "I don't blame you. He's been a monster."

Carmela's eyes blazed. "So have they all. All our old neighbors, our friends. They pass me in the streets. Their heads turn away."

"Let us in," Dinah said. "It might be better, if you opened your door."

This is not Dinah, Carmela said to herself. This is not a child. She gives commands. . . . She widened the crack of the door, said, "Shalom," and let Teddy and Dinah into her house. "Asi," she called out, "Teddy has come to see you."

Asi edged around a doorway and stood staring at them.

Dinah pushed Teddy again. "Shalom, Asi," he mumbled from Dinah's side.

"Shalom," Asi answered him.

She prodded her brother. "Go on. Say the rest."

Teddy took one step toward the doorway where Asi was. "I apologize," he quavered. "For throwing the shrapnel." He looked back at her, begging support.

"Go on," Dinah said.

He threw her a despairing glance. "And for everything else," he half-shouted, and precipitately, lest she force the ultimate admission, he ran toward Asi. "Come play with me, Asi. Will you play with me?"

Asi looked at his mother, saw her slow, assenting nod. His eyes brightened, began to glow. "Can we play in your yard? I am sick and tired of my yard." His arm was around Teddy's shoulders, Teddy's arm around Asi's waist, as they ran from the house.

Carmela said, "Dinah, sit down. You have done me honor. Now, tell me about the Negev, please."

"No," the girl answered. "Not yet, not here. You will hear it in my mother's house. You will come with me."

Edith opened her arms and Carmela flew into them. They stood locked a long while.

"I have missed you, my friend," Edith said.

"I have missed you."

"You should not have closed your door."

"You should have broken it down."

"Will you go to Lillie Gross, too?" Edith asked afterwards.

"Should I, Imma?"

"You went to Carmela."

"That was different. She and her children were not to blame for what happened to him. Those others let their son stay away, kept him away. That is hard to forgive."

"Do what you wish," Edith said. "You are no longer a child. Do what your heart tells you to."

When the water cart came at noon, Dinah insisted the pails were too heavy and she must help carry them in. Edith laughed. "I don't carry the water. The water carries me," but the girl wouldn't listen to her.

"You're the mother, I'm the child," Edith said. "You tell me what to do."

All afternoon, neighbors streamed in, Ida's whole family and the Winklemans. They brought small presents for Dinah, a few apples, oranges, a tomato, half a kilo of sugar, a few grams of coffee and demanded details of all that had happened down in the South. They made a circle around her in the living room, keeping her separate, as though she were Marco Polo, come from far journeys, with fantastic tales. Udi snored at her feet. Teddy and Asi sat open mouthed on the floor.

Everyone clucked and exclaimed, "What do you tell us! . . . Can you believe it!" When she was out of breath and insisted, "You talk. Tell me what happened here," invariably the reply was the same. "It was nothing. We had a siege. We were shelled. We did the best we could do. . . . Tell us more, about the Negev."

Toward evening, Jacob arrived, announcing, "Some of my colleagues are coming tonight with their wives. And some of our nurses, to hear what went on in the South. I told them, 'No coffee, no drinks.' 'No need,' they said. 'We want nothing more than to hear Dinah tell about her kibbutz.' "

Professor Gross and his wife came in the evening, when the room was filled, and took seats in a corner. While the others were saying goodnight they went up to Dinah and Professor Gross said, "Forgive us for coming tonight, uninvited. We had to see you. We have been greatly stirred."

"We are proud of you," Lillie Gross said. "You, too, are our child."

It was late, close to midnight, when the last guest was gone. Teddy was yawning. He went up to bed, but Dinah and her parents lingered a few minutes more.

"All my life I have not talked so much," the girl said. "Is this why we fought in the South, to become tellers of tales?"

Her father caressed her soft hair. "Dearest, these are legends. These will be history. To hear them from you, at first hand—"

"Tell me about Jerusalem," she said. "All day I have tried to find out. Don't say again, It was nothing."

Jacob shook his head gravely. "No, it was not nothing," he said. "It was different." She saw his expression alter, become more sober and thoughtful than any she had ever seen on his face. "We were civilians. Ours was a test of endurance. To hold fast, do our work every day in the presence of death. Jerusalem was saved, not by the Davidka, not by arms—we had none—not by an enemy's cowardice —make no mistake, the Arab Legion is brave and it knows how to shoot. But by discipline and by stubbornness. By the drivers of the food convoys, the bakers, the water carts . . ."

"And the doctors," his wife put in.

He smiled at her. "And the housewives." They moved together, touched hands. Then Jacob said, musingly, "I wonder how history will deal with us. Will it tell the plain truth? How we cooked kvacker and beans on woodfires in the yard. How we used the same water over and over again. How our homes and our bodies stank. How we sat, sometimes scared, sometimes bored, by candlelight in our smothering hot rooms. How desperate was our need for a few moments of peace and of privacy. How we ran, always running and crouching, like animals. No, little one—" he pressed Edith's arm, shook his head—"they will probably try to make bloody heroes of us. And that was not the truth. We were frightened and hungry and very tired. There will be some who will tell you we withstood the siege because our faith was so strong it moved mountains and worked miracles. I tell you the truth. We had no choice. We were here, in our city, our home. We had no escape, not even a road on which to run if we wished. So we stayed. We thought the world had forgotten us. All the world had, except our own Israel. It fought for us." His shoulders braced themselves; his head came up. "You. An outpost, cut off, bombed and shelled day and night, pitting your bodies against tanks, you were the heroes, not we."

Dinah rose, covering her mouth. "The plane will be here at five o'clock. I must go to bed."

They were contrite. "We've worn you out." Her mother's arm was around her. "You will sleep, haviva, in your own room."

"Perhaps I had better not go to bed, I may not wake up in time."

"We'll wake you. Do you think Imma and I will sleep tonight?"

They went up, three in a row, jamming the stairs. Edith had put fresh sheets on the cot. "Haviva," she ventured, "if you would like, I'll heat up our water. You'll have a bath."

"I've had a bath, Imma. I've bathed more than you." Her brown hand ran sensuously along the sheet. "Do you know how long it is since I have slept in a bed?"

After she had blown out the candle, her mother came back to sit on the cot. "Haviva, are you asleep?"

"Foolish question."

"God has been generous to me today."

"Imma, we shall have more happy days."

"I know, haviva, I know." Her hand ran along Dinah's shoulder and arm. "Haviva, I have a confession to make. Long ago, in April, when Arieh fell, I was confused. I thought I had a problem, a question of choice. I asked myself, which do I want more, the Nation which was my life-long hope, or you, my child? Did I want the Nation at the price of Dinah Hirsch?"

The girl laughed. "Now you have both. Are you satisfied?"

"The taste of triumph is delicious," her mother said. She bent to kiss Dinah's forehead. "Thank the American flyer for us."

"Imma." The girl found herself timid, yet eager to tell. "Imma, you always worried I would be an old maid."

"No, haviva . . . Yes, haviva," eager to hear.

"I think there is someone."

"At Gan Darom?"

"The flyer, Imma . . . The American."

"Oh!" Edith stayed silent a moment. "What is he like?"

"Like . . . like no one I have ever met."

Her mother's soft laugh was young and amused. "It is always so. The one is always like no one you have ever met. I thought the same thing when I met Jacob."

"You will meet Al. You will see I am right." She crossed her arms under her head, raising herself. "Some time when there is more time, I will bring him here."

"But you are in a kibbutz," her mother said. "And he is a flyer. An American. Suppose he is here for only the war?"

"He will stay, Imma." She spoke confidently. "I will make him stay." She let her arms down, stretched her legs straight, relaxing.

"Haviva, do you mind if I sit here till you are asleep?"

"I do not mind."

Her mother leaned over, kissed the girl's lips, cheeks, eyelids. "Sleep well, darling, in your own bed."

The girl lay motionless, breathing evenly. Edith thought she had fallen asleep, and she rose, stood close to the cot, straining through the darkness to glimpse the body's young grace beneath the white sheets. "Imma." The loved voice was drowsy. "Be sure you wake me up."

Jacob said, "She seemed so glad to be home. Do you think, when it is over, she will wish to come back to us?" He struck a match to see his watch dial as he had a dozen times through the night. "Four o'clock. Shall we wake her now?"

"She must dress. She has to walk to the field. She daren't be late."

They went into her bedroom together and stood beside the cot. "See how she sleeps!" Jacob said. "A pity to wake her."

"Wake her. She must not be late."

"Let her sleep," he said fiercely, under his breath. "She deserves this rest. Let her sleep. Let her stay."

He is right, Edith thought. Why must we wake her? She's been through enough. Let her stay here and rest. The sharp struggle was over almost before it began. She touched the girl's arm, kissed her cheek. "Wake up, soldier," she said.

They woke Teddy, too. He came downstairs, rubbing his eyes. They gave Dinah cold coffee, wrapped her presents of vegetables, fruits, sugar and coffee in a clean linen towel. They all kissed her. "L'hitra'ot," they said.

She was waiting on the field when the plane landed. Al dropped his passenger and small load and she climbed in. "How was it?"

"Wonderful."

"What did you do?"

"Talked. Talked and talked."

"I bet. How were things with them?"

"They would not tell. They wanted to talk just about us."

"They feed you up?"

"I had tomatoes and fruit."

"And a bath?"

"Certainly not. In Jerusalem nobody bathes."

"Next time, I'll run you into Tel Aviv first. Hot showers and strawberries and cream."

"My parents were grateful to you. They would like to meet you sometime."

"Me, too," he said. "We'll do this again, and again and again."

The trip was short, up in the air, down again, and just time for a "toda raba," and "l'hitra'ot" before she ran to hop on the back of a truck.

Ketti was out of bed, helping to clean the hospital bunker, when Dinah brought the fruit there. She gave Ketti an apple, since that is specific against the shil-shul.

Ketti said an apathetic thanks and squatted on her bunk.

"How are you?"

"I am tired being sick."

"Then get up and be well."

"How can I be well if I am not well?"

"If there were no truce, if we were attacked, would you be well?"

Ketti looked at her hard. "If I had to save my life," she said laconically, "I would save my life." She bit into the apple. "How was your airplane ride?"

"Very short. Very good."

"Did he make love to you?" Ketti champed the apple noisily.

"Make love to me? It was not for that he took me in the plane."

"How little you know! A minute before, I thought you were clever. Now I know you are not." She swung her bare legs over the edge of the bunk and chewed the apple. "How was it in Jerusalem?" she asked after a while.

"They have had a bad time."

"Did you tell them we also have not had a good time?"

"I told them. They made me talk about us all the time."

Ketti laid the apple core down. "Remarkable! That they listened to you. No one has ever been willing to listen to what I have been through."

She gave Ketti a push. "That isn't true. I listen to you."

"And how much have you learned?" Ketti snapped. She saw an

angry glitter in Dinah's eyes. Her tone softened. "What news do you bring?"

Dinah crouched beside her on the bunk. "Ketti, in Jerusalem, I heard a strange thing. Yora, a neighbor, an old close friend, was shot as a traitor, a spy."

"Well?" Ketti asked, with indifference.

"They treated his family cruelly." She laced her brown fingers together. "My little brother did a terrible thing to Asi, Yora's son, his best friend."

"Well?" Ketti said coldly again.

"Well, what? Well, nothing. I believe the man was no spy." She spoke with heat. "Yora did what he had to do. He died in the line of duty, like all the rest."

Ketti shook her head slowly. "What makes you so sure?"

"He was one of us."

A bitter smile curled Ketti's mouth. "Does that make a difference? Since when are we saints? It can be true. I have known such things. There are reasons—no one else can know—why a person needs sometimes to do evil things."

"But, Ketti, if he is innocent, then we behaved like Hitler himself."

"Yes," Ketti answered. "That could also be true. We are people, yes? Therefore we are capable of everything. We can be brave and wonderful. And we can also be stupid and cruel."

II

In a modest but persistent fashion, Judge Winkleman of Jerusalem had been making a pest of himself in Tel Aviv for several days.

He had a room at the Gat Rimmon on Hayarkon Street, an extremely hot cubicle, for the coastal plain stewed and simmered in July's muggy heat and thick blackout curtains barred any relief from sea breeze. Yet he slept soundly, not even annoyed by the radios which blared from beachfront cafés, since, when evening came, he was worn out by the day's running around.

He had come to see the Prime Minister. Before May fourteenth that would have been simple—walk up a street, ring a doorbell. But Judge Winkleman's one-time Jerusalem neighbor was now the Premier of a State, and position and title erect barriers. Though the Judge was determined, he was not a pushing man. Proper connections, he sensed, was how to do this.

It was his purpose to locate a friend who might make an appointment for him. He struggled with the telephone, but whoever believes he can conserve energy by using Tel Aviv's phones is a great optimist And so he walked sweltering pavements and jammed himself into buses which were like steam baths. His old acquaintances were glad to see him. "So you survived, eh? Came through the siege! How was it? Let us hear." He tried to inform them. Usually they listened a minute or so, before they broke in, "Ah, yes, but we went through something, too. You should have been here the night we took Jaffa. The shooting! The noise!" As for arranging an appointment for him with the Prime Minister, that was impossible. "He cannot be bothered with private matters. He is too busy, you must understand. He has time for nothing these days but the war."

Before the Judge said "Shalom" his old friends invariably remembered from where he had come and invited him to have a bath.

He decided to knock on official doors and took a taxicab out to

Sarona, on Tel Aviv's outskirts, the bucolic settlement created by German Knights Templar in the last century, a charming small village, now re-named Ha'Kirya, the seat of the new government. He meandered up tree-shaded lanes, wading in dust churned by taxicabs, trucks and new motor cars. He inhaled construction's pungent aromas—wet plaster, fresh paint. He entered, hat in hand, awed by the mere notion that this was a State's capital, the little, neat dwellings, resembling Bavaria, where farmers had lived, and where brazen fieldmice now nibbled at sandwiches Cabinet Ministers brought for their lunch. He inquired for former Jerusalemites who he knew were at the Kirya. These one-time friends were busy, too busy, they sent word out to him, to leave their own desks—if he chose to make an appointment, next week possibly. He spoke with secretaries, of whom some were rude and some were forbearing. One told him the Prime Minister was tied up with conferences; another that he was away; another that he was too occupied to see anyone except his Cabinet or his military staff. They made Judge Winkleman feel superfluous and small.

He went out of the Government's cottages and crouched on a motor car's running board, resting his feet and nursing his hurt dignity. He watched bureaucrats, with bulging briefcases, climb out of taxicabs, clamber through ditches to get to their desks; bulldozers widening the paths; carpenters sawing and hammering; gardeners trimming the lawns and bright flower beds. Busy. Everyone busy. Too busy. What did I expect? he thought with rancor. In Jerusalem, Judge Winkleman is a somebody. Here he is nothing at all. A fool. A romantic, come on a quest. For justice. For Carmela's husband. . . . The Prime Minister has far more important things on his mind.

That was true, undeniably. There was, for one matter, the imminent peril of a civil war. All Tel Aviv buzzed about it. Etzel had just attempted to bring a ship, the *Altalena,* loaded with arms, into Tel Aviv harbor, in defiance of the rules of the truce. The Army, at Government's orders, had fired on the ship, Jew killing Jew. The vessel itself, a charred hulk, rocked on the Mediterranean's blue swells, beneath the windows of the Judge's hotel. When such things were troubling the State, was it reasonable to ask the Prime Minister to take time to examine the matter of Yora Levine? I'll go back, he thought. I'll tell Carmela it was not possible.

There is a law of averages, however, which governs affairs of men. Luck cannot always run bad. Judge Winkleman saw a familiar figure, in khaki shorts and sports blouse, emerge from a cottage, carrying a thick sheaf of papers in his one hand. The man cut across a lawn to another small house. Judge Winkleman scrambled up from the running board and ran to him. "Shalom, Nathan!" he cried.

The man wheeled. "Judge!" There was surprise in his voice and expression. Judge Winkleman always, even during a siege, proper and neat, now was disheveled, shirt glued to ribs, shoes grayed with dust, face moist with sweat. "When did *you* come here?" Nathan asked.

"Three days ago."

"Where do you stay?"

"Gat Rimmon."

"You are lucky. People are tearing their hair to find a bed."

The Judge smiled sourly. "The Gat Rimmon has not forgotten who I am."

Something in the jurist's tone—a hint of self-pity, perhaps—made Nathan wonder. Is he hunting a job, Supreme Court, possibly, or a Cabinet post? Or needing a personal favor? These old-timers may become a nuisance. Have we a new problem, displaced Zionists? Well, find out. Be that courteous to a neighbor. "What brings you here?" he asked.

The Judge answered truthfully, "I wish to see the Prime Minister about the execution of Yora Levine." He saw Nathan blink, then look down, biting his lip.

"If I were you," Nathan said harshly, "I would not trouble him. He has more important matters."

The Judge shook his head. "What is more important than justice?"

"The security of the State," Nathan answered him.

Something he had heard and let slip from his mind came back to Judge Winkleman. He recalled that Nathan had been at the trial and had given evidence. The soldier who had brought him the news that morning in June had mentioned it, but the details had been driven from his mind by the shock of awareness that he himself had set in motion a chain of events, through Gordon Leake, which had brought this tragedy upon Carmela Levine. I have found the right person, he exulted to himself, Nathan will explain everything. He put his hand on the other man's arm and said sternly, "Where there is no justice there is no security. I hardly need to tell this to you."

He saw creases deepen in Nathan's face. The man's mouth drew tight. He stood an instant, not answering, then jerked his arm free. "Excuse me, I am busy. Shalom."

After his supper, the Judge closed the blackout curtains, switched on the lamp in his tiny room and sat down to compose a note to the Prime Minister. One chance remained, appeal direct.

Writing the letter was difficult, stating the case, laying correct emphasis, accusing no one, yet denoting the areas of doubt, and indicating how this concerned the integrity of the State. Sweat dribbled from Judge Winkleman's forehead, streamed down his cheeks.

There was a sharp knock on his door. He mopped his face hurriedly, thrust the letter paper into a drawer and opened his door. Nathan stood there, scowling, as though he had come unwillingly by a peremptory summons. "I have half an hour only," he said. "I have a meeting."

"Then why have you come here?"

"Because you have," the man answered him.

Gravely, they eyed one another, before the Judge said, "Come in. Sit."

The man came into the stifling, narrow room and crouched on the edge of the bed. He crossed his knees and uncrossed them with evident nervousness. He took out a brown box of cigarettes, offered them, said, "I forget. You do not smoke." Clumsily, with his single hand, he flipped his lighter open, lit his cigarette. "In Tel Aviv, we live in luxury." He was trying to make the set-at-ease preliminary talk. "A man can offer another a cigarette." He inhaled deeply, pushed the smoke through his nostrils, and then leaned forward and asked, "Henry, why have you come to Tel Aviv?"

The Judge settled himself upon the straight-backed chair before he replied. "I was troubled about this affair."

"Why?" Nathan asked.

He knotted his hands. "I wanted to know, I needed to know the truth. To learn the truth I required help from the highest source."

"Why?" Nathan asked again. "What is your interest?"

The Judge stared at the yellow stones of the floor. A sweat bead bounced off his forehead, rolled, tickling his nose. He wiped it impatiently with the handkerchief before he glanced up. "Why? I shall tell you why. Because a Jerusalem woman in deepest distress came to me and asked for my help. She wished to receive her husband's death as a death *for* the State, not as an enemy of the State. This was a mistake, she insisted, and the mistake must be known and acknowledged. She asked it, that Israel might understand what justice means." He paused. "You were at the trial," he went on. "You gave evidence."

For a second, dismay in Nathan's eyes. "Who told you?"

The Judge felt himself reddening. He mopped the back of his neck. "A man who was there."

Nathan shrugged. "Then you know everything," he said. "You know he confessed."

"What did he confess?"

"That from time to time he gave lists of our vital places to a Britisher."

"With what intent?" Judge Winkleman asked.

He saw Nathan frown, the Adam's apple in his throat bob as he swallowed his spittle. "To provide current for us," Nathan finally said.

The judge bent forward. "Was that a crime? You must have known—or surmised—he was doing something like that. That was his task, was it not? A difficult task, assigned to him, for our defense. He worked out this plan. The plan had its dangers. Every plan we made last spring had its own risks. Nathan, when have we not had to run risks?"

Nathan drew on his cigarette a moment. "It was reported the Arabs used his lists as a map for their shell fire."

"Reported? By whom? By a British informer?" Henry Winkleman heard his own voice, level, calm. "I know that person. I know him perhaps better than you. And I know the sources of his information. And so now I say, we had no right to take a man's life because this informer reported gossip that Yora's list might have been used by Arabs—because something went not according to plan."

"There were other facts," Nathan said stiffly. "You do not know the whole thing."

The Judge folded his hands in his lap. "Then tell me the facts."

"Levine was personally intimate with Duncan. He was seen drinking with him at the King David bar."

The Judge raised his head. "Was that also a crime?" he answered coldly. "I know our laws well. I never have seen a statute forbidding Briton and Jew to drink at a bar. Look, Nathan—" He slid forward to the edge of his chair. "You accused a man of treason on the word of a British informer." He choked slightly, recalling his own part in this, but went on. "Did you learn a motive? Was he paid? Was he promised reward? Did you bring witnesses? Did you permit the accused to have legal counsel? No, you did not. You did none of these things. You were accusers. You were judges. You were executioners."

"We were at war." Nathan laid his cigarette down. "The security of the State was involved," he said. "It was no time for legal formalities."

"Nonsense." The Judge snapped the word out. "You had no proof. . . . Where was your proof? Answer me. Where was your proof?"

The face of the man opposite grew set and hard. "The machine-gun post," Nathan said.

The Judge looked up sharply. "What was that? That I do not know."

Nathan crossed his legs and he smiled, a lift of self-justification. "There was a post on your street. On the Doctor's house."

"I remember that."

"The house was hit two separate times. On my advice, the gun was removed. Levine suggested a new place, in a street where there had not been shelling, a street near several legations. That very night the new place was shelled. The gun and six soldiers were lost."

"I remember." The Judge leaned back. "I recall it now. It was just before the Old City breakthrough. There was some talk then of spies."

Nathan nodded. "There was talk. Even I thought at the time, perhaps some one in one of the consulates . . ."

"Perhaps," Judge Winkleman said.

Nathan reflected a moment before he shook his head. "This, added to the other. There you had it—the whole picture of guilt."

"And that was your proof? . . . Nathan, a picture of guilt is no proof." The Judge heard his voice rising, shrill, womanish, and paused to recover composure. "Suspicious circumstance. It was no more than that. The plague of justice is suspicious circumstance. The symbol of justice is bandaged eyes and balanced scales. We who are judges do not dare look on what you call the picture of guilt. We need to listen, seek facts, seek proofs, and weigh carefully. Nathan." He pounded his fist into his moist palm. "It was shameful to employ an informer's gossip to condemn a soldier of the State. It was a disgrace to all Israel to deny a citizen the protection of law. It terrifies me, that in the heat and excitement of war, a coincidence which seemed to point to one man—"

"Stop!" Nathan cried. "Change the tone of your voice. Am I on trial?"

"Yes," Judge Winkleman said.

The man stood up, angry and flushed. "I was concerned with security," he rasped. "You quibble with law." He glanced at the door, took a step toward it, but instead, turned and walked a few paces to the window, stood fingering the heavy curtains as though to draw them apart. He heard Judge Winkleman, saying levelly, "Nathan, you are on trial, you and each man who had part in this. The death of this man is a personal tragedy to his family. But, more than that, above and beyond, you, all of you, harmed the integrity, the very purpose of the State. If we, who have suffered so much from injustice, ourselves act this way, with injustice, too, then have not our children died all in vain?"

The man at the window turned slowly. "It is over," he said wearily. "Levine is dead. The thing is finished. Nothing can be done."

"Levine is dead," Judge Winkleman echoed him. "Nothing we do can bring him back. But the thing is not over. It has only begun. If we have the courage to face our own acts, our own reckless deeds, to say, Yes, we have made a mistake, then our stature will heighten and grow. We will gain in respect, in the world's eyes and in our own. All men, everywhere, will be assured that in Israel, justice is a triumphant and living thing."

His voice dropped and died. In the hot little room, there was for the moment the sound of a radio bleating a marching song of Palmach. And when the music ended, there was merely the muffled swish of the sea. Then Nathan came across the room and extended his only hand. "I take my responsibility," he said quietly. He shut his eyes as though he were in pain. "I have done much for our Nation," he said. "I shall do one thing more." He opened his eyes. "Tomorrow, we go together to see the Prime Minister."

Judge Winkleman was white with dust from the terrible road and sore in all his bones when he limped up the street to Carmela's house. "I have seen the Prime Minister," he told her. "He has promised a full investigation. He has assured me justice will be done. I believe him. He is a great man."

"I thank you." Carmela bowed her head. "You have been more than kind. This will not bring my husband back. But it is a comfort to know I have a good and brave friend."

The news was on the wireless and in the newspapers. Jerusalem was first startled, then dazzled by it. The Prime Minister had concerned himself with the facts in the case of Yora Levine. He had learned there had been no fair trial, no proof. A shocking miscarriage of justice had taken place. The State apologized, knowing words could not restore a husband and father, but it promised to try and to punish those who had been to blame, and to make what reparation it could.

The Scoutmaster rapped on Hirschs' door. "We meet at the school at three o'clock," he told Teddy. "In uniform, to parade."

"Where do we parade?"

"Here, up this street. Before Asi's house. The Prime Minister has ordered it. His father died in line of duty and we must honor the son."

A small stone got caught under the flapping sole of Teddy's worn shoe and he lagged behind the others to remove the pebble.

"Come on, hurry up," a boy called back to him. "We're going into the house."

"So what." He waved his hand. "I've been there already. Did you think I ever believed that traitor chisbat?"

Shoshanna opened the door. When she saw the boys in khaki and Ata blue scarves, she cried, "Oh!" before she called, "Asi, Asi, the Scouts are here."

They filed into the hall, big-eyed, red-faced, unnaturally solemn. Carmela stood watching as each boy in turn stepped forward and shook Asi's hand. Asi was flushed; his eyes glistened; his round chin quivered a bit but he held himself straight, with dignity. "Like a soldier's son," Carmela found herself thinking. "His father would be proud of him."

III

AFTER THE NINTH of July, there was no longer time for Scout parades in Jerusalem or gossip in Gan Darom's hospital bunker. The cease-fire had ended without bringing peace and the Tegart Fortress on the rise above Gan Darom again was shelling the settlement. Lorries scudded back and forth to the base every night, but no longer to transport people for showers.

July's heat tormented the desert. Men stripped to their shorts. Gan Darom's bunkers grew even more crowded and stank horribly. The young men who slept in them now were new immigrants who spoke little Ivrith.

The tank was moved; the wall was patched up. In all the pillboxes there were new guns.

Al still ran his airlift to the base every night, a better plane now, a larger one, though he wished it was not, since at Gaza, the Egyptians had competent ack-ack and a larger target is that much easier to hit. He asked the boys at the Base what news from Gan Darom? They said so far, all was well, which meant nothing more than that the kibbutz still held out. He left messages for Dinah. He got no messages back.

One evening he ran into the red-bearded boy who was the head man at Dinah's kibbutz. They passed each other in the dining hall. Dan did not reply to his greeting, but marched ahead, as though he had never seen Al before, to a table where there were several High Command men whom Al had just flown down from the coast.

Too big for his breeches, Al thought. The swell job they've all done has gone to his head. And he's paying me off, because I spent a night watching the moon with the best-looking girl in the place.

What Al did not know and could not possibly guess, was that Dan was telling the headquarters strategists, he thought he could do what had to be done. This would be a job for sappers. He had several competent people. He did not mention that one was himself, one, Joshua, whom he loved as a brother, and the other the girl with whom Al had watched the moon. If reinforcements could be brought up— artillery as well as men—after the breakthrough, he thought there was a reasonable chance the Tegart might yield.

If Al had known that, he might not have flown, whistling, back to the coast, telling himself, Dan hates my guts. That must be because I've made time with the girl.

They moved in tarry blackness, inching forward, their bellies flush with the rough, hard-baked terrain. They moved in small groups. The first was to locate and clear away enemy mines, and lay new ones. The second was to cut the heavy barbed wire around the Fortress. The third carried explosives strapped on their backs. In the third group were Joshua, Dan and Dinah Hirsch.

Bren guns, two three-inch mortars, and infantrymen with good new rifles were a way back, waiting for the signal to attack.

The ring of wire had been cut and the sappers were crouching, ready to crawl through the openings to blast off the Tegart's iron doors, when from the window and roof of the Fortress, guns started to blaze, point-blank fire. Joshua caught the first blast. It hit the load on his back. As the others scattered to run, they saw him explode.

Dan had time for one action—just one—to seize Dinah's arm, for she would have gone lunging ahead into the spitting guns—before he loosened his own lethal load.

The artillery halted. Dan finally came up to the guns, crawling, belly-flat, soaked with blood and with both his legs smashed.

When it received the brief wireless report, the base asked that survivors come over next day to give details, and the High Command men flew up again to learn precisely why the attack had failed. A young girl appeared with Gan Darom's men.

Al saw her go into the concrete pillbox where the officers were but she did not see him. An hour later he saw her come out and go with them to the dining hall. He went up to her then. Her face was dirt streaked, her eyes bloodshot. She greeted him somberly, "We are in trouble," she said. "Last night we tried to take the Tegart Fortress.

We lost twelve good men and our explosives. Dan was badly wounded."

He gaped at her. "You were there?"

"Of course," she said. "They are shelling us steadily now, what you call softening us up. There will be bombers. There will be a tank attack."

He asked, though it was pointless to, "You're going back?"

"We have a jeep. We start right now."

"In daylight?"

"We came in daylight, we return in daylight. We are beyond fear." Then she left to speak with the officers again and return briefly to him. "If you go to Jerusalem, do not mention, please, that I was in the Teggart attack. I would prefer they do not know."

The jeep was waiting outside the barbed wire of the base. He walked out to the vehicle with her, fifth wheel, a boyish Lieutenant Colonel walked along, too, and held her attention with military matters, no doubt. Before she climbed into the jeep, she shook hands with Al, said "l'hitra'ot" and smiled, and from the front seat, leaned out and waved to him.

He watched the jeep start. He saw it stop a few yards down the road. He saw her speaking urgently to the driver, tugging his arm. He saw men pile out and run for a ditch. He saw her stand up in the jeep, a second's unsureness, as if she too were readying to jump.

She stood alone, her black hair streaming, her bosom thrust forward, like a carved figurehead on a ship. Then he was aware of whirring over his head and realized he, too, stood alone, and he and she were crazy because a plane with the green crescent and star had just let a bomb go. He leaped for a trench. While he sprawled there, the ground rocked. He heard the short, panting puffs of the anti-aircraft at the base and the diminishing of the drone of the enemy plane. When he could hear it no longer, he climbed out of the trench. He saw his plane blazing out on the field, felt a brief pang of distress but he didn't go toward it, but out to the road, where the jeep had stood. He saw something lying at the side of the road and he picked it up, and held it because it was her worn, muddy shoe. He sat holding it, while the others gathered the fragments of what had once been a beautiful girl, and arranged them hastily in a hole hacked from the parched earth. He stood up when the men from her settlement, who had jumped into the ditch, heaped stones above a small mound, and he heard them speaking in Ivrith, with faces of sorrow and anger and upraised fists. He knew they were pledging themselves to avenge her death.

"Dinah," he said to her through himself, "I'll avenge you too. I'll stay here. In your country, your place." And he thought, deeper down in himself, Staying here, I remain with her.

He took a long look at the bleak bareness of the plain and the burning, pitiless sky from which her death had come. He saw birds wheeling high over the spot where the jeep had been, circling down. He shut his eyes, not merely to shut out this horror, but to lock within himself the image of a slim, brave and fanatical girl.

When the others finally left in a lorry which belonged to the base, he went with them because that would keep him near her a little while more and he could not bring himself yet to think finality.

One of the men in the lorry recognized him, saw he was carrying the shoe, and said, "We will give you the rest of her things, to bring to her family in Jerusalem." The man who had been driving the jeep sat with his head in his hands, muttering. An argument started between two men, went on, till the driver cried, "Sheket." It was all in Ivrith. Al couldn't imagine what they were quarreling about, and thought miserably, this is no time for debates, common decency ordains silence, out of respect for the dead.

The first word they had at Gan Darom was when the lorry arrived. The men jumped out and went directly to Dan in the hospital bunker, without asking Al to join them, and he found himself wandering alone. He made his way to the rubble heap which had once been the house for the children, and stood there, still holding the shoe.

The Fortress was lobbing shells toward Gan Darom. He saw one strike the wall, blow cement and gravel sky-high. People with better sense stayed in the trenches, down in the ground. When wonderful young girls like Dinah can die, he thought bitterly, why should I save my carcass?

It occurred to him he was being dramatic, behaving just as she had, baring his breast, and he repeated clichés to himself, Better a live coward than a dead lion. He who fights and runs away, lives to fight another day. You were a soldier, Dinah, you should have known better, too. A second too slow, timing off. She died of being too brave. But you knew nothing else, Dinah. That's how you were raised.

Someone plucked at his sleeve. "Dan wants to see you, in the hospital bunker," a girl said. It was Chava who'd worked in the kitchen cave with Dinah. She looked at him queerly, with pity, he thought.

"Of course," he said to the girl. "I saw it. For the sake of the record, let's give it straight." Were they cowards or not, they who jumped into the ditch? he kept asking himself. They were better soldiers than she. Part of good soldiering is to know when not to be brave. But if I tell that to Dan, he'll think her a fool. She wasted a life. . . . No, he decided. She would want me to tell them the truth.

He hadn't the chance. The jeep driver already had told them, but because Al had been there, and he was a guest, to whom one owed courtesy, the white-faced, bearded boy who lay in plaster casts on a hospital slab made the man tell it again, in halting, guttural English.

"She saw, I saw the Egyptian plane," the driver said. "She told to me, 'Drive straight ahead. Keep going. Don't stop.'"

It drove a searing flash through his brain. *Drive straight ahead. Keep going. Don't stop.*

Step on the gas, beat out death.

"I say, 'No, stop. Jump, quick. No chance.'"

The pain-filled eyes of the man on the bunk knifed the driver so that the man looked away. "If you had listened to her," Dan asked, "is it possible the girl and the vehicle would have been saved?"

The man bowed his head. "It is possible. If we had gone very fast."

Drive straight ahead. Keep going. Don't stop.

"I have lost both of them. My best comrades. Joshua. Dinah. I loved them the most." Dan's eyes were marbling. The men stared at him in amazement for no one had ever imagined Dan knew how to cry.

Al turned to leave and heard Dan calling him back. "When you go soon to Jerusalem, please take her things. She would wish it so." He extended his hand. "Come back to us. Shalom. L'hitra'ot," he said.

IV

SHELLING FROM THE Arab positions was especially heavy in the Holy
City the day of the air raid on the Negev base. Power lines were
struck. The newspaper's one press had no current to get out its daily
run. Even the field telephones did not work and with the full fury of
the renewed war, the short-wave radio was occupied with more
crucial matters than the death of a single girl. It was not till the following day that Jerusalem knew Dinah Hirsch had been killed.

A messenger ran through shell-fire from Army headquarters to the
hospital, for it was decided it would be kinder if the father knew first
and he tell the mother the best way he could.

Jacob was in the operating room when the messenger came and
the man had to wait in the hall until nurses wheeled out a stretcher
with an ether-reeking, mummy-swathed form and the Doctor
emerged in his bloodied hospital gown. When the man gave him the
news, he staggered and groped for the wall. Then he asked, "Are
you sure?"

"There were witnesses. The news comes from two places. Gan
Darom and the base. They buried her where she fell, at the base."

Jacob bowed his head. He stood, unable to speak. A nurse came
out to the corridor and touched his arm. "Ready, Doctor," she said.
"We are waiting for you."

He shook himself. "Thank you for bringing the news," he remembered to say to the messenger before he returned to the operating
room.

A young girl, twelve years or so, lay on the table, the ether cone
over her face, her olive-tinted belly with a long scarlet slash, bared
in a round opening within white sheets.

"This time a little variety, Doctor," the anaesthetist greeted him.
"No shrapnel. Knife. The foolish child went out this morning to pick
apricots. Our cousins were in the neighborhood. . . . Pick apricots

in a war! Children have no caution, no sense."

"We will do what we can for her," Dr. Hirsch said. He glanced at the long, curving black lashes on the narrow, swarthy face, the silky tendrils of ebony curls at the rim of the towel turban. An Oriental, he thought, possibly from Iran, a pretty child. He drew on his rubber gloves. A nurse tied on his gauze mask. His hand was steady as he probed the tender flesh across the navel and sutured the slashed gut.

When he was done, he drew off his gloves. "Call someone else for the others," he said after the nurse had removed his mask. "I am exhausted today." He laid his bloodied coat aside. "I have just heard," he said. "My daughter Dinah is dead."

Edith cried out, as everyone, everywhere, cries at such news, the denial, the single word, "No!" She turned her face from her husband, crept to the furthest, darkest corner of the living room and sat there alone. He went upstairs and locked himself into the W.C.

After a while, Teddy came in, shouting, "Imma! Imma!" and when he saw his mother he asked, "Why are you sitting there? What's happened to you?" and she got up, drawing her breath in painfully, to tell it to him.

There was a matter of hours before the news spread and the rush of condolence came. By that time the shock had been borne and Edith Hirsch had only to show what she wished, the accepting Jerusalem face. Jacob took to his bed, behind a closed door. It was she who met callers, calm, upright, alone.

Ida Goldstein came first with Carmela Levine. These three who had all been bereaved clung together, like one. When finally they drew apart, to sit side by side on the couch, Ida said, "She was brave, like my Arieh. She was beautiful like my Deborah."

"She was wise," Carmela said. "Beyond eighteen years. Do you know what that girl said to me? 'G'veret Levine,' she said. 'If you know in your heart he was innocent, you must not rest till you prove it was so. The main thing, always, is how much you believe.' She said to me, 'If you know the truth in your heart, try not to mind what anyone thinks. Open your door. Hold your head high.'"

She heard her friends without hearing them, for the anaesthesia of shock had set her apart, within the veiled and numbed world of grief, where all sensation, all thought concerns itself only with that which forever is gone. Was Dinah afraid? Was she in pain? Did she, at the instant, cry out for me? . . . What use are these eulogies? She will not return. The hour, long-dreaded, has finally arrived.

It was Carmela who stayed to fix supper and urge the mourners to eat. The Winkleman sisters came while she was there. She said "Shalom" to them and they had no choice except to answer "Shalom," although after that they hurried to Edith and conversed with nobody else. "Unbelievable," Maida Winkleman said. "Every house on this street has had death. Even ours."

Every house. Yes, that was so. Arieh. Madame. Yora. The Afrikaaner. My beloved Dinah . . . And on the corner, Tamar, Herr Prinz, the Viennese blondes. Bereavement, like the water and bread, is rationed, an equal portion to every dwelling. Does that make my portion easier to bear?

Lillie Gross did not come till the following day. She came early at an hour when no one else was likely to be in the house and she brought a cake she had baked. She set it upon the dining table and stood beside it, not certain whether to leave it and go, or to stay.

"Thank you," Edith said coldly. Margarine, sugar, eggs, she thought. Will the waste of her whole week's ration make us good friends? Hers was the one household spared.

"Edith," Lillie's voice shook, "I did not know what to do when I heard. 'Not Dinah,' I cried to Ezra, 'not Dinah, our very best.'"

Edith moved her head slowly from side to side. "They all are our best. Each life was precious. No one was more than anyone else."

Tears sprang to Lillie Gross' eyes. She felt she could not stay and knew she could not leave. I must explain to her, she thought, this dare not be allowed to fester between my old friend and me. "Edith," she began again, "David is trying to get passage home. We had a letter during the truce."

"About time," Edith said.

A silence, chilly and tense, fell between them. Lillie Gross broke it, speaking rapidly, "We did not tell him to stay, Edith. And we did not tell him to come. We could not tell a grown man what to do." Edith was looking directly at her. The reproach in that gaze was unbearable. "Could we say," Lillie cried, "'David, leave medical school. Give up your whole life's ambition.'? Could we say, 'David, come home. Lay down your life for this land'.?"

"No," Edith answered after a while. "You could not say it. You could only hope that would be what he would wish to do."

"That is so," Lillie said, her voice rising defensively. "That is precisely what he wished to do."

Edith lifted her eyes to meet the glance of her old friend. "If there is blame," Lillie was saying, "the blame is mine. But who can blame me for wishing to save my child?"

A long minute passed before she replied and as if with great weariness, "Not I. I cannot blame any mother who would save her child."

V

ON THE SECOND afternoon of the second truce after a ten-day renewal of war, Al Brody had his first glimpse of Jerusalem's streets and felt as if he had had a relapse to serious sickness. Here were London, Dieppe, and Frankfurt. Here were all the world's cities, senselessly battered and broken by the fury of war, for everywhere rubble looks precisely the same and the sight makes one physically ill from sorrow that men have so patiently built and even more patiently hoped for progress and peace. All they ever have asked is the chance to live with the things they have wrought, but those known as statesmen never give them that chance.

Yet here it was worse than anywhere else, Al told himself, for this was the Holy City, beloved by man and by God. Hands should have shriveled and wasted away before they launched shells. Sacrilege to employ that blue sky as death's passageway. God, what's the matter with You? he demanded. Why did You let them wreck Your home town?

As he plodded through street after street and everywhere saw devastation, he wondered how one single person had remained alive through Jerusalem's cruel ordeal.

Being a stranger in town, he had to ask where to go, and it was late afternoon before he walked up the quiet street. He noticed the brilliant gardens before he saw the jagged scars of the siege. He lingered at the gateposts to examine the Doctor's blue on white sign. He dawdled on the path, looking over the dusty pepper tree and the bougainvillea vines, wondering what their names were. He studied the lanky geranium hedge and the dejected roses in their parched, weedy beds. He knew his behavior for what it was, stalling, the naked dread of what might transpire after he knocked on a door.

Drive straight ahead. Keep going. Don't stop. He made himself go up the steps at the side of the house and rap on the door.

The woman who opened it had been sewing. In one hand, she held a khaki blouse with needle and thread still attached. She was gray haired and sweet faced and small, plainly attired in a faded cotton print dress. A word sprang to his mind, one he had never thought or spoken before. A gentlewoman, she was.

She appeared surprised to find a stranger in a nondescript uniform with a small duffle bag standing there, but not displeased at his looks, his boyish, open countenance, rumpled, curly hair, and his nonchalant air. Then she saw the duffle bag, with the name in Ivrith, and she gripped the frame of the door.

By the way she looked at him, he knew she had guessed who he was and why he was here but he said, "Shalom, I'm Al Brody. I'm Dinah's friend."

Her hand came away from the door. "I am Edith Hirsch, her mother," she said. "Shalom. Please come in." She gave him her hand, mere finger bones, gloved in cool flesh. There was some resemblance to Dinah in the small, refined features and the way this woman held her head up, proudly, an aristocrat, but in no more than that. Dinah was glowing, vibrant. This woman looked haggard and drab.

She went ahead into a large living room. A brindle boxer rose from the stone floor and padded toward him, sniffing his shoes. He stroked the dog's head. "Shalom, Udi," he said. "Dinah's dog," he said.

"Dinah's dog," her mother repeated. "She told you, then?"

"About Udi and her whole family."

He looked around. The room impressed him. They had been well-to-do, he could see, and probably they still were. There was expensive furniture, a baby grand, more elegant household goods than he had ever found in any home he had visited. Across the room's length, from the piano lid, from a silver frame, Dinah's almond-shaped eyes looked at him. He felt his tears rising and he bunched the rough cloth of the duffle bag in his clenching hand.

Edith saw it. She saw everything, since she was attentive for all he might say and do and all he could not. She said, softly, "She was sixteen when that picture was taken. As you know, she changed very much." Then she said, "Please, sit down."

He sat in an armchair with a carved walnut frame, covered with old rose brocade, and placed the duffle bag carefully on the stone floor.

It occurred to him that Dinah must have sat in this chair. Why, she knew intimately everything in this room. This was the house which had shaped her, had taught her to spoon soup like a lady though she ate in a cave underground. This luxury she had left to live in the earth, under rubble, beneath the desert's floor.

Dinah's mother pulled a small armchair close to his and set a sewing box on the table near her. "You will not mind if I go on with my work?" Her accent was unlike her daughter's, as though they were of a different race. "We have little current to sew by at night and my young son is threadbare."

"Teddy," he said.

"Teddy." She nodded, pleased that he knew. "Every blouse Teddy owns is worn out and there's nothing to buy in town." She spoke without self-pity, mere statement of fact.

"Please go on with your sewing," he said and he thought how much better this was, her busy work, stalling, both stalling the time when one must . . . *Drive straight ahead. Keep going.* . . .

"Did you have trouble finding our street?" she asked, like any hostess with conversation to make.

"I asked directions."

"This is your first time in Jerusalem?"

"My first."

"It is a pity you see it this way, torn apart. It was one of the world's most beautiful cities, you know. Our Rehavia alone was so serene and secure, with its gardens and trees. We used to say it was Cambridge, transplanted to the Middle East."

He kept eying her, watching her hands flicking the needle through the faded cloth, listening to her pleasant, modulated voice. Here sits a woman, he said to himself, who has lived through violence of the most shocking sort, and by her very presence, here, in this spot, has made history, a woman whose daughter has only just died in a war, and she sits quietly, patching a boy's khaki blouse, like anybody's mother in Brooklyn or the Bronx. That's ridiculous and it is right. It was as though all she was inherently had rejected extraneous disturbance and left her the ordinary housewife she always had been.

The dog loped toward them again and nosed the duffle bag. She noticed that, as she noticed everything, and she said, each word separate, as though it were being drawn, like a tooth, "Are those Dinah's things?"

"Dinah's things." A pulse in his throat started to throb. He slid the canvas bag an inch or so nearer to her.

"The dog knew." She reached out but drew her hand back. "You were kind to bring it," she said and began sewing once more.

"None of her comrades could leave," he said.

"They are having a very difficult time?" She spread the boy's blouse on her knee and flattened the square of a patch with her palm.

"Very." He crossed his legs. He was aware of how hard she was trying to keep this encounter easy and casual and he was grateful. My Old Lady, he thought, if this was me, would have called out the cops with her carrying on.

"Will they hold out?" her quiet voice asked.

"So far, they have. And now that there is another truce, for whatever these truces are worth—"

She nodded, fell silent, let her sewing lie on her lap, and then in a strained, taut voice, asked, "Did it happen there?"

His nerves drew together. The time was now, no more putting off. "No," he managed to say. "Near the base. She had come in to report to some Headquarters brass," he went on. "I'd flown them down. That's how I happened to be on the scene. The day after the attack on the Tegart Fortress."

Her needle halted, her pale lips divided. "She was in that attack?"

He bit his tongue. Dinah had said not to tell them. Can it matter? They're past worrying. "She was very brave," he said.

Her breath made a sucking noise. Her chest rose and fell. "Do you know how it happened?"

He nodded yes.

She gripped her hands and bent toward him. "Will you tell me?"

He shook his head. "I'd rather not."

He saw her hand rise to her heart and he was aware of a dull emptiness in the house while he waited for what she might ask after that. The question was one he had hoped not to hear, "Could it have been prevented?" she asked.

His fingers closed and stiffened. His nails bit his palms. "In war," he replied, "hindsight is remarkable. When you've split-second decisions to make—"

"You haven't answered my question," she said. She took two stitches in her seam.

"I'm doing the best I can."

She kept still, then she asked, "Did she know it was happening to her?"

The tip of his tongue wet his lips. "I'd rather not answer that either." He saw her face working. "Because I'm really not sure," he blurted out.

Her needle ran in and out of the cloth. "You were there? You saw it?"

"I did." He squirmed in the chair. "Please, don't ask me. I'd rather not tell."

He saw her lips compressed and the shadows of imagined horrors flickering over her gray face. "How awful for you!" was what she said.

His chest constricted. "Please believe me," he managed to say. "She wasn't afraid. That's all I can tell you. But of that I am sure."

"I believe you." She snipped off a thread, folded her sewing, leaned away from him to put spool and scissors into her box. She got up, then, still calm, still poised, "Now, may I have her things?"

He rose, too, and carried the duffle bag to her, though she stood less than two feet from him, but it seemed right to do this with a flourish, like handing on a torch. Her fingers fumbled with the knots in the cord. "Shall I help?"

She shook her head sharply, and he left her and walked down the room, past the framed photograph, up the short flight into the dining room, to the window there. The dog followed him. He stood looking out, on a wall covered with morning-glories, and he stroked the dog's brindle head. He wondered whether he dared to ask her to let him have Dinah's dog.

"But there's only one shoe!" he heard the girl's mother exclaim.

He bit his lip hard before he wheeled and came back. She had spread the things out on the sofa—some pink underwear, a crimson sweater, some scarves, handkerchiefs, a few books, a notepad, a mechanical pencil, a hairbrush and comb, a wrist watch with a torn strap. But she held the shoe in her hand.

"I couldn't find the other," he said helplessly. "I hunted and hunted, but I couldn't find it." And he thought, shuddering, that shoe and that foot are down in the Negev and buzzards are picking those little bones clean. He begged, as much of himself as of her, "Don't cry, please, don't cry."

Her answer came with a quiet pride. "We do not cry."

He sat down abruptly and covered his face with his hands.

After a long while, he heard her again. "Mister Brody," and he let his hands down. She was standing. She looked ravaged and worn but she had laid the shoe with the rest of the things. She touched his arm. "I'll fix you a drink," she said. He began to protest but she said, trying to smile, "You are a guest. You have come a long way. . . . I'll be no more than a moment. Please make yourself at home."

He lit a cigarette, crossed his legs and uncrossed them, got up, paced the room. A painting behind the radio cabinet attracted him. He was studying it when he heard a child yelling, "Imma" and turned to see a yellow kid with enormous black eyes and cup-handle ears. "Shalom, Teddy," he said.

The boy's mouth popped open. "How do you know my name? Who are you?"

"I'm Al," he said.

"Are you the flyer who brought Dinah here?"

When he said that he was, the boy walked over and shook his hand. "That was good of you," Teddy said. "I appreciate that." Then he goggled at Al, and swooped toward him. "Your ashes are dropping. . . . Wait, I bring you something." He ran out and came back with a curved bit of metal. "From our own pagaz," the boy said. "The one that hit our own house. A twenty-five pounder, it was. You can have it. . . . From me . . . I make you a present of it."

His mother came in, then, bearing a silver tray, polished, exquisitely etched. In its center lay a drawn linen square and upon that, two glasses of pale yellow fluid. She set it down on a carved table. "I am sorry we have no ice or charged water," she apologized as though she had to. "I'm afraid it's a bad lemon squash."

He remembered the hot afternoon at the Park Hotel and would have laughed at this joke on himself but he saw the boy eying the tray with such genuine longing, he was ashamed of himself. "Yes, Teddy," the boy's mother said. "You may take the other. We can't often spare water for lemon squash. Drink it quickly and run out and play. We want to talk."

The boy made a grimace of protest but he got the drink down in three gulps, set the glass on the tray, winked at Al, like an old comrade, and said, "L'hitra'ot." At the door, he called back, "Don't go away. I want to introduce my friend, Asi, to you."

Dinah's mother pulled her chair up to his and folded her hands in her lap. "Now," she said. *"Now.* Now we can talk. . . . Speak about Dinah to me."

He set down his glass, half-emptied. "I don't know where to start."

"Begin anywhere. There's so much to be said."

Yet he waited, unsure where to start. "I never met anyone like her," he began finally.

She smiled. It was an odd little smile, as though she knew a secret, but she said, "Every mother likes to think her child is unique," and shook her head. "Dinah was typical, a typical sabra, like all of our children, you know."

"I *don't* know," he replied. "I never knew people like her. A new human dimension." He found himself blushing and felt he had to explain why he blushed. "It embarrasses me, using big words like that. You see—" He stubbed out the smouldering ember of his cigarette. "We make a thing in the States of talking slang, talking tough. It makes people feel you're a regular guy. Now and then I'd find Dinah looking at me sort of queer, I'd been using American slang. She knew English all right, but not my kind."

Edith Hirsch smiled again. "She paid you a great compliment, speaking English with you. That was one of her quirks. Out of hate of the British, she wouldn't speak English, though she knew it perfectly well. Her mother was born in Boston, you see."

He nodded. "She told me that. It struck me queer. There was nothing Boston in her." He paused. "She belonged," he said. "She belonged right where she was."

"Yes," her mother said softly. "There's that about our children. They belong. They know they belong. It makes a great difference when you know you belong."

He bent toward her, his words tumbling over each other. "That's it, that's the crux of the thing, belonging, knowing where you belong. Now, I, me, we—" he drew a deep breath—"American Jews, *especially* American Jews, where do we belong?"

"Here." Her index finger pointed down. "You belong here."

"I wish I knew that." He ran his hand under his collar. "I wish I was sure. Your daughter tried to give it to me, her sureness, I mean. She knew where she stood. She knew what she had to do." He looked directly at her. "And what she had to do," he went on to say, "was exactly the same as what she wanted to do." Yet while he was speaking there ran through the back of his mind what Dinah had told him that night, in the pretentious phrases which he had felt were not her own, and her wistful moment of wavering when she had said, candidly, "I think we are jealous of them," and he wondered whether what he was thinking showed in his face. I dare not give her away, he thought, not even hint, and repeated, with more emphasis than the small words demanded of him, "She did what she wanted to do. She gave her life for the country she loved."

There was a pause. "Do you think," her mother asked then, "that my daughter wanted to die?" She shook her head slowly. "No one does, not a young girl who is loved."

He bowed his head, mumbling, "That's different. She had no choice."

He wasn't sure Dinah's mother had heard him, for she made no reply, but sat braiding her fingers. When she once more started to speak it was with the thin, detached remoteness of recalling a past. "A few months ago, I sat in this very room," she said, "with a neighbor of ours. She had just heard that her son—one of Dinah's old friends—might be dead. In the Easter battle on the Bethlehem Road."

"I was there," he broke in and flushed, recalling his failure that day, and was relieved she did not halt but went on, "A fearful dilemma possessed me that day—and all through that night—a problem, I assure you, which wasn't just mine. Every mother, every father, of a child in this Land, each one of us who had come here out of faith, of ideals, tormented himself with that cruel riddle. Which do we want most, the State which has been our life-long dream or our living children?" Her head came up; her eyes were clear. "For ourselves, there was no question. We had made our choice. Coming here was our time of decision. But our children? Dared we to sacrifice them for what we believed?"

He shook his head firmly. "You needn't have asked the question. Dinah believed as much as you did," and was surprised to hear himself saying the words with assurance. I've cleaned the slate, he thought, wiped out my own moment of doubt about her.

Edith Hirsch rested her chin on her hand and regarded him thoughtfully. "Yes," she said, slowly. "I had no choice and she had no choice. Mister Brody, my daughter's life and her way of death were decided for her long ago. By her parents. Us. By her grandfather. He was a friend of Theodor Herzl, you know." She waited a moment. "And long before that," she went on. "In this very Jerusalem two thousand years before this, when the Temple was razed and the Nation dispersed. What happened to her, and to all of us, was part of an endless striving, a desperate need to come home." Her words came sharply, each one incisive, a surgeon's blade. "To belong. To be human beings, what you might call just another guy. That's not more and not less, than the basic yearning for home." She paused to swallow, to restore her breath. His half-emptied glass on the tray caught her eye. "You didn't like lemon squash," she said, reproaching herself. "I should have made coffee for you."

He said, "Please, please don't think about me." He snapped open his lighter and started a fresh cigarette.

She moved back in her chair. "My daughter, you understand," she started again, "had no choice, no chance to be otherwise than she was. The factors were weighted for her, by our coming here, by the society in which she lived, by all that had happened to the people of which she was part. So you see—" She twisted the gold wedding band on her finger. "She had no free choice." Her chin came up. "Nor do any of us. I know that now, so clearly I wonder why I was ever confused."

"She may have had a choice at the final moment," he said carefully, "between living and dying, but her courage was something she couldn't compromise with."

"Do you really think that?" Edith Hirsch bent toward him again. "Do you believe any of us are heroic, out of mere choice?"

He had to remember himself over Germany, falling, pulling a parachute cord, flailing those people with sticks and stones in their hands, one man against a multitude. Did I want to do all of that? he asked himself now. I did not. I was brave, hell, yes, I was brave, but what choice did I have?

"We were ordinary people," this sweet-faced woman was saying in her New England accent. "We did not choose to be heroes. Believe me, we did not. All we have ever asked of the world is the chance to raise our children, do our work, live graciously and in peace, and in time's fullness, die. No one, no country, no era, has let us. Never. At any time." She ran her hand over her forehead. "We're fearfully tired of being a problem, of making headlines."

"Even your daughter—" He started then to tell her about the poem Dinah had wanted to write, but she was speaking again before he could get his words out.

"It's so uncomfortable to make history. We're drained and exhausted. Time and again, we've found ourselves asking ourselves, 'Why should it have been us?' We envied, we even hated, those who had quiet nights, water, food. Yes, we were even angry with Tel Aviv." She laughed softly then. "Why, we told each other, they've had to take nothing. Just a few air raids, that's all . . . But we were here. Sitting ducks, shelled night and day. The world wasn't lifting its little finger to help us. Stay and take it. The siege was our fate. Understand." She shook her head decisively. "We are vehicles only, a kind of—" Her glance fell on the silver tray on which the glasses stood. She smiled faintly. "A kind of silver salver, on which a State is served. We would prefer it to be otherwise. In our hearts we crave, how much we crave it you can never know, to have peace of mind, comfort, hear music, read books." She stopped suddenly. "Are you bored with me?"

"Far from it," he said.

She smiled again. "I cannot remember when in my life I have talked as much." She rose then. "I feel," she said, "As if I'd been talking to my own son." Her hand pressed his shoulder and choking tears rose in his throat. "Dinah spoke of you," she said. The secretive smile was again on her lips.

"Oh!" He was pleased, yet in that instant unsure of himself. He laid his cigarette down on the metal shell. "What did she say?"

"That you were unlike anyone she had ever met. She said about you exactly what you said of her. . . . It was that night, before she fell asleep. . . . That's why you saw me smile. It's what every girl says when she's found her love."

His tears spilled finally. He let them, for a moment or so, then mopped them with his hand and looked up, into her face. "Mrs. Hirsch," he said gravely, "you have met me. You know what I am.

Now, I bring you a present. I bring you Dinah's last spoken words."
He saw her lips part, her blue eyes bulge. "I had not meant to tell
you how your daughter died. I tried not to, really. But you deserve
to know. You can take it. You can face facts." He drew a long
breath. "She took it standing up, like a soldier." He rose as if to act
out his words. "She was in a jeep on the road when the plane came
over. The men ran for the ditch. She did not. Her last words were
to the jeep driver. Listen, listen carefully, it's something to have, it
adds the whole business up. She said, *'Drive straight ahead. Keep
going. Don't stop.'*"

He saw her lips soundlessly moving, her hands cross on her breast
as though she were hugging the words to herself. "Dinah," she
breathed. "Dinah! . . . Then it wasn't all wanton waste." She lifted
her eyes. "But there's something I don't quite understand. If the
driver had agreed with her, it might not have happened. Isn't that
so?"

"Please, Mrs. Hirsch, don't ask me," he begged.

She said, "Oh!" merely "Oh!" and then, piteously, like a child,
"I am fearfully tired. Do you mind if I sit a while by myself?"

She moved away from him to the sofa where the girl's things
were and she looked so spent he felt it was time for him to depart,
but when he came over to say "Shalom," she put her hand out to
detain him. "This may be our only chance. We've still so much
to speak about." But she said nothing for a long while and he
smoked a cigarette through and got up and strolled over to the corner where the dog lay, and crouched scratching the animal's throat
and feeling Udi's ribs through his pelt. The air in the room had
grown heavy, with the thickening dusk.

"Mr. Brody!"

He rose and turned.

She had come back to her armchair. "Please, sit down, do."

He returned slowly and crossed his legs, waiting for her. The
room was quite dark and through its shadows, her face seemed
softer, her eyes had a faint glow.

"Did you and Dinah spend much time together?" she asked.

He shook his head. "We really had only one evening. I had run
into her at the base, that time she gave me the first message for you,
and in the first truce, I got a Shabbat leave and went out to Gan

Darom. We sat in the ruins of the—"

She did not allow him to finish. "She was beautiful, wasn't she?"

So beautiful, too beautiful, don't let yourself think of how beautiful. "She looked a good deal like you, her features, her carriage, her smile."

That pleased her, he could see. "But her eyes," Dinah's mother protested. "She had her father's black eyes and did you notice their almond shape? A bit of the Tartar, my husband would say."

"She was rare and lovely." He clasped his hands. "A very real woman in spite of being Palmach."

She nodded. "More feminine than she would admit," then, bending forward, "Did you love her very much?"

He bowed his head and stared at the evening-grayed stones of the floor, before he could bring himself to say, "Yes, I did."

"And she loved you?"

His head came up. "I don't know. I think so." Then he made an effort to alter the moment's mood. "This will amuse you," he said. "The first time she met me, she slapped my face."

She was dismayed. "Why did Dinah do that?"

He grinned, waved his hand. "She must have thought I was getting fresh, the way we make a pass in the States."

Her "Oh!" startled him. She was all at once fidgety, began moving about, an aimless fluttering, picking up her workbasket, laying it down, piling up the scattered garments and nicknacks on the sofa. He thought her restlessness meant she could not converse any more and, again, he got up to go.

From the opposite side of the room, he heard her, speaking so faintly he had to strain to be sure of what she had said. "Did you make love?" she had asked.

He gaped at her. "After a fashion," he said.

"But you were together. She was pretty and young."

He said, "Please!" The time he had placed his hand on her breast came back now, in a flood of shame, and his nerves tensed and bunched, like a drawing boil.

Edith Hirsch moved toward him slowly, to stand facing, her hands folded upon her bosom, as if in prayer. "Tell me," she said with a strange urgency. "You can trust me. Tell me all about you and her."

"I kissed her once," he managed to say.

"Yes," she breathed, leaning forward, lips parted, question in her manner and voice.

A sudden anger swept him. What right has she to ask? What does she want to know? Why is she prying? She had seemed so intelligent, controlled, sensitive, but now he was sure she was mad. In the best of them, grief turns a screw loose.

"Tell me, please do," she was pleading. "Tell me everything."

All the regret and the sorrow, the long night's frustration, the putting off for a later day, was mounting, was tearing at him. "There was nothing, I tell you," he all but screamed. "We did nothing but talk." He stopped. He knew he was glowering at her. "Is that what you wanted to know?"

There was silence. Then words broke from her and hurtled into the shadow-filled room. "Not even that," she cried out.

He got up at once because he knew if he stayed, he would break down and bawl.

She hurried after him, met him at the door. "Forgive me, please, understand. You must stay, if you can. You must meet Dinah's father. You must break bread with us."

She lit a candle and they talked, calmly, after that, about his parents, about his life in the States, and a little about his future plans. He was thinking of staying, he told her, or of returning, eventually. They had asked him to join them at Gan Darom. That he had to think over, had to be sure whether he would fit in. "Dinah would like it," she said.

Teddy came in with a blond youngster of his own age. "This is Asi, my friend," Teddy said. Asi and Al shook hands formally. Edith left them together to go to the kitchen and start fixing a meal.

"We have an important matter to speak with you," Teddy said. "Do you have time?"

Al said he was at their service, what could he do for two young gentlemen?

"Tell me." Teddy stood in front of him. "You have seen New York?"

Al said he lived in New York. Teddy glanced at Asi and beamed. "Then tell us." He hitched his skidding shorts up. "Is it true there is a road under the water where big lorries and buses can go?"

He said yes, that was true.

The boys traded glances. "Then Dovidl wasn't a liar," Teddy said.

"Some time I would like to see that," Asi said. "I do not think I will ever have the chance." The blond lad had a sadness about him, as though he labored under a handicap of some kind. Teddy seemed aware of that, too, for he kept his arm around his friend while they sat on the floor at Al's feet.

"Tell me," Teddy demanded again. "You are a flyer. Is it true planes can fly three hundred miles—miles I mean, not kilometers— in one hour?"

He said yes, that was true, too. He told them about different planes he had flown and jet fighters of which he had heard. From their rapt attentiveness, he got the impression the boys believed they were listening to God.

Teddy nestled against Al's legs. "Once I thought I would like to be Palmach and live in the Negev, like my sister, Dinah," he said. "Now I know I am going to be an airplane pilot like you."

"Me, too," Asi said. "I would like to fly one of those jets." Then he got up, looking harassed. "It's suppertime. Imma will worry if I am late."

When he had gone, Al asked Teddy what was wrong with the lad, he seemed depressed. Teddy studied the tips of his shoes before he replied, "His father died in the war. It was a very sad case." His lips quivered, his face got red, and Al changed the subject to Udi, the dog. "He is my dog," Teddy said firmly. "Dinah gave him to me. We have been through a siege together. I will keep him always. I will take him in my plane when I fly."

Dinah's father came late and Al was somewhat surprised at the man's looks, thick lips, unshaven blue jowls, coarse features, more of a peasant, a proletarian, he concluded, than a professional type.

Edith Hirsch introduced them. "This is Al Brody. Dinah's friend. Our friend."

The Doctor's "Shalom" seemed careless, indifferent almost. "You must excuse me if I am not good company. I find myself very tired." He turned to his wife. "Is it not strange, little one, for me to be tired?"

After a scanty supper of tomatoes, olives, cheese, coffee and bread, Al sat with them in the living room, and Dinah's mother and he made small talk. She told him how bad the shelling had been and how they had managed the rationed water business, and after Al brought it up, Dr. Hirsch discussed the painting above the radio cabinet. He had done it two years before, he said. "I was a better prophet than a painter. Storm clouds over the Old City Walls. The storm is subsiding, but we can never forget how it raged." Then Al mentioned the piano and asked who played. "I used to," Edith Hirsch said. "When we had time and mind to think of such things." She asked did he care about music and he said he did, very much, and she wanted to know what he liked. "I'm old-fashioned, Beethoven and Brahms." He told her that what he liked best of all he had ever heard was a broadcast of Horowitz and Toscanini doing Beethoven's "Emperor." She seemed greatly pleased with his choice and said, a shade wistfully, so that she sounded almost as Dinah had, "I should like to hear that, too, someday, on a recording, perhaps, when there is time for such things."

The boy said "good night" and "l'hitra'ot" to Al and went upstairs with the dog. Al saw that the Doctor was nodding and he announced it was time for him to leave. Dr. Hirsch forced his eyes open. "It is a precious thing, our State," he mumbled drowsily, as though he had been reviewing these words in his sleep. "See how much it cost. Six million in Europe, and our . . . And our best . . ." His senses sharpened. He seemed to be hearing those very words, spoken before and in this room. He broke off, grasped Al's hand. "My wife told me you brought our daughter's things and her words. I thank you," he said. "'Drive straight ahead. Keep going. Don't stop.'" He looked into Al's face. "You do it," he said. "We are very tired."

They went upstairs immediately after Al left. "He seemed nice," Jacob said while he took off his clothes. "It was a pity," he said.

As always, he fell asleep at once, but he slept fitfully. He tossed and moaned in his sleep and once he sobbed.

He's thinking of her, Edith said to herself. He is dreaming of her and he weeps. She turned on her side and stroked his rough cheek, tenderly, to comfort him.